Dear Reader,

The editors at Harlequin and Silhouette are thrilled to be able to bring you a brand-new featured author program beginning in 2005! Signature Select aims to single out outstanding stories, contemporary themes and oft-requested classics by some of your favorite series authors and present them to you in a variety of formats bound by truly striking covers.

We plan to provide several different types of reading experiences in the new Signature Select program. The Spotlight books will offer a single "big read" by a talented series author, the Collections will present three novellas on a selected theme in one volume, the Sagas will contain sprawling, sometimes multi-generational family tales (often related to a favorite family first introduced in series) and the Miniseries will feature requested, previously published books, with two or, occasionally, three complete stories in one volume. The Signature Select program will offer one book in each of these categories per month, and fans of limited continuity series will also find these continuing stories under the Signature Select umbrella.

In addition, these volumes will bring you bonus features...different in every single book! You may learn more about the author in an extended interview, more about the setting or inspiration for the book, more about subjects related to the theme and, often, a bonus short read will be included.

Watch for new stories from Janelle Denison, Donna Kauffman, Leslie Kelly, Marie Ferrarella, Suzanne Forster, Stephanie Bond, Christine Rimmer and scores more of the brightest talents in romance fiction!

We have an exciting year ahead!

Warm wishes for happy reading,

Marsha Zinberg
Executive Editor
The Signature Select Program

SAGA

JEAN BRASHEAR
MERCY

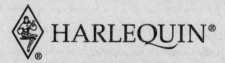

HARLEQUIN®

TORONTO • NEW YORK • LONDON
AMSTERDAM • PARIS • SYDNEY • HAMBURG
STOCKHOLM • ATHENS • TOKYO • MILAN • MADRID
PRAGUE • WARSAW • BUDAPEST • AUCKLAND

ISBN 0-373-83650-3

MERCY

To librarians everywhere,
for opening the world to all of us,
with special mention of the staffs of the Georgetown,
Deaf Smith County and Austin Public Libraries.
For the countless hours of pleasure I've spent,
from childhood to now, wandering stacks
and partaking of the wealth you make available,
please accept my deepest gratitude.

Special appreciation to Georgetown librarians Dixie Hanna
and Ethel Barnes, who read my early efforts, assured me
this day would come and cheered me all along the way.

And, as always, for Ercel,
whose existence is my most treasured gift.

ACKNOWLEDGMENTS

My thanks to Lois Samuels,
who graciously shared with me her New York,
and to her dear Stu.

To Marsha Zinberg, my deep appreciation
for this wonderful opportunity. Special thanks to
Alethea Spiridon, for being such a pleasure to work with.

Heartfelt gratitude to my editor, Beverley Sotolov,
without whom this book would still be sitting in the closet.
Your constant faith in my talent and expert guidance
are pearls beyond price.

The quality of mercy is not strain'd,
It droppeth as the gentle rain from heaven
Upon the place beneath. It is twice blest:
It blesseth him that gives and him that takes...

Though justice be thy plea, consider this,
That in the course of justice none of us
Should see salvation: we do pray for mercy;
And that same prayer doth teach us all to render
The deeds of mercy.

William Shakespeare
The Merchant of Venice

PROLOGUE

Attica

COLD, STERILE WALLS. Harsh lights. Worn furniture and ugly floors. Violence buzzed outside like a cloud of angry wasps. Hopelessness hung thick as a shroud. Decades of misery and bad news, broken hearts and hate lay as coats of yellowing varnish on this room he had never seen before.

After almost twenty years in prison, this was the first visitor Lucas Michael Walker had ever had.

Twenty-something, bad goatee, eyes sharp and sly, the visitor picked up the receiver. Pasted on a smile. "Lucas Walker? I'm Brian DeForest from the *New York Post*."

Lucas looked at him but didn't respond.

DeForest's dark eyes twitched to the side, then back. He sucked in a quick breath, wiping one palm on his pants. "Bet you'll be glad to be out, huh? Not long now."

Lucas had been fresh kill for these carnivores twenty years ago. He would walk out on this lowlife right now, except that time dragged on forever the nearer he got to the end.

And because he wanted to hear why he was news again.

But he was much less impulsive than he'd been at seventeen. Lucas knew waiting the way he knew his own skin.

So he watched the kid sweat.

DeForest's hand slid into his pocket. A tape recorder emerged in white-knuckled fingers.

Lucas's eyes narrowed to slits. He rose, slammed down the receiver, kicked back the chair. Heads swiveled in their direction. The nearest guard lifted his hand toward his belt.

"Wait—don't go." DeForest's dark eyes shifted toward the recorder. "Is it this thing? Okay—all right. I'll put it away."

Lucas glared until the silence stretched into a twanging, catgut scream. Then slowly he settled back into the chair, but didn't pull it close. Arms crossed over his chest, he stared the man down.

DeForest gripped his receiver, darting hummingbird-fast glances at the one on the other side of the glass.

Finally, Lucas picked his up. And still said nothing.

"You wonder why I'm here?" When he got no answer, DeForest continued. "Martin Gerard's seventy-fifth birthday is coming up soon. Lots of hype. Kennedy Center award, that sort of thing. He's going to do his first performance in years, *King Lear,* two weeks each in

New York and Washington. Tickets are being scalped for ungodly prices—the leading Shakespearean actor of our time returns to the stage for one last run."

Lucas's gut clenched. He wanted nothing to do with Martin Gerard. All he wished for was to be left alone.

"So I'm working on a piece about his life. Checked out your case, wondered if you might have a comment."

Goddamn vultures—when would they forget? With effort, Lucas merely shook his head.

DeForest's face reddened, but he pressed on. "In talking to the guards, I ran across mention of a letter." His eyes turned sly once more. Lucas dug his fingers into his thigh.

"I hear you almost killed a man for stealing it. Word is, Gerard's late wife wrote it after you murdered their only son. Care to tell me what it says?"

Lucas lunged for the glass. His chair crashed backward. The phone he'd dropped bounced off the shelf.

Footsteps pounded behind him.

Lucas grappled with fury he couldn't afford. He gripped the desk and shut his eyes. Raised one hand to the guard in reassurance. Shooting a glance at the reporter's ashen face, Lucas prepared to leave.

"Walker!" DeForest yelled. "There's a rumor that the other twin might be marrying a friend of Gerard's. Look—I've got a picture."

Lucas's head whipped around. His gaze settled on the grainy black-and-white photo of three figures. Martin

Gerard and his longtime benefactor, Carlton Sanford, flanked a slender blonde Lucas had tried very hard to forget.

"She's a recluse. Most people have forgotten she exists. Why does she hide, Walker? What's wrong with her?"

Lucas ignored the questions shouted over the partition. He couldn't take his eyes from the picture. Tansy hardly seemed older than she'd been at age sixteen, when he'd last seen her. For the first time, he spoke. "Married—" he cleared a suddenly clogged throat "—to Sanford?"

DeForest nodded.

Oh, God, Tansy, no. Lucas shot the reporter a murderous scowl. Everything he'd spent twenty years trying to bury had just roared back to life. Slowly, he picked up the receiver again.

"Tell me where she is."

CHAPTER ONE

Manhattan
Early March

THE LAST MONTH BEFORE spring was the one that came nearest to killing the soul. The weather could slip from cold to warm in the blink of an eye—and back to freezing just as quickly. Today the sun teased, playing peek-aboo from behind gray clouds sagging like wet wool. Mona Gerard stared out her midtown office window and silently begged the sun to come out and play.

"Kat, I need your help with Daddy's party." Mona rubbed her temple while picturing her younger sister's features screwed up in a frown at the other end of the phone line.

Kat swore under her breath. "I told you—"

Mona sighed. "I know, I know. But what I'm asking is for Tansy, not for Daddy."

"Oh." Immediately, her sister's rebellion subsided.

Six years younger than Mona's thirty-five, Kat was

part Annie Lennox—spiky, short copper hair included—and part Madonna, before motherhood reformed her. Owner of her own emerging Chelsea gallery, statuesque Kat was cutting a swath through the New York art world as though it were the AIDS-innocent eighties again. Mona's lectures on caution fell on deaf ears.

"What are you asking?"

"For you to take Tansy shopping for a dress."

"Yeah, right," Kat jeered. "Me and whose army? There aren't any decent dress shops in the neighborhood, and Tansy won't venture farther."

"Damn it, Kat, would you just help me for once?" Mona hated hearing her voice go shrill. She dropped her forehead to the flat of her palm. The whole party was a nightmare. She didn't have time for this. She had an issue of her magazine due at the printer's in a week, and her plate was so full she couldn't see the table.

"Hey…what's wrong?" Kat's voice was instant softness and sympathy. "I'm sorry. You're still shaken over what happened to Fitz, aren't you?"

Mona wanted to confide in her sister, tell her how strange things had been in the weeks since the terrifying forty-eight hours when her reporter husband had been held hostage by a deranged gunman.

But Mona had an image to uphold. She was the one who coped, the one who had risen to the challenge after their brother, Paris, was murdered. After Mama died.

"Nothing's wrong," she lied through her teeth. Something had changed with Fitz, though he protested otherwise. Something new switching the current rushing over the bedrock that was the only man she'd ever loved. Thank God they were going away this weekend, never mind that she couldn't afford the break. Things would get back to normal if they could only be alone for a bit.

Kat snorted. "Well, *I* was scared to death, and Fitz isn't even my husband…more's the pity."

Mona's lips curved at that. Kat had always proclaimed loudly how she coveted her sister's husband. Fitz and Kat disagreed vociferously and often on almost everything under the sun, but he was just as fond of her. He was the big brother Kat had lost when too young. "Fitz is fine, and so am I. I'm just terribly busy at work, and this party is consuming every spare second."

"Carlton's hosting. God knows the leading prospect for ambassador to Great Britain can afford to hire a party planner. You should be cuddling with your hunk of a husband, not adding this to your load. The old bastard doesn't deserve it, Mo. Why do you do this to yourself? He's never going to appreciate what it's costing you. Don't you get it? We're not important to him. We never were."

Paris was. Mona was sure her sister would be thinking the same thing. But their elder brother had died at age sixteen, his bright golden hope extinguished on one violent night.

Paris had died a hero, defending his twin from rape by Lucas Walker, may he rot in hell.

Mona blocked out the chaos outside her office door and concentrated on a to-do list a mile long. "It's an important night for him, the first performance in almost ten years. His seventy-fifth birthday. He's our father, Kat." She sighed, rubbing her temple again. "Maybe he wasn't the best one, but—"

"Please," her sister responded dryly. "Don't start with the excuses for him. I'm eating breakfast."

"It's one-thirty." Mona smiled in spite of herself. "Don't tell me. Reheated pizza." Her sister's knockout figure certainly couldn't be attributed to the quality of her diet.

"Okay, I won't. And it was a long night." Her sister's voice got that cat-in-cream purr. "Wanna hear about it, old married lady?" Kat teased, good humor restored.

"No, I do not wish to hear the details of your lurid sex life. Just promise me you're being careful."

Kat laughed. "Careful is no fun. With the big three-o staring me in the face, caution is the last thing on my mind."

"Life doesn't end at thirty, goose."

"It's sure as hell not going to with me. I met this guy last night who is hung like—"

"I'll be saying goodbye now, Kat."

Her sister's throaty laugh made Mona chuckle, too.

"So will you do it? Make sure Tansy has something new to wear?" Mona hastened to add, "Think my taste, not yours." But she was smiling, though Kat's penchant was more for leather than lace.

Kat sniffed. "My gallery caters to all different palates, Mo, not just mine. I can see the appeal of other styles—I just don't want to wear them."

"You have excellent taste," Mona soothed.

"Not that Tansy will notice. She'd just as likely wear sackcloth as silk."

"But Daddy will—his friends, too. I don't want anything to mar his big night."

"God forbid that anything should get between Martin the Magnificent and his grand ambitions."

"Kat…"

"All right, all right." She surrendered. "Anything else?"

"Who are you bringing?" Mona nearly bit her tongue for asking.

"Fitz is taken, right?" Her sister giggled. "In that case, I think I'll torture you awhile longer."

"What does the new guy look like? Is he of legal age?" Kat had a thing for young flesh.

"He's got an all-over tattoo and he's not much on wearing clothes. Daddy's friends will love him."

"Kat—" But she didn't get any further.

Her sister whooped. "Gotcha."

"Bring Armand. Please. I'll beg if I have to."

"Armand? Get real, Mona. We don't do social."

"He's perfect."

"Perfect to keep me in line, you mean. God, Mona, Armand's too old to be any fun."

"He's barely forty and the most charming man in town."

"Forty-four, and I don't need a chaperone."

"Consider it, that's all. He'd help you get through it. And Tansy loves being with him."

Mona could almost hear her sister's brain whirling. There was nothing either of them wouldn't do for Tansy. Neither was willing to give up on the fairy princess, lost in her dreamworld for so long. The oldest at thirty-six, Tansy was perfectly preserved in girlhood. She shouldn't be moldering in that haunted apartment Daddy refused to sell.

Mona's assistant appeared in the doorway, using their signal for a special call. "Kat? I have to go. Please—just think about it, all right?"

"Yeah, okay." Dramatic sigh.

"I'll be dropping by Daddy's later. Can I tell Tansy to expect you?"

"Yes, Mother."

Mona ignored her tone. "This week?"

"Go away, Mo. Love you." And with that, Kat hung up.

I love you, too. Kat was flashy and temperamental, Mona's opposite in almost every sense, but she was the only real family Mona had left. They shared more than their father's penchant for naming his children after Shakespearean characters. Paris and Titania. Desdemona and Katharina.

Her bond with Kat was one forged in exile. Once possessed of a rich, full life in New York with a famous, if distant, father and a gorgeous, adoring mother, all four children had been sent by Martin to Texas to live with his mother-in-law when Juliette fell ill with cancer. He'd been determined to focus on saving his dying wife. They had been thoroughly and completely abandoned in a strange, raw place, banished from his mind until the day he'd inexplicably sent for Paris and Tansy and left the two younger girls behind with Nana.

Then the life they'd known in New York shattered forever. Paris died, Tansy retreated into a world where no one could follow, and Mama died a few months later. Mona and Kat were forgotten in the wake of a family's destruction. Texas became more real than New York. Then one day Nana, too, was gone.

But Mona understood Daddy's devotion. Mama had been so beautiful, so magical. She didn't blame Daddy.

It was Lucas Walker who was responsible. The friend Paris should never have trusted, the viper Mama should never have welcomed to her breast, to her comfort.

It was not Daddy but Lucas Walker who had destroyed them.

JUST OUTSIDE THE DOORWAY of her father's living room, Mona paused to watch Martin Gerard, his carriage that of an aging king, pace slowly over the shabby Persian rug that had once glowed like a ruby in the apartment he'd inhabited for forty-two years. The West Side Highway roared dully through closed windows overlooking the bare trees of Riverside Park.

"'Tell me, my daughters—since now we will divest us both of rule, interest of territory, cares of state—which of you shall we say doth love us most? That we our largest bounty may extend where nature doth with merit challenge—'"

He gestured expansively toward the slender blonde across the room. "'Goneril, our eldest-born, speak first.'"

Still out of sight, Mona observed her sister, older by one year. Tansy's long pale hair glowed under the Tiffany lamp. Once honey-blond, her hair had turned almost white after that night when everything changed forever.

The daughter Martin had named after Titania, the queen of the fairies, was heartbreaking in her beauty, a delicate hothouse orchid trembling at the arching tip of a thread-slender stalk. Curled in the overstuffed, once-burgundy sofa almost as old as she herself, Tansy lifted her twinkling blue gaze from the script, her voice melodious with the amusement she tried to stifle. "'Sir, I love you more than words can wield the matter; dearer than eyesight, space and liberty….'"

Her smile slipped away, replaced by the gentle, soft-focus glow that was uniquely hers. She spoke the words without glancing at the page, her eyes locked in the distance. "'Beyond what can be valu'd, rich or rare; no less than life, with grace, health, beauty, honour; as much as child e'er loved, or father found; a love that makes breath poor and speech unable; beyond all manner of so much I love you.'"

Shakespeare's Goneril had been mouthing sentiments; Mona knew Tansy meant them. Her father stopped and watched, on his face the tearing pain of grief. His bright twins, he'd called them, Titania and Paris. Both lost in the span of one single night, one to death, one to oblivion.

Damn Lucas Walker for the beauty he had ripped from this world.

Then Tansy noticed Mona and smiled, rising to float across the room with her singular grace. "My king, behold another devoted daughter. Methinks 'tis past time for tea. Perchance my sire's bones require warmth?" She dipped a curtsy, then embraced Mona, her eyes alight with a rare impishness that brought back memories of the very different girl Tansy had once been.

Mona accepted the hug, touching Tansy's spindrift hair and smiling past the ache. Once, Tansy had been all mischief and shimmering energy, complete and fearlessly safe in her bond with her brother.

Martin responded in an echo of Tansy's teasing tone. "'How sharper than a serpent's tooth it is to have a thankless child'…who will not run lines with her dear old father."

His lips curved, but in her father's gaze Mona saw the heartbreak. She squelched old pangs of envy. No matter how she wished he'd just once look at her with such devotion, she understood how special Tansy was. To resent her would be to resent starlight or a perfect rose.

Tansy laughed, the sound bell-pure. "I'll go ask Mrs. Hodgson to bring tea." She left, barely stirring the air as she passed.

Martin glanced at Mona, then at the train clock beside the playbill Mona had preserved from his last London run. He sat down heavily, his face leached of color.

"Are you all right?" she asked.

He nodded. "Merely a combination of age and Lear. Titania and I have been running lines since just after lunch. An old man needs his afternoon lie-down, I fear."

Mona studied him, seeing him in a new light. His always regal carriage had diminished, his proud, leonine head slightly bent. Standing above him, she saw tender pink skin and realized that the thick white mane was losing purchase.

For a second, the ground beneath her shifted. She closed her eyes against the unwanted view. "You'll never be old, Daddy."

But in his face she saw weariness. "This is my swan song. Ten years away from my life's blood…" He stared into the distance. "Twenty years without my Juliette. Where did the time go?"

"You still miss her."

"One cannot help but miss the heart when it has fled the body. If it weren't for Titania—" He faltered. Shook his head.

"What, Daddy?"

Martin captured her with those fierce eyes that could still mesmerize an audience. "I worry about your sister. Every day my eyesight dims more, my body aches in new places. Lear will tax me to my limits."

This brutal honesty was new and shocking. Her father never shared confidences with anyone but Carlton. Mona moved closer, pride a new song inside her. "Should you be doing this? Have you seen a doctor?"

He harrumphed, for an instant the imperious king of theater again. "Lear is the one role I've not tackled. My career would be incomplete without it." Disdain colored his tone. "I understand Lear now. I have my own thankless children."

Why was it that this man could reduce her—a woman who controlled her own kingdom, who influenced hundreds of thousands of people by her decisions—to a girl again, one whose most fervent wish had been to be like the golden family into which she'd been born?

The grown woman wheeled to leave. Martin's imperious voice stopped her. "Desdemona…"

She crossed toward the door, her insides a nasty mix of shame and rage and, goddamn it, longing. "I'll let myself out."

"Wait…" A new note crept in. Tentative. Almost… pleading.

She paused but didn't turn around.

"Please. It's about Titania. Carlton has offered again to marry her so she'll be safe when I'm gone."

Mona whirled. "Carlton once wanted to put her in an institution. She's not his business. Kat and I will care for her anytime you're willing to let go."

Lines of strain on his face relaxed. He started to speak, but just then Tansy reentered the room, the hem of her long, pale-blue gown gliding over the rug. She resembled their mother so much. Mona watched her father accept the cup Tansy brought, watched the way Tansy spread his napkin in his lap and smoothed her hand over his hair. She reminded Mona of a little girl playing mother, the gestures slightly fussy and nervous, lacking the confidence of a true adult.

When she had her father settled, Tansy drifted away, her skirts swishing against the floor. She began to hum a little tune, her face dreamy as she danced across the carpet.

"What makes you sing, sweet?"

"I dreamed of my prince last night, Daddy. Mama promised me he'd come one day to take me under the fairy hill." She knelt on the floor before him, yearning visible in every line of her face as she clasped his hand. "She said I would recognize him when he arrived. I hope he'll be here soon."

Martin frowned. "Perhaps your mother was only telling a pretty story…."

Mona understood her father's concern. Tansy was too gentle for this world. The eldest, but by far the most innocent. He'd protected her for twenty years. They all had. She lacked essential elements required to fend for herself in a universe that would chew her up and spit her out.

Tansy's eyes glowed in the golden light. "He'll come, Daddy. I'm sure he will." Then she reached for her cup, her face pensive. "I've painted his form, but I can't quite see his face." She peered up at her sister. "Would you like to see the painting, Mona?"

"Sure."

"Are we finished for today, Daddy? After I show Mona, I need to go see Paris."

Her father's eyes flashed. Tansy didn't say it often, had learned not to speak of her belief that her twin waited for her in Riverside Park. They'd tried over the years to make Tansy understand that Paris was dead, but a remnant of her former stubbornness surfaced at such times. Paris was not dead, she insisted. She would know. She would be dead, too.

Mona and her father traded glances. He lifted his shoulders in resignation, and frankly, Mona had to agree. If not for going to the park to see Paris, Tansy would never leave this apartment. Mona had argued with Martin, urged therapy, medication—anything to get her sister back. He wouldn't hear of it. Tansy was so fragile that all of them sensed how critical the delusion was to her well-being. All in all, it was relatively harmless. She visited Paris most afternoons at the park, seldom straying more than a block either way.

For the first time in a while, Mona reexamined their truce and wondered if she should try again. Now wasn't the time, however. Maybe after the premiere…or maybe not. Perhaps they should let her be.

"Yes, sweet. We're finished." Martin accepted the brush of her lips on his cheek and stroked her hair. "Thank you, princess."

She smiled and slipped away. Mona followed.

Tansy's studio was an old, cleared-out butler's pantry, with barely enough room for her easel and paints. Rolls of canvas and wood for stretchers were stacked on high shelves. She'd painted a mural on the wall behind the shelving, with its unicorn and butterflies and rainbows.

On the easel, the beginnings of a knight clad in armor greeted Mona. The body of Tansy's prince was there, strong and tall, but just as she'd indicated, the face was missing.

"I wish I could remember his features," Tansy said wistfully. "I've waited for so long. His hands…they make me feel safe."

Mona slid an arm around her sister's shoulders. She and Kat were tall, but Tansy was a good five inches shorter. Kat leaned her cheek on Tansy's hair. "Do you feel unsafe here? Or in the park?"

She shook her head. "No. It's…" Her voice dropped to a whisper. "The other dream." She moved away quickly and traversed the hall to her room, alight with rainbows cast by the crystals hanging in her window.

Once inside, she stopped beside the bureau, where she kept Nana's scarves.

"What dream?"

But Tansy turned a face as blank as slate to her. "Do you ever think of Nana?" She pulled open the slender right-hand drawer, then closed her hands around them, the bright, frothy squares of blue and red and lilac, still faintly smelling of Nana's lavender sachet. Nana had always worn one over her hair for protection when she went outside, and Tansy followed suit.

"Of course I do." Indignation stirred. Hadn't Mona been left behind with Nana when Tansy and Paris were allowed to come home to New York?

"Nana's house was a safe place. I loved her spice cabinet. Do you recall it?" Tansy buried her nose in the bright froth. "I loved the way she'd hold me and stroke my hair."

Mona's stomach jittered. "Tansy, tell me about your other dream." It was unlike her sister to be so troubled. Was she remembering?

Tansy hunched her shoulders slightly.

"Tansy…"

Blinking, she turned and smiled. "I need to see Paris. Are you sure you don't want to come?" She drew a pale-blue scarf from the drawer to match her dress, then slid the neat triangle over her hair as Nana would do, and tied it beneath her chin. Then she stood there, eyes impatient.

"I…" Mona wasn't sure what to do. She glanced at the Rolex on her wrist.

"It's all right." Tansy crossed to her, pressing one hand to her cheek before bestowing a kiss. "Go home to Fitz. I'm fine, I promise. Paris is waiting."

Mona watched her go, heart aching.

CHAPTER TWO

FREEDOM WAS TWO GATES away.

Lucas Walker had long ago quit dreaming of that land of trees and air, of sunlight and birdsong, of steps in any direction he chose. It had been crucial to cut off all hope of them—or go insane. Yet here liberty lay, just past the bars. So close his chest ached and he could not breathe. A wild, buried anger stirred. Today, for the first time in twenty years, he would be a free man.

Unshackled in body, that is; his spirit would never again be unfettered. He'd lost more than his friend that autumn night when he'd been seventeen and street savvy. Still innocent enough, though, to succumb to the lure of the Gerards. To glimpse, now and again, himself as Juliette had viewed him. To believe that lives could change, even one as worthless as his.

"Don't get too excited, hard case." The guard beside him sneered. "It ain't no picnic out there. World's changèd since you was last on the loose." He shrugged, then his wide lips split in a parody of a grin. "You'll be

back. But don't worry—we'll leave the lights on. Keep
your cell warm."

Lucas stared straight ahead at that last gate, still remembering the sound of doom clanging shut like the
gates of hell looming over him that long-ago day. The
severity of the crime had caused them to try him as an
adult, and he could still feel the shudder that had racked
his spine when he'd heard the gate close and lock out
hope…choke the life from the pitiful dreams a boy had
barely begun to have.

In the pocket of his too-crisp shirt, with its cardboard
folds crisscrossing his chest, the yellowed letter burned.

Juliette Gerard. Angel. Mother of his dreams. Mid-
wife of his stillborn hopes. To a boy abandoned as so
much garbage by his own mother, Juliette had seemed
a miracle. He'd read her letter a thousand times that first
year, then never since—but it was still his most treasured possession.

He'd beaten a man half to death once for stealing it,
taunting him, holding it over a flame. He'd been in solitary for a year that time, afraid every second that the
letter was forever lost—and along with it, what was left
of his soul.

But Mose had saved it. Rescued Lucas, too. His only friend had understood that the letter was all that kept
Lucas sane.

Written on pale lavender linen gone brown with age,
to him it smelled of roses, as she always had.

Mercy was its message.

The mother he'd have sold his soul to have, forgiving Lucas for murdering her beloved son, even though she was so sick herself that death caressed her like a lover.

The final door clanged behind him, but Lucas never heard it. Like north on a compass, Juliette's mercy called him back to New York to face her daughter once more.

IN SOME CIRCLES, to be behind the times came treacherously close to a cardinal sin. The most acceptable speed was full-throttle, the proper direction forward. For all its sophistication, New York was a very small town. Reputations could be made—and destroyed—with that same lightning pace.

Which was why Kat Gerard hadn't eaten all day, almost breathless with the risk she'd taken to mount this show. Yet there was nothing she loved more than hanging out over the edge…in this case, a precipice appropriately named Gamble Smith.

She paused in shadow, listening. Observing the stage she'd set and the players now assembled. Delicate chime of crystal champagne flutes. Soft waterfall of harp strings. The bouquet of a hundred women's perfumes mingled with crisp, almost-great champagne, melted Brie and a subtle undertone of chocolate. Voices murmuring in fascination, city dwellers lost in a fantasy they'd try to dismiss when moonlight fled and day returned.

Kat strolled across Oriental carpets she'd begged

from hither and yon to capture the mood of the paintings, surveying the opening-night crowd for Gamble's
show. And smiled.

No one had left yet. The air all but sizzled. She'd tak-
en a chance on him; in her outré world, the blatant romanticism of the Texan's work could easily be mocked.
Her circle did not suffer fools—or romantics—gladly.

But it appeared she had won. The place was packed
to the pearl-gray walls. Kat might not be able to paint
as Tansy could—the true sorrow of her life—but she
damn well had a killer instinct for good art. When she'd
slammed against the wall of her limited talent, it had
crushed her for a time. She'd given her brushes to Tansy, unable to bear even looking at them, and walked
away from the whole scene.

But a year later she'd known her soul was withering.
She returned to her favorite haunts and began talking to
her art school friends. She mounted her first exhibit in
the loading dock of a Chelsea building scheduled for
renovation. Two more shows followed, in equally un-
orthodox locations.

At the third show, she'd met Armand Delacroix.

The renegade scion of a patrician Boston family, Armand continued to resist his family's pleas for his return to the life to which he was born. He was a man of
many contrasts: opera patron with a taste for old,
scratchy blues records; a brilliant thinker with a penchant for breakneck sports; an entrepreneur who made

pots of money without seeming to try, and who shared it with others easily. Suave and handsome, Armand was often seen with strikingly beautiful women on his arm, but he was also a man who, despite his inborn elegance, numbered among his friends as many starving artists and tradesmen as prominent public figures. He ran every day and piloted his own plane, had once played polo with abandon and still liked the challenge of tackling the world's highest mountains.

Despite the wishes of his family that he come home to Beacon Hill, Armand found Boston too limiting, his family too inclined to want to peg him in one neat niche. If any city had a hold on him, it was ever-changing New York, his Gramercy Park pied-à-terre manned by an aging butler Armand refused to put out to pasture.

The wealthy patron and the neophyte had hit it off, and Kat had learned more from Armand than any school could have taught her. Two years ago, on a wing and a prayer and a shoestring—and Armand's not-so-gentle nudging—she'd leased a permanent space and moved into the back room. Six months ago, she'd taken her own apartment ten blocks away.

She would never produce works that others would buy, but it almost didn't hurt anymore. If she couldn't set the world on fire with one talent, she would use another. No matter what, the world would notice Kat Gerard as her father never had. Tonight was an important step.

Diandra Salud from the *Voice* stared raptly at a painting that was blatantly après-coital. The female figure re-clined, one leg softly spread in total surrender. Absolute trust. Complete lack of defense against that too-deadly species, the human male.

Instead of the usual buzz that accompanied the con-troversial shows Kat mounted, the room hummed with something different. A silent eroticism charged the air, coupled with, of all things, a sort of peace at odds with life in this city.

Gamble Smith looked like a cowboy and painted like a fallen angel. He brought to mind a different world, something at once earthy and voluptuous, yet more ethereal.

Kat wondered if he made love that way, as well.

Perhaps she would find out. She avoided getting down and dirty with her artists until after a show; be-fore that time, she preferred them sharp and hungry. Teasing was great—it put them both on edge, crisped the air with appetites unappeased. She and Gamble had been fencing for weeks.

But no touching, not until afterward.

It was almost afterward now. Tonight. Here, perhaps, surrounded by his work.

Or in his studio. More than once, Kat had experi-enced the possibilities of paint application as it related to the human body.

She sized him up as he stood across the room, sur-rounded by preening women. Raw, angry and towering over them all, he was impatient, uncomfortable. Furious eyes met hers.

Kat smiled and lifted one brow. There was nothing he could do about it. She'd made sure of that. Gamble Smith resented the hell out of every person who wanted a piece of his art. He was pissed off that he needed food and a place to rest his head. He spent as little as possible on both, living and working in the sordid warehouse he called a studio. He had found one of the few remaining spaces in Manhattan an artist could afford. There were hardly any of the basic amenities, but plenty of great light and room for his rangy, rough-hewn body to move, for his big hands to turn paint into dreams. Into beauty that called like a siren.

He slept on an old mattress on a platform he'd built himself. He cooked—when he remembered to eat—on a hot plate. He had no phone. To see him, she had to dig him out herself. Only the most dire of threats had him here this evening.

His eyes narrowed. Kat brushed her fingers across her thumb in the ancient symbol for money. Filthy lucre required to buy more paint, more canvas. And she smiled in triumph.

He was a wild being, barely restrained, hardly civilized. She saw his nostrils flare, his strong jaw clench. *Go to hell,* he mouthed. Kat lifted an eyebrow and bit her thumbnail at him. With a curt nod, he cocked his dark head toward the simpering woman directly in front of him.

One more hour. Then the revelry began. There was nothing quite so satisfying as being a patroness of the arts.

"Stop torturing the talent, Katharina."

Kat started at Armand's voice. "But that's half the fun."

"Here." He handed her champagne. "Leave the man alone to do his work." He sipped his own. "A successful show once again. I salute your intuition."

Kat slid her gaze to her friend. Just under six feet, Armand was a striking figure, the premature silver hair in contrast with his athletic build. "You found him."

"But you had the nerve to showcase a blatant romantic in the heart of Sodom and Gomorrah. You sensed the hunger that exists in the heart of the jaded." He cocked one eyebrow. "A reflection of yourself, Katharina?"

Only her father had called her that damn Shakespearean name, until Armand. He did it simply to tweak her. Kat snorted. "There's not a romantic bone in my body."

"Indeed? I disagree."

"You enjoy arguing with me." She scanned the room again. Satisfied, she turned back to Armand. "You don't approve of much that I do. You're worse than a father."

The lines around his green eyes crinkled. "I'm hardly old enough to be yours. Not that you'd know about a father's guidance."

"Touché," she murmured, concurring. "How would I, indeed? The old bastard certainly never bothered." She smiled at him sweetly and patted his cheek. "Speaking of which, you will be my date to all the festivities, right? The Lincoln Center gala, Mona's godforsaken party and all that crap?"

"Poor Katharina. Mona's requiring you to bring a respectable escort."

Kat snorted. He understood her family too well. "You're a natural. Cary Grant returned to life. You can't let me down. I'll never figure out all the forks and shit."

Tolerant amusement brightened his expression. "Your years in Texas weren't spent on the range. I have it on good authority that they use full place settings there, too."

"Nana tried to teach me, but it didn't stick." She lifted her chin. "I'm telling you I'm desperate, pal. You can't let me down." Then she cocked her head. "Want to help me take Tansy shopping?"

Armand laughed. "Mona must be utterly desperate if she's asking you to dress Tansy for Martin's big night."

"I have taste." Offended, Kat sniffed, gesturing around them. "People pay for my taste."

He scanned her attire. "Red toreador jacket, see-through lace bra and long white spandex skirt. Red stilettos." One eyebrow lifted. "No panties, if my eyes don't deceive me."

In his green eyes, she saw a twinkle. She'd never been able to shock him. Nor had she been able to tempt him—he'd passed that test and won her over. That was the beauty of their relationship. He'd become her mentor and best friend. Men to fuck were a dime a dozen. A true friend was priceless.

"So?" she challenged.

"Not exactly Tansy's look."

"You sound like Mona," Kat muttered. "I don't have to adopt other styles to appreciate them." She gestured around the room. "Witness Gamble Smith."

"Ah, yes. The romantic barbarian. Tonight's the night, I suppose."

Kat's eyes closed to slits. "I don't screw all my artists."

"None of the women—so far, anyway."

"Asher Domel," she sniffed.

"Ah, that's right. No grandfathers, no females, no men over thirty. Perhaps Gamble Smith can breathe easy. He's probably thirty-five."

"I'm leaving now. I have guests to entertain." She turned away, only to have Armand grip her arm. "Let me go. I have paintings to sell."

"The pieces are flying off the walls." He tilted her chin upward with one long finger. His normal sangfroid slipped just a hair. "Becoming thirty will not be the end of your life, Katharina. It isn't all downhill from here."

"Go to hell, Armand. I'm not afraid."

Intensity fled as quickly as it had appeared. With a chuckle like that of a favorite uncle, he leaned closer, kissing her on the forehead. "Yes, you are. You're terrified. That's why the men in your life get younger by the week."

Then he released her. "Tansy is special. Call me when you're ready to go shopping, and I'll ride to her rescue."

"Bite me, Delacroix."

"A tempting prospect for some, I'm sure. Enjoy your conquest, Katharina." He moved away, quickly swallowed up in the crowd.

Kat swore viciously, than raked impatient fingers through her short, spiky hair. Drawing a deep breath, she surveyed the room, then abruptly decided to head for the prissy caterer. She could use a good fight right about now.

MONA JERKED AWAKE on the sofa at the sound of a key in the apartment door lock. She hadn't meant to fall asleep, but she was always tired lately. Fingers tightening on the page proofs spread over her chest, she blinked a few times and shook her head, then rose from her afghan swaddling. "Fitz?" She glanced at the stainless-steel clock: 1:00 a.m.

The refrigerator door swished gently.

"Fitz?"

He appeared in the doorway of the living room, taking a long pull from the brown glass bottle of his favorite beer. As she watched the strong muscles of his neck tighten while he swallowed, yearning shimmered through her body.

He didn't speak, both of them waiting, she supposed, to test the winds. Nothing had been the same since that night.

"Long day?" she ventured.

He shrugged. "It was all right."

He was so still. Too still. Unease rippled down her spine. "Are you upset that I couldn't go to that party tonight?"

"If you'd skip your own sister's opening, I couldn't very well expect that you'd choose a retirement party."

"Fitz, I wanted to. I adore Ben. It's just that—"

"You always mean well, Des." He frowned. "You're special to Ben. Even if you skipped that, Kat's your sister. Surely the magazine could have survived without you for a few hours."

"Fitz, I—" She started to defend herself.

"Forget it," he said, his voice too neutral.

They'd always argued loudly and often. They made up just as passionately. This aloofness was new, unsettling. And he'd never viewed her this way, never studied her like a bug on a pin.

Six foot one of boxer's muscles, the crooked nose in character with a man whose appearance disguised a razor-sharp mind, James Fitzgerald was a man's man to the bone, life grasped in two fists for every one of his forty years. He could have had the decency to grow a paunch, lose some of his thick, sandy hair, let endless long days and late nights show up in his hazel eyes.

But no—her husband played handball regularly at his downtown club. Worked hard as the city's premier investigative reporter, always the first on the big story, ever in demand. Sex on the hoof was Fitz Fitzgerald.

"Hungry?" she asked, dodging another argument over her work habits. She didn't know why, though; she hadn't cooked in weeks and the refrigerator offered only beer, olives and butter. They caught dinner together when they could, but it was usually out somewhere, not at home.

He shook his head. Started to speak, then didn't.

"Are you all right?" She could have kicked herself. He'd never liked it if she hovered, even less so now that everyone kept watching him for signs of stress from that night. "I'm sorry. I didn't mean…"

Finally, Fitz chuckled, and Mona relaxed slightly. "It's okay. Join the parade. Hank asked me today if I wanted to see a shrink."

"A shrink?" The idea startled her. "You?" His behavior was off, but not *that* off.

He shot her the crooked grin she loved. "Post-traumatic stress syndrome, some crap like that." He shook his head, then crossed to her, setting down the bottle before drawing her to her feet.

Fitz drew her hair back from her neck with one finger. He nipped at her skin, and Mona shivered.

"Christ, they act like I'd been a POW or something."

Mona shuttered her eyes. She still couldn't stand to think about those two endless days and how close he'd come to death. They'd made fierce, almost violent love the night he'd been released, but in the two weeks since, nothing. It wasn't all the extra hours she'd been putting in, either. That had never stopped them before.

She wanted her husband back, but she still hadn't seen the man who'd gone to work that fateful morning. "You were in real danger, Fitz. Anyone would be shaken."

"I'm not shaken," he murmured against her ear. His tongue slid along the outside curve. "I'm glad as hell to be alive."

She couldn't help digging her fingers into the long muscles of his back. She'd been so terrified that she'd never again be able to touch him. Have him touch her. She tightened her arms around him with every ounce of her strength. "Oh, Fitz, I…" She buried her forehead in his shoulder and struggled not to cling. "I am so very glad you're safe."

He pulled her deeper into his embrace. "I just kept thinking that I had to make it out because I couldn't leave you alone."

She'd been alone all her life, and he had saved her. Just as important as his love was the promise he'd made never to abandon her. He knew a Mona no one else did. He was the only one who'd ever put her first. Made her feel good enough, just as she was.

The tears she hadn't let herself shed wouldn't be held back. She burrowed more deeply into his arms. "I love you so much. Fitz, I was so scared." She stared into those hazel eyes she adored. "I'm a strong woman. I can survive whatever I have to endure, but—oh, God—" Her throat tightened.

He leaned his forehead against hers. "I was scared, too, Des. I had a lot of time to ponder what's important." His eyes blazed, alight with a new tenderness.

She relaxed against him. Desire stirred to life.

"Make a baby with me, Des." His mouth lowered to hers, brushed across her lips.

It was a slap of ice-cold water. "Wha—" The back of her neck prickled. She couldn't have heard right. She wanted him so badly, craved the comfort only Fitz could provide, but his words made her shudder as if she had palsy. "Fitz, we always said…" They'd agreed—no children.

He placed a finger over her lips, then teased a long caress down her throat. "I remember what we said." His eyes went dark and serious. "I didn't believe I cared, as long as I had my job and you. But I've changed. I realized that night that we're only living on the surface. Look around at this place." His arm swept out, encompassing the cool Scandinavian décor they'd painstakingly assembled, leather and blond wood and clean lines of metal. "At how we're living. There's more to life than cold ambition, Des. Much more."

"Our life is good." But even as she scrambled to marshal arguments, a chill ran through her. She wasn't enough after all. The man she'd loved for ten years suddenly needed more than she could give him. She tried to pull away, but he wouldn't let her.

"Shh," he whispered, tightening his arms and stroking her hair, pressing a kiss to the top of her head. "It has been good, yes. But lately… We're missing so much. I didn't see it before, but all of a sudden I'm realizing that I wish for what my parents have."

She stiffened against him, his words sinking into her like a stone. She couldn't give him what his parents had, that big, utterly normal American family. She didn't know the first thing about normal.

"Hey," he murmured, rocking her gently, soothing her with his hands. "It's a switch, but we could do it, Des. You and me, we could have it all. Just think about it, okay?"

He held her close, and all Mona could focus on was what she could say to make him forget this crazy notion. She had no desire to hear about babies. She needed to be enough for Fitz all by herself. He couldn't alter everything so abruptly. Couldn't just kick the legs out from under her.

He'd been shaken; she understood that. Anyone would be. But the two of them would get past it. In time things would go back to the way they'd been, if she stayed the course. In the manner that she'd learned over so many years, she squeezed her eyes shut and concentrated on blocking out the words she didn't want to hear, re-forming them into a reality she could tolerate.

She lifted herself to her toes and drew him down to her kiss. Kept her eyes closed so she wouldn't have to lie to him.

He soughed out a gust of relief. "God, Des, I love you." He met her mouth with his own, his clever hands roaming over her body with a new urgency.

Luxuriating in the unique pleasure only Fitz could bring her, Mona ignored how she was letting him believe she agreed. He would come out of this strange mood and be Fitz again if she'd only be patient. So she concentrated, instead, on binding him to her, bringing him back to what they had, how good they were together.

He bore her down to the ivory leather sofa, his lips following the path of skin his fingers bared. Mona gloried in his touch, in the knowledge that he was safe and alive and back with her, and shut out the words he would forget in time. She tore at his clothes, desperate for the touch and taste of his skin. He joined them savagely, and Mona welcomed the surge of power, the sense of connection. She needed this, needed him. Needed to grasp that they were together once more, that the terror was over. With a cry at the unbearable sweetness, she let Fitz carry her away into blessed forgetfulness, reveling in the rightness of this moment...of this man for whom she had surely been made.

"SO HOW DID WE DO?" Kat gnawed at the cuticle of her right thumb and paced the honey-gold oak floors she'd stripped until her fingers bled. As she crashed from the high of the packed crowd, she found the risk she'd taken stole her breath away. Making this month's rent was going to be dicey.

Gregory Adams never faltered as his fingers danced over the calculator. "If you'd stop hanging over me, I could get this done faster. A 'watched pot' and all that," he said mildly.

She should go outside, of course. Babysit the talent. With every tick of the clock, Gamble's glower had darkened. Maybe the busty blonde was still amusing him and he'd wait a little longer.

She couldn't leave yet; she had to know. "I never should have gotten my own apartment," she muttered to the navy beret covering Gregory's thinning, light-brown hair. "It was too soon. I shouldn't be paying you so much."

A small snort issued from his still-lowered head. "You're not paying me anything yet." He'd wandered in one day and bartered framing labor for a workroom in the back of her space.

"Then I should be charging you for the pleasure of being here." She ripped away a sliver of skin and hissed at the sting.

He sighed and drummed his fingers. One glimpse of her books, and he'd banned her from her paperwork weeks ago. "Go away. I'll call you when I'm finished."

"Not on your life. I'm suffering here, damn it. Keep working."

His head lifted. Sympathetic pale-blue eyes studied

hers. "Armand would help you out if you'd just ask," he reminded her.

"Great. So I'd have two wolves breathing down my door."

"Breathing down your neck," he corrected, as his fingers flew. "Or blowing down your door." Gregory had been an English major as well as a failed painter. "You're mixing your metaphors."

"Bite me," she countered.

"Oh, I believe I'll leave that to the glowering giant outside the door. He's far more likely to be interested in your backside. Speaking of which, why don't you already have him naked in your apartment?"

She waved a comment away. "That's only sex. This is money."

His grin was quick and shrewd. "Yeah."

The door behind them opened. The caterer stood there with palm out. Kat had beaten him down unmercifully on his price, exchanging a promise to distribute his cards liberally, but she couldn't get off scot-free. "Ms. Gerard, we're finished out here."

"I'll be right with you." She closed the door in his face and turned to Gregory. "Well?" she whispered. "Will the check bounce?"

Gregory held up a hand, did a little more finger magic, then frowned.

Kat's heart sank. "I screwed up, didn't I? Should have put on the show of pieces done with bedsprings."

He looked up, a sparkle in his eyes. "As long as you don't eat but once a week, we'll be fine." Then he grinned. "Just kidding. Actually, we'll make expenses this month. Only by a hair, but enough. And we've got more pieces coming in to sell on the buzz."

Kat shrieked and threw herself across the space between them. She clasped his face between her hands and smacked a big wet kiss straight on his mouth. "We're saved! Oh, Gregory, maybe I'll pay you after all." She twirled around the desk, then jerked open the door to let the goggle-eyed caterer inside. "Write this man a check, Gregory." Over her shoulder, she winked at the slender man. "And then go get laid. I intend to."

Behind her, Gregory's laugh buoyed her. For tonight, she wouldn't worry about next month's bills. That was next month. Tonight, the juices were flowing. She was still in business, despite everyone's predictions that she wouldn't stick with this any longer than she'd done anything else. She began mentally running through her list of potential partners for the evening, but realized that none of them was what she wanted.

Then she glanced across the gallery at the figure seated alone in a dark alcove, his posture, even at rest, projecting a barely leashed inferno.

Kat smiled. Definitely…a bad-tempered artist was exactly what the doctor ordered.

He stared across the wide golden floor between them.

Kat licked her lips and watched his eyes darken. She

took a deep breath, knowing exactly what that did to her generous cleavage. "Well now, Mr. Smith. It appears that you're a hit with the cognoscenti. This calls for a celebration." She scooped a bottle of champagne from the caterer's waiting stack and crossed the gallery floor. "My place isn't far."

He rose to his feet, towering over her own tall frame. An insolent scan of her body had her blood heating dangerously fast.

Ah, yes. This brooding artist with the rugged hands so at odds with his romantic bent might be just the ticket for a night's pleasure. With effort, she resisted the urge to sink in her nails and wrap her legs around his hips…but just barely. Later. In ten minutes, she could have him in her bed. Already, hunger buzzed its way up her spine.

Gamble Smith seized the champagne, walked over and set it back on the caterer's stack. Kat followed his movements, her gaze drifting over the powerful, rangy body simmering with anger.

"Send my check when it's ready." He stalked to the door.

"Gamble…" She stopped, confusion yielding to fury. He was walking out on her, damn it. Men didn't take a powder on Kat Gerard. It wasn't allowed. "Half the men here tonight would kill to be in your place."

He turned back at the door, his eyes unreadable. "I

did your dog and pony show, Kat. I don't do flavor of the day. Go get one of your little boy toys for that."

He barged into the night without her.

CHAPTER THREE

AT BROADWAY AND Seventy-ninth Lucas emerged from the subway, blinking in the flaccid late-winter sun. Countering every instinct for solitude he'd honed in prison, he joined the crowds and walked toward the Hudson, headed for the building where a dazzled teenager had once dared to dream.

Around him, the street roared with buses and cars, horns and screeching tires. Voices. Tension. Hustle and bustle that had once seemed normal.

He'd never intended to enter Manhattan again. Through all the years of being caged, he'd planned to head west the minute he was clear. To start over, to lose himself in wide-open spaces that held nothing of this place, of memories at once too dim and too crisp. He'd thought to search for Cherokee ancestors his father had claimed had the same angled cheekbones, whose raven hair was Lucas's own. His mother's family he'd never met. After she'd left, his father had kept them moving, always a new town. Always the fresh start that would be their big break.

Now Lucas had no one. If his mother was still alive, he had no idea where she might be, nor did he care. His father had given up on Lucas when Attica's gates had slammed shut. There was nothing in this city for him but pain, nowhere he wanted to be.

But Juliette's mercy called him. He had to find Tansy first. Find out if the reporter was wrong about Sanford.

Sweet Jesus. Carlton Sanford and Tansy. The final betrayal.

Martin Gerard would never agree to let him near her, he knew. If Paris's father had had his way, Lucas would have breathed his last in a dungeon, would never again have seen the light of day.

He shouldered his way through the crowd, eager to be done with this duty. His new life was on hold until then.

The stink of prison still coated his nostrils. The crowd pressed in on all sides, buckling the walls he'd held in place for so long. With fists and force of will, Lucas had declared a dead zone around himself all these years. Only Mose had trespassed.

Someone to his left jostled his neighbor. Lucas went on alert, every muscle tense. Unexpected movement meant danger. He couldn't draw a breath. For anxious seconds, the world grew too narrow, the air too thin, the people too close. Within a knife blade's reach of countless hands, Lucas forced himself to stop, to focus on the gray sky, to remember that he was not in prison anymore, that these people were not the savages with whom he'd spent the last twenty years.

No one wanted to kill him for an imagined insult, for his place in the yard—or just for the hell of it. No one knew him. No one cared. The crowd around him surged and waned, muttered and rushed, but it was just normal New York hurry, nothing more.

He was alone, and he had the power to determine his next step. Lucas stood perfectly still, the knowledge finally sinking in that no one would lock him up this night. No one would tell him what to eat, where to sleep. No one in this faceless crowd had any idea who he was or where he'd been.

No one would control his destiny ever again, he swore. He'd paid with twenty years of his life, and what was left was his.

And at that moment, on a crowded New York sidewalk rife with the sounds and scents of hundreds of people too busy to notice, Lucas Walker breathed the sweet air of freedom and began to believe the nightmare might be over at last.

For one second, features long ago schooled into granite relaxed into something resembling a smile. He had no idea where he would sleep, what he would eat, and the money he'd saved from his prison job wouldn't go far. He was what he'd always been: the scum on a shoe sole, the dregs of humanity. An ex-con who would never totally forget what it was to be locked in a cage.

He was out now. Free to starve. Free to freeze. To die as he'd lived: alone, with no one to care.

But the air around him, stinging with hot dogs and exhaust and grimy concrete, was his to breathe. His to suck down lungs that had forgotten the taste of hope. Only one duty restrained him.

Tansy.

The reporter had to be wrong. Dead wrong. Until he was certain, though, he must put off discovering if he could remember how to live as a normal man in a world that rubbed at him with the pinch of too-new shoes.

He rejoined the flow of the crowd past the next corner, then stopped stock-still.

There it was. Nineteen stories, prewar, rust-and-cream brick, it appeared too normal, the place where he'd once so very foolishly thought to sidestep who he really was and what people like him deserved. Where he'd dared to dream of a life in which beauty reigned, where love held sway. Where a naive half-breed, cast-off boy could dream that the golden fairy Titania might look past a peasant and see a prince.

Until one night of unspeakable darkness had shattered more than foolish fantasies.

He craned his neck upward to the sixth floor of a building he'd once known like the back of his hand, wishing he could see through walls so he would have to get no closer.

Lucas Walker was young no longer, a fool no more.

He'd been a nobody, then a prisoner. Now he was only a man who wanted to forget the past and find some small measure of peace. He walked away from the building, headed to the park across the street.

For the sake of a woman named Juliette, he would face that past again, no matter how much it squeezed his chest, made his long-dead heart sink. He would find a way to see Tansy again, to be sure she was safe.

Then he would leave New York forever, and make what he could of the rest of his life.

KAT PULLED HER COAT tight around her, drew a deep breath and stepped off the M5 bus as if facing her own execution. Ahead of her was the building that should have felt like home. Thanks to her father's self-absorption, it had ceased to be her home when she was eight years old. She stayed away from the place as much as possible; only the need to touch base with Tansy from time to time drew her back.

The elevator operator nodded. "Afternoon, Ms. Gerard."

"Hi, Jerry. Doing okay?"

"Right as rain, I am. Come to visit your father? Not long until his big day."

She didn't bother to correct him as they headed upward. Every day was Martin Gerard's big day. As far as he was concerned, the world revolved around his whims. How had her mother stood him? Why would someone so beautiful and talented have let her own star be eclipsed by his?

Juliette Clark Gerard had been stunning, if somewhat shy. Kat had spent hours poring over Nana's photo albums and scrapbooks filled with clippings. She'd had plenty of opportunity in those lost years; Dimmitt, Texas, was not exactly the hot spot of the world.

Kat had read every review of her mother's work, watched over and over the one movie she'd made. Juliette had been a star in the making. She could have had everything, could have risen to the top. Instead, she'd fallen in love with the wrong man, one whose monumental ego couldn't bear the competition of a more famous wife. He might have been the premier Shakespearean actor of his day, but stage could never compete with screen for star power.

The part of Juliette that had found fame excruciating welcomed the care of a man who'd offered to hold the vultures at bay. A man who'd fathered children to keep Juliette busy, but never bothered to get to know them.

There'd always been another production, another rehearsal. As richly as their lives had been filled with Juliette's love, it had been utterly devoid of fatherly interest. The only one of his children Martin had cared for had been The Son. And when Paris was gone, Martin had forgotten the rest.

Except Tansy, the eternal reminder of the mother she so resembled…and the son Martin had lost.

Screw him. Kat would never make her mother's mistake. No man would have the chance to take away her life. No man would get the best of Kat Gerard.

Which brought to mind one Gamble Smith. The night before still stung. She could send his check by messenger, but that would be a cop-out. He wasn't important enough to brood over. She'd keep to normal procedure and deliver his check herself.

But thinking of him, she was frowning when the door opened. Her father's housekeeper frowned right back. Mrs. Hodgson had never approved of Kat, never would. The feeling was mutual. She was a dried-up old prune who was foolishly indulgent of a tyrant. But she was devoted to Tansy, so for the sake of her sister, Kat attempted a smile. "Good afternoon, Mrs. Hodgson. I'm here to see Tansy." One day, she would take Tansy away from this place forever. Teach her how to live in the world again.

"I'll get her." Unsmiling, the woman turned her back without hesitation.

Musty air clogged Kat's nose, dust motes dancing in the weak light trying in vain to pierce the umber shadows. The apartment was a mausoleum, and Tansy was buried alive inside, whether or not she realized it. It was her sister's gift that her presence made the air fresher somehow, that light clung to Tansy as though she were dusted with gold. But how much more alive could Tansy be if she ever broke free? If she lived in a place where the paint wasn't yellowed with age and sorrow, the carpets moldering with dreams long dead?

Kat refused to set foot farther inside this place haunted by memories. She stared at the floor, studiously avoiding the entry wall crowded with photos of her father's triumphs, until she heard a crash in the living room. Frowning, she rounded the corner.

Her father sat suddenly, phone in his hand, his face drained of all color.

"What is it? What's wrong?" she asked, hearing the dial tone. Damn. The old bastard was supposed to be invincible.

Her father didn't answer for a moment. She moved near and reached for the phone. He pulled it away, then frantically punched in numbers.

"What is it?"

He blinked once, then focused on her. "Katharina. What are you doing here?"

His normally mellifluous voice was unforgettable even when he was not onstage, but at this moment, his imposing frame sagged and he looked as old as she'd ever seen him.

"I'm here to check on Tansy," she snapped. "What's wrong with you? Are you ill?" She hadn't known what to call him in years. Not Daddy or Dad or Father. *Old bastard* was closest to what she felt, but for Tansy's sake, she called him nothing.

He squeezed his eyes shut for a moment, then, when

a voice said hello, started to speak. "Carlton, thank God. A reporter just contacted me. Walker was released today."

Kat sucked in a breath and barely resisted the urge to grab the phone and make her father tell her the details. Of course he would contact Carlton first. She'd never understood why a man as overbearing as Martin Gerard had danced to another man's tune for so many years. Especially a pompous one like Carlton Sanford.

"What will I do if he comes here?" Martin listened for a moment, then his voice crackled. "He's an animal. He raped my daughter and murdered my son. He should have been executed, wiped from the planet. I want him dead, Carlton. I don't want him walking this earth, breathing the same air. I must find someone—"

Kat heard Carlton's voice, both commanding and soothing, and she tried to catch what he was saying.

"How can you be sure?" Martin retorted. "Perhaps Walker wants revenge."

Let him come, Kat thought. This time she wasn't a child. This time she wasn't exiled to Texas. She'd like to tear out Lucas Walker's black heart herself.

"No," her father said firmly. "She can't be at your place, Carlton. You know that. She stays here."

It was at Carlton's apartment that Tansy's nightmare had unfolded. Kat paced, waiting for her father to finish. She had to call Mona. Good God, *Walker.* Free when Tansy was still a prisoner of that night.

"No, I'm certain she doesn't remember. I don't want her to. There's no need to put her through that." Martin listened again, distress plain on his face. "No. I won't hear of it. She's too fragile. I don't care how expensive the facility—I won't have Titania locked up. Promise me that will never happen." He washed a palm over his face. "If only I'd kept him away from the twins—"

If only you'd looked past your own nose, you old bastard.

"Yes, all right. I'll leave it in your hands." Her father sighed deeply. "Of course I'll be ready for the opening. Lucas Walker has stolen too much. He won't have that." His voice softened. "You've been a good friend. I'm getting old, but I'm not ready to let go yet. I long to be remembered, Carlton, not fade away."

And that, in a nutshell, was their childhood. Her father's dreams and ambitions had always held first place.

He smiled faintly. "I know Titania's safe as long as you're in charge. Thank you, my friend." He hung up and slumped back in the chair.

"You are some piece of work."

"'Sharper than a serpent's tooth'," he muttered.

"Don't quote Shakespeare at me. I hate your precious Bard."

"Why, Katharina? What is it I've done?"

There was the crux of it. He'd never seen, never understood. Never paid attention. Never would.

"The discussion would take years you don't have. Tell me what's going on."

"Walker's been released. Carlton doesn't think he'd return here, but I cannot help wondering…"

She'd never liked Carlton, but Kat felt a certain gratitude for his role. She desired nothing to do with the care of a man who didn't give a damn about her.

Carlton Sanford was the true ruler of this place. He had dated her mother before her parents met—had, in fact, introduced them. He had been woven into their lives since before Kat was born. He had become a hero the night Lucas Walker had assaulted Tansy and murdered Paris.

If Kat had been there, if she hadn't been banished to Texas, she'd have stopped Lucas Walker. She might have been only nine, but she'd already been in her first fight, delivered her first black eye. She'd have fought like a demon for her sister.

She'd never understood how Carlton and Paris hadn't been able to protect Tansy or themselves against one young hood, even one armed with a gun.

Her father spoke again. "I have no idea what to do. I'm tied up in rehearsals, and she won't want to attend. I don't like leaving her here alone."

"She hardly ventures farther than the park."

"Perhaps she shouldn't go there."

"You'd cage her in this place?"

"It's for her own protection."

"Daddy, if you really cared about her, you'd get her help." In her anger, Kat forgot that she refused to call him by any name. "You'd bring her out of this gilded cage and let her fly free."

"She doesn't want out."

"Because she doesn't believe she can fly," Kat shouted. "You've clipped her wings, kept her helpless, encouraged her to live in that other world. But what about when you're gone? What then?"

"Carlton will guard her."

"Carlton is almost as old as you are. Surely you aren't considering that ridiculous marriage idea. He isn't family. I heard what you said—he's ready to put her away."

"He gave me his promise that he would never do that."

"You've already made him executor of your estate. He'll have too much power over her life."

"He cares about Titania as much as you do."

Kat saw red. "She's my sister. He doesn't understand her. I'd let her grow up, not keep her a prisoner."

"Your sister is not a prisoner. She's not well. She doesn't want to remember, and I am only protecting her from that pain."

"Women get raped all the time. They deal with it."

"Your sister isn't most women. She's not as strong as you."

She used to be fearless. And I didn't want to get strong, but I had no choice. Kat didn't bother saying either. He still didn't look past his own concerns. She might as well be invisible.

Suddenly, her father's face grayed. He sat down heavily again.

Her anger dried up. "What's wrong?"

"Nothing. Just a little tired. I'm not so young as I once was, Katharina."

To think of him as mortal shook her. He'd always been too big, too strong, too commanding. Something to fight against, not someone to protect.

Then he lifted his head. "Promise me you'll watch over Titania when I'm gone. I wish she were strong like you, but she isn't. And I worry." For the first time, she saw indecision in that proud face. "Perhaps I shouldn't have closed the world out so firmly. But I'd lost Paris, and so soon after that, my Juliette. I couldn't lose Titania, too." His voice turned to a whisper. "It was so close."

You still had two daughters, Kat wanted to say. *But you never remembered. Never sent for us. Didn't let us mourn together as a family should.*

Bringing it up wouldn't do any good. He wouldn't change.

So she answered, but not for his sake. "Of course I'll care for her. Mona, too. We don't need Carlton. Tansy is family." To Kat, that said it all—everything that he should have noticed but never had.

Just then Mrs. Hodgson returned. "Tansy isn't in her room. She must be in the park."

Martin's head lifted. He rose heavily.

"Stay." Kat held him off with a hand. "I'll go after her."

"Don't tell her why, Katharina. Don't make her remember."

Before she could fire off a retort, Kat left the apartment.

TALL BUILDINGS CAST shadows that marched across the park as the sun slid westward, making way for a cold and mournful evening. Lucas sat beneath the silvery-brown trunk of a tree, its naked branches devoid of any sign of life. Everything he owned in the world was stuffed in a plastic bag on the ground beside him, the bag, with its red heart proclaiming affection for New York, struggling to inject cheer into the unrelenting grayness. He tried to shut out the hiss of buses pulling to a stop, the constant roar of cars on the West Side Highway, the chatter of joggers and the barking of their dogs.

He craved silence and open spaces. This ribbon of park along the Hudson was a pale substitute. He'd grown up in cities up and down the eastern seaboard, always one step ahead of the landlord, until his father had found the job as super in the building where the Gerards lived.

Lucas should be accustomed to noise; it had surrounded him from the day of his birth. And Attica was full of it—clanging doors, shuffling feet, sharp, violent explosions when angry men collided. The prison itself nestled in a bucolic setting, a small, lovely village scarred by high walls and razor wire. Even at night, Attica reverberated with sounds of men snoring, moaning, shifting in restless sleep.

Lucas had had to find his own silence within the clamor, and he'd managed, sometimes just barely. A dead zone where his mind could rest from the screaming need to shout out the truth no one would believe.

But that was over. He was almost free. If he could just get away from this cursed city and all its memories, all its demands.

One more task, and his life would be his own again.

Why couldn't he leave the past alone? He told himself that he owed it to Juliette, to a mother who had shown sweet mercy to the murderer of her only son.

But that wasn't all of it, not by half. Every night of the past twenty years had been haunted by the memory of a terrified girl who'd held his heart in her hands. Lucas had never truly believed that he and Tansy had any chance, but he'd treasured the fantasy in those two years before the darkness fell.

Lucas Walker had no use for make-believe now. His breath escaped in a long gust. Night would come soon, and he had found nowhere to sleep. For a moment he toyed with the idea of crashing right here. The thought of walls of any kind made it hard to breathe.

But it was March in New York, and he didn't have so

much as a jacket. After so long in a cage, he was not about to die his first night out because he didn't have the sense to find shelter.

So Lucas stretched and started to rise—and then froze when he spotted the figure bending to pick up something from the ground twenty yards away.

Dear God, she looked just the same.

Lucas blinked, sure he was seeing things. Tansy would be thirty-six now, but she still seemed sixteen.

And fragile as a ghost. Her hair was white-blond, not honey-gold anymore, and covered by a pale scarf that some old lady might wear, but it glimmered like sunlight glistening on water.

With the stillness he'd learned the hard way, Lucas crouched right where he was, intent upon watching Tansy without being noticed.

She held up a feather, studying it against the sky as she drifted like a cloud, her feet hardly appearing to touch ground. Her pale-blue dress floated about her legs, far too light for the chill still clutched in winter's hand. Over the dress, she wore a bulky pink sweater that could not disguise the delicacy of her frame.

And she was talking. To the air. Walking beneath a tree, her slender hand caressing its bark, the worry on her face transfigured by sudden joy.

He rose with great care to get closer, and all the while he was wondering how it was that she could appear the same when every cell of him had been transformed.

How was it he could recognize her in an instant—and would she recognize him?

Not likely. His once-bony frame was layered with muscle, his face lined from twenty years in hell. His hair was long, and he had a scar on one cheek. His voice had deepened. And who he'd become on the inside had erased every trace of the boy she'd known.

But the fear that she might somehow see past all the changes kept him hanging back behind her, though he wanted badly to watch her face.

"Do you know, Paris?" she asked. "Did Mama tell you and not me?"

Paris? Dear God.

And then she laughed. "Don't tease. Mama promised my prince would come, and I don't believe a word you're saying."

Her laughter was a melody out of tune with her words. The Tansy he'd known was gone, and her mind with it. Despair settled over his shoulders like a shroud. Of all the scenarios he'd imagined, this was never one.

Tansy twirled and laughed, then stopped abruptly as she spotted Lucas.

Too late, he began to move away, afraid of what would happen next.

But her head only cocked slightly, her eyes alight. "Hello."

Lucas said nothing.

"I haven't encountered you here before." Her smile

was dawn after a night of storms. Shyly, her head dipped, then lifted again. "You look tired."

There was a kindness in her voice that made Lucas want to sink to the ground, lay his head in her lap and find peace. He was afraid to speak for fear that he was wrong, that she'd recognize him and run.

"Have you traveled from far away?"

He nodded. Four hundred miles and a lifetime.

Her smile widened in wonder. "You can hear me." Her head cocked again, her eyes worried. "Can you speak?"

That was very much like Tansy. She'd had a lot of mischief in her, but she'd also had more than her share of compassion. He'd once tried to save a bird that she'd found in this very park, and had felt himself a total failure when he couldn't.

His voice emerged rusty. "Yes." And he waited, breath held, for her reaction.

Not a trace of recognition, only pleasure. "Where do you live?"

Still cautious, he shrugged.

With one finger, she stroked the feather held in her other hand. She peered at him from beneath lowered lashes. "Is your kingdom pretty?"

Kingdom? "I beg your pardon?"

Color washed her cheeks. She glanced around her, relief in her eyes. "Oh, good. He didn't hear me."

Lucas glanced around. "Who?"

"My brother. He doesn't believe in my good dream."

He spoke past the ache in his heart. "What dream?"

Her face suffused with color, she cast her gaze downward. "It will sound foolish."

The vulnerable line of her neck made him long to reach out, protect her. Though he'd taught himself not to dream, he liked it that she still could. "Maybe not."

"I dream of a man...." She lifted her head suddenly, eyes wide. "He has dark hair...like yours." Her voice dropped to a whisper. "Are you my prince?"

A sharp bark of laughter rose in his throat. He'd had delusions of being one, a lifetime ago.

Then he saw that he'd hurt her. "I'm sorry. It isn't you, it's...me." She turned away and he wanted badly to draw her back. "Tansy, I—"

Her head swiveled sharply, her gaze locking on his. Then her whole face glowed. "You know my name." The smile was crafty. "You weren't supposed to say it, were you?" Her laughter pealed. "You made a mistake." She clapped her hands. "Ooh, I like this story."

Dear God. He hadn't saved her after all. The Tansy he'd cherished was gone...gone crazy.

He had to get away, to think. This was nothing he'd expected. He had to—

What? What could he do?

"Tansy, where are you?" An unfamiliar voice called out.

Both of them jumped. He searched for the source.

A tall woman with spiked copper hair strode through the park, her long legs eating up the ground with determined steps, though nothing could disguise the overt sensuality in the swing of her hips.

"Over here, Kat," Tansy called out.

Kat. Hell. Her youngest sister.

He began backing away.

"Wait," Tansy pleaded. She grabbed his sleeve. "Don't go."

He shrugged her off gently. "I have to."

"Will you return?"

He shook his head. "I don't think so."

"I've waited for you so long." Her words were said quietly but he felt a hand clench around what was left of his heart. "Please don't leave me."

"You don't know who I am, Tansy. You don't want to."

Blue eyes held a conviction he couldn't seem to fight. "You're wrong," she said. "I understand exactly who you are."

Lucas shivered at the unearthly light in her eyes. Was it madness or a knowledge that had survived time and agony? "Who am I, then?" he said softly.

That beautiful smile lit with a thousand suns. "You're my prince. You've finally appeared, just as Mama said."

"Tansy, I'm not…" Her sister was getting closer. "I have to go," he said with real regret.

"But you'll come back. Please. I'm here every day."

Lucas studied her for longer than he could afford. He shouldn't. He should leave on the next bus, get the hell out of Dodge.

But she was damaged, his beautiful Tansy, and he still hadn't found out about Sanford. He couldn't go yet.

"All right," he said. "I'll come back."

Then, with her sister only a few yards away, he grasped his meager belongings and loped off.

"TANSY, WHO WAS THAT?" Kat frowned after the tall form, the shaggy dark hair, of the man disappearing into the trees.

"He's lonely," she murmured. "But he says he's not my prince."

Kat stared down at the wide, innocent blue eyes and wondered how many times a heart could break. Mindful of her conversation with Martin, she regarded her sister. "You can't just talk to strangers, Tansy. You can't be sure who might hurt you. He could be anyone. He could—"

Tansy giggled, then reached up to brush slender fingers over Kat's forehead. "Hi, Kat. I'm glad you're here."

But the thought of someone like Lucas Walker harming her again made Kat's voice go sharp. "Tansy, I'm serious. You can't just…" She exhaled in a gust. "No one knew where you were. We were worried."

Immediate contrition filled the blue eyes. "I'm sorry." Then too-wise eyes peered into hers. "But I visit here every day." She trailed a tender touch over Kat's brow again. "What's worrying you? How did the show go?"

And that was Tansy. Lost in fantasy most of her life, then abruptly very right-here-in-the-present. Tansy was a great sounding board, though Kat was never sure how much she really heard. But her presence was always comforting, and sometimes Kat unburdened herself more than she intended. Tansy never passed judgment.

So to Tansy she'd confided her worries about putting on such an overtly romantic show in hip Manhattan. Kat couldn't help but smile now. "It was a roaring success. We sold almost every piece mounted, and the phone's been ringing all day with people wanting more."

Tansy's smile was serene and proud. "I had no doubt you'd do it." She tucked her arm in Kat's and led her across the grass toward the smooth, rounded top of Mt. Tom, a bump they'd once pretended was a mountain. "Stroll with me, sweetie, and tell me all about it."

And so it was that Kat found herself talking about success and Gamble Smith. She left with Tansy's reluctant agreement to go dress shopping in a few days, and by the time she realized that her sister had never agreed to stop talking to strangers, Kat was almost downtown to Gamble's warehouse.

The stranger in the park wouldn't be the first lost soul Tansy had picked up, but doing so still wasn't wise. Kat would continue to caution her, and they'd all keep an eye peeled, but Kat couldn't truly imagine Lucas Walker wanting to come within miles of any of them ever again.

And woe betide him if he did.

CHAPTER FOUR

LUCAS WALKED UNTIL it was almost dark, blind to the streets around him; for once, his concentration was so complete that even the crowded sidewalks didn't register.

He stepped off a curb, and a cab's tires screeched, the yellow paint halting within a breath of his body. Lucas jerked back to the world around him. He stopped his headlong charge, his fingers clenching automatically. Violence sang in his blood.

In the middle of the throng, he looked around. Chinatown. Good God. How long had he been walking?

"Whassamatter wit' you?"

He heard the muttered curses, but people moved around him the way a stream eddies around a boulder. Eyes downcast, passersby gave him a wide berth.

Lucas inhaled their fear and made it part of his shell. Solitude, his old friend, settled back into his bones. Suddenly, he was as exhausted as he'd ever been in his life. He needed sleep, needed space from his thoughts. Needed to forget…

Tansy. *Christ, Tansy, what have they done? Didn't anyone notice you slipping away into madness?*

Her prince. He pinched the bridge of his nose. Good God.

Desolation sucked up the adrenaline that had sent him racing away—from her, from his memories, from all he could never have. The best thing he could do was leave New York forever. Hunt for those empty miles where he could lose himself for good.

But the plea in Tansy's eyes...

A harsh voice broke in. "What you starin' at, asshole?"

Rage shot through him. His hands fisted; he took one step forward.

The man must have seen something in his eyes that unnerved him. Flipping Lucas the finger, he mumbled and pushed into the crowd.

But all Lucas could see was Tansy, the too-young, clean-slate look of her. A woman trapped as a girl. At sixteen, she had been innocent, but sharp. Funny. Restless and full of life.

At thirty-six, she was more child than woman. And lost, so lost. Protected only by the soft lambswool of her delusions. Anyone could hurt her. Anyone could—

No. You're done. You can't protect her anymore.

He'd given up twenty years of his life for her—and witness what they'd let happen. What the hell had gone on all this time? Was no one paying attention to what she'd become? Where was the help that had been promised? Where had the bright mischief gone?

Lucas cut across the sidewalk, shuffling like an old man. He leaned against the cold stone of a building and slid down to a crouch. All at once, he saw the waste his life had been, the foolishness he'd clung to the way a starving man hoards the last crumbs.

Christ. It was supposed to be over. He was supposed to be free.

He shuddered, sucked in a deep breath, exhaled in a gust. Juliette's mercy mocked him, bound him. She was the only one who'd ever believed in him.

Except Paris. And Tansy. All dead but her.

Please don't leave me.

Oh, Tansy. He squeezed his eyes shut as long-ago agony washed over him. A very rusty door inside him creaked.

She was gone. The girl he'd loved had died when Paris had died, and Lucas had never known. All this time he'd believed she was safe.

At once too drained to walk another step, too hopeless to fight anymore, Lucas Walker turned his side into the cold stone, curled his body in on itself. Alone as he'd always been, he closed his eyes on his fate as darkness fell.

The moment. One moment at a time, that's all. Do what's required and don't think beyond this.

His belly rumbled. All right. He would search for food. A place to sleep.

Just those. Just now. Nothing more.

KAT LEANED ON Gamble Smith's buzzer again, hard. "Come on, you big jerk. Answer the freakin' buzzer."

He might not be home, but she'd trekked all this way to deliver his check, it was getting dark and she'd be damned if she'd do it again tomorrow. *If* she ever decided to handle his work again, a post office box—and his agreement to check it daily—would be a minimum part of the deal.

She regarded the filthy sidewalk, the run-down building with distaste. *And* a phone. *And* a recorder.

Artists. Why hadn't the Fates seen fit to grant her the talent? *She'd* be smart enough not to squander it being rude and unrealistic.

Finally, she heard an answering buzz, the inner-door lock sliding open.

Kat smiled grimly. He *was* here, damn it. She'd give him his check and escape this neighborhood before the night creatures crawled out and the gauntlet got too thick. Two steps at a time, she stalked up the stairs.

His door creaked open. Framed inside stood Gamble Smith, his dark hair spiking out in some demonic nimbus, eyes shooting sparks. "What do you want?" he thundered.

"You have a mother, Gamble?"

He recoiled, his thick, jagged brows drawing together. "Yeah, why?"

Kat cocked her head, arching one eyebrow. "I'd think she'd have taught you some manners."

"You don't have any. Why should I?"

"I've got money in my hands. If you want me to hold on to it a little longer, then go ahead—act like the championship asshole you usually do."

He stared at her, nostrils flaring. "You always get your way?"

Her chin jutted. "Always."

He studied her with those penetrating blue eyes. Kat resisted the urge to squirm. At last, he spoke. "Keep the money." He revolved on his heel, shoving the door closed.

Flabbergasted, Kat barely got her hand inserted in time. She leaped through the opening. "If I leave right now, you'll never see this check."

He crossed his arms over a bare chest with an amazing amount of muscle. "I don't think so. Your gallery won't make it if word gets around that you cheat the artist." What might almost be a smile lit his eyes. "Best I can tell, that gallery is the only thing you understand how to love," he drawled in the Texas accent that reminded her too much of life with Nana.

"What would you know about love?" she countered.

Something that might be pain flickered across his features. "Not a damn thing," he growled. Then his gaze lifted, pinned her. "But more than you, with your pretty boys you can fuck and forget."

His scorn pushed her to strike back. He stood there, lean and long, looking dangerous in the half light of the dying day. His feet were bare, her boots with four-inch heels bringing her closer to eye level.

A wiser part of her cautioned that she should ignore his words, hand him the check and walk away.

But Kat didn't often listen to her wiser part. Instead, she crossed the three feet between them, grasped a handful of his hair and sneered, "I can forget you, too, Gamble Smith." Then she laid her mouth on his, pressing her curves all along the length of him.

And felt him go hard. Her mind shouted in triumph. She stepped away and smiled, ignoring a jitter. "You desire me."

"That doesn't mean anything."

"Sex doesn't mean anything," she retorted. "It's just fun. You *have* heard of fun?"

"You don't want to get involved with me, Kat." His tone turned ominous.

"I never said I did." She thrust his check at him and started to go.

Then froze at the sight of the painting on his easel.

"Get out," he commanded, inserting himself between her and the portrait.

Kat shoved past him, mesmerized. The canvas literally glowed with color, rich and ripe and glorious. It was an ode to beauty, his most romantic piece yet. Her first glance showed her a woman of stunning passion, yet such delicacy that she might have risen from mist. Her flowing gown rippled; her head tilted with a tender grace. Her eyes were open and shining with a love that could break your heart. Kat took a big step forward, then rocked back on her heels in shock.

The face was hers, red hair falling down her back. She could almost feel the filmy gown swirl over her legs, feel her hand stretched out for something she'd ceased to yearn for years ago. With every heartbeat, she edged closer to an innocence she'd left behind long ago....

Kat pressed one hand to her chest, literally robbed of breath, so thunderstruck that she hardly registered Gamble stalking past her, covering the canvas with a dark cloth.

He remained with his back to her for a long moment in which she, for once in her life, had no idea what to say.

Then he turned, but she could read nothing at all in his face. They didn't move for time that seemed endless, simply staring at each other as if one word would be too much.

Finally, the silence weighed too heavily. "Gamble, I—" She broke off. "Is that really me?" she whispered.

Instead of his usual barely restrained rage, his face was cold now. Closed in and lights off.

Then he spoke, his voice distant. "It's what you could be. But you waste it. Every day you throw away more of yourself."

"You can't..." Her voice scraped like rusted tin. She swallowed hard. "You don't know me." She felt naked, crazy naked as if her chest had been ripped open, and the air stung like a thousand razors slicing the tender pink inside.

Indecision tore at her. She wanted to uncover that painting, to see the woman she didn't recognize, to stand in front of it until she could find the traces of that woman inside her own skin.

And she wanted to back away from Gamble Smith and this terrible knowledge of his. Out through that door and back to the life she recognized.

"Who the hell are you?" she whispered. All at once, Kat understood cultures whose people feared the camera would steal their souls. He'd stolen something from her, some part hidden and precious. He'd reached deep into longings she'd cast away with childhood.

That was private. He had no right. Fury restored her voice back. "I'll buy that painting. How much do you want?"

"It's not for sale."

"You can't work on it any longer. You can't let anyone—"

One dark eyebrow lifted slightly. "It's mine. I can do whatever I wish with it."

"Gamble, you can't—it's too much. I can't bear…" Where was fury now? He'd stripped her defenseless. Shoving weakness away, she closed in, set foot on familiar ground. "You have a price—what is it?" One scarlet nail slid down his chest as she arched to bring her breasts closer to him.

Gamble caught her wrist in a crushing grip and shoved her back. "It's not for sale." His jaw flexed. "Nor am I. Get out." He took a menacing step toward her.

She pointed one long, scarlet-tipped finger. "Don't you let anyone else get their hands on that painting." He'd exposed her, opened her up to ridicule. She wasn't that woman, but an almost visceral longing plagued her.

"Don't you cross me," she warned. "I'll ruin you."

"You're not as tough as you pretend to be."

"You understand nothing about me." She straightened to her full height. But deep inside her, something shivered. "I'll leave now, but I'm warning you—our contract calls for me to handle all your work for the next year. There are no provisions for reserves. That painting is mine." With a toss of her head, she strode to the door, then tried to ignore that her hand was shaking as she gripped the knob.

He didn't say a word as she left, but she could find no comfort in his silence.

LUCAS JERKED OUT OF the half sleep that was as far as he had dared go in the doorway that had been his bed during the night. He'd walked for hours returning toward Tansy, stopping only to grab a quick bite, unable to force himself inside an enclosure, even one he was free to leave.

The faint gray of dawn dusted the tops of buildings, but here on the street, deep shadows still held sway. He stood and stretched. Shivered, rubbing his arms, wishing for even the thinnest blanket.

Damn this place. The city noises drove him nuts. And it was cold. He wanted to be somewhere warm and solitary and quiet, but he had to face facts. He was going nowhere yet. No matter how his soul yearned for space and a new start, one image stalked him and wouldn't be erased.

Tansy. More beautiful now than the girl he'd thought beyond compare. Delicate. Gentle. And vulnerable, too vulnerable.

Lucas knew that he could not leave until he understood what had happened. Until he'd determined for himself that Tansy would be all right. Would be safe.

He had to take immediate steps to conserve his meager funds. He must find work, and soon. With what he had now, he couldn't afford anything but a flophouse for a room, and he was not going to any shelter for the homeless. Never again would he sleep in a mass of men where despair hung in a smothering cloud. He had paid with his youth, had spent all his hope inside concrete walls, had learned to be brutal to defend his life.

Sleeping in a doorway was not the night under the stars in the wide-open spaces he longed for; however, it was better than any of his other options.

He would do it again tonight if he had to, but he

would find a job today and soon he would have a bed of his own, however humble. Four walls inside which he was king and no one could trespass. No guards. No cons. No father's fists.

And as soon as possible, he would depart this god-forsaken city forever.

Hours later, Lucas understood that he would never be finished paying for a night that was not of his making. That he'd educated himself in prison didn't matter. He'd already applied for eleven jobs and been rejected for every one. No one wanted an ex-con with no references.

The only jobs he'd been offered were selling dime bags to kids and selling himself. He hadn't fought off the advances of bigger inmates only to give in now that he was free.

So as he walked into the topless joint with the Help Wanted sign in the window, he battled with desperation. He couldn't let it be the same old story here.

The place was as dark inside as the windows were dirty on the front. He counted four men scattered at tables, halfheartedly watching a dancer long past her prime. She shot a glance at Lucas and cupped her beyond-belief breasts in her hands, grinding her pelvis in his direction while her tongue slid over cherry-red lips.

He'd been a long time without a woman. Hell, he'd hardly gotten started learning women when he'd found himself locked up.

But he wasn't that desperate. Resignation slid

through his bones. He was ready to call it quits, when, from a tiny corner of his mind, Tansy's face rose.

Goddamn it. *How much is enough?* he wanted to cry out. When did he get to live *his* life, the one ripped away on a night when he was a stupid kid?

You've had a difficult life, Lucas, Juliette had written. *There's goodness in you; I can't believe you intended it to happen. I've asked Martin to help you, to forgive you as I do.*

Well, he didn't, Juliette. He helped them to bury me.

But that didn't change what she'd done, what she'd asked. She'd believed in him when no one else had. She'd granted him mercy in her dying twilight. Him, a kid whose own mother hadn't believed him worthy of saving.

All Juliette had ever asked of him was that he take care of Tansy. Long before that night, she'd asked a streetwise kid to watch over her impulsive, naive daughter. That girl was gone, but Lucas's debt remained.

Christ. He squeezed his eyes shut, tried to block out all the noise in his head. After a long moment, he opened them again and saw sympathy in the face of the dancer.

Life trapped people in different ways. She was here because she had nowhere else to go, and Lucas didn't, either. He smiled at his fellow prisoner, and when she smiled back, her face was almost pretty.

Lucas steeled himself and headed for the bartender.

"What can I get you?" Dark eyes viewed him from a weary, lined, dark-chocolate face.

Lucas nodded back over his shoulder. "I want to see the manager. I'm here about the job."

"Ain't much of a job, just washing dishes."

"I don't care. I need the work."

The eyes scanned him. "When you get out?"

Shit. Lucas met the gaze evenly. "Yesterday."

The head cocked. "And you already lookin' for work? Not out whorin' and drinkin'? How long you in?"

His heart sank. "Twenty years."

The eyebrows lifted slightly, but the man kept polishing the glass he was drying. "You kill a stranger?"

The length of time he'd served was a dead giveaway that violence had been involved. "No. And I can do the job. I know how to work."

"So you killed somebody familiar. How close?"

He forced his fingers to relax from the fist he'd formed. "I've done my time. The past is over."

"Past ain't ever over, son. It's with us till the day we die."

"Let me talk to the manager."

"You lookin' at him. Manager, owner, chief cook and bottle washer of this fine establishment."

To give up and walk out was tempting. He was so damn tired of fighting. Tired, period. He forced himself to remember that picture of Tansy and Carlton Sanford.

"I can cook, too. The warden had me cook for him."

"Don't need no cook."

Lucas glanced around. "Good food would bring in more people."

"Younger tits would bring in more people. I can't afford them, either."

From somewhere deep, Lucas dug for strength. "The sign says you're hiring help. If it's washing dishes, I wash dishes. Sweeping floors, I sweep floors." Jaw tight, he waited a second. "You don't trust a con, I'll make you a deal. I'll work free for two days."

The old man's eyes narrowed. "You really mean it about workin', don't you?"

A tiny hope flared. "I do." He paused, dug deeper. "I'll beg if you want." The word *beg* stuck in his throat, but Lucas didn't have the luxury of pride right now.

The old man studied him for a long moment. "You don't have to do that, son. I spent some time behind bars myself in my younger days." Slowly, he extended a hand across the bar. "Albert Jackson. You got a name?"

Lucas's heart beat a deafening tattoo as he lifted his own hand. "Lucas Walker, Mr. Jackson."

"Cool Hand Luke? You call me Al." He shook hands firmly. "Don't you make me regret this, boy. I won't be made a fool."

"You're not a fool, Al. I'll do the work."

Al went back to his drying, though surely not one drop of moisture remained. "You got a place to stay?"

"Not yet."

"Got me a cot downstairs for nights when I'm too

tired to make the trip uptown. "'Spect you could use it until I find out if you work out." He glanced sideways at Lucas. "Oh, I ain't no fool. Money goes home with me at night. But I don't believe you're a thief, Luke Walker, are you?"

Pride knotted in his throat, but he swallowed his bitter retort. "No. I'm not a thief."

"And you didn't murder no stranger, so as long as I don't get to be your friend, I ought to be safe, you think?"

Finally, Lucas noticed the twinkle in those dark-chocolate eyes. For one second, he thought he might embarrass himself as the kindness of a stranger hit him hard. Swallowing around the tightness, Lucas found a small smile. "You'll be safe."

The twinkle vanished as dark eyes went serious. "Don't disappoint me, son."

Lucas drew himself up to his full height. Met Al's stare with one of his own. "I won't."

"Then go pick up your stuff from wherever you got it stashed and get on back here. You go to work today."

Lucas started to head toward the bus station where he'd rented a small locker. "I'll be back in thirty minutes." Then he stopped and turned. "Thank you."

Al jerked his head toward the door. "See if you're still saying that tomorrow. Now, go on. Get your sorry white butt here in thirty minutes and try to convince me you can really cook."

Lucas nodded and headed for the door. As he passed the small stage, the overblown blonde waved goodbye. Lucas winked and blew her a kiss.

CHAPTER FIVE

TWO DAYS LATER, Lucas burst out of the subway car and took the steps upward, two at a time. He'd told Al he had an errand to run before work, but he didn't have much time before he had to be back at the bar.

It was a fool's errand, hoping for Tansy to come to the park again just because he'd spotted her there around this time before.

But then, it wouldn't be the only time he'd been a fool over Tansy Gerard.

He could still remember the day he'd first seen her, a laughing sprite usually inseparable from her bigger twin. Lucas had met Paris in the basement of the building the day before, when Paris was being punished with laundry duty. Lucas's father, the new building super, had put him to work mopping the laundry-room floor. An angry Paris dumped clothes without sorting, scattering soap on the floor Lucas had just mopped. One temper butted up against another, and soon they were pummeling each other with abandon.

They became friends in the space of one fight.

The next day Lucas's father beat the hell out of him after Martin Gerard figured out who had dared to touch his precious son. Threatened with firing, Harry Walker stormed in the door, fists swinging, pounding a promise out of Lucas to stay away from those who weren't his kind. Their luck had improved at last, and Lucas was not to screw it up.

It was far from the first occasion on which Lucas had felt the bone-cracking force of his father's fists; it wouldn't be the last. But Lucas was growing every day, and he swore that the last time would be sooner than Harry Walker wanted.

His sixteenth birthday was only months away, and Lucas planned to be gone when that day arrived. To promise to stay away from Paris Gerard was no hardship.

Until Tansy came downstairs that same day.

A year older than the twins, Lucas at fifteen was already tall if not yet filled out. Paris and Tansy were halves of a whole, but not equal halves. Both slender, both blond; still, brother topped sister by half a foot, and Lucas topped Paris by several inches.

Tansy was a reed, already living up to the promise of her heartbreaking beauty, but though she looked like a fairy princess, she was as fearless as her brother, twice as impulsive. She was a genius at sneaking out without getting caught. Equal parts curiosity and mischief had brought her to see this boy who dared to touch her golden brother, The Son, the apple of Martin Gerard's eye.

Curiosity might have incited her to beard the lion in his den. Compassion made her stay.

Lucas could still feel the touch of those dainty fingers as she'd fussed over the new cuts he tried to shrug away. He'd bandaged them himself, just as he'd done many times before, but nothing would do except that she must clean them better and bandage them again.

Lucas had barely stopped her from dragging him upstairs for a dose of her mother's tender care. Only when he'd grudgingly explained about his father's job had Tansy relented, but she'd told him where to meet her and Paris after school the next day, taking it for granted that he would defy his father.

She'd been wrapping her own sire around her finger for years, covering for Paris when he got into his many scrapes. When Lucas joined them and became their Third Musketeer, he was astonished at Tansy's talent for duplicity. Soon, she'd worked her magic on his father, too. Neither man could stand in the path of Tansy's charm, Tansy's sweetness, Tansy's implacable will. She wasn't spoiled or temperamental. Tansy simply made you feel that you'd be turning down magic if you didn't join in whatever enthusiasm held her in its sway.

Paris was no different. People thought Tansy followed him like a shadow. It was a few weeks before Lucas realized that their worst mischief was often Tansy's idea, which Paris seemed to absorb without words. The communication between them was remarkable...linked by a cord invisible to the naked eye, the two were separated only by skin. In heart and mind, they would always be one.

And they were magic, pure and golden. To be with them was to swallow sunshine, to walk inside a spell that kept all harm away. Life had never been so rich, so full for Lucas Walker. Dazzled by their beauty, he felt himself the luckiest kid alive simply to be allowed near. For that, he had Tansy to thank. He was more than half in love with her, but willing to wait until she was ready, until the woman replaced the girl.

And in the meantime, there was Juliette, who took him in and replaced the mother who'd discarded him and run away. Over and over since childhood, Lucas had asked himself what made him so easy to leave behind, but deep inside, he knew. He came from bad blood, bore the taint of it. He'd never be any different. His mother had seen it and cut her losses.

Juliette would have realized it someday, too. Martin Gerard had figured out who Lucas was—a truant and a rebel—and his disdain had been clear. But Gerard was seldom there in body or spirit, always playing a part, ever onstage. His work was his life, his family an afterthought, except for Juliette.

Juliette of the Sorrows, Lucas called her in his most private thoughts. The most beautiful woman he'd ever laid eyes on, she was also the saddest, the most in need. She gave everything to her children, to the husband who put her on a pedestal and expected her to stay there. She would have had a dozen kids if Gerard had agreed; instead, she adopted a stray like Lucas. She drew him out of the cesspool of his life and brought him into the enchanted circle despite her husband's protests about taking in a cur. Slowly, she wooed Lucas from wildness. Inside the circle of her compassion, she made Lucas want to believe he could be more than he was.

He would have died for her, would have killed for her.

In many ways, he had.

So on this day more than twenty years later, Lucas darted across Riverside and stopped at the rock wall near Eighty-second where he'd sighted Tansy before, but there was no sign of her anywhere. He glanced at the cheap watch he'd bought on a street corner and noted that he had only a few minutes left before he must head back to Al's. He vaulted the wall and scrambled down the hillside toward the Hudson, swiveling his head this way and that, hoping to spot her.

But what he really craved was to find the Tansy of so long ago. Not the Tansy who'd returned from exile in Texas only a few short weeks before it all ended. Not the Tansy he'd seen two days ago…

Juliette had entrusted the old Tansy to him, had believed he could protect her. But he was certain now that Juliette couldn't have guessed what her daughter would become, a wisp of the enchanting creature who had first brought Lucas in from the cold.

No hint remained of that Tansy, and Lucas possessed no sorcery to restore her.

Freedom beckoned. Tansy wasn't here. He could walk away now, leave today. Remember that he was only a man, an ex-con who had lost twenty years of his life to a doomed impulse. Shoving his hands in his pockets against the chill wind blowing off the Hudson, Lucas recognized himself for the fraud he was.

He was no Galahad, no St. George to fight the dragon of Martin Gerard, of Carlton Sanford. To get near enough to Tansy to help her would be an impossible task—

But he would have to try, anyway.

Hunched against the wind whistling through his one clean shirt, Lucas quickened his steps and climbed back to Broadway to catch the downtown train.

"MONA, THE LEAD ARTICLE still hasn't shown."

"Mona, Artie's layout for Health and Beauty sucks."

"Mona, the warehouse guys called and the roof leaked last night. We've lost a whole pallet of the next issue."

"Mona—"

Mona blinked against the screaming Chinese-red of the walls and their pulsating yellow chrysanthemum accents, her stomach rolling. She made her way down the hall to her office, her staff hanging from her like leeches. Her head was primed to blow and her eyes were so scratchy she was wearing her glasses. Her father had been on the phone at seven this morning, complaining that she hadn't called him back last night.

And Lucas Walker was a free man.

"Mona, I need—"

She whirled. Held up one hand. Sucked in a breath. Counted to ten.

When around her the leeches fell quiet, she singled out her assistant, Gaby. Cool, calm Gaby, who had come to New York from Texas to eat nails for breakfast.

As Mona once had.

"I will deal with each of you beginning in ten minutes. Gaby, make a list. Everybody out."

Then Mona walked into her office, closed the door and leaned back against it, knowing that aspirins were six feet away and the strong cup of coffee Gaby would bring would be here by the time she opened the bottle and shook them out.

A baby. Christ, Fitz, my whole life is dealing with babies. Some of them twenty-three and one of them seventy-five.

Mona glanced at the stack of messages on her desk, heard the chime of incoming e-mail and pondered having it all.

I don't have time or room for it all, Fitz. Dear God, please come to your senses soon.

They'd passed as strangers in the night ever since his

shocking request. He'd been gone when she woke up this morning.

She wanted nothing more than to curl up and take a nap. With a shake of her head, she crossed to her desk and had barely removed the cap from the aspirin when she heard the door open quietly, and smelled the coffee.

"You are henceforth forbidden to marry or have children, Gaby. You can't ever leave—my first decree of the day."

"Bad night?" The voice was both sympathetic and teasing.

Mona turned, hand outstretched for the life-giving elixir. Popped the aspirin, saw the glass of water, drank. Then clutched her coffee as though it were salvation. After a sip, she looked up.

"My only mistake was waking up."

Their smiles met, nodded, mingled with care. Gaby would leave when she was ready. Mona understood that; she'd been a bright young girl herself.

You can't have it all, Mona wanted to warn her, though it wouldn't do any good. *You think you have it wired, and then fate steps in. Shakes the balance.*

"Your ten minutes are almost over. Drink up," Gaby urged.

The magazine. Yes. *Her* magazine. Her baby.

Fitz would snap out of it. He would.

Mona drank deeply, sighed. Ignored the rebellion in

her stomach. Rolled her neck like a boxer, then looked up and grinned. "Bring 'em on."

THAT AFTERNOON MONA SAT beside her father in Carlton's limo, accompanying him to the theater for the first time. The cast had been rehearsing the principal parts in a private studio. She was too busy for this, but when he'd asked her, she didn't have the heart to refuse the chance to be present for his triumphal return to the stage.

She was shocked to feel him trembling, like a child approaching kindergarten, as he rose, slowly and with less grace than he would wish, from the back seat of the limousine Carlton had put at his disposal. For a moment Martin stood at the stage door, seeming almost afraid to enter for the first time in ten years. Was he worried that it would not be the same—or that it would?

"Mr. Gerard, a real honor, sir."

The wizened face at the doorway belonged to a slender, slightly stooped man who gazed at her father as though he were the Second Coming. When her father didn't respond, he added, "It's Charlie, sir. Charlie—"

"Howard. Charlie Howard, you old dog. Of course I remember. How could I forget you?"

"If you don't mind me saying so, sir, it's been too long. We've missed you. The theater has missed you. No one like you anymore, Mr. Gerard."

She could see the pleasure straighten her father's

spine, even as he brushed at the air. "Now, Charlie, there's some fine actors treading the boards these days."

"None to compare with you, sir. Not even close. Welcome home, Mr. Gerard." With a flourish, Charlie opened the stage door.

Martin paused on the threshold, his expression reverent. Mona stopped, as well, unsure what to do. "Three thousand days and nights," he murmured, his eyes suspiciously damp.

She tried to imagine how it must feel to be him. A heart attack had forced his retirement; ten years had passed since he'd last breathed the air of this world that had been his marrow, his very life blood. The jealous mistress who had claimed the love his children had craved. Mona had no idea what to say, so she merely waited.

When the door shut behind them, Martin hesitated and closed his eyes, his chest expanding as though breathing oxygen for the first time in years.

"Not a smell like it, Desdemona, anywhere else. Every theater is different, yet every one the same…the perfume of greasepaint, the undertone of ruined dreams, the top note of triumph beyond imagination. The *tristesse* of the love affair with every opening night crowd, when hopes and dreams and fears all crash together in a mélange that will distill, in the course of one performance, into salvation's exquisite kiss…or failure's sweaty embrace."

On his face she saw rapture, a lover returning home after decades in exile. "I've been half-alive," he whispered. "Now I'm young again."

Just then a woman walked down the shadowy corridor and sucked in a breath. "Mr. Gerard…oh, Mr. Gerard…" She sighed—

And dropped into a curtsy.

Another time Mona would have laughed, but somehow today it was appropriate. Grand as a monarch, he reached to lift her to favor. Suddenly, he was no old man, no quavering father. He was Martin Gerard, who'd owned this world for half his life.

"Come now, my child. You make too much of one old man."

"Oh, no, Mr. Gerard. You'll never be old. You're the best there is. Theater has not been the same—welcome home."

Mona saw for the first time in many years the world's leading Shakespearean actor. Far from old, he was ten feet tall again, striding young and strong to conquer the great stages of the world. He reached down, drew the young woman out of the shadows—and froze.

He stumbled backward, his cry hoarse and choking.

"Juliette. My God…Juliette."

CHAPTER SIX

"MR. GERARD? MR. GERARD?" The young woman hurried to him, face screwed up in concern. "Are you all right? You look as though you've seen a ghost."

His own face drained of color, Martin pressed one hand against the wall to steady himself. "Who...are you?" His voice was weak and thready as an old woman's.

Just then a larger shape moved out of the gloom. "I see you've met Ms. Hart, Martin. She'll be understudy to your Cordelia," said Carlton. He turned. "Mona, how are you?"

She glared at him. "What is this, Carlton?"

Martin's glance jumped to the young woman again, then back to his trusted old friend.

"It's all right, Daddy," Mona soothed. She snapped out an order to the young woman. "A glass of water, please."

Carlton merely lifted an eyebrow and smiled. "Remarkable, isn't it?"

"Ms. Hart..." Martin called out.

The young woman paused. "Oh, call me Julie, please. Is—is something wrong?"

Julie. It was too much, on top of all the other memories Lucas Walker's return had dredged up from the abandoned riverbed of their past. "The water, Ms. Hart," Mona reminded her.

"No, wait…" Martin straightened, his eyes aglow with a fanatical light. He grasped for her hand. "Nothing is wrong, my sweet. Nothing at all, not now."

"Daddy, this isn't—"

But her father wasn't listening. He'd turned his back on her, tucking the young woman's hand into his elbow. "Perhaps you'd be my consort as I make my reentry to the proscenium arch."

She blushed with pleasure. "I'd be delighted, my king." She nodded with a grave dignity beyond her years. Together they walked away.

"What's going on, Carlton?" Mona hissed under her breath.

He shook his head, staring at Martin and the young woman. "I'd wondered if I were the only one who saw it."

"You can't let this pass." Stepping around Carlton, she headed for her father.

Carlton grabbed her arm, held her back. "Look at him. Not as your father but as an actor. He's energized. I haven't seen him that way since—"

"This is ridiculous. What's wrong with him? He can't believe that's Mama—"

"This is who he is, Mona, an actor. He lives for make-believe. He's not suited for real life."

"But he can't possibly think she's—"

"Notice that spring in his step. Would you deny him the fuel necessary to make his triumphant homecoming?"

"Why would she do this? It's dishonest."

"She's ambitious, of course, as only an understudy can be. But what's the harm in make-believe if it helps him out?"

Mona turned to the suave older man who'd been in their lives before she could remember. "Did you plan this, Carlton?"

His grin was quick. "No. Sheer coincidence, my dear. I can stop it now, if it bothers you that much." He waited a beat. "He'll admit it soon enough himself, in any case. He doesn't really believe she's Juliette. It's only a comforting memory. Come, Mona. You're not a child anymore. What's so bad about boosting an old man's ego?"

Mona struggled to put away her resentment. Martin had had little to say to her since they'd left the apartment, but he was already regaling this girl with story after story.

Clad in capri pants and ballet flats, but carrying herself like a queen draped in satin, this pale substitute for Mona's mother accompanied her father on his grand entry.

Leaving Mona behind, once again utterly forgotten.

"OH, GOD, SHE'S WEARING another one of Nana's scarves," Kat muttered as she and Armand stood in the doorway of her father's apartment, waiting to take Tansy shopping.

"Shh," Armand soothed. "She'll be fine. I know a saleswoman at Bendel's who'll treat her with kid gloves."

"Bendel's? Armand, she'll come out of there clothed like some doddering East Side matron."

"Hush. Your ignorance is showing." He moved toward Tansy, holding out his hands, a broad smile on his handsome face.

"I was thinking SoHo," Kat muttered. "Or Chelsea." But Armand had clearly taken over as captain of this adventure.

Tansy's lovely face lit up as she caught sight of Armand. With a musical laugh, she launched herself into his embrace.

Kat wondered where the cynical sophisticate had fled as Armand's entire demeanor softened, his face revealing a tenderness she'd never seen before.

"Hello, princess." He placed a gentle kiss on the head that snuggled into his chest, and a pang seized Kat as she watched them.

Then Tansy stepped back shyly, and Armand held her hands out wide. "You look lovely. Are you ready for our adventure?"

Tansy cast her sister a frightened glance. Then she squeezed Armand's hands and drew herself up straight, though Kat could sense the effort. "I want to make Daddy proud. It's his big night, after all, isn't it?"

Kat's heart went out to her too-fragile sister. Tansy's world had shrunk to a few blocks, and this couldn't be easy. But when Tansy loved, she loved fiercely, even now. Her nerves showed, but this outing would be good for her. Perhaps she would discover that her world could be bigger. Perhaps she would at last attempt to free herself from the prison of the past.

God knows the old bastard would never do it.

Kat moved closer, ran her hand over her sister's arm and squeezed the hand clenched at her side. "We'll have fun, Tansy. I promise."

Tansy licked her lips with a nervous swipe and squeezed Kat's hand back. "Will we take the bus?"

Kat couldn't tell whether the light in her eyes was terror or anticipation, but the former seemed more likely.

"Oh, no—Armand's car and driver are here. No commonplace cabs or trains or buses for Princess Tansy, the belle of the ball. Your fairy godfather is transporting you in style."

"A car?" Tansy's eyes rounded. "I haven't been in a car much since…" Again her gaze darted to Kat.

Kat nodded and grinned. "Since Nana's monster of a Buick, right?"

Tansy fingered the edges of the scarf, lavender today to match the flowers in her long skirt, and nodded.

"Remember Nana turning corners and running up and down over the opposite curb?"

Tansy's eyes filmed, a tiny crease appearing between her eyes. Suddenly, she grinned, and it was almost as if the old Tansy stood before them, mischief dancing in her sky-blue eyes.

Then an amazing thing happened.

Tansy laughed.

The old laugh, like a hot July day at the top of a Ferris wheel when you're full of cotton candy and the summer seems endless and ripe. The laugh of a Tansy Armand had never met and Kat had almost forgotten.

Kat rejoiced with the big sister she'd lost so long ago, chuckled from deep in her own belly as she hadn't in years. She reached out, marveling, to grasp the sister she should have had all this time. Drew her close as tears stung her eyes.

Tansy clasped her around the waist and hugged her hard. Kat peered over her sister's head at Armand, surprising an expression naked with longing and helpless pride.

Longing? For Tansy? He'd never said, not a word.

Tansy pulled away, her eyes dancing. "I have to remind Paris about the time he decided to drive Nana's car while she was taking a nap." She squeezed Kat's hands, then whirled around. "I wonder if he recalls the spanking she gave him with that willow switch." She whirled back. "I'll go tell him quickly, all right?"

Kat's heart plunged to earth in a sickening dive. From

the top of the Ferris wheel to the bare dirt below, her hope crashed. Shattered. She couldn't look at either of them. "The car is waiting, Tansy." She couldn't acknowledge her sister's sickness. Within her, rage rose. *Paris is dead,* she wanted to shriek. *If I could, I'd kill him myself so he'd let you go.*

No—that wasn't true. She'd loved Paris, too, had stood in awe of his golden perfection, his favored place as The Son. Her adored big brother. Who she really wanted to murder was Lucas Walker. He'd taken her sister, her beautiful, saucy sister, and slain her as surely as his bullet had stolen Paris's life.

Kat couldn't speak as she watched Tansy's face settle into resignation. Back into madness. *Damn you, Lucas Walker. Damn your soul to hell.*

"Perhaps you could visit Paris when we return," Armand suggested. "You'll be able to regale him with our adventure, as well." As smooth as ever, Armand waltzed into the breach stinging with tear gas, and dispelled it with the fresh wind of reason and uncommon grace.

Kat could almost hate him, too. No one wanted Tansy to wake up. Everyone was afraid of what would happen if Tansy ever did.

Kat started to speak, to say it out loud. *Wake up, Tansy, damn it.*

But Armand caught her intent and shook his head, his green eyes hard as emeralds. "Kat, would you please inform Mrs. Hodgson that we're leaving now?"

Dismissed, she fumed. He treated her as an irresponsible girl, while he behaved as if her child of a sister was a princess who would crumble, should the light of day ever land squarely on her illusions.

Illusions, hell. Delusions. Kat stalked toward the kitchen, not sure who made her angrier, Tansy for being so weak or Armand for protecting that frailty.

But as Kat returned to the living room and saw her sister's fair head leaning against Armand's shoulder in a posture so trusting and vulnerable it could break your heart, all the venom leaked out of her like air from a punctured bicycle tire.

The thought of her sister being brutalized by Lucas Walker made the gorge rise in Kat's throat. Kat could stand such a thing; she'd survive. But Tansy had lost half her soul that night when Paris died, and Lucas Walker had savaged the rest.

Guilt rode Kat hard, never mind that she'd been nine years old and far away when it happened. The bright spirit inside Tansy might have been lost forever, and shame forced Kat to step back from her rage. Perhaps the others were right. Maybe their shared complicity made them all search for ways to spare Tansy from remembering.

Perhaps their father and Mona knew better than Kat. They believed it was up to those who loved Tansy to guard what was left, even if that meant wrapping illusion around her like cotton batting.

"Come on, gang." She roused herself to cheer, false though it was. "Our adventure awaits."

Armand led Tansy to the door, where he stopped and gazed back with something Kat didn't often see in his eyes.

Approval. And pride.

Past the lump in her throat, she summoned a smile. Then she looped her arm through her sister's and led her out.

They were encouraging Tansy brave only a few blocks, but perhaps that was the way it would be, this opening of Tansy's world.

One step at a time. Patience was not Kat's friend and never would be.

But for Tansy, she'd try.

"WHERE DID YOU FIND HER?" Kat glanced from the efficient but warm saleswoman toward Armand. "She's too old to be one of your devoted conquests."

Armand merely lifted one of his jet-black eyebrows, which contrasted with his shining silver hair. He'd gone gray in his early thirties, and the contrast with his youthful bronzed sailor's skin was striking. He was one of the most handsome men she'd ever met, but there were layers and layers to him beyond his looks.

"I'd prefer to think of myself in a more benevolent light. I appreciate women far too much to want to ravish them." He gave her a wry smile. "Seduction is so much more satisfying. A willing woman is a man's greatest triumph."

Kat snorted, glancing from the dressing room door toward him. Under the miracle saleswoman's firm ministrations, Tansy's nervousness had fled, and now she insisted on surprising both Kat and Armand with each selection. "I see plenty of willing females, but few who get a repeat performance. A commitment problem, my friend?" The more she considered it, the more the idea of Armand languishing for love of Tansy took hold. Kat would never have thought about it before, but perhaps Armand's confirmed bachelorhood had its source in a deep romanticism.

Kat was torn. Tansy and Armand… He would guard her fiercely, of that Kat had no doubt. But what would a world traveler such as him do, chained to such a fragile flower?

Still, Tansy could not have a better champion. Armand was, despite his air of world-weariness, a deeply decent and honorable man.

"What's placed that cat-in-cream smile on your face, Katharina?"

"Oh, nothing." She nudged him with her elbow. "Look lively, pal. Tansy's headed our way."

Flushed with an inner sense of accomplishment, Tansy approached the chairs where they idled, her head high, her eyes fevered in a manner Kat had never seen.

"What do you think?" Tansy lost her nerve in that instant, her head ducking, her eyes flicking toward them and then away.

The dress was nothing Kat would ever have expected Tansy to wear, with her penchant for flowing, formless gowns in pale, demure colors. It was a slim column of gold and ivory, beaded from neck to hem with bugle beads and tiny white pearls, a strap over one pale, slender shoulder only, leaving the other bare in a manner that was both tender and sensual. Tansy's delicate collarbone stood in relief, the glimmering waterfall of fabric caressing her breasts and hips before flowing downward to end in beaded fringe at her ankles.

For the first time in her life, Kat saw her sister as a woman, a shy fawn emerging from a slumber as deep as Sleeping Beauty's. In this gown, Kat could envision Tansy as she might have been, a woman full-grown. Still far more delicate than Kat herself, but bursting with the promise of sensuality heretofore hidden from the eyes of the world.

Kat had thought of her sister as a girl for so long that it was startling to see her as a woman. Kat's own sexual nature seemed overdone in contrast—too much the Valkyrie, when Tansy was the fair maiden. Kat couldn't find her voice.

Armand tried, but even he had to clear his throat first. "Lovely. Truly perfect, Tansy. It accents your natural beauty without overwhelming it."

When Tansy's head rose, her cheeks alive with hectic color, there was on her face a smile so beatific yet so hesitant that Kat was inexplicably moved to tears.

Tansy quickly shifted her gaze to Kat's. "What do you think? Is it…will Daddy like it?"

Kat bit the inside of her cheek and closed the distance between Tansy and her, managing not to say that she couldn't care less what the old bastard thought. "He'll burst his buttons he'll be so proud." She clasped her sister's shoulders, feeling the fine trembling in her frame. "You did a fabulous job of picking this out. There's not a woman in New York who won't gnash her teeth in envy of how beautiful you are."

Tansy reached out and hugged her sister. "I feel beautiful," she whispered. "And I'm not so afraid with you here." She pulled away and approached Armand slowly, her head high. "Thank you, Armand."

His smile could have lit up the world. "You're exquisite, Tansy. It is my pleasure. I intend to claim the first dance at the gala, if you'd be so inclined."

Tansy dimpled in a way Kat had never seen before, and dropped to a curtsy. "I'd like that."

Gravely, Armand clasped her hand and bowed with an elegance that would suit a courtier.

"Shall I wrap this, Armand?" the saleswoman inquired.

"I—is it too expensive, Kat?" Tansy asked. "I don't—I'm not sure how much—"

The dress cost the earth, but Kat was willing to mortgage her soul to help her sister emerge from her cocoon.

Armand spoke before she could. "Please, Tansy. If you'd consent, I want to make this a gift. It would please me enormously. Will you do me that honor?"

Tansy's cheeks flared with bright spots of color. She glanced toward her sister. "Kat?"

Kat couldn't afford the dress. She wasn't sure her father could do so, either. Mona made a bundle and had intended to buy it, but—

Armand's formidable will assumed center stage. He nodded toward the saleswoman. "I insist on the privilege. Please have this delivered, Mrs. Simone." Pride and assurance marked his face; a subtle possessiveness leached through his gentle touch on Tansy's elbow, then he turned toward the cash register to make arrangements.

Why had she never seen it earlier, this silent love he bore her sister? Kat wondered. A shadow crept over her heart, and she realized it was disappointment. Tansy deserved a man such as Armand; he would take superb care of her. It was just that Kat had always thought she'd have a shot at him whenever she wanted to exercise the choice. Not that she would, of course. He wasn't her type. But he'd always been there, ever since the day they'd met.

"Will Mona think it's pretty?" Tansy asked. "I feel like a princess."

Filing away her musings for later perusal, Kat turned her attentions back to her sister, reaching for her hand. "You look like one. And yes, Mona will be so proud."

She pushed herself further for her sister's sake. "And Daddy will be the proudest of all."

"I can't wait to show Paris," Tansy exulted.

Kat squeezed her hand. "I wish Paris could be there, Tansy." She was surprised to discover that she meant it with every fiber of her soul.

Her sister's eyes glowed with certainty. "He will be."

Kat refused to let the triumph of this day dim. "Go get changed. Armand's treating us to the Palm Court for tea."

Tansy's eyes widened, a tiny fear sparking. But in the tradition of this magical day, she only nodded. "I'll be quick."

One step, Kat. Every inch of progress was important.

When Armand rejoined her, Kat silently relinquished his heart to her sister, ignoring a dull new ache. She smiled and tucked her arm through his. "Come on, hot-shot. We're not through spending your money just yet."

Armand laughed. "Two beautiful women on my arm, with spring just around the corner? I certainly hope not."

They stood in companionable silence and waited for their fairy princess to emerge.

MONA RACED THROUGH the apartment door. "I'm sorry— the printer phoned just as I was leaving, and then Daddy called with a question—" She stopped abruptly at the anger on Fitz's face. "What?"

"Bradshaw could have handled the printer, couldn't he?"

"Maybe, but you know I—"

"I know that we were supposed to leave the city three hours ago. Traffic's going to be murder." A muscle in his jaw leaped.

Mona sighed and closed her eyes. Their stolen weekend wasn't getting off to much of a start. "I didn't want any of this to happen, but what am I supposed to do? Don't tell me Bradshaw could handle it—of course he could, but I've told you he's after my job—"

"Forget it." Fitz headed for the kitchen.

She followed him. "Forget what?"

He grabbed bottled water from the refrigerator and shrugged. "Any of it. All of it."

"What are you saying? Don't you want to go? Fitz, we need this weekend—"

He rounded on her. "You sure as hell don't act that way. I passed a big story to the new kid who's dying for my job, just because you were so set on getting an early start. Hell, I could have had the story done by now."

"You don't understand—"

His short, sharp laugh hurt her ears. "Oh, I understand just fine, Des. I comprehend that we're on very thin ice here. The question is, do you?"

"What?" She couldn't believe her ears. "Fitz, you can't be serious. We're not—we've always worked hard. Both of us. We…" The expression on his face was scaring her. "Okay, listen. We're both tired. The downtime will be good for us. It won't take me five minutes to throw my things in a bag and we'll be gone."

He drew a long sip from the bottle before he answered. "Maybe this is a bad idea."

"No. No, Fitz." She grabbed his arm with one hand. "Don't do this. I'm sorry. I should have let Jack handle it. I'm just…" *Going out of my mind, trying to be there for everyone.*

But then she looked, really looked at him and saw the smudges beneath his eyes. He'd been sleeping poorly ever since that night. He needed a break, and so did she.

He let out a long sigh. "I'm sorry, too. I just…" His hazel eyes softened. "I want this time with you. Just you. No damn magazine. No Martin. Just you and me, babe."

Mona closed her eyes and turned her cheek into his hand, a hand that was as dear to her as her own. "Me, too. I'm really sorry." She opened her eyes and lifted her palm to his strong jaw. "Five minutes, I swear it."

He grinned the cocky smile of a man who knew her too well. "I'll believe that when I see it. Come on, I'll help you." He slung one arm around her shoulders, and she nestled into his side as they crossed the living room.

Two hours later, as they drove northward for their stolen weekend, Mona glanced again at her husband and tried very hard to forget all she'd left undone at her office. Worked on ignoring the exhaustion, the knot in her stomach. Once past their quarrel, Fitz was lit from within by an almost manic glow, but he refused to divulge their destination. He'd told her to pack casual clothes, mentioning only that she might want to include that deep plum peignoir he'd once all but torn off her, his eyes gleaming in a manner she'd missed more than she'd thought possible.

On the drive north, the first hour had been strained, but gradually the traffic eased and each of them put the tension of their late departure behind them. Fitz's big hand moved to her thigh, stroking ever higher until she had to cross her legs and squeeze them for relief.

Mona wanted to cry at the luxury of his touch. Once he and she had been ravenous, had hardly been able to keep their hands off each other, greedily feeding on every inch of skin, every dark curve, every hard contour. In those days Mona had been late for work more often than not, had missed untold hours of sleep waiting up for Fitz to make his deadline, caring little about anything beyond the glory of his body against hers.

Marriage had not quenched that flame at first. Fitz would drop by her office and spirit her away for lunch in shadowy hideaways where they'd fondle each other beneath the table, barely able to remember what they'd eaten in their rush to find an elevator, a hallway, once even the women's restroom in an unfamiliar office building that just happened to be close when they could no longer bear it.

Though she and Fitz both worked long hours and threw themselves into their careers with abandon, in the secret hours of the night, their bodies still sought each other. Perhaps less often, perhaps less crazed, but the craving was replaced with commitment and caring so strong she'd have sworn it could survive fires, famine and flood.

When had that ceased to be enough? When had they supplanted long, leisurely Sunday loving with the *Times* and bagels? Still, she'd accepted it with grace, knowing deep in her heart that they were growing older, that they had more than most people ever dreamed, that they were the best and the brightest, and life could go on this way endlessly with no complaint from her.

And then came the two days that changed everything. Now slowly, insidiously, she was losing her husband. And try as she might—and she did try, God knows—he had gone somewhere she couldn't follow, had turned inward and refused to bring her along.

So his hand trailing beneath her skirt was more than welcome—it was salvation, little less than a miracle. Mona had survived much in her life, had always accomplished what must be done, had been strong when others were weak.

But Fitz had saved her. His love had made her whole. Without him, she was quicksand. She'd meant to not ever depend on anyone, but he'd stolen past her caution, and something shivery inside told her she would not survive the loss of him, though she'd never say that to a living soul.

Damn him, she thought as she played with the tawny curls at his nape. He had no right to change the deal. She couldn't be anything other than what she was.

Then Fitz sent her a glance so hot her fingers tightened in his hair. "Ow!" he complained, but his grin made promises and his eyes raked her. He kissed the inside of her wrist, then nipped at her skin.

Mona laughed, uncrossed her legs, letting her skirt ride up high—and raised the ante.

"Christ, Des—no panties?" he croaked. He closed his eyes and exhaled. Then he swerved, slammed on the brakes and jerked her close, grazing teeth over the tender skin of her throat. At last his mouth slid upward and took hers in a scorching kiss.

Mona luxuriated in the kiss, glee and power swimming in her blood. It would be all right. They would be all right. Fitz wanted her badly. She wanted him. They had it all, everything important. They loved. They could laugh. Each respected the other's mind, appreciated their differences.

And they were great in the sack.

Mona pulled away, breathless, and pressed her hands to his rugged jaws. "I'm all for pastoral sex, but there isn't quite room in this car for what I'd like to do."

Fitz leaned his forehead against hers, his breath still unsteady. "A few more miles," he muttered. "God, Des, I love you."

She traced a tender line over his lips. "I love you,

too…" Her throat closed up. She managed to whisper, "Get me there, Fitz. I need you so much."

He shifted into gear and they hurtled down the road.

"'NIGHT, KAT," Gregory called. "Sure you don't want me to stay and finish that last piece?" But in his face, she could read his eagerness to leave, to return to his loved one.

He would go home to a hot meal, to the warm glow of refuge. Once, a long time ago, she'd had that refuge and thought it normal. "No, thanks." She waved him away, holding the tape measure in one hand. "If I don't do some framing now and again, I'll forget how."

"See you soon, then." He had the next three days off.

"You and Patrick have fun in Boston."

Gregory nodded, opened his umbrella out the door and left, smiling despite the gust of wind that swirled through the opening.

Kat watched him leave. He had someone to go home to, someone with whom he'd built a life. Someone to plan with, who expected him home. Mona had someone. Even their father did, embarrassing as his obsession with a woman Kat's own age might be. For just one moment, melancholy crept in past the raindrops, and Kat shivered at the chill draft that swirled from Gregory's exit.

Metal tape clutched in her hand, she paused and looked out toward the gallery floor. Her eyes roamed the walls where Gamble Smith's work remained for another two weeks, part of her agreement with the purchasers.

But in her mind's eye, she was visualizing another work, a different collection of strokes. That was all it was, really. Oil and colors ground and mingled, caught on sable bristles, applied to canvas primed as the resting place for random thoughts transmitted through nerve and bone and muscle.

Gamble Smith hadn't really stolen her soul. She was not that woman caught in his fierce eye, not the honeyed limbs, the eager, dewy beauty who surrendered herself, who yielded her heart with utter trust.

For a moment, Kat thought of Tansy, so fragile and afraid of the world. Tansy could love that way, if her prince would truly come. But not Kat. Never Kat. Kat was power and strength, Kat said *Fuck you* and meant it. Kat was an Amazon who leaned on no man, never would.

Unlike her beautiful, doomed mother or Tansy, who were both too gentle. Too soft.

Kat had been bitter for years that her mother hadn't fought to bring all her children back to New York in those last months. She understood now that Juliette had been too ill to do anything but battle for her life. It was her father who had wanted his son beside him, and the twin who looked so like his Juliette. His younger daughters had been abandoned. Forgotten. Thank God they'd been left in Nana's care—Nana who understood being strong. Who would have been a terror in these days of liberation. Who'd raised a philanderer's daughter by herself and taught Kat all she'd learned about standing alone.

We hide behind others, little Kat. We think they can save us. In the end, we are alone, and we can only save ourselves. My poor Juliette thought Martin was her answer. Answers are inside, KitKat, not in any man. Love if you want, honey, but never need. Never give away the strongest part of yourself. Hold to yourself, child. Hold to yourself.

Kat laid down her tools, crossed the floor to one of Gamble Smith's works. Reaching out toward those lying brushstrokes, she touched the oils…traced the play of light and shadow.

He was gifted, no question. Brilliant and self-absorbed. But he didn't know her. Couldn't… Yet he'd bared her naked in a way no one else ever had. That made him dangerous. Kat was not her mother; she'd worked hard to root out weakness in herself. She was strong; everyone understood that. She used men until she was through with them; not for her, Juliette's mistake. Kat was strong enough to be alone, to protect Tansy. Tough enough to fight Lucas Walker for her sister's soul, if it came to that.

But Gamble Smith was different somehow. He intrigued her; he annoyed her. She wanted nothing to do with him; she burned to have him. No matter; she must erase the lie he had painted, reclaim the treacherous flaw she'd somehow missed. There was no space in her life to be a woman who could abandon herself that way, and that woman's very existence was dangerous knowledge in the hands of a stranger like Gamble Smith.

CHAPTER SEVEN

LUCAS STEPPED OFF the M5 on Riverside near Eighty-second and hunched against the slap of the wind, the ancient field jacket he'd bought for five dollars failing the challenge. He shoved his hands into the pockets and glanced at the Tootsie Roll–brown bald head of Mt. Tom.

He was late today, but he had no idea if that meant anything. He'd spotted Tansy once, missed her once—his idea of attempting to catch her at the same time of day might be futile. Did madness preclude having some kind of routine?

Was Tansy truly insane? Her imagination had always been robust, vivid…fuel for the beautiful drawings she could dash off with ease. Did she still draw, or had her hands gone mute just as she'd slipped into silence after that night…that unspeakable night that had destroyed them all?

You promised you'd get her help, you bastard. You promised…

Lucas squeezed his eyes shut. Swallowed down rage.

He'd been so damn naive. Thought he'd been such a ne-gotiator, believed he could save her, that pale, still mar-ionette, her limbs naked and too vulnerable, her eyes staring at him unblinking as he lay on the floor bleed-ing, trying to take in what he'd done.

Christ, he'd banished that image to the far reces-ses of his mind, but encountering her brought it all back. Tossing and turning on Al's narrow cot, he'd felt the weight of failed dreams and lost chances sitting on his chest, while freedom strolled out the doorway, mocking.

But Tansy as she'd once been stood silent in one sin-gle shaft of light. And Tansy as he'd seen her in the park called to a mustard-seed-size remnant of honor.

She'd rescued him from years of hopelessness and made him reach out for that apple, that Fruit of the Tree…brought him from the darkness into sunlight, giv-en him the mother of a boy's broken dreams.

He had no idea why those around her had not been able to halt her descent into madness, had no reason to believe he could do more.

He only knew he had to try.

A streak of color roused him from his reverie. Lucas uncoiled from the broad tree where he'd huddled against the wind's bite, and leaned to see more clearly.

And smiled.

Her coat was not the black or gray or dark brown of most New Yorkers. It was not the pale blue-and-pink of the day he'd first found her. Her coat was the first evidence he'd seen of the Tansy he'd once known.

Bright Kelly-green.

He watched her stop to speak to an old woman who sat on a bench surrounded by all her belongings, watched the old woman's face light up in welcome. He understood the feeling.

With steps made lighter by hope, he quickened his pace. When he was a few feet away, she turned. Her face lit in a smile. "Oh—you're here. Come meet my friend Darla."

Lucas looked down at a woman who'd suffered a hard life. Her eyes were warm with affection for Tansy. He sympathized completely.

"Darla, this is him, my prince. I told you about him."

Brown eyes hardened with caution. He understood that, too, and steeled against flinching under the weight of her disapproval. But Tansy's obvious delight in bringing them together made him reach for manners he'd forgotten.

"Pleased to meet you, ma'am."

Silently, the old lady studied him. He met her scrutiny, wondering just how much she divined.

Finally, she nodded as though she'd found what she needed. "You be good to her, boy." Years of smoking made her voice rough.

"He will," Tansy blithely assured her. "He's my prince." As if that was all that had to be said.

Lucas met the old woman's gaze and nodded.

Tansy leaned down and kissed Darla's cheek. "See you later." Then she was gliding away, chattering to Lucas as though assuming he'd follow. He did.

"Yesterday I went on a trip to a big store. I think my mother took me there once when I was a girl. For Easter." Lost in thought, she fixed her gaze on the ground. "Mona got a hat, I got a hat, Mama got a hat," she chanted. "We were Daddy's pretty girls." Her mouth twisted in chagrin. "Baby Kat was too little."

Suddenly, her gaze lifted. "I rode in a car. I tried on dresses, and Armand bought me the prettiest one. He said I was beautiful. Kat said it, too." A shadow drifted over her face. "Paris couldn't go. I wanted to wear it to show him, but Armand told them to deliver it later." She studied Lucas. "I was scared. I don't like to leave Paris. He stays here." Then she smiled. "If you would go with me, Prince, I might go farther. I wouldn't be scared if you were there."

Oh, God, Tansy. I'm no prince. And I couldn't protect you after all.

She grasped his hand too abruptly. Lucas recoiled, fighting twenty years of conditioned response. Touch meant danger. The shock of contact rippled through to bone, but soon the feel of her reached into the beast he'd become and spread the oil of kindness over waters long troubled.

She opened his palm and placed in it a bird. Not a real one, but a fanciful confection of eggshell and shiny beads and feathers in blue and white. As fragile as Tansy. As easy for him to shatter.

"It's beautiful. You made it?"

She smiled and nodded. "It's a bird."

"I can tell. Is this for me?"

She nodded again, shyly.

"You like birds?"

Her eyes grew distant, her face wistful. "Sometimes I wish…"

Lucas stood quietly, waiting for her answer as she pondered the sky. When no response came, he prodded. "What do you wish? Would you like to fly?"

Still she focused into the distance on dreams he couldn't see, but wished he could. Frowning slightly, he dared to touch her hand. "Tansy?"

She snapped back to him then, dreams scattering as dust. "Paris needs me," she said matter-of-factly. Like the sun emerging again, she smiled and captured Lucas's free hand. "Come on—I want to show you something."

He should pull away, but he couldn't let go. He hadn't known he'd been so hungry for touch, for the sweet pressing warmth of human skin. For twenty years, he'd been on guard, violence his only experience with contact. It had been a journey back to his father's fists, a lifelong procession interrupted only once, for those magical months in the oasis of Tansy and Juliette.

Tansy glanced back. "Hurry, slowpoke. Time's a'wastin'." For a moment, he caught a glimpse of the old Tansy again. She'd brought back that drawled phrase from her grandmother in Texas.

Lucas returned the smile, but his face felt stiff and awkward. She squeezed his hand, and his treacherous, misguided heart responded.

She's little more than a child, he cautioned himself. *Far too trusting.*

But when she tugged at him again, laughed with pure joy and began to skip, what was left of a long-dead boy ran with her.

MONA AWOKE TO THE PRESS of lips on her throat, sending a shock of pure hunger jolting through her body. Drowsily, she smiled, eyes still shut.

The down comforter descended, and she felt the kiss of cool air on her skin. Silken heat closed over one nipple, and she didn't even try to stifle the moan.

"I know you're awake." Fitz's voice, low and hoarse.

"Nuh-uh…only dreaming."

Goose bumps danced as the comforter vanished. With one quick slide, a human blanket replaced it. Fitz parted her thighs, pinned her hands to the sheets and thrust inside her.

Mona growled and wrapped her legs around him. The night had been everything she could wish. Her Fitz was back, whole and strong.

Oh, yeah, baby. Very strong.

Her pelvis rocked in a dance they both knew intimately. Mona refused to open her eyes, lost in fantasies of staying in bed all day. They would love and laugh, drink coffee and get crumbs in the sheets; they would be as they'd been in the beginning—

"Look at me, Des. Open your eyes, love."

Slowly, her lids lifted. His nostrils flared, his face intent. "Look at me and understand how I love you."

"I do, Fitz. Oh, God, how I do."

The hazel eyes she'd adored for so long held hers, something there that she couldn't quite read, dark and intense, something so fierce...

Thanksgiving filled her, bringing tears to her eyes. *This is all we need. This is who we are. Like this, we're incomparable. Invincible.*

Thank God. My Fitz is back. As if saying a rosary, Mona whispered tiny prayers and rejoiced. She wound her fingers into his and held on, abandoning herself to ecstasy with the man who had finally returned from the darkness.

They slept then, curled together like puppies, arms and legs a jumble, skin seeking skin. The sun was high when she felt a faint breeze against her hair, a tickle at her ear.

She opened her eyes and smiled sleepily. "Hi."

"Hi." Golden motes of sunlight danced in the hazel. Then he smacked her behind. "Get up, lazybones. We can't sleep all day."

She gripped the hair on his chest and pulled. "Sure we can. Sleep and...interludes."

His eyebrows lifted. "Interludes, you say?"

Mona grinned and nodded. "Interludes."

He pressed a kiss to her lips, then caressed her behind with one big hand. "Hold that thought, but right now, we have an appointment in an hour."

Mona frowned. "Appointment?"

He ran one hand over her hair and avoided her eyes. "Just an experiment. To see what you think."

She lifted herself on one elbow, unease stirring. "About what?"

"Living outside the city."

"What?" That brought her upright in a hurry. "Fitz, I can't live outside the city. Neither can you. Our jobs, the hours we work—" She threw up her hands. He was as aware as she was of what their lives demanded.

Then it hit her as though he'd slammed a fist into her chest.

"Fitz…no." She shook her head, trying to make sense of what had happened. "This isn't about—oh, God, it is, isn't it?"

"Just take a look, Des. Lots of people live outside the city and commute. You could have an office at home, go into the city three days a week—"

"And Jack Bradshaw would have my job in a month. Fitz, this is insane. You can't cover your beat from the country, for chrissake. You can't possibly put in the kind of hours…"

He rose from the bed and shrugged on his jeans, his

shoulders stiff and unyielding. "Maybe I don't want to put in those hours anymore." He glanced over his shoulder at her. "I've got an idea for a book. Maybe I want to take it easier, smell the flowers. Maybe you do, too."

The enormity of his betrayal was finally sinking in. "I've worked like a dog to get where I am. I'm not giving it up to play Rebecca of Sunnybrook Farm. Jesus, Fitz, you can't ask this of me."

He grew very quiet and still. "I can't ask the woman I love to understand that my needs have changed? To care enough about me to compromise?"

"This isn't compromise. This is abdication." She leaped from the bed, put her hand on a stomach tumbling with nerves, and searched for something to cover herself with. She grabbed his shirt. The smell of him made her want to cry for all that they were losing.

They had so much. Why couldn't he see?

"Look, Fitz." She struggled for a reasonable tone. "Of course it was traumatic for you, what happened. Anyone would be shaken. But you'll get over it. You just have to get back into your routine, give yourself time to settle—"

"Goddamn it, don't patronize me. I'm not sick, I'm not deluded. I'm viewing things as they are for the first time in years. You're the one who's in denial. You think that a job is a substitute for real life. You're so fucking trapped in the past that you refuse to gamble on the future."

"What does that mean?"

"I'm not your father, Des. So he's a self-centered bastard. So your mother died. Everyone doesn't betray,
Des. Everyone won't let you down. You keep clinging
to me like a leech, afraid to share me with anyone, even
a child. But it doesn't have to be what you had. Families aren't always screwed up. Families can make you
stronger, make life richer. If you hide in your work forever, you're letting the best part slip away."

All she could hear was *leech...clinging...afraid*. Humiliation was a sirocco, roaring in her head. "I'm not
the coward, Fitz. You're afraid to get back in it, aren't
you? Afraid it could happen again?"

His face paled, and she knew she'd gone too far. Suddenly bone-deep afraid, she soothed. "Anyone would be
scared by what happened to you. It's no disgrace."

His face turned to stone.

"A book is a great idea. There's room in the loft. We
can rearrange, make an office for you, get some new furniture...." She stopped babbling, watching the man she
loved becoming a stranger.

Nothing made it past the white noise of her fear. She
was losing him, and she had no idea how to stop it. "Fitz,
please..." She crossed to him, reached up to place a
hand on his cheek.

He recoiled from her touch.

At that moment, she felt more dread than any day of
her life except when she'd realized that her father would
never send for her, never let her and Kat come home again.

Fitz examined her with eyes that seemed years older. Eyes that pitied.

Damn him. He was the one to feel sorry for, not her. Mona Gerard needed no one's charity.

He gave a deep exhalation. "There's a train that will take you back to the city. It runs on the half hour."

A dagger to the heart couldn't have hurt worse. "And where will you be?" Was that her voice, so thin and high?

"I'm going to look at houses." His voice warmed, entreated. "Just try, Des. You might be surprised." He stepped toward her, held out his hand.

Mona stared at that hand that had taught her love, had guided her and protected, stroked and caressed, and she couldn't speak around the boulder lodged in her chest.

Finally, the hand dropped.

"Fitz, I…" The planks of the oak floor wavered through her tears.

His sigh was heavy, drained. "I'll drive you to the station when you're ready."

She thought she felt his hand brush her hair as he left the room.

CARLTON'S HOUSEMAN OPENED the penthouse door. "Your coat, Ms. Gerard?"

"No, I won't be but a minute. Where is Mr. Sanford?" Mona rushed past the man. She was wet and she'd had to wait forever for a cab. She'd tried to work after leaving Fitz, but she couldn't concentrate, so she'd switched her focus to the plans for the party at Carlton's sumptuous Fifth Avenue abode.

"He's in the library. I'll announce you."

"No, thanks. I'm familiar with the way." *Announce me. Sheesh.* She shook her head. Some days Carlton's sense of self-importance was more than she could take. He would only get worse if the rumors were true that the president was going to appoint him ambassador to the Court of St. James. The plum of all ambassador-ships… Mona wondered what he'd had to do for that little jewel.

The library door was half-open. "Carlton?" she called out as she knocked faintly and kept going. "Thank you for—" She jerked to a stop, staring.

Carlton quickly shoved the photograph in his hand into the top left desk drawer, rising to his feet, on his face an expression she'd never seen and couldn't name. Quickly, he smoothed it over. "Mona, where is Hanson? He should have taken your coat." Patrician displeasure laced every syllable.

But Mona didn't care. She was still staring at the desk drawer where the photograph had disappeared. "Is that my mother?" Juliette, very young. A picture she'd never seen, she was certain. She lifted her gaze to his. "May I look at it?"

She noted the war in him—breeding at odds with anger—but she didn't back down. For a long moment, they stood locked in a silent struggle.

Once again, Carlton wiped his face clean of all expression, his posture stiff. "Certainly." With noticeable reluctance, he opened the drawer and drew it out.

Mona stepped forward to accept it. For an instant after her hand closed on it, Carlton refused to relinquish control. Then he did so, turning and walking to the high windows that overlooked Central Park.

The room with all its rich, dark woods, its smell of leather bindings and cigars and expensive brandy, receded. Mona examined the face of a woman she'd never met. Young and alive, fresh with the promise of a different future than the one she would be given, Juliette Clark gazed out from the photo with a beauty and sweetness that could break your heart.

"I've never seen this photo," she murmured. "Nana didn't have one."

"She had it made for me." In Carlton's voice was an odd note.

Mona was shocked to hear vulnerability in his tone. "How old was she?"

"Nineteen. It was shot prior to her departure for Los Angeles to act in her first film."

"I didn't realize you'd known her so long before…" Mona halted, awkward in the thick stew of emotions swirling in the air around them.

"Before she met your father?" His smile was anything but amused. "Before I introduced them, and he swept her off her feet?" An edge returned to his voice.

"I encountered Juliette when she first came to New York. She never told you how we met?"

Mona could only shake her head, torn about hearing more.

"She was a waitress in a diner near the Theater District." He smiled, and it was all fondness now. "Even then, she planned ahead. She wanted the additional edge of being seen by agents and directors outside auditions. She'd accept any break she could get. She was living in an apartment with four other girls and hardly making ends meet, but even half-starved, she was the most beautiful thing I'd ever seen." He gazed into the distance, a light in his eyes as he peered beyond this moment, this room.

"She was your waitress?"

"Hmm? Oh—no." He blinked. "Some drunken fool was giving her a hard time, and I stepped in." He smiled. "She ordered me to butt out. I asked if I could wait for her after her shift. She told me not only no, but hell no." His eyes sparkled. "She said it just that way, in the Texas accent she hadn't yet lost. I, of course, waited anyway and walked her home. She let me, but only barely."

This was a woman Mona had never met. How had Juliette gone from tart-tongued ambition to the woman who'd renounced everything for love?

"She doesn't sound like…"

His eyes cleared. "She was different then. Before fame and your father…"

Good manners should have precluded her asking,

but Mona doubted she'd ever have such a chance again. "Why didn't you marry her? If you knew her first?"

"We were inseparable for months. I'd never run across anyone like her, so fresh and original. But Juliette wasn't the only one with ambition. My chance was here, in New York. Hers was in Hollywood. Neither of us was willing to yield." His voice grew quiet. "We didn't think we'd have to, that there'd be plenty of time. I let her go, planning that when I'd made enough money, I'd ask her to marry me. By then, she would have gotten acting out of her system. She'd realize what I could offer. How much better her life could be. Then she was cast as Annabella, and everything changed for her." Bitterness tinged his voice. "She changed, as well."

Annabella. Mona owned a copy now. Sometimes when she couldn't sleep, she watched it, just so she could hear her mother's voice. "But you saw her again. You introduced her…" Mona fell quiet.

His mouth twisted. "To your father, yes. She was in New York for publicity. Called me up, asked me to meet her for drinks." The faraway expression was in his eyes again. "I had it in mind that maybe the time was right. I wasn't where I wanted to be, but I could have supported her in far better circumstances than—"

He broke off, rounded his enormous mahogany desk and sat heavily in the leather chair. Face composed again, he lifted his hands, palms up. "Well, the rest is history. Martin was there—I introduced them.

Fate had its own plans." He looked at Mona. "I'm sure your schedule is as tight as mine. Perhaps we could discuss the party plans now." In his voice was command, not request. She'd gotten all she would gain from him.

But she'd finally recognized what she'd witnessed in his face earlier, when she'd surprised him. Love and pain, mingled with a deep anger. After all these years, he still hadn't resolved his feelings for her mother. So why had he stayed so close to their family? Why would he put himself through that? Why would he make himself such a guiding force in her father's career, when it would mean seeing Juliette constantly? Why help the man who'd won her?

Mona looked down at the stunning face in the photo, a face that, once viewed, would never be forgotten. Mona and Kat had speculated more than once on whether or not Carlton had a crush on Mama, but what she'd heard today said that he had never forgiven her, either. Why he remained in their lives after Mama's death was another matter. He did enjoy wielding power, and her father certainly granted Carlton more than Mona thought was wise.

No surprise there. Her father was a selfish man, and he had often taken the easy path.

"Mona?" Carlton's voice was sharp. "If you please…" He held out his hand.

Reluctantly, she returned the photograph to him. With

a practiced move, he slipped it into the desk drawer, then folded his hands. His eyes forbade her to ask more.

She inhaled sharply. "Yes. The party plans." She flipped open her briefcase and drew out a folder.

TANSY SCRAMBLED UP the caramel surface of the huge outcropping, her lithe, supple steps outpacing Lucas's longer strides. Halfway, he glanced upward and saw a streak of bare calf. He watched her slender hips sway as she climbed, saw the sweetly curved bottom as she bent forward. One pure stab of desire raced through his body. He ducked his head quickly, so unsettled was he to know that this child woman should be the one to make him remember that he was a man with all his parts in working order.

One foot lost its purchase in the hasty movement, and he scrambled to recover his balance, carefully guarding the bird in his hand.

"Are you all right?" she called from above him.

"Fine," he snapped.

"Wait there. I'll come get you…."

"No!" He heard the savagery in his voice, aware she could have no idea why. He cursed silently, turning away from her until he could get himself under control.

A mistake, a mistake, a stupid goddamn—

So lost was he in self-loathing that her touch almost jolted him out of his skin. "Don't—" he barked.

She recoiled from his fury, her face gone as pale as milk, her eyes blue and huge and hurt.

But oddly, not scared.

Fighting for control, he wrestled with the beast inside. "I don't— Don't touch me." If there was anyone on this earth who should scare her, it was him. He'd lived among animals for twenty years. Been one himself.

But Tansy only smiled, then slowly extended her hand and traced the scar on his cheek. "Did someone hurt you?" Her voice was soft and sad and tender.

She undid him. Lucas found himself closer to tears than he'd been since that night of soul darkness when he'd realized that he was well and truly trapped. Crouched over, he dropped his head into the arm that rested on top of his knees, and struggled to breathe just the next breath. To not think past this moment, this second, the way he'd learned to survive in his cage.

At last, he could speak. "Tansy, you should go home."

But she didn't move, not a muscle. For a long time, they sat at the halfway point up the scarred face of Mt. Tom, on the path worn by the feet of countless children, including his own.

And bit by bit, he relaxed. Felt peace steal over him.

Then he lifted his head, ashamed to face her but also needing to view, just once more, the sight of this too-tender creature with power far beyond her size.

She sat very still, her legs folded beneath her, hands clasped lightly in her lap. On her face was infinite patience…and a wistfulness that he knew to his bones would break both their hearts.

"I'm not a prince, Tansy. Surely you can see that now. Please…go. I can't be what you need. You'll be hurt, and you've been hurt too much."

Into her eyes he saw the faint and poisonous bloom of a dark knowledge he should welcome, for it might save her from making this very big mistake. A tiny shiver ran over her delicate frame.

But as quickly as it cut through her composure, it vanished, and along with it, the faint ghost of a frown that had flitted over her forehead.

He waited, breath held, afraid of what he might have stirred.

Then she blinked as if awakening, and her lips curved in a smile. "Tell me your name, my prince."

"I'm not—" He cut off the protest, swearing under his breath. Then he drew a deep breath and reminded himself that she wasn't wholly sane, that the moments just passed were a fantasy and had nothing to do with him, not really.

The look she bestowed on him was one of such forbearance and single-mindedness that Lucas felt amusement bubbling up, however out of place. Perhaps the girl Tansy had matured in some ways not immediately recognizable. This sort of stubbornness had been delivered with much less subtlety and grace when she was young.

Finally, he did laugh. And she joined him.

Two could play her game. "What do you think my name should be?"

She pretended to study the subject, head cocked, gaze sweeping the trees and the sky. After a bit, she turned her attention back to him. "Galahad."

Lucas's eyes went wide. A long-buried yearning leaped in answer, one he'd thought safely smothered in the ashes of his life. A lump crowded his throat. Only he understood just how badly he'd failed that dream. "You can't imagine how wrong you are."

Her lips curved. "Maybe you're the one who's wrong." Her blue eyes danced, and Tansy's pure bell-like laugh floated, high and dear, in mischief he hadn't heard from her in twenty years.

She jumped to her feet and began climbing again.

"Why Galahad?" he called after her, watching her nearing the top.

To understand what she'd said took a minute, and by that time, she'd vanished over the top.

Come back tomorrow and maybe I'll tell you.

Lucas raced to the summit to explain why he wouldn't come back. Couldn't. Shouldn't want to. He tensed to run after her, to catch her and tell her no.

But she was already halfway across Riverside, heading toward the door of her building.

And getting out of a limo at the curb was her father.

Lucas could only observe as Tansy launched herself with abandon into the arms of the very man whose neglect had set her nightmare in motion.

CHAPTER EIGHT

KAT SHUT OFF THE LIGHTS in the gallery and strolled halfheartedly toward the front door, unaccustomed to feeling blue. Surely Armand's defection could not mean so much to her. They were still friends, after all. Nothing had truly changed. He'd been her mentor and conscience for five years now, and neither had wanted more. Wished for more.

And Tansy deserved him. She was far kinder than Kat would ever be. She would need shelter and caring, but in her own way, Tansy gave both back. Anyone she loved, she loved unselfishly, holding nothing in reserve.

No matter how Kat rebelled at his advice, at his reasoning hand staying her from what he considered rank folly, Armand was as good a man as she'd ever encountered, and he was entitled to the kind of love Tansy could give. No matter that she might never be more than half child, Armand's life would be richer for her presence in it.

So why did that make Kat feel as if she were a toddler who wanted to flail her fists and scream? She had no claim on Armand, had never wanted one.

Still, she'd thought…

Kat laughed at herself. She was behaving like the petulant girl he'd often called her, and that was not to be borne. She didn't want Armand, didn't appreciate his interference in her life and plans. Didn't require anyone telling her what to do.

So why was she so blue?

She felt old suddenly, emptied by chances lost, roads not taken. Thirty would be just as bad as she'd feared. It spelled the end of any claim to girlhood, to carefree, kick-ass life on the wild side.

Didn't it?

Kat smiled. The hell it did. She was a force to be reckoned with. The art world had better be alert—Kat Gerard was a tigress, and she was hungry.

With confident strides, she resumed course for the front door. She would go down to Hogs and Heifers and do some damage. Pick a fight, tease a cock, break a heart—maybe two. She would get stronger with age, not weaker, and she would take her pick of only the best— lovers, friends, works of art, you name it.

Watch out, Manhattan. You ain't seen nothin' yet. The man who can break my heart hasn't been born.

"You 'bout finished, boy?"

Lucas looked up from sweeping the kitchen floor. "Just have to mop, then I'm done."

"Good. Then I'll be headin' on home." But Al paused. "You got somethin' on your mind?"

Lucas shook his head. "Nope."

"You been mighty quiet all night." When Lucas said nothing, Al hesitated, then spoke again, his reluctance obvious. "Freedom ain't all fun and games sometimes. Ever'body has tough times, but they pass."

Humbled by the gruff caring he heard in that voice, Lucas leaned on his broom, wishing he could explain to Al what was eating away under his skin.

But he wasn't sure himself. "I'll manage."

Al nodded and turned to go.

As he reached the doorway, some rusty instinct toward decency prompted Lucas to speak up, hard though it was. "Al?"

"Yeah?"

Lucas would like to be better with words. "Thanks."

The older man gave a quick salute. "It'll get easier, boy. I'll see you tomorrow."

Lucas followed his progress for a minute. Then he started sweeping again.

"Lucas?" The voice was so quiet he almost didn't hear it, lost in his thoughts as he was.

"Hey, Gloria. What are you still doing here?"

Al's lone dancer leaned against the doorway, lush

curves displayed in a tight sweater worn over skin-hugging jeans. "Thought maybe you could use some company."

For a second, Lucas lost the rhythm of his sweeping. He kept his eyes on the floor, not sure if he was misunderstanding her offer. He darted a glance at her, then resumed the strokes with his broom. "I've still got some work to finish."

"I'm not in a hurry." Her voice was alluring and warm. Her body would be warm, too. He could lose himself in a woman's sweet flesh, something he'd fought to forget. Something he'd barely gotten started learning when he'd been locked away.

But his mind was full of Tansy.

What a laugh. Tansy might as well be on the moon. Responding to her as a woman had shaken him as nothing else could. She wasn't in her right mind, for God's sake—she was more child than woman, more spirit than bone.

She was nothing like the girl a boy once had hot, sweaty, long-night dreams over.

"What is it?"

He shook his head. "Nothing." He faced her. "Gloria, I'm not good company right now."

Her shoulders curved in protectively. "I…see. I—I thought maybe you hadn't…" Her cheeks reddened. "Just getting out and all, I figured it had been a long time and maybe…"

Humiliation washed hot over him. "I don't need charity," he said stiffly.

Her head jerked up, and in her eyes he could tell that he'd guessed wrong. Chagrin fought with something else.

Shame. And sadness.

Chastened, he gentled his voice. "Honey, you can do better than me."

Strangled laughter crawled from her throat. "A washed-up stripper working in a place like this? You're wrong." She lifted her head into something resembling defiance, but the slump of her shoulders defeated the effort. "Sorry. I should have known better." She turned to go, but he heard the tears in her voice.

"It's not you," he said.

She halted, one hand on the doorjamb. "You don't have to spare my feelings. I'm aware of what I am."

"It has nothing to do with you. The problem is me."

She scanned down his form with a practiced eye. "Appears to me that everything works just fine."

Lucas felt his face redden. His body wanted what she was offering. All he had to do…

She was here, a warm and willing woman. He could say yes and give his aching flesh respite. Dear God, the very thought of it sent a shudder of lust up his spine. The body he'd forced into numbness for so long was roaring back to life with a vengeance.

But he could sense a sorrow in her, a feeling that this was all she merited—a furtive coupling on a cot in the basement of the place where she submitted every night to the greedy gazes of any man willing to pay money to watch. With an ex-con she barely knew.

She was entitled to better. And he might not deserve much, but maybe he was, too.

"I won't try to tell you I'm not tempted. You're a pretty woman, Gloria."

She snorted softly, her mouth twisting.

He pitched his voice low. "You don't think I understand about having to survive?"

Her glance was startled, her eyes, for once, naked and vulnerable.

"There are things that you don't—" He looked away, shook his head. Then he focused on her again. "No matter how much I want to take you up on that offer, you have a right to more than the trouble I could bring you."

Her mouth tightened again. "I don't need the bullshit, Lucas. I understand."

"No, you don't." He took a step forward. "What I'm saying is that I…" He let out a huff, then inhaled deeply before continuing. "I could use a friend right now. Sex is easy to find, but friends…well, that's a lot harder."

He didn't much like touching or being touched—except, he'd discovered, by Tansy. But this woman seemed as though she could use a friend as badly as he could. So he held out a hand and ran it over her hair very lightly.

She leaned into his palm, and tears spilled. "Friends

can make love, unless…" She studied him. "There's another woman, isn't there?"

"Not…" He sighed. "I don't know. It's…complicated."

"Want to talk about it?"

For a moment, he was tempted almost more than by the offer of sex. Confiding in someone, trusting someone…

No. That kind of faith had deserted him years ago.

"Maybe later. Right now, I'd better get finished. Want me to walk you to your train before I do?"

Gloria's lips curved slightly. "You know what your problem is, Lucas? You're a nice guy. Anybody ever tell you what happens to nice guys?"

Lucas frowned. "I'm not nice. Don't kid yourself."

"That what's holding you back from this woman? You think you can't be her knight in shining armor?"

"I can't."

"I suspect that you're wrong. Maybe she does, too." Gloria stood on her toes and pressed one soft kiss to his cheek. "I'll be fine, but thanks for the offer. See you tomorrow." With that, she slipped out the door.

They were both wrong. He was a landless knight with rusty armor, a champion without a sword. He lived in a basement room and slept on a cot. Carlton Sanford had money and power and—

And if Lucas stayed away, Sanford might have Tansy.

Hell. He would go back, there was no sense lying to himself. As Lucas stripped and washed himself and carefully folded the secondhand clothes he'd bought to replace prison-issue new, he faced himself in the tiny, cracked mirror and wondered what the hell Tansy saw.

Because he saw old eyes, tired eyes in a face that was still prison-pale. A man who'd survived, but just barely, and had no business tilting at windmills.

But inside him, Tansy had spread peace for those few moments, had stirred a reckless hope. She made him want to believe that he could be more. Could be enough.

Sliding between sheets worn to smoothness, lying in the warmth of a scratchy, ancient army blanket, Lucas rested his head on his hands and stared up at Tansy's bird perched on the box that served as his nightstand.

And admitted to himself that he wasn't going to leave her. Not until she was safe.

Lucas muttered the first prayer of his life, spoken to a God in whom he did not believe. Prayed that he was not making yet one more mistake for which Tansy would pay.

KAT ENTERED THE TINY, smoky bar safely locked behind a plastic forest of decals shielding the windows from the slimmest possibility of light. She sucked in the cigarette smoke to relieve the stink of the streets outside, the mingled odors of fish and bones and blood. The streets were hosed down every day, but ancient cobblestones had absorbed the smells of generations of butchers whose gory wares graced the tables of the finest restaurants in town.

Why this little bar had become a hotspot for the trendy, she would never understand, except that the dilettantes of New York were constantly on the prowl for virgin territory to proclaim their own, to be absorbed in the timeless ritual of those who create nothing, but feed like vampires off those who do.

Residents of Bohemian SoHo had moved to Chelsea, then been displaced again by vampires too trendy or too poor for the West Side. Way down on the food chain, artists had lost their havens, forced farther and farther from those who feasted on their blood and bones. Many no longer lived in the city, but had retreated to Brooklyn or Queens.

Kat was aware that she could be called a queen of the vampires herself, but she chose to consider herself a patron. In truth, she had no more money to her name than those whose work she showcased.

Danny, the lesbian bartender who ruled this roost when Tim Mulgrew, the owner, was gone, shot Kat a look loaded with her usual loathing. "What the fuck do you want?"

Kat bared her teeth. "Good evening to you, too, *Dan-i-elle*." She'd found out Danny's given name and used it relentlessly.

"Fuck off."

Kat leaned over the bar, showing generous cleavage, cognizant of just how offensive it would be. "I'd like Sex on the Beach, Danielle," she said with a sweetness sure to rot the teeth.

"Why don't you just take that tramp ass home and get out of my face?"

"Danny, the lady bothering you?" The deep voice spoke over Kat's shoulder.

A quick shiver shot through Kat's body. Of all the nights, all the places.

"First off, she's no lady, Gamble," Danny retorted. "Second, the day that little twat bothers me is the day I hang up my spurs."

"And wouldn't that send legions into despair?" Kat reached for the very dry martini Danny had mixed, instead, knowing Kat's true tastes.

Behind her, Gamble unbent long enough to laugh, and the sound of it sent sparks down her spine.

Danny smiled at him and nodded dismissal to Kat.

Equally satisfied with their exchange, Kat nodded back.

"You going to turn around, or are you afraid to face me?" he asked.

Kat took a long sip first, closing her eyes to steady herself. Then she complied, drawing in a deep breath and watching his gaze drop to the very low scooped neck of her skintight black cotton top, then travel down her hot-pink excuse for a skirt. "The man who could make me afraid hasn't been hatched." She offered him the thinnest pretext of a smile, then perused his body with insolent languor. "What are you doing out of your cave? Won't it ruin your art to have actual congress with humans?"

He spared no answering smile, his face a blank—except for those eyes that burned a vivid blue. "You sharpen that tongue every day? Use a whetstone or a strop?"

Kat felt the day's melancholy slide away. God, she loved a good, rousing fight. "Sometimes I practice on small children, just to keep the edge gleaming. Though I prefer better sport." She shrugged elaborately. "One can't always be picky."

His mouth quirked in a reluctant grin. "So you come here when you need a little extra honing from Danny?"

Kat cocked one eyebrow and sipped again, taking her sweet time. "Careful, Gamble Smith. I might get the idea that you're interested." She perched one hip on a bar stool, aware that her skirt would ride up her thighs.

His blazing glance followed the flash of skin. He swept down his lashes, and the room abruptly dimmed. Cooled.

She found that she wanted that heat back. So she crossed her legs, sure that her skirt was almost up to her crotch now. Holding the bar with one hand, her drink in the other, she leaned toward him and whispered, "Are you, Gamble? Interested?"

His eyes shot open, pure blue flame roaring out. He stepped close, grabbed her shoulder, sent her martini sloshing over her hand as he jerked her toward him. With one knee, he shoved her legs apart and stepped between them, bringing his mouth to within a breath of hers.

"You think you hold the power, teasing every man

you meet until he's stone-ached half out of his mind. You think you're safe because you choose when to stay and when to leave."

His harsh whisper stung her ears, and she wrestled down a tiny spark of nerves. "Get your hands off me." Her own voice shrill with unaccustomed fear.

"Isn't that what you want? To drive every man you meet to distraction? Isn't that why you dress like a trollop and cock-tease your way through the male population of New York?"

"Trollop?" Kat had been working up a good high dudgeon until he said that word. Now she started laughing. "Good God. Trollop." It set her off again. "I haven't heard that word since I left Dimmitt."

Gamble's rugged face couldn't seem to settle into one expression. Fury turned to outrage, outrage to a wry grin. Wry grin became outright astonishment. "Dimmitt? Texas? You've been to Dimmitt? No way."

"Way." She held up one hand in a Scouts' promise. "Spent from eight to eighteen there. Shoot—" she was surprised at how easily she slipped back into the drawl that had become a child's refuge "—I've even been to Amarillo, sugar."

He laughed, the free, easy, straight-from-the-belly kind. "Well, hell. If you've been to Amarillo, why would you ever need to come to New York?"

The glowering artist morphed into someone she might actually like to know, God help her.

"It's home."

"Is New York ever truly home?"

Kat thought about how hard she'd fought to make it back. "Yes. For me it is…always was," she said softly, lost in recollection of days when she'd been much younger, the world brighter. "I was born here…and it took a long time to find my route back."

"Careful." His eyes were very, very serious. "You just might make me feel sorry for you."

"Do that, and I'll have to kick in your teeth," she growled. But they both understood she was playing this time.

He grew too still. "This is a problem, Kat." He held her gaze until she yearned to wriggle away, but he stood too close. "I don't want to like you, damn it."

She slid off the stool, her body unavoidably grazing his. He reached for her, but she danced out of his grasp, tossing her head and backing away, slanting him her best hellcat smile. "I don't want to like you, either." She turned to go, casting one last sally over her shoulder. "So let's just don't."

He grabbed her arm and spun her around so quickly the smile was still firmly in place. The man she faced was big and rugged and smoldering beneath the surface. Her smile vanished under the intensity of his gaze.

"I'm not one of your boy toys, Kat. You come with me you won't leave until I let you."

Molasses-slow heat oozed through her blood while

needles of something akin to fear prickled over her skin. For once in her life, she was devoid of a snappy retort. Part of her wanted to run from something she could not name, something preternatural that put every nerve in her body on alert.

But then there was no time. His head lowered. The heat of him surrounded her like a second skin.

Something inside Kat shivered. And for the first time in many years, she didn't stand and fight. Instead, she skimmed to the side like quicksilver, veering between packed bodies, headed toward the dark hallway leading to the restrooms.

Gamble moved to pull her back—

Kat ran. And cursed herself.

CHAPTER NINE

MONA PEERED down at Forty-second Street from her office window, and wondered how long ago darkness had so securely closed the door on the day. She vaguely remembered Gaby telling her she was leaving—a date, had she said?—but Mona had been too busy seeking a way to make the figures before her lie. Or murmur sweet nothings in her ear, the way Fitz used to do when he—

She squeezed her eyes shut, whirling back to the computer screen and the dreaded numbers. Circulation was down for the third month in a row, and Mona's arm muscles screamed from the strain of preventing failure from dragging her over the edge of a very steep cliff while Jack Bradshaw looked on, amusement on his too-smooth, vulpine face.

The numbers weren't terrible yet—still slight enough to reverse with socko changes in layout, with the new blood she was determined to infuse. But the advertisers would notice soon, if they had not already, and she would lose the money to effect those lifesaving amendments.

And Bradshaw would be there. He was waiting for her to fail, had been for the whole year since she'd been given the plum of editor-in-chief of the magazine he thought should be his.

Fitz had offered more than once to rearrange Bradshaw's features for her. She'd laughed it off, sure that she'd moved ahead in a decisive manner, that she wouldn't feel the bite of his fangs nipping at her heels for long.

Maybe she should ask Fitz—

Mona shook her head. First she'd have to see him; they'd have to be in the room together, awake—something that hadn't happened since last weekend. Some mornings there was evidence that he'd slept beside her, but never in the old way, never in that sleep-softened tangle of limbs, of waking in the night and hearing the steady beat of his heart beneath her cheek, feeling the crisp sandy chest hair, the weight of his arms and legs as she cuddled into the comfort of his body.

Theirs was a correspondence of notes and messages on the recorder, of obstacles to shared dinner, of showers and breakfasts grabbed alone. She couldn't begin to guess what he was thinking lately. She didn't even know if he'd found a house he liked because she was dancing so hard around the chasm that had opened up before them.

Fitz was, too. Normally a man who confronted problems head-on and dispatched them, he seemed to be paying his respects to what had always been so alive be-

tween them by not disturbing a truce so fragile it might
be spun of sugar. A candy-coated replica of what had
always been so real but now felt utterly insubstantial.

Mona longed to tell someone how scared she was,
but there was no one she could trust. For ten years now,
Fitz had been her confidant, the only one who knew how
hard she ran to keep from falling into the abyss that had
always been there, waiting for her. From childhood,
Mona had been alone. Paris and Tansy had been one en-
tity, the light of Mama's eye, and all Daddy had ever
cared about was Mama. When Kat had come so many
years after, Mona had tried to love her, but Kat had never needed anyone's love. Exile had drawn them closer,
but seven years was a lot of distance to bridge when it
connected a teenager to a child. Now they were grown,
and the distance of age had given way to one of lifestyle.
Kat made her affectionate contempt for Mona's choices
only too clear.

Mona's gaze fell on the teacup and saucer that sat on
her credenza. The set had accompanied her everywhere
since the day she'd picked it out of Mama's things as
her keepsake. Nana had told her that Mama always
loved the porcelain so thin it was translucent, the tiny
scarlet rosebuds intertwined on cup and plate, the deep,
glowing green of leaf and stem, the tiny gold dots for
accent.

There was a minuscule crack at the base of the cup,
but within Mona, a faint memory stirred, of days when

the crack didn't exist. Of having tea all by herself with Mama in the dusty golden light pouring through the high windows of the apartment. She didn't remember where Paris and Tansy had been or why she'd been granted this rare boon of time alone with her mother, of feeling the diamond-bright radiance of Juliette's full attention. All she could recall was that she'd handled the cup and saucer with exquisite care, terrified she'd spill tea or drop the cup and the magic would vanish, that she'd find herself invisible again. Back in the shadows cast by all those radiant beings: her achingly beautiful mother, her famous father and the twins just one year older but also bathed in the golden light. Mona was the darkling child, the pentimento…the umber shading no one really saw.

She'd been very, very careful, and she'd been rewarded. Even now she could hear her mother's voice, clear and so lovely it made your heart ache, made you want to sit quietly at her feet and simply listen. *You're a very good girl, Mona. You always try so hard.* Juliette had been heavily pregnant with Kat then, so there had been no room for Mona to sit in her lap as she'd fervently wished. But the words and the tone had hugged her close, had warmed the dark, hungry place that gnawed inside her.

The screensaver suddenly swept away the figures on her computer, and Mona blinked. She'd been a good girl all her life, and where had it gotten her?

Her glance skimmed over the papers spread on her desk, across the folder with her notes on the party for her father. All of a sudden, she was swamped to her eyeballs with her good-girl deeds, with the chains around her neck dragging her under. The magazine. Her father. Tansy, for whom she'd be responsible for the rest of her life.

And Fitz. Fitz and his damn baby craving. What the hell would he do with an infant? He'd get over this funk and go back to his hard-driving life—and who'd be stuck in the sticks being the good girl, attempting to be enough for some poor kid when she couldn't even be enough for herself?

Her mother had done that. Been seduced into sacrificing everything for her father—her career, her identity, her bright, shining light. Mona would not. Fitz had known from the first how important it was to her never to be invisible again.

With choppy strokes, Mona shut down her computer and began gathering up her usual mountain of work to take home—then, quick as a lightning bolt, it hit her. She didn't want to drag any work home. She wasn't even sure she had any desire to go to the place that seemed now to be prison, not refuge.

Maybe she would call Kat. Kat never worried about being good. Never had. Mona felt like raising hell tonight, not that she had any experience at it. But Kat did.

Mona's hand hovered over the phone, ready to dial.

Then, very slowly, she pulled her fingers away and stared out into the millions of lights outside her window. If she called Kat, she'd have to explain her behavior—no way Kat would let this ride. Mona was not prepared to explain about Fitz to anyone. A crazy part of her was still hoping he'd relent, go back to being the real Fitz. Whether or not he did, though, Mona was not ready to concede the upper hand. Her role as the family's Rock of Gibraltar was hard-won, not something she was ready to give up. However rebellious she felt tonight, Mona was, above all, a practical woman. One who did not take impulsive steps lightly.

Rebellious. Mona's mouth curved in a smile that, reflected in the smoky glass window, looked altogether the Cheshire cat. She studied the woman there, in her simple black knit suit, pearl studs in her ears, tasteful make-up and all, and she wanted to tear that woman's hair out. Muss it up, at the very least. Discard that slim gold watch, ditch the pearls and leave the jacket opened all the way down to *there*. Replace her panty hose and sensible pumps with a garter belt and spike heels. Ditch the panties as Kat would.

Mona stared at herself as she removed one pearl stud and asked the woman in the glass, *Who are you?*

She didn't answer, but her brown eyes were huge and scared and…

Excited. Fever bright.

Mona grabbed her purse and left everything else exactly as it was, feeling in her palm the prick of the post of the earring she knew she would not replace. Not yet, maybe never.

With her so-sensible pumps clicking softly, Mona made her way out of the building and caught a cab.

But instead of telling him the address of her apartment, she simply said, "East Village. I'll tell you when we get there."

And with the post of one earring biting into her tender palm, Mona waited to find out what this new woman might do next.

KAT EMERGED FROM THE HELL of the filthy bathroom after staring into a cracked mirror for far too long, ignoring the banging on the door. She scanned the crowd, not sure whether to hope Gamble had left or stayed. When she didn't see him, her heart gave a curious lurch before it settled gracelessly into relief. Nowhere did she spot his towering frame.

But despite her best intentions, the night lost its color. Gamble was a dangerous game, but the most intriguing one she'd had in a long time. Kat surveyed the room, saw no better opponent than Danny and decided it was time to call it a night.

Gregory would have a good laugh. Eleven o'clock and Kat was headed home. She snagged her coat, slapped some money on the bar and walked to the door.

Outside, the wind off the Hudson hit her, and she

shivered, shaking out her coat before she donned it, wishing she hadn't worn such a damn short skirt.

"Here. Let me."

Kat whirled at the sound of his voice. Gamble emerged from the gloom outside the door, his expression troubled. He stepped forward and held her coat. She expected him to keep her at arm's length, but instead, he wrapped it around her and drew her close with careless strength.

And for once, she dragged her feet, wary as an animal in enemy territory.

Gamble bent down, his frame blocking out the streetlight.

Kat arched away, but his grip meant that her movement only brought their lower bodies closer. "Gamble…" Whose voice was that, so high and thin?

"Shh…easy…" Deep and low, his voice soothed. He licked at her lips, and the hair on her nape rose. As iron to a magnet, she swayed toward him, rising to her toes, plastering her body against his.

But hard hands held her away, letting the cool air come between them as if it brought reason with it. "Last chance, Kat. I won't love you, and I won't be good for you."

A deep shudder shook her, and she hesitated, sensing that some hint of truth lay beneath his words.

She grasped for the reserve that had always been so easy. Pah. He was a man, and men didn't scare her. Her father had force-fed her the best education a girl could have. She would never be left again, never ignored again.

So Kat disregarded the still, small voice and gave him her best go-to-hell smile, then licked her lips with slow, lascivious care. "I don't like men who are good for me. I thought you were smarter than that."

He studied her for a long moment, his eyes older than time. Then, with a muffled oath, he turned and pulled her after him, crossing the street with determined strides. "Don't say I didn't warn you."

Kat's throaty chuckle felt oddly like whistling in the dark.

He stopped at the far curb and wheeled, his mouth closing swiftly on hers. But before Kat could kiss him back, he took off again, still clasping her hand while she tried to keep up with him.

They crossed the last few blocks in that fashion, Kat stretching her long legs to maintain his pace. They neither spoke nor touched again except where her fingers were caught fast in Gamble's steady grip.

Within Kat sang three discordant notes: a catgut string of anticipation drawing tighter with every step, a low bass hum of ever-growing need…and a faint, tinny quiver of warning that she just might have met her match.

A few feet from his door, she was seized by an overpowering urge to stop. To think. To reconsider. "Gamble, wait." She dragged her heels against cement.

His face was drawn tight, all sharp planes and angles. In the streetlight, the hollows cast him in the too-possible role of sorcerer, a sense of power enveloping him like night-dark robes. But his eyes were what gave her most pause; no longer glowering, for one brief second before he shuttered them, they held shadows of profound pain.

He shifted away from her and busied himself with the lock, as though he didn't care. "Second thoughts?" His smile was false, a pasted-on, brittle one. "I won't make it simple for you, Kat. I won't push your buttons. I won't let you turn this into a pissing contest so you can tell yourself you're just keeping the upper hand the way you need to do so badly."

He held the door open and gestured inside. "You walk through this door you're doing it as a grown woman, not a spoiled brat. You won't order me around and you won't fuck with my head. For some godforsaken reason, I want you, and you want me. Body to body, we'll come together—no promises, no regrets. No tears when it's over."

Stung pride demanded its due. "I never cry. Or have regrets. And I don't need promises."

"You don't have the first idea what you need." His eyes were surprisingly calm now, almost soft.

"Ever think you might be the one shedding tears, Gamble Smith?"

His grin was anything but cheerful. "Tough to the last, huh? Just remember I warned you." He opened the outside door wider. "Now, you in or you out?"

She closed the gap between them, then pressed her

pelvis against his, wrapping one leg around his calf and grasping a handful of hair to bring his mouth closer to hers. "I'd like to have you in, if you'd ever stop talking." She laughed against his lips and heard his chuckle. And the night's colors came rushing in.

"I'll give you this, Ms. Gerard—you're definitely not boring." He backed her against the wall and yanked her thigh up higher, bringing himself snugly against her as he devoured her mouth.

"Now, Gamble. Damn it, I want you now."

He picked her up, and she clamped her legs around his hips, nibbling at his jaw while he climbed the steps, then fumbled at the lock on his loft door.

Finally, it was open, and he swept them both inside, heading across the floor. Kat tossed her head back and laughed as his mouth worked down her throat, his tongue sliding toward one breast as he hitched her upward and ran his hands under her skirt to grasp her hips and bring her tighter against him. She could feel the matching tension in his body, the hard evidence that he wanted her, the faint trembling of his arms, the groan as he discovered that she had nothing on under the skirt.

She smelled oils and turpentine, heard the rasp of his zipper just as he spread her on a mound of cushions covered by an ancient quilt.

Towering above her, he appeared to be some avenging angel, a son of the morning fallen from grace. He held her hips in his big hands and his eyes locked on hers. Without a second's hesitation, he entered her in one savage thrust. There was no need for foreplay; Kat had been ready for him for days.

Then he stopped, hard and full inside her. She wanted to scream for him to keep going. Every nerve in her body was strung wire-tight; her very blood boiled. She clutched at his arms, her nails scoring his skin. She rocked her hips to seat him deeper, arched her back to force him to move.

He smiled, slowly and wickedly, one eyebrow cocked. But she could see the strain in him, too, could feel a matching quiver in muscle and bone.

"I'm going to make you scream, Kat."

"Oh, God, I hope so," she sighed. "Please, Gamble. Now."

He held her still one second longer, staring into her eyes with an expression she couldn't read, but one that made her remember the painting where he'd stripped her naked.

And then she spotted it, over his shoulder. She shivered, feeling both voyeur and spectacle.

He saw where she was looking. "First this, until we both collapse. And then I'm going to paint you this way."

Caught between thrill and fury, Kat only tightened her legs around him. "You talk too much."

CHAPTER TEN

LUCAS STOOD ON THE sidewalk in the darkness, staring at Tansy's window. This part of town was too quiet and still at this late hour. It was cold, the buildings were mostly dark and where there were lights, they were not for him. Solitude was a deep hollow in his chest tonight. He'd been alone for a long time; he thought he'd gotten used to it, but now there was Tansy.

Loneliness lost its edge when you didn't know any different, but Tansy had opened him up again. Made him feel the sharp ache the way he'd only experienced it twice before: the first night in prison, and the night his mother had left.

On the latter, he'd awakened with a nightmare and crept quietly from his room. He was eight years old, too big to seek out comfort, he'd been told. But the dream gripped him in a huge fist, his pajamas soaking wet with the sweat of fear.

So it was that he slipped down the hall and across, quietly. Very quietly. The old man might hear. And in the silence Lucas realized two things: one, that his father, with his smell of sweat and whiskey, was gone from the apartment. And two, that his mother was whispering into the phone.

"Pick me up now," she said. "I can't stay another minute with him." There were tears in her voice. Then a gasp. "No—are you crazy? Don't come up here. Stay around the corner. I'll be packed in ten minutes, and I'll meet you there."

Packed? They would go far away. They would be free at last. Hope danced a little jig in his heart. Barely able to breathe for the joy crowding in, Lucas forgot all about the bad dream and raced back to his room to pick out what to take.

As he'd done before when they'd skipped out just ahead of a landlord, Lucas stripped the case from his pillow and began stuffing in his belongings. First, he set aside the sock monkey his mother had made when he was a baby; that would go on top. Clothes—he grabbed jeans and T-shirts and his secondhand jacket with the Phillies badge worn almost colorless. In went the toy truck he'd had since he was five, along with a book he'd read until the pages were falling out. Last went George the monkey, his mother's attempt at re-creating the Curious George who'd made Lucas laugh and laugh as a child.

One ear alert for her progress down the hallway, Lucas was pulling a sweatshirt over his head when she appeared. "I'm ready, Mom," he said. His head popped through the top almost as fast as the joy was rising up his chest.

And then he saw her shock. For one endless moment they regarded each other. "Oh, baby..." In the sinking of her voice, Lucas heard the sound of the end of his childhood.

"Mom?" But he already knew.

Her eyes, gray as his, slid to the side. "Baby, I'm just...I've got to go out for a little while, but I'll be back."

He wasn't sure where he got the nerve to push. "Take me with you." When she didn't answer, he didn't let go. Couldn't. "Don't leave me here with him."

Soft gray eyes, a little shiny, met his. "I can't," she murmured.

Can't? he wanted to say. *Or won't?* But his adult moment was over. Not an innocent anymore, but still a child. His eyes stung, and he wiped them with the back of his hand as his heart shriveled like a balloon when the party was all over. He blinked hard and tried to figure out what he could say, how he could convince her. *Please* was the best he could do, and it wheezed out of him like an old man's defeat.

"Please," he said again, louder now, and rubbed his eyes again, then sought her out.

But it was too late. She was already gone. Not for a little while, but forever.

Tonight as Lucas stood on the sidewalk waiting, he

was not a small boy anymore. He had long ago abandoned illusion. But he wished for Tansy, for her sweet smile. After five long days, he hadn't been able to stay away, even though she would be in bed asleep. Al had been down with a flu, so Lucas had been working long hours to keep things going. It was the least he could do to repay the only person who'd given him a chance since he'd returned.

But he'd worried about Tansy every hour of those endless days. No way he dared to phone the apartment to explain. Tonight he had felt the call of her so strongly that he'd risen from his cot, weary to the bone, and come anyway, certain he wouldn't see her.

And suddenly, he did.

Like a pale, beautiful ghost, she appeared in her window as if conjured up by the force of his need to look upon her bright head, to feel the calm that stole into his bones when he was with her. To gaze into her sky-blue eyes and feel hope stir.

Tansy, don't come out.

Tansy, come—come now. I need you.

Lucas raked one hand through his hair and stared at the ground. She was not his Tansy, this one, yet somehow it didn't matter. That she was softly, sweetly mad did not change how she lightened his world-weary heart. The days without her had shown him that his desire to protect her had not died, but only cloaked itself to save him all those long years he was locked away.

An unlikely savior he was, more so than ever. He owned the clothes on his back and nothing else. He could not support her even if she were so foolish as to want him. He could barely support himself. Tansy was too bright and precious, too fragile and lovely to subject her to the vagaries of his very dim future.

And he owed her. More than he could ever repay.

But none of that seemed to matter to his ancient, scarred heart, too stubborn to die, a foolish bundle of cells steeped in long-ago dreams.

Then she was running toward him, and his heart literally leaped. Without stopping to remember why he shouldn't, he opened his arms, and Tansy flew into them as though it had happened many times before and not only in dreams.

Lucas felt her tremble, those delicate bones, the finely drawn curves, quivering as if she were some small, wounded bird. He tightened his arms around her and brushed his lips over her hair. "What is it, Tansy? What's wrong?"

She didn't answer, only pressed herself closer as though to crawl inside his skin. Lucas yearned to sweep her away, to find some still, quiet place to take her, warm her…keep her safe.

For an instant, he thought about swooping her up, carrying her off, leaving this town and their past forever. Spiriting her to some haven of sunny skies and fields of green, simple white houses and sheltering trees. A sanctuary where no one knew them and no one would care.

He would heal her. He would make it all up to her. He could do it, and he would. With time and space enough, he would find a way to knit her whole again.

"Tansy…" *Come away with me,* he wanted to cry.

Then he recalled his mother, worn and beaten by all the moves, by the constant, grinding poverty, the mean surroundings of dingy walls and scarred furniture. Even before she'd left, her once-startling beauty had faded to a monochrome shadow of the woman she'd been.

Tansy lifted her face, her blue eyes swimming with trust and hope. "What?"

He had a room on sufferance, a few changes of clothes. A job, in a dingy bar, that could vanish tomorrow.

He shook his head. "Nothing." Carefully, he stepped back from her, pulled her hands from his sides, feeling tender pieces of him ripped away as he withdrew.

She seemed bereft, stepped closer. "You didn't come."

He shoved his hands in his jacket and looked away from the impossible lure of her. Forced all warmth from his voice. "I was busy."

"You're here now." Quiet satisfaction hummed in her voice.

"You shouldn't be out here. It's not safe."

Tansy laughed, like clear spring water singing in a brook. "You're here. Nothing can hurt me."

Impotent fury scorched through him. He turned on her. "You're wrong. It can." It already had.

In the streetlight's glow, he saw something flicker, a dark shape swimming beneath the surface of her gaze. Her slim, graceful fingers tangled together, twisting. Her eyes darted to the side. "I dreamed—"

A hot ache crowded his chest. *No, Tansy. Don't.* He had to get away from here, away from her. He should never have returned. "I have to go," he said abruptly.

Blue eyes locked on his. "I dreamed a name. In the bad dream."

The air went still around them. If there were sounds, he couldn't hear them for the rasp of his own breath, the dread that choked out everything else.

"A name," she said. "The bad dream came, and no one could help me. I was so afraid and I couldn't breathe and Mama wouldn't answer. I cried for Paris, but he—he wasn't there. No one could help me, I was all alone and I…" Her breath was only quick gasps, and terror smothered the light in her eyes.

Lucas longed to shield her, to guard her, to chase away what he feared was not dream but memory, but he was afraid that any move he made could be the one that brought it all back.

"The name made me not scared." Her clear blue gaze lifted to his. "Michael—that was the name."

His middle name. Lucas Michael Walker. Once, Juliette had told him in front of Paris and Tansy that it stood for a warrior angel, an archangel wielding a sword. Paris had teased him, calling him St. Michael for days, but Tansy had told him it suited him. From that day, she'd dubbed him Michael.

Was she remembering? A cold black hole opened inside him. There was not one word he could think to speak, not one breath that would emerge. Suspended over a crevasse, he could only wait, frozen. *Dear God, don't let her remember.*

She spoke again as though nothing had happened. "I woke up and crawled into the corner. I said that name to myself, over and over. Then Paris told me to go to the window, to look out at the park. I was scared and I wished to keep hiding, but Paris wouldn't let me. He said he'd leave me forever if I didn't get up." Slender fingers twisted and turned. Wove. Gripped. Unfurled, then clasped again.

"I didn't want to, but I can't lose Paris. If I lose him, I'll die. We can't live alone, either of us. We were born together and that's how we'll die."

Oh, Christ. If her memory returned…what would happen?

Then Tansy smiled, and it was the sun breaking out after endless days of gray, after a long dark night you think you won't survive.

"And there you were," she said. "My prince, ready to save me." She took one step toward him, and he couldn't move. One more brought her to him, and she slid her arms around his waist and snuggled against him.

"I'm going to call you Michael. I feel safe as long as

you're here." She sighed and settled her head against his chest in complete trust. "Please promise me you won't leave."

What a sick irony that she would use his own name, the one only she had preferred. How long a step from that before other memories stirred?

He was no savior. Instead, he feared to his marrow that he would be her doom.

No one knew what he'd done but Tansy and Carlton Sanford, and any information she possessed was locked deep inside. She was vulnerable; she could not guard herself from the dangers of the past unless she remembered—but that very recollection could kill her.

If I lose him, I'll die.

If Lucas left, she was vulnerable. If he stayed, she might recall everything. And if she did, he feared for her life.

Lucas needed an ally, someone who cared deeply about Tansy's welfare.

But the only two he'd had were dead almost twenty years. Everyone left who cared about her would prefer to see *him* dead.

He had to have time to think. "Tansy, you have to go back now."

Innocent, trusting eyes opened wide. "Why?"

"Because…" *I'm dangerous.* Instead, he settled for something was more likely to accept. "Because it's late, and I have to work tomorrow."

"Oh." Her long lashes fluttered. "I'm sorry. I should have thought—will you be all right?"

He grasped her delicate hands and brought them to his lips, searching for suitable words. He was never all right—except when he was with her.

But he was also her biggest threat.

Lucas settled her hands at her sides and framed her face with his fingers. With all the gentleness he could muster, he leaned down and placed a butterfly kiss at the corner of her left eye.

And tried not to wish for more.

"I'll be fine, sweet Tansy. Don't worry about me. Just go upstairs and sleep in peace." With effort, he backed away.

Pale fingers rose to touch the spot where his lips had pressed, her eyes huge and dark and innocent. "Will you return? Please promise me you will. I need you."

"You shouldn't." He shook his head sadly.

The stubborn tilt of her chin was a sight he'd almost forgotten. Then she smiled. "You'll come back, Michael. You will."

With a wave, she departed, leaving him alone to hear, over and over, the haunting sound of her voice saying his name.

All the while unaware of who he really was.

FUCHSIA FOG SWIRLED through inky darkness, tracers of laser-green slicing staccato bursts. The floor shot deep thumping vibrations up through Mona's chest. She glanced around and wondered what she was doing in this club where she was at least ten years older than anyone she could see.

Rebellion. It had a funny metallic taste on her tongue. She took a long sip of her drink to rinse it away.

Frozen in place, she watched the dancers writhe and felt invisible and oddly…safe. She began to relax as the seductive warmth of the alcohol smoothed jangled nerves. No one here would care about her, no one expected anything of her, and there was freedom in that.

She should go home, return to the life she knew. She had work to do, must be her sharpest, her most aggressive to keep climbing to the top.

But right now she wanted to be just where she was. Relishing the delicious escape from all that bound her.

"Hey, baby." A baritone voice slid over her shoulder and down her throat. "You sure you in the right place?"

Mona tightened for a second, glancing down at her trim suit. Touched the one pearl stud in her ear. "No." She tried for cool dignity. "I'm not."

"You lookin' for someone?" He moved in front of her, just her height, a leather vest with a deep scoop baring a chest ornamented with a jewel-toned dragon, one nipple forming the eye and the other circled by the tip of the dragon's tail. He invaded her space. "You want some help, baby?"

Mona fought twin urges: to step back, and to dance

near the flames. Reason won. "No, thank you. I was just leaving."

"Such a lady." He tilted his head, long dark hair brushing his shoulders, and studied her with chocolate-brown eyes. A wide, mobile mouth almost too pretty to belong to a man split in a grin. "Scared, are you?"

"No, of course not. I simply…" The sly grin made her furious. Kat would be laughing at her if she were watching.

"Oh, yeah." He nodded slowly. "You plenty scared. But I could take care of you, show you the ropes."

"How old are you?" she snapped. God. Kat would die.

He raised one dark eyebrow. Lifted a finger and traced the line of her sleeve. "Old enough."

She felt his touch through the fabric but resisted the urge to shrug it off. She didn't sense danger from him; his eyes weren't wild with drugs, his stance didn't menace.

What would Kat do?

Mona smiled faintly. For all she knew, this *was* Kat's boy toy who was hung like—

He laughed, and she realized that her glance had dropped. "Yeah, baby. Old enough for that, for sure. You want some? That why you here?"

She sniffed. "I'm married. I don't need that."

"Oh, I think maybe you do, but we don't have to worry about that yet." He grabbed her hand. "Come on."

She resisted. "Come where? I told you I'm leaving—"

"You too chicken for one dance? Maybe you ain't sure what you after, but least I can do is send you home with something you didn't have before." His grin was engaging. "Hey, baby. It's just a dance."

"I…" She should probably pull away, but the image of Kat rose before her, shaking her head in pity. And what did Mona have to go home to, anyway?

What the hell. "All right. One dance. But no funny stuff." God. She might as well move to Westchester, talking that way. When had she gotten old and fuddy-duddy?

He laughed, something sparkling in his dark eyes. "I won't if you won't."

She laughed, too, and gulped the rest of her drink, then set it on an empty table as he slipped through the jam of bodies, drew her with him. They were quickly swallowed up in the crowd, and she completely lost sight of the way out. She wasn't sure she knew how to dance anymore, it had been so long. But if there was a style she should copy, she didn't see it. The music, so strange at first, slid under her defenses. The bass vibrated through the floor, and the air around her sizzled.

Time slowed. Thought stopped. Heat pressed in, scented with sweat and the perfume of hundreds of bodies. Mona peeled off her jacket. Lacking another choice, she tied it around her waist, the midnight-blue camisole beneath soon sticking to her.

Her skin bloomed with a sheen of moisture, and Mona removed the pins from her hair, letting it fall heavily to her shoulders. She closed her eyes and tilted her face to the ceiling, hair swaying across her back with the rhythm of her movements. She glided into a groove, melting into the music, emptying her mind of everything but this moment.

His hands clasped her hips, and Mona started to open her eyes but decided against it. Soon, his thighs brushed hers, weaving in and out between them. He leaned nearer, and she felt the warmth of his chest against her nipples through the thin silk.

His breath ruffled the hair against her neck as he spoke. "You are choice, baby. Don't never think you too old. You are hot, honey girl. Hot and sweet." His lips grazed her throat, and Mona wanted to drown in the sensation.

Then he pressed against her, full-length, and she felt how hard he was. His tongue slicked down and fastened on her breast through the silk, and Mona's knees went weak.

And Fitz's face blossomed in her mind, his mouth on her breast, his sandy hair beneath her fingers—

Mona jerked away. Crossed her hands over her chest, her breathing ragged. "I'm sorry. I can't…" Dizzy, she stumbled as she whirled to flee, but he grabbed her arm and spun her back.

She raked her nails across his face and snarled, "Get your hands off me."

He recoiled from the blow, lifting his hand to touch his cheek, seeing blood on his fingers. "You bitch. Run to your white-bread house and white-bread life, where you belong." He took one menacing step forward.

Mona ran. Shoving through the crowd, shouts following her; fumbling with the knot at her hips, desperate to cover herself. She couldn't find the door. Panic sent her tumbling to the floor. With a ragged sob, she pushed to her feet and glanced back, watching for him to come after her.

But he didn't. She wasn't that important. Just another white-bread woman, seeking a thrill.

Mona scrubbed at the wet spot over her nipple, trying to erase the feel of his mouth. Even as she shoved her arms through the sleeves of her jacket, she kept scrubbing, but finally she settled for covering it up. She wanted a shower badly, but what if Fitz was home? She couldn't show up looking this way.

She needed some means to gather up the scattered strands of what used to be her perfect life with Fitz, so right not that long ago. The first step was to put her appearance back together before she went home. But where could she go?

Tansy would invite her in, would never ask a question. But Daddy would be there, too, and that would never do.

Kat had a black belt in rebellion. Mona could barely stand the thought of explaining anything to her, but Kat was her sister, after all. Mona had gotten Kat out of more scrapes than she could count. Humiliating or not, it was Kat's turn now.

She retrieved her cell phone and punched in Kat's

number. No answer but her machine. All the better. Mona had a key to Kat's apartment; she would shower and do her repairs and never have to say a word.

KAT SLID INTO WAKEFULNESS by inches, her body soft with inner sunshine, freed from the restlessness that normally plagued her. She touched the spot beside her and found it cool. Sprawled on her side, she felt the kiss of frigid air and reached for her duvet…instead, she found a very old quilt, silken with age.

The unfamiliarity of the bed registered. Memories flooded her brain. She shifted to her back, pulling the quilt beneath her chin as she peered through the pool of golden light to make out a shape in the darkness.

He slept on the floor beside the mattress, naked, one edge of the quilt thrown haphazardly over his torso. Around him like abandoned petals were pages from his sketchpad, each covered with bold strokes she couldn't make out from here.

Curious, Kat rose carefully, and gave him a wide berth. But she knew before she snatched the closest sketch.

She lay on the page, exposed in sensual bliss, every line of her body shouting that she'd been well and truly fucked. She clasped the sketch and crept across the floor to find more.

Gamble muttered in his sleep, and she stilled, her heart beating against her chest like a trapped bird.

Freezing on the cold floor, still Kat explored, crawling like a crab to pick up first one, then another, feeling more naked by the second. She'd never been a prude, was proud of her body. But this…

They were scattered pieces of her soul. Kat ranged over the scarred floor, gathering the sketches. Fear tottered in shaky steps up her spine. No one had ever exposed her this way. Only Gamble Smith.

She couldn't bear it.

Hardly breathing, she dressed quickly, then tiptoed away, rolling the sketches in a cylinder with as much stealth as she could manage.

But one of them crackled, and Gamble stirred. Opened his eyes as she neared the door.

He cast his gaze around, searching for the pages. "What are you doing?" he thundered.

She jutted her chin, fear a snake writhing in her belly. "Taking what's mine."

"Those are *mine.* Give them back."

"No. Gamble, this isn't right. You've—you can't have this part of me."

"Why are you so afraid? It's the best work I've ever done." He muted his voice, getting to his feet slowly. "I'll make you famous. You'll be bigger than Wyeth's Christina." At ease with being naked, he moved across the floor, his the stride of a powerful lord, secure in the allure of what he offered.

"I don't want to be famous. And I want that painting, or I'll ruin you." Kat struggled into her other shoe.

He snorted. "Don't play power games you can't win." Then his voice went molasses-sweet and warm. "You're scared, Kat, but there's nothing to fear. You're beautiful. Let me show the world just how much."

For a second, she relaxed under the caress of his tone. Then, lightning-fast, he grabbed for the sketches.

Kat jerked open the door and ran, hearing him roar her name all the way down to the street.

MONA TURNED OFF the blowdryer, thinking she heard a noise. The front door clicked shut. She gripped the edge of the sink and waited for the ax to fall, for Kat to crack wise about her being here instead of at home.

"Mona?" Footsteps down the hall. "If you're not Mona, then get ready for a world of hurt. I'm already pissed, and I'm going to beat your ass before I call 911."

Mona couldn't stifle a faint grin. Life would never defeat Kat. She'd go down swinging. "Relax, Kat. It's me."

Her sister appeared in the mirror behind her, frowning. "What the hell are you doing here this time of night?" Quickly, she took in Mona's damp hair and the towel wrapped around her body. "Uh-oh. This doesn't look good." Her expression went stricken. "Oh, God— you're having an affair. Oh, Jesus, how can you cheat on Fitz?" Suddenly, she seemed six years old and as if someone had just told her the truth about Santa Claus.

Mona averted her face. "Nothing's wrong."

Kat recovered her poise. "Bullshit."

"I told you nothing's…" Mona's chin dropped to her chest. Tears sprang to her eyes. She'd been on autopilot since she'd left the club, but now the night and the upheaval of her life crowded in. "It's not…" Kat adored Fitz; she'd never understand.

But Mona had sold Kat short. "Oh, sweetie, what's the matter?" They were both tall, but Kat was two inches taller. She wrapped one arm around Mona's shoulders and pulled her close, making nonsense noises and soothing as though she were the older sister. The reliable one.

Mona fell apart.

She was barely aware of Kat removing the towel and bundling her in a thick, fluffy robe. Of Kat drawing her into the living room and settling her on the couch. Sitting right beside her, patting her shoulder awkwardly. Awkward but there. Caring. It seemed a million years since Mona had had anyone to lean on.

Except Fitz. Fitz, who'd changed all the rules.

Fresh tears spilled. Kat yanked a handful of tissues from a box and thrust them into her hands. "Go ahead and cry it out." Her voice went sharp. "Men are such assholes." She rose. "I'm going to make us some tea and then we're going to indulge in some serious hen talk."

Hen talk. It had been Nana's term for baring the soul, for the cathartic release that men didn't understand and women needed like breathing. Memories washed over Mona, of bad dates and not making cheerleader, of having her first period without her mother there… But Nana always made it better. A little hen talk and the world righted itself again.

And now her much-younger sister was trying to assume Nana's place. Just that quickly, she'd taken Mona's side without even knowing what was wrong.

Mona laid her head back on the thick cushion and let out an exhausted sigh. She settled her feet on the trunk that served as a coffee table, one foot brushing a thick roll of sketch paper that was beginning to unfurl. Mona thought about examining it, but she was too tired to rise. She closed her eyes and drifted…and tried to think what Nana would do.

"Screw tea. We're going for the strong stuff." Kat strode in with her usual panache, but when Mona opened her eyes and sat up, she realized that Kat was pale, that she was off-kilter.

"What is it? Did something happen to you tonight?"

Kat's glance slid to the roll of papers, then darted away. "No. I'm great. And anyway, we're discussing you."

Mona straightened. "Talk to me, Kat."

Her sister shrugged. "No big deal. Just a guy." She handed Mona a goblet and filled her own. Holding it high, she met her sister's gaze. "Here's to women without men. Who needs 'em, anyway? Mud in your eye and all that rot." She tossed back her wine as if it was a shot of whiskey.

Mona was still worried. "Kat…"

Kat ran one long-fingered hand through the spiky red hair. "It's no big deal. I swear." Then her eyes narrowed. "So tell me what's going on. What are you doing here?"

Mona bought time by taking a long sip. "Mmm, good wine. What is it?"

"Mona…" Kat's voice held warning. "I'm big enough to sit on you and tickle if you don't start spilling. And you know how you hate that." She wiggled fingers in the direction of Mona's armpit. "You have about seven years of tickles coming for all the times you sat on me and tortured."

Mona couldn't help a small grin. She'd forgotten how ticklish Kat was. They shared a moment's amusement.

"So dish. What did you do tonight that must be washed away?"

"I tried to be you."

"You what?" Kat's double take made Mona grin.

She sighed and leaned her head back. "I'm afraid my marriage is in trouble. And I'm sick to death of being good." She lifted her head. "So I went clubbing and found me a guy with a tattoo." She giggled at Kat's expression and sipped again. "I can't say if he's hung, though. I think so, maybe." She tried for blasé, but failed miserably.

She'd never seen Kat speechless.

"Holy shit." Then Kat threw back her head and laughed. "I would have paid a million bucks to witness it." She fell against the couch in a gale of laughter, then sat up quickly. "You're lying to me. Not Mary Mother of God Mona. No way."

Mona grinned, and for a moment, the night seemed funny. She pictured herself in her perfect black suit, one earring gone, dancing with a tattooed guy with a hard-on. "Way. I ditched my jacket. All I had on was a camisole. One earring."

"Nuh-uh…oh, this is great…" Another wave of laughter rolled over Kat. The sound was so infectious that Mona joined in. Kat swirled one finger in a circle. "More. Tell me there's more."

Between giggles, Mona continued. "I took the pins out of my hair while we danced. He had a dragon right—" She choked out the word between gasping for air, pressing her hand to the center of her chest. "Right…here."

Kat grabbed her sides. "Oh, God, you're killing me." Another wave overcame her.

"Hey, it was a pretty dragon." Mona shoved at Kat, and Kat tumbled to the floor. She lay on her back, giggling.

Mona set down her wine, sloshing it over the side. She lay on her stomach on the couch, peering down on her sister. "I think he was hung. He was damn sure hard. He grabbed me and—"

Her laughter died as her throat went tight. Fitz. She'd wanted Fitz so badly, and now what would she do? She'd never had a story she couldn't tell Fitz before. Mona pressed her face into the cushion and felt the hot rush of tears. "Oh, God, Kat. I feel awful. I don't know what to do."

Kat's laughter stopped instantly, and she rose to her knees, leaning over Mona to press a kiss to her hair.

Nana had done that. She was a big believer in the healing power of hair kisses. Hers always worked. Always.

"I miss Nana so much," Mona whispered. "She was tiny, but she made me feel so safe."

"Oh, baby." Kat stroked Mona's hair. "What happened with Fitz?"

Mona grabbed her hand and squeezed. "Can I stay here tonight?"

"Of course. But won't Fitz worry?"

"I guess." Mona shook her head. "I'm not sure."

"I'm going to call him and tell him that we went out and drank too much and now I've tied you to the couch." She bestowed one more kiss on Mona's hair, then walked away. "And then I'm coming back, and you're going to spill your guts."

Mona grabbed her hand before she got out of range. "Thanks, Kat."

Kat squeezed back and smiled. "No sweat. I'm always glad for an excuse to flirt with Fitz." Her voice went soft. "I'll be right back, sweetie. You just rest, you hear?"

Kat playing Nana—would miracles never cease? Mona stayed where she was and smiled.

FAINT LIGHT BROKE the shadows where Lucas huddled for warmth. It made no sense for him to be standing guard over Tansy, snug in her bed across the street, but he'd been aware when he'd gently urged her back home a few hours ago that sleep would not visit him this night.

Some Galahad he made. Don Quixote was more like it. Or Sancho Panza. His own search for a permanent solution to Tansy's safety was more doomed than the search for the Holy Grail.

As long as Carlton Sanford was alive, Tansy would never be safe. Nor would Lucas Walker. Somehow, he had to find someone concerned enough about Tansy to listen to the man who had been sent to jail for murdering her twin. But he had to be careful, for the spider had many legs and a huge web.

For half the night, he'd pondered how he, an ex-con with a prison education, could take on Carlton Sanford without alerting him. He'd spent a lot of time in the prison library; his education had come not from classes but from reading to keep himself sane. He'd devised his own plan of study, fumbling his way through the library until he'd learned how to research almost any topic.

That was where he'd start. He'd research Sanford's life until he found a hole, located some leverage. And while he was digging, he'd wait for Sanford to trip himself up.

But he didn't have long. Not now that Tansy had said his name.

He didn't want to steal her away and condemn her to a life he could afford; that would be his last resort. But rather than let Tansy be placed in the hands of Carlton Sanford, Lucas would grab her and run.

The odds against him were terrible, even he could tell that. And if Tansy's memories were stirring…

He could lose her again. And he wasn't sure he could bear it.

CHAPTER ELEVEN

MONA JERKED AWAKE and tried to remember where she was. A line of Tansy's birds marching across the purple-and-green Indian scarf draping the scarred footlocker was all the clue she needed. Kat's place. On the ancient overstuffed sofa.

Bundled in Kat's robe, with one of Nana's quilts covering her legs. Kat playing Nana, having to call Fitz. *Then I'm coming back and you're going to spill your guts.* But they'd never made it to the gut spilling, Mona was almost sure. Instead, she'd fallen asleep to the sound of her sister laughing with the husband Mona had come within a hairsbreadth of betraying last night.

She groaned and rolled over, drawing her knees up to her chest, and memories spilled out like overturned garbage. Earsplitting music, the clash of perfume and sweat. Darkness and violent color. And hands. On her. Another man's hands. Not Fitz. Dragon tattoo on young flesh—

Mona leaped from the sofa, banging her toes on the trunk, and hopped around the room, cursing. Pain and shame collided. Her stomach queasy, she sank to the floor, holding her foot and fighting back tears.

Oh, Fitz, what happened to us? Never in a million years would she have believed they could drift so far apart. Anguish sucked her under. She couldn't breathe. "Oh, God," she whimpered.

"Mona?" Kat's voice, husky with morning. "Are you all right? I heard…" She moved into view, and Mona attempted to hide behind the arm of the sofa.

But too late. "Oh, honey, what is it?" Kat settled beside her, brown eyes soft with worry.

Mona shook her head but couldn't speak.

Kat's arms went around her to pull her close and rock her. "Tell me what's wrong, Mona. I've never seen you this way. Tell me what happened with Fitz."

Before, Mona would have stood up, dusted herself off, denied it all. Years of ingrained behavior battled with a choking need for comfort, for someone to give her answers she didn't have.

Then Kat began to hum the melody Mona had last heard from Nana. And she cracked. "I'm so scared, Kat," she whispered through hot, painful tears. "I'm going to lose him, and I don't know what to do."

It all poured out: his captivity, the baby, the trip to Westchester. How insidiously their entire understanding had collapsed. How she didn't know Fitz anymore, had lost her trust. How she'd tried to rebel last night, and the taste of ashes lay bitter on her tongue.

Kat listened quietly, and Mona was relieved that her sister didn't attempt to justify why Fitz's new dream of family made sense. The daughters of Martin Gerard had learned better.

"I've never had a single secret from him in ten years." Mona sought to smile. "I can't even keep mum about his presents—I always give them early." She stared into her sister's eyes, her voice dropping to a whisper. "How do I remain silent about last night—but what happens to us if I tell him? He's my best friend, Kat, and we're barely speaking."

"He loves you, Mona. You can't think he doesn't."

"I'm not sure that's true anymore." She glanced away, sliding the fingers of one hand through her hair. "I'm not certain of anything."

"I hear that."

Something emphatic in Kat's tone brought Mona's head swinging around. "What's up with you, anyway? Who is this 'just a guy' you mentioned last night?"

Kat shrugged. "Nobody important." But she wouldn't meet Mona's gaze.

Mona placed one finger beneath Kat's chin. "Uh-uh. Now I'm not buying."

"We were talking about you, not me."

But the break had brought Mona back to herself. Acutely conscious that she was the one who listened, who gave advice, not the one who asked for it, she drew the mantle of big sister around her once more. "I...it's not your problem. I'll figure it out. I always manage, don't I?"

"God, I hate it when you do that."

Mona recoiled. "Do what?"

"Did it ever occur to you that nobody asked you to be the pillar of this family? That maybe somebody else might appreciate being needed for a change?" Kat uncoiled her long-limbed frame and rose from the floor, stomping off toward the kitchen.

Mona was honestly shocked. "Kat, I don't see—"

Kat snorted. "That's the problem. You're too busy organizing all our lives to notice that we can manage just fine on our own."

A huge crevasse opened up before Mona, and all her certainties tumbled away from her feet. She teetered on the edge, fear making her vicious. "Tansy can't take care of herself, and Daddy leans on me, too. And you—" she shot one arm out, gesturing wide "—you're too busy screwing your way through the city to pay attention to what anyone else needs. Left up to you—"

Kat whirled, teeth bared. "You are such a bitch. Who died and made you God?" With the subtle, devastating accuracy only a sister can wield, she slid in the knife. "How can Fitz stand it? You're so damn rigid."

Angry words, killer words, harsh words meant to wound whipped through Mona's brain, toppling over one another so fast she couldn't catch them. Couldn't catch her breath for the edgy, ugly pain spreading in her chest.

She struggled to defend herself, to make Kat see. To get all of them to realize that she had never asked for this. Never wanted to be the tower of strength, but she'd had no choice.

Couldn't anyone but Fitz understand that sometimes she had wanted to be the one to lean?

"Never mind," Kat muttered. "I'm going to make coffee." She left the room.

Mona stood where she was, feet bare, heart bare, her life a mess…and suddenly, she was so tired her bones ached. She sank to the floor, leaned back against the sofa and closed her eyes. Stretching out her legs, she bumped her toes into something.

The roll of sketch paper she'd spotted last night came unfurled. Half of one sheet was in view. The model was someone Mona knew well.

Kat. Naked. Relaxed, almost serene in a way Mona had never imagined, yet she glowed with an earthy sensuality so stunning that even a sister could feel the allure. Mona pulled the sketch toward her and perused it.

Kat had always been the most striking one of them all. Larger than life, sometimes rude, sometimes caustic…unbearably arrogant to boot. But the artist who'd drawn this had unmasked Kat. Whoever it was understood that the brash Kat had a tender side. That the Kat who hissed had once dreamed of being a princess, and melted around babies. That her bravado hid a cry for love.

Eagerly, Mona unrolled the rest of the sheets, digging her teeth into her lower lip as she studied the quick, devastating sketches that peered into her sister in a way few ever had.

Mona noted one thing more. This artist was a man. And he'd made love to her sister.

"What the hell are you doing?" Kat screeched. "Put those down."

Mona held one hand over them calmly. "This is him, isn't it? This is 'just a guy.' Who is he, Kat?" She glanced down. "These are stunning."

Kat plunked the coffee mugs on the table, and brown liquid sloshed over the side. She yanked the sketches away from Mona and rolled them carefully. "I don't want to talk about it."

There was hurt here, and confusion. Kat, who discarded men as though they were tissues, had hit a snag with this one.

"Yes, I'm a bitch and you can criticize me all you wish, but even I can tell that he has incredible talent. If you don't want to keep those, give them to me. They should be framed. They're gorgeous."

Kat's jaw hardened. "No one is going to ogle these."

"Because you're naked? When did that ever bother you?"

Her sister's head whipped around, and Mona was

shocked to spy the sheen of tears. "You think I'm a slut. I understand that. I deserve it most of the time. But this is different, Mona." Her voice fell. "He'll probably be beating down my door for them, anyway. I'm surprised he hasn't already."

Curiouser and curiouser. "Why?"

"Because I stole them from him." Kat's chin jutted. "I'm going after that painting next."

"What painting?"

Kat just shook her head, clutching the roll so hard that Mona feared for the sketches. Gently, she withdrew them from Kat's grasp. When Kat resisted briefly, Mona reassured her. "I'm only going to set them down. Even if no one else gets a look at them, you don't want them wrinkled, do you?"

Kat stared in that direction, but she was seeing something else. Finally, she inhaled sharply, as if emerging from a dream.

"Gamble Smith."

Mona blinked. "Pardon me?"

"The artist from my latest show, the one you had to miss for your deadline. That's who did them."

"The romantic." Mona remembered now. "The reviews were glowing. One of my editors was there. She said she nearly swooned."

Kat laughed, but there was bitterness in it. "A common reaction."

"What's he like?"

"Big. Glowering." She turned to Mona, her lips curving upward. "He's from Texas—you believe that? I can't even consider what he'd look like on a horse. Hell, *I'd* swoon."

"He intrigues you."

"He makes me furious. He's a rude, ill-mannered, bad-tempered brute who—"

Mona couldn't help herself. She started laughing. "A match made in heaven."

Ire rose in Kat's eyes, but just as suddenly, she laughed, too. "The hell of it is, he got to me, Mona. I've never felt this way before. If I hadn't woken up and spotted what he'd done…"

Mona frowned. "What?"

"Those." Kat pointed an accusing finger at the sketches.

"What's wrong with them? They're gorgeous. Women would kill to have a man view them that way."

"I have no desire to be…" Kat raked unsteady fingers through her hair. "That woman doesn't exist. He can't show these to anyone, and I'm going to get that painting if I have to—"

Mona grasped her shoulders. "Is it so bad for people to discover you have a soft side?"

Anguish filled Kat's eyes. "Mama was soft. Tansy's soft. The world destroyed both of them. You, of all people, should understand."

Mona leaned her forehead against her sister's, her

amusement more shaky than merry. "We are a pair, aren't we? You spend your life telling everyone to go to hell, and I tell them how to get there and what to pack." She sighed. "We had to be strong. Everyone left us."

"Everyone but Nana," Kat insisted. She wrapped her arms around Mona.

Warmed but sad, Mona agreed. "But in the end, she left us, too."

They stood there in silence, each lost in thought. At last, Kat spoke up. "What are you going to do about Fitz?"

"What are you going to do about the bad-tempered artist?"

They drew apart and looked at each other, speaking in tandem.

"Hell if I know."

Each cracked a smile, then a giggle. The giggles broke out in full-throated hilarity, and they fell onto the sofa, made helpless by mirth. Soon they were wiping their eyes, drained by twin urges to giggle and sob.

Finally, Kat lifted one arm, palm turned out. "Here's to sisters, bitches though we may be."

Mona slapped palms with her, and their hands closed in a clasp. "How much money do you have in your purse?"

Kat grinned. "Seven dollars and change."

"I've got plastic. Let's ditch everyone and live on some beach with hot and cold running lifeguards."

Kat nodded. "No names exchanged. Just sex, then

kick them out and replace them. No one spends the night."

"No panty hose."

"No shaving legs."

Mona grinned. "No high heels."

"No alarm clocks," Kat added.

"Alarm clocks!" Mona bolted upright. "Ohmigod—I have a nine o'clock meeting. What time is it?"

Kat shot a glance into her kitchen. "Nine forty-five."

Mona shrieked and leaped to her feet, headed for the phone.

THAT AFTERNOON THE DOOR to Mona's office swung open, and Fitz walked in.

The night that had vanished under the day's pressures roared back. She caught his somber expression, and wished there were a way to make the phone call she was having last forever.

She signaled to him to wait, and he nodded.

"Yes, George. I understand." She pitched her tone to soothe. "You're very special to us here at *Bijou,* never doubt that. We would tell you if there was anything wrong. This dip is simply seasonal. The weather is depressing everyone, but that won't last." She struggled to listen to the magazine's most important advertiser while Fitz filled up her mind. "Let me take you to lunch next week, all right? I'll put Gaby on the phone to arrange it. Can't wait, handsome," she said, kiss-kissing into the phone.

She slammed the receiver down. "Pig. Prick. Bastard."

"Bad day?"

She had to force herself to meet his gaze. "The worst."

"Tsk-tsk. You never could hold your liquor."

She smiled. "Seems I recall you liked that about me from time to time." When his eyes smoldered, she wondered what she'd been thinking last night. He was still the sexiest man she'd ever met.

He leaned over her desk, arms outspread, hands flat. "You and Kat had quite a night, huh?"

She studied the long fingers, the wide palms. Thought about how happy she'd always been to have those hands on her.

She tried to remind herself that she hadn't done anything serious. Not even a kiss. But she could feel the dragon man's hands on her hips, his mouth on her breast.

"Des?" That voice that she'd loved for years. "What is it, babe?"

She played with a pen, sliding it over and over through nervous fingers. "I love you, Fitz. You know that, don't you?"

The air between them was suddenly sharp and crackling. Fitz pulled his hands away without touching her. Went rigid. Voice strangely neutral, he spoke while jamming his hands into his pockets. "You weren't at Kat's last night, were you?"

"Yes, I was. I slept on her sofa." The lie crowded her throat.

One eyebrow cocked. "But before that?"

She didn't know what to do, what to say. *Please, Fitz, can't we go back? Where did it go, the perfect life we had?*

"I…I went to a club, that's all." She swallowed hard. "Nothing happened." But she'd stayed silent too long, she could tell.

"A club." He shrugged. "Harmless, right?" His voice sounded anything but. "What club?"

Ever the reporter. Always digging for details. "I— I'm not sure."

His snort condemned her without a trial.

"I didn't do anything, I swear it. Just one dance." Begging to be believed. Had it come to this? They'd never kept tabs on each other. Never needed to.

He rocked back on his heels. A deep sigh escaped him. A shake of the head. "I've been kidding myself, haven't I, Des? You're never going to compromise. You like this life, empty as it is, and you're not willing to change."

"Compromise?" Rage displaced shame. "When have you offered me a compromise? Have babies, move to Westchester, become a hausfrau like your mother?"

"My mother's a good woman. You can't say that she isn't."

Mona sank back in her chair, despair crowding in. "Your mother's an angel. She's absolute perfection." She wasn't being sarcastic. His mother *was* perfect. That was the problem. "But I'm not her, Fitz. I never have been." She couldn't keep the hurt from her tone. "You said you loved me the way I am."

"I do love you, but there's more than this, more than what we have."

Not for me. I'm spread so thin I'm becoming transparent. She looked up at the man she'd loved for ten years, and pondered when they'd become strangers. She summoned the nerve to ask, "What about our agreement? You didn't care about kids. You understood who I was and what I wanted, and you said you felt the same."

"You haven't been listening to me. Everything's altered for me. Everything. We're living a half life, Des, a selfish existence. We're not on this planet to be famous or win awards or—" he went for the killer thrust "—run our competitors out of business. That's for people who think they have all the time in the world. All that is vanity. Two nights spent with a gun to my head taught me that I've been a selfish bastard, focused only on my career, or pushing and shoving my way to the top."

He leaned over her desk again, in his eyes a zealot's fire. "What we're doing is bullshit, babe. Pure crap. We can't be certain that we have past the next second, yet we act as if we've got all the time in the world." His voice went low and urgent. "I realized those nights that I've been skimming along the surface. That you have, too. I want children, sweetheart—I always did. I thought you'd get over being so scared and inflexible. I believed you'd come to understand that I'm not like your father. I'd be the best damn dad in the world." His eyes locked on hers. "I want children, and I'd prefer them with you."

Prefer? What kind of commitment was that? The shock of it stole her breath.

Terror made her brusque. "And if I can't want them? If I suspect that you're just unnerved by what happened and you'll recover, given time?"

Fire turned to shock. Then to ice. "Christ. I thought you'd change, but you aren't interested, are you? You're so damn sure yours is the best way that you aren't even willing to try."

"You can't send babies back if it doesn't work out."

Learning that the man who'd made her feel whole had been secretly hoping she'd change one day, that their relationship had been based on a hidden lie…Mona reeled from it, her world shattering around her. She did the only thing she could figure to do, what had worked before when she'd seen her life splinter.

She pulled back from the stranger who stood before her. Retreated into a silence that would protect her, even as her heart cracked. "I guess we never really knew each other, did we?" She shuttered her gaze, forcing her face into a polite mask. "Perhaps we could talk about this later?"

"You're just amazing." Harsh laughter escaped him. "Sure. Later is great. Hell, it's only our lives." Fury rode hard on his frame. "You just go back to work, Desdemona. After all, your damn career is more important, isn't it?"

Rage claimed her, too. "You backed me in this. I told you what I was, what my goals were. You had no right to change the rules." She clamped her jaw shut. Felt a trembling begin. Sensed the sands shifting beneath her feet, but she held fast.

Fitz stalked to the door and grasped the handle. "I won't wait forever, Des." Honest regret shouted out from every feature. "We don't have forever. I want more, sweetheart…" He paused, as close to pleading as she'd ever envisioned. "But I wanted it with you. I only wish you longed for me as much."

Then he was gone, leaving silence, sharp and painful, in his wake.

Mona groped for her mother's teacup, fingers shaking so hard she had to grip it in two hands. Through a glaze of tears, her vision was drawn to the crack at the base. She traced it with one fingertip, seeing her life reflected there. What she and Fitz had had seemed so beautiful and indestructible, but a tiny flaw in the foundation was widening. She'd never viewed the crack as such before, blinded by love and work and the sheer relief that Fitz accepted her as she was.

Once.

He didn't understand that she was trying to save them both. That even if she was too strong to give up everything as her mother had, she was quite likely capable of her father's self-absorption. That had been fine for Fitz, a busy man himself.

But children deserved more. She would never doom a child to her own fate, but she understood herself too well to take on her mother's long-suffering mantle. Mona was no hausfrau, no earth mother. And neither was Fitz. Any child of theirs would wind up starved for the kind of nurturing that should be every child's birthright.

Mona set the cup into the saucer, careful not to put stress on the crack. With that same caution, she would shepherd her marriage until Fitz came to his senses. She would do nothing to widen the fissure, and she would pray fervently to the Fates that it would not widen on its own.

Time. They just needed time. To heal, to mend. To find their love again.

Squeezing her hands until the knuckles turned white, Mona summoned every last ounce of strength she had.

Then, drawing in a deep breath, she reached for the next paper in her stack.

CHAPTER TWELVE

TWO DAYS HAD PASSED since Lucas had left Tansy, endless hours of reminding himself that he was doing what was best for her, and that was staying the hell away.

He'd scrubbed pots that didn't need cleaning. He'd rearranged all the supplies. He'd washed every glass in the place during the long hours when he couldn't sleep for thinking of Tansy with mingled fear and longing.

Carlton Sanford was more powerful and connected than Lucas could have imagined. Long sessions spent poring over microfiche had shown Sanford with prominent politicians and businessmen, raising money for fashionable charities. At the helm of a Fortune 500 company, Sanford was respected by legions, had impeccable credentials to his name.

Lucas Walker was an ex-con with a pedigree that led straight to the toilet, a child whose mother hadn't thought him worth saving. Bad blood flowed through his veins, blood that could not be cleansed.

Tansy was better off without him, that was for sure.

But she wasn't safe with Carlton Sanford, and that worried Lucas. Kept him up at night, aware that he was powerless to protect her.

But if the reporter was correct…he had to find a way. Sanford could not be allowed to get his hands on Tansy. If the rumor was true and Sanford really did plan to marry her, he had to be stopped.

Short of murder, Lucas had no idea how to do it. All the power was in Sanford's hands.

Misery swamped him. Tansy had opened up the protective casing of his heart when he wasn't looking, and loneliness ate away at his resolve. He missed her with an ache that had teeth and claws. He longed to be with her, wanted the right to care….

But he could not risk being her doom.

Sinking down on his cot, he buried his face in his hands. Then he heard the noise. Quick as a cat, he was on his feet, a knife at the ready.

"I'm sorry. I didn't mean to scare you." Gloria. The stripper with the soulful eyes.

He shoved the knife out of sight. "No problem. I just…" *Learned to have hair-trigger reflexes in the night.* "You okay? Al's not here. He's already gone home."

She smiled and moved across the darkness, moonlight scattering across her features. "I didn't come to see Al."

"Oh." Lucas went on alert.

"I'm worried about you."

Lucas shrugged uneasily. "I'm fine."

"You're not. You're wound tight as a top." Slender hands drifted over his chest, down the front of his jeans. The body that hadn't had a woman in twenty years leaped to life with shocking speed.

"Gloria, no—" Lucas grabbed her hand.

"Shh. You've been good to me. Treated me as a real person, not a whore. You won't ask, but I'd like to give something back," she whispered, then covered his mouth with hers.

He stiffened, ready to shove her away. It wasn't right, no matter how much he craved the release. How much he craved the oblivion. How badly he wanted to feel again what it was like to lose himself in the sweet heat of a woman's body. God, he was tired of taking care of it himself.

Lucas groaned as hunger dug in with claws so sharp he thought he'd lose his mind. "Gloria—" He tried to say, *I can't.* Tansy stood in his mind as a beacon, so pure and so fair. So innocent.

And so off-limits.

"Shh," Gloria soothed. "No strings. Just let me do this." She had his jeans open, drawing him out, hot and hard, into her hand.

Lucas fought with himself as savage need pounded against the dreams of a boy who wanted only one shining girl. A girl who was not ready, might never be ready for him. A girl he should walk away from now, whose only experience had been of violence and pain.

Expertly, Gloria touched him, and Lucas was sorely tempted to let go. To stop the fight. He was only a man, flawed and all wrong for Tansy. One who'd spent twenty years locked up. He'd battled to survive hell, had lived for the day he could do just this—fill his hands with a woman's breasts, place his mouth on her nipples, run his fingers over every soft curve until he remembered what it was like to be a man again and not a caged creature, barely half-human.

Gloria slid down his body. "Let go, Lucas. It's all right," she soothed.

"No. I can't—" But something inside him tore.

Her eyes were dark and ancient. "Please, Lucas. I've watched you—something's wearing at you. You haven't been sleeping, have you?" She stroked him, and his hands clenched. "You never look down on me the way everyone else does. I needed a friend, and you've been that." Sorrow crossed over her face. "I understand your heart isn't free, but…I'm lonely, too. Let me fight the darkness with you."

"Gloria, this isn't the way—" But her words were even more seductive than her skill. He was weary to the bone…and so damn empty.

"Shh, Lucas." She took him into her mouth.

"No…" he groaned. He wanted to wait. *Tansy might never be ready,* whispered temptation.

No. He bunched his fingers in Gloria's hair and tried to fight off the surge, but his body didn't listen. *Tansy…* He keened silently with the agony of a man who has lost his last sight of hope—

And with a cry torn from his depths, Lucas let go. His mind went white. He sagged against the wall, drained… for one glorious moment unable to think.

But all too quickly, bitter truth returned with a vengeance. *Oh, Tansy.* Lucas sank to a crouch, head in his hands, despair crowding in, darker than the worst day of his years in the hole.

MONA RODE UP IN the elevator, leaning against the wall, lost in thought. She dreaded the impending darkness, wondering, once again, if Fitz would come home. He hadn't been there for two nights now. She was so exhausted, a constant state lately. Maybe she would take a nap first and hope it would recharge her, make her more able to face his absence.

She opened the door and stopped in shock. Home at a very early hour for him, Fitz whirled toward her.

"Hi," she ventured.

He nodded. "Hi."

He appeared as tired as she felt. "Tough day?"

He shrugged. "Nothing special." No explanation for the missing nights. He shifted on his feet. His gaze flickered to meet hers, then away.

All at once, she longed for nothing more than for him

to hold her. When words wouldn't work, physical contact always did. Setting her briefcase and purse aside, she crossed to him.

To her shock, he stepped back. Only one, but he might as well have hit her.

When he glanced at her, she spotted regret in his expression…and something more.

"Des," he murmured. He studied her for a second with something that seemed too much like pity. "I've found a hotel room. I…" He huffed out a breath. "I would have been here earlier and gotten out before you came home, but I got a call from a source and had to meet him. I could wait until tomorrow, but—"

"No." It was all she could think to say. Then her voice lowered, into some supplicant she'd never met. "Fitz, no. You can't mean—" To her horror, her voice broke. "All this over babies?"

She began to pace. "I don't understand. How can we live in Westchester? What happened to all our plans?" She turned back. "Florence. We were going to do Florence this year."

"You wanted to do Florence, not me." His eyes were at once gentle and resolute. "Babe, that's the problem. We have no idea what the other one wants anymore."

"You're wrong, Fitz." A voice she hardly recognized slid into shrill. "After ten years, we know everything about each other. You enjoy cigars and brandy and talking Kant and listening to Sinatra." She moved closer, desperate to make him see. "You have a mole under your left shoulder blade. You understand how I like to be kissed."

God. Was she begging? She didn't beg. Ever.

"Des." Oh, that voice she'd loved for years. "You have no idea what stories I'm working on. You don't even realize that I turned down an offer to go to *Newsweek*."

She blinked. "Why didn't you tell me? Oh, Fitz, that's wonderful! But why would you turn it down?"

One tawny eyebrow lifted. His eyes were sad. "Because ambition isn't as important to me as it is to you."

A surprised bark shot from her throat. "You'd kill over a breaking story. You love your work. It's who you are," she insisted.

"Not anymore," he said softly. "But you haven't been paying attention enough to realize that."

"It's just this stupid party. It'll be over soon. A little longer and we're home free."

"Don't, sweetheart." He clasped her shoulders gently, but it was to keep her at bay, not to bring her near. "It's not just that you'll never let it go with your father."

"Daddy doesn't have anything to do with this."

Fitz's jaw hardened. "Don't try to bullshit me, Des. And don't lie to yourself. You're never going to quit trying to become Daddy's favorite, to make him admit he was wrong in ignoring you. You'll never stop wanting him to look past Tansy and Paris and see you."

She jerked away. "You don't know what the hell you're saying."

Suddenly, Mona's blood chilled. "Who is she?" That must be it: another woman.

He sighed. "There is no 'she.'"

"Then why leave? You're lying. You've found some little homebody to create your nest and give you babies. Who is she? Where did you find her? Was that who you were with last night?"

Her hand lashed out almost of its own accord and slapped him. "Damn you, Fitz. Why did you change the rules? You said it was fine. You told me all that wasn't important—you only needed me. *Me,* you bastard." A harsh sob scraped her throat as she stared at the red imprint of her hand on the cheek that even now she wanted to press against her own.

In horror, in grief, in pain that threatened to break her, she dragged out the question she'd been asking herself for days. "Why? You loved me. You said I was all you'd ever want. Why did it change? We've had so much."

One big hand rose as if to soothe her. Mona held her breath, craving to be nestled in his arms more than she'd ever wanted anything in her life. But she wouldn't move toward him. He'd torn them apart. He was the one who'd changed. She'd kept to their agreement. She wasn't mother material. Never would be.

And then his hand dropped to his side and his head lowered. She thought she saw tears in his eyes.

"Fitz…" she whispered.

His head lifted. "Not an inch, will you, Des? You grant the ghosts of your past everything, and you won't compromise one iota for anyone else." He walked around a chair to avoid her. "I'll only pack one bag and get the other things later, when you're not here."

He disappeared into the bedroom, where they'd laughed and loved and argued and wept.

And Mona felt despair of a sort she'd never thought to live through again. This was like when her father sent them away. When Paris died and Daddy wouldn't let them come home. When Mama died and he forgot everyone but Tansy.

Now the man she'd let become too important was abandoning her, too, and he wouldn't listen any more than Daddy had.

Why did they have to have children? They had each other. Their life together had been so good.

Fitz had been the one who taught her that she could scale mountains if she dared. He couldn't walk away, now that she was nearing the top.

She heard him coming back. A crushing ache choked off any words. There were none, really, not for this. Not unless she pleaded, and she was through begging for crumbs. She'd been too forgettable when she was young. She'd never be overlooked again, and if Fitz thought he could put her out of his mind, he was fooling himself. They were part of each other, blood and bone. He'd take some time away and he'd remember how right they were together.

He just needed some space. She'd concentrate on this godforsaken party and her magazine. It would be plenty to keep her from crawling, even if she should lose her mind and want to try.

Fitz emerged from the bedroom. "Des…" he said softly. "I'm sorry. I—" He cursed beneath his breath.

She could feel him waiting for her to turn around, but he was kidding himself if he thought she could look at him now. If she didn't have Fitz's love anymore, then her dignity was all she had left.

She heard him exhale wearily. Heard the door open. She still didn't budge.

And then the emptiness stole into her heart, telling her that Fitz was gone.

Mona collapsed into a chair and curled up, fighting the knowledge that, once again, she was all alone.

BONNIE RAITT CROONED slow, smoky blues. Kat unrolled the sketches and spread them out on her dining table, weighting the edges. She slipped out of her heels and walked from one sketch to the next, swirling the wine in her glass, rubbing the goblet against her cheek.

Here, in solitude, she could study them at will. Drink them in, though terror still nibbled at the edges of hard-won calm.

How? How could he see past her careful defenses? How had he stripped her down to ancient dreams?

Kat laughed silently, shaking her head. That defense-less girl was so long gone she could barely remember her. All traces of her had been firmly routed out like weeds in a garden, she'd thought.

But like all weeds, dreams were difficult to kill. Somewhere, seeds had germinated in the dry crust over Kat's heart…and Gamble had spotted the tiny, nearly dead tendrils.

A knock on her door jarred her from her musings. She wasn't expecting visitors. Had Mona come back? How had things gone with Fitz? With a frown, she peeked out, then whirled and sank against the door.

It wasn't her sister.

Gamble knocked again. "Kat? I know you're there. I have to talk to you."

The music gave her away. Damn.

With a deep sigh, she opened the door, reassembling her armor. "We have nothing to talk about."

He brushed past her as though invited, larger than life and twice as threatening to her peace of mind. "Yes, we do." He spotted the sketches and approached them, studying them with a frown on his face.

"I'm not giving them back, Gamble."

Lost in contemplation, he stirred. "What?"

"I said, I'm not giving them back."

He held up a tube. "It doesn't matter. I have more."

She pushed away from the door. "What? How—" She grasped for the tube.

Gamble held it out of reach. "I have a photographic memory. What I saw is in here—" he tapped his forehead "Forever."

"Gamble…"

He stepped toward her, his smile as much caustic as genuine. "Want to wrestle me for them, Kat?" Husky and low, his voice brought back the most electrifying hours of her life.

Then he was there, a heartbeat away. She could feel the heat of him, the pull of polar north to magnet. "Come on, baby…best two out of three." His head lowered.

"Gamble, this is crazy." She should be able to turn him away.

He nipped at her upper lip, and she sucked in a gasp of pure lust. "You think I want this?" he asked, blowing a soft breath over the tender skin beneath her jaw. "I don't have room in my life for you, Kat." One sizzling stroke on her throat had her blood singing. "Tell me to leave."

"You're no prize, buddy."

His chuckle was more than a little harsh. "I don't like you, either." He slid one arm around her waist and drew her close.

Kat dug her fingers into his shoulders and leaned into him.

The tube hit the floor with a thud. Any playfulness

vaporized. In its place was hard, aroused male, ready to mate.

"I don't want to want you," she muttered, scraping teeth over his jaw.

"Ditto." He slid his kiss down her throat, lifted her up and fastened his mouth on her nipple. "Damn it, Kat, I need you. Now."

She dragged him down with her onto the nearby sofa, their mating all fury and thunder. Temper swept gentleness out of its path, making way for hunger, knife edged and huge. Clothing parted only enough to gain access—then he was inside her, and she couldn't remember why she'd ever left his loft, why she'd been so scared. Ragged and crazy, they clawed their way to an explosive release, then lay there, panting. Still joined. Eyes wide.

"What the hell was that?" Gamble asked.

Kat attempted to speak, wet her lips. Tried once more. "I don't know. But let's do it again."

His face split in a rare smile and he laughed. "Yeah."

Kat found herself laughing with him, something she would never have dreamed could happen. Loving the pure, crazy freedom of it. The improbability. She laughed again, full throated and delicious, and when she felt him hardening again inside her, she rocked her hips and waggled her eyebrows at him.

Then laughter made way for lovemaking of a tenderness she would never have believed possible from a rough, raw, angry man like Gamble Smith. He slipped away from her, and she protested with a moan—until his mouth began to do things to her that had her melting, then arching in a plea. As ecstasy spilled over her once more, he rose above her, capturing her gaze with eyes gone somber even as he moved inside her once again.

And Kat forgot, for a moment, to be scared. To shield herself. That men were the enemy, to be fought at all costs.

Instead, she spun out on the edge of fantasies she'd thought long gone, held in a gentle cradling of strong arms, drawn out of herself until she dared to be soft…to surrender. With a silken sigh, Kat gave herself up to the man who had captured her dreams on his canvas.

And then she fell asleep in his arms, trying not to wonder if he'd be there when she awoke.

CHAPTER THIRTEEN

"COFFEE, MONA?" Gaby asked.

Sitting in the meeting with the circulation manager, Helen Cantrell, and Jack Bradshaw, Mona accepted the cup gratefully. She'd slept very little the past two nights. Her newly solitary bed still smelled of Fitz because she hadn't been able to bring herself to change the sheets. She'd awakened this morning with his pillow clutched to her breast, damp from tears she hadn't been aware of shedding.

She felt a thousand years old and wanted nothing more than to climb back under the covers until the hurt went away. Since that wasn't an option, she raised the cup to her lips. Instantly, her stomach rebelled. Clenching her teeth she attempted to focus on the spreadsheet before her, but the smells in the room pressed in on her, making her gorge rise.

With shaky fingers, she grasped for the water pitcher and poured herself a glass. The first sip told her that was a mistake. She saw Helen's speculative glance just as Gaby leaned forward. "Are you all right, Mona?"

Mona rose from her chair. "I—I don't feel very well." She seized on the first excuse that rose to mind. "Last night's dinner, I guess." Though she'd hardly touched a bite. She had to get hold of herself. Couples separated all the time—not that she'd breathe a word of Fitz's departure around here.

"You sure you want to go on with this meeting?" Bradshaw asked.

"Of course I do." Mona gritted her teeth.

"Coffee's hard on an upset stomach. When I was pregnant with my first, just the smell of coffee made me violently ill," Helen observed. She lifted her mug to her lips. "I should have known from the outset that Annelise would turn out to be a hellion. I was never so exhausted as when I was pregnant."

Pregnant. The word was a lightning bolt right between the eyes. Mona scrambled to dissemble. "Well, I can't blame anything but the Chinese takeout around the corner." All too aware of Bradshaw's narrowed gaze, she pushed forward, swallowing around the nausea that had her breathing light and shallow. "Okay, let's talk about this report."

For half an hour, she battled danger. Jack wanted to pin the blame on editorial, but Helen, thank God, was armed with statistics about the sales staff. Mona fought to listen with her normal intensity, but beneath her every thought lay the thumping heart of terror.

No. No way. She'd been on the Pill for years.

Finally, the meeting ended.

"He's out to get you, Mona." Gaby smiled.

Mona tried to summon her usual disdain, but she craved silence and peace to order her thoughts. "He wants my job, but he'll have to dismember me to get it."

Gaby smiled, a half-grown shark increasing in strength every day. "He'll have to get through me first."

Mona was absurdly touched. Tears burned behind her eyelids and scared her half to death. She was the ice queen. She ate nails for breakfast. She did not cry. "Thanks" was all she could manage.

"So…how are you feeling, honestly?"

"Fine," Mona said, her insides trembling with her need to be alone.

Gaby didn't seem convinced.

"I could use something carbonated," Mona said. "The shrimp…I'm never ordering from there again." Then she cloaked herself in her usual command, her voice cooling. "If you don't mind?"

"Oh—yes. Right away," Gaby said. "Then we can go over this afternoon's appointments?"

"Absolutely," Mona replied. "Just give me half an hour to clear some of this." She gestured with a quick sweep of her arm.

"Sure thing," Gaby replied, gathering up an armload

of files. "I'll get the cola, then I'll guard you from the barbarians."

Mona forced a grin. "Great."

When the door closed, Mona reminded herself not to fall apart just yet. After Gaby reappeared, she would lock the door. *Just don't think. It can't be.*

Gaby deposited the soft drink on her desk and grabbed some more files. "Thirty minutes. The only one who gets through is Fitz."

"Right." Mona didn't glance up, because if she did, she'd cry for sure. Fitz wouldn't be calling yet, but he would, one day soon.

And what would she tell him? *You got your wish? I hope you're happy?*

She glanced at the cola can in her hand, struck by an entirely new thought. Were soft drinks bad for a baby?

Ridiculous. There was no baby.

Suddenly, she recalled that for two days when Fitz was in danger, she'd been so unnerved and distracted she'd forgotten her pills. But she'd caught up as soon as she'd remembered. And it hadn't been the first time she'd skipped one with no ill effects.

Her fingers shaking as if palsied, she placed the can on her credenza and stared out at the city she'd always wanted to take by storm.

It couldn't be true, her mind said, over and over again. She tried the word on her tongue, but she could barely whisper it, so foreign to anything she'd ever applied to herself. "Pregnant." A sound so soft it could barely register as a feather on the wind. Fate could not be that cruel.

Helen's remark had nothing to do with her. Mona had changed nothing about her life; ergo, life couldn't change the rules on her. But then she considered that her husband of almost ten years had left her; thus, the rules had already changed. Her nice, neat, orderly life was coming unraveled after all she'd done to assure that it never would.

Her beloved husband had betrayed the very foundation of their concord, had altered the carefully lettered script of the agreement they'd made from the first. Had her body, so attuned to his, turned *its back* on her, too?

She sat down at her computer and logged on to the Internet, searching for symptoms of pregnancy. Nausea could be anything.

As the words scrolled by on the screen, she could barely breathe. Nausea, yes. Unusual need for sleep during the day. Sensitivity to smells. She sank back in her chair. Her hand drifted downward, pressed against her belly.

And despite all the reasons she needed to be wrong about this diagnosis, something deep inside her knew.

She'd felt so at sea recently, adrift from the normal ebb and flow of her life ever since the night Fitz had been restored to her. The Fitz who'd returned to her arms was not the man who'd left two days before. Had the same forces that had changed him at the cellular level altered her own chemistry? Tiny pills were no barrier to the urge to celebrate life. To cement the bond between them in a manner older than time. They'd come together in heartfelt thanksgiving, grateful beyond the power of words to be restored to each other again.

Everything had changed then. She just hadn't realized it.

Dear God. She was carrying Fitz's baby inside her, will she or nill she. It was not a possibility she'd ever considered, and it terrified her now.

The choices before her glittered like jewels and crocodile teeth, the dangerous beauty and sparkling menace of them striking fear in her heart.

In her corner office, Mona stared out at the world she'd wanted to rule, arms locked tight around her waist. Endless moments passed before she realized she was crying…for the husband she could regain with one single call…and the life inside her she was not sure she was brave enough to keep.

"WHERE IN TEXAS ARE YOU from, Gamble?" Kat asked as she lazed on the pile of cushions.

He scowled. "It's not important. Stop wiggling."

She forced herself to still, though she really wanted to leap up and dance. "It is to me. Tell me about your family. I know you have a mother because we've already established that her lessons in manners didn't stick. What about your dad? Brothers or sisters?"

He stood before the easel, bare-chested, jeans half buttoned, hair tousled, and looked good enough to eat. "Why does it matter?"

Kat laughed, too thrilled with the day to let anything annoy her. "Something to hide? You on the lam?"

He didn't answer; instead, he emerged from behind the easel and tipped up the picture hat that was all she was wearing. Then he walked behind her and adjusted one shoulder.

The touch of his hands on her skin, as always, got her insides humming. Kat leaned back, viewing him upside down. Languor gave way to the urge to jump up, to climb his body, to revel once again in the raw electric charge of their lovemaking.

"You couldn't be still if your life depended on it," he complained. "Come on—surely a few more minutes won't kill you."

"With all the money I'm generating for you, you can afford to pay a model." The hat fell off, and she slid one hand up his thigh. "But you can't—" Kat stopped, horrified at what she'd been about to say. *You can't make love to her.* Good God. She was never jealous.

She rose and grabbed for the nearest clothing: Gamble's flannel shirt. "I want some coffee. You have anything but that rotgut instant?"

He grabbed the tail of the shirt as she passed, and reeled her in. "I'm not through with you yet."

She pushed at his chest. He only laughed and drew her closer.

"Don't. I don't want to—"

"Bullshit." He was hard and ready. He jerked open his pants and lifted her in one smooth move. Despite her nerves, she wrapped her legs around his waist, and he thrust inside her. Kat's head fell back and she moaned.

"Forget everything but this. It's all we need to understand," he said, his eyes burning flame—hot blue.

That had always been true, until him. She'd never cared before to know more about the men who'd come into and been dismissed from her life. It shouldn't matter now who Gamble was, where he'd been, who he'd loved.

But it did. Once her body was satisfied…just as soon as she'd had enough of him, one more time—only once more surely—she'd start asking again. And this time she'd get answers.

Later. Kat tightened her legs around his waist and met him, thrust for powerful, mind-stealing thrust.

Later would be soon enough.

AFTER A MORNING SPENT trying to keep her head above quicksand, Mona was positive she would scream or cry or otherwise disgrace herself if she didn't get away where she could think.

She was desperate to talk to someone who would understand, but one by one, she discarded names, forced to face the reality of her life. She had friends galore, but none to whom she could confide something of this magnitude. Staggering across shaky ground, she dared not open up to a soul.

And then she thought of Tansy.

Mona was aware that Kat sometimes confided in Tansy and that Tansy never told a soul. She kept the silence of the confessional, whether by design or inner flaw. Mona herself had never taken advantage of it, content to share all her secrets with Fitz. But even she had experienced the power of Tansy's serenity to banish terror.

Serenity seemed as far away as the galaxy's edge. All morning, Mona's every thought had been ambushed by wonder and terror and debilitating indecision. She had considered buying a pregnancy test and enabling herself, perhaps, to laugh away her fears.

But part of her was already certain. And part of her cringed from confirmation, because then she would have to act. She would have to take steps…to end or to begin. Each was fraught with fear, ponderous with implications.

What Mona desired more than anything else was to put off any reckoning. Her queasy stomach roiled in a sea of tumult, and her mind swayed precariously atop the mast.

So it was that she found herself at her father's apartment while he was out once again with Julie Hart. Mona resisted the urge to comment on how often that was happening, instead exchanging perfunctory greetings with Mrs. Hodgson. Then she walked down the hall to

Tansy's bedroom, drawn toward her sister as lodestone and savior. In Tansy's refuge, would she find answers?

Tansy sat on the floor, an ancient hatbox in her lap. Photographs lay like a shower of rose petals on the rug around her. With one delicate fingertip, she traced the faces in the photo held gently in her hand. A sweet, sad smile played on her lips.

"Tansy?" Mona said quietly.

Her sister turned, the unfamiliar glitter of tears in her eyes. To Mona's knowledge, Tansy had seldom, in all these years, cried over anything. She drifted through life with a calm that Mona envied, protected somehow by the spindrift of her dreams.

"What's wrong?" Her own problems superceded, she moved to Tansy's side. "Why are you crying, sweetheart?"

"Look, Mona. It's Mama with Paris and me."

Mona accepted the offered photo of her mother with the infant twins in a rocking chair Mona could almost hear creaking. "Nana's front porch." She sank to the floor beside her sister, stung by longing, sharp and bittersweet. For a moment, she could hear Nana's rooster crowing, hear the constant West Texas wind playing the bass note beneath a quiet so deep it settled into your bones.

"She seems so happy," Tansy said.

Mona couldn't take her gaze off the photo, suddenly feeling a kinship with her mother she'd never experienced. Her mother had experienced this sea change not once but three times. How had she felt? Had she been terrified, too? Or had she possessed something lacking in Mona, an inner certainty that she would be enough? Had Juliette been afraid or elated? Had she realized the cost she'd bear? She'd had a career far more glamorous than Mona's.

"She loved you both so much." If her mother had ever had doubts, it seemed they'd been dismissed when the twins arrived. Mona couldn't begrudge Tansy their mother's devotion. Twins required a lot of care, and she'd been born too soon after.

"She loved you, too. She called you her Rose Red."

Mona reared back in surprise. "I'd forgotten."

"Her dark-haired beauty. The good princess," Tansy teased. "Paris and I were her handful—recall her saying that?"

Mona grinned. "Someone had to behave. You seldom did."

Tansy giggled, then returned to digging in the hatbox. Soon, she found what she sought, and placed it in Mona's hands. "She had enough love for all of us."

Mona glanced down, and her breath stalled. It was her mother and herself, perhaps when Mona was five. Memory stirred. Her first day of kindergarten, and her mother had insisted on taking her there, just the two of them, while the housekeeper escorted the twins to school. Mona could almost feel the crisp morning air of September, the brush against her leg of the bag of pencils and crayons and scissors. Her hand clutching her mother's as they walked up the sidewalk toward the school steps.

Then her mother knelt before her, one hand outstretched. In her palm lay a bracelet with one tiny charm. A heart.

As she fastened it around Mona's wrist, Juliette spoke. "I'm sending my heart with you, sweet girl. I'll be there with you every minute. You're going to have a wonderful time at school, but if you ever feel the tiniest bit lonely, just touch this heart and feel my arms around you." Juliette embraced Mona. "You're my brave, good girl. You're going to be your teacher's pride and joy." Leaning back, she held Mona's shoulders. "After school, it's your job to return my heart to me. And I'll be waiting to hear every single thing about your day. All right?"

The grown Mona could hear the tears the child had not. She cupped her hand around the photograph of her beautiful golden mother and the darkling child and wondered where the charm had gone. "I wanted to see her again, Tansy." A long-buried sob crowded her throat. "Why did she let Daddy abandon us? Why couldn't I be with her one more time, too?"

"I don't know," Tansy soothed, gathering her into a hug. "She had our pictures by her bed in the hospital. She held yours and Kat's in her hands while she slept."

Mona reared back. "You remember that?"

Tiny lines appeared between Tansy's brows. "I…"

Her gaze turned inward. Quietly, she continued. "She was still pretty. So pretty. She hugged us, but it hurt her to be touched. Paris hugged too hard, and she made this sound—"

Mona held her breath, wondering why, after all this time, her sister's memory was rearing its head.

"Paris cried. He asked to stay, but we had to go back to Carlton's." She wrapped her arms around herself, fixing her gaze past Mona's shoulder, her slender frame rocking.

"Tansy?" Mona touched her elbow, but Tansy pulled away and rose to her feet. She walked to the window and stared down at the park, still holding herself. Still rocking.

"Tansy, what's wrong?" What was she recollecting?

Tansy's head shook from side to side with the steady beat of a pendulum. "No," she whispered. "No, Daddy, I don't want to go."

"Where?" Mona frowned. "Where don't you want to go?" When her sister said nothing, she tried again. "Tansy?"

"Don't let him take me away, Mona."

"Who? Take you where?"

But her sister didn't answer. Instead, Tansy pirouetted, her skirt lifting in a graceful arc with her movement, her mood suddenly light. "I dreamed of my prince, and now he's here, just as Mama said. He'll save me."

Oh, Tansy. She'd gone away again. Mona would hear no more about her mother.

Tansy's eyes spoke of sorrow. "I miss him so much. He makes me feel safe. But in my dreams he still comes to me." She glanced up. "I painted his face. Would you like to see?"

Mona couldn't care less about Tansy's imaginary prince, but she stifled the urge to weep and rail at the Fates that had stolen her sister from her just as surely as they'd taken Paris and her mother. She summoned a smile. "Absolutely. Let's have a look."

She followed Tansy into her tiny studio. The painting was stunning, a bold knight on a white charger. The knight's helmet had tumbled to the ground, and raven hair spilled around his shoulders.

At first glance, he appeared handsome and strong, just as she'd expect. But when she stepped closer, she realized his was not a young, smooth face. This knight had eyes older than time. Though he smiled, it was not the triumph of an invincible champion. The weight of great suffering shadowed his face.

"Who is he?" she asked, frowning. Something about him…

"My prince."

"No, I mean who's the model?"

"My prince." Tansy reached out as if to stroke the face, but her fingers halted just shy of the still-wet paint, her eyes soft and her mouth tilting slightly at the corners.

Mona sighed and turned away. She didn't give a hoot about some imaginary prince. She needed to go back to the pictures, to dig deeper and find out if Tansy had other memories of their mother's last days that might give Mona the answers she needed.

She wanted to confide in her. *Tansy, I think I'm going to have a baby.*

But Tansy had slid once more behind the mists. Mona grasped for a way to bring her back, though she knew from experience that you had to take what you got with Tansy.

Then she remembered one task she hadn't yet completed, though her father's party seemed frivolous and unreal to her now. No matter; she'd promised. "I'd like to see your new dress, Tansy. May I?"

Tansy's eyes danced with delight. "Want me to try it on?"

"Sure." Mona cast one last glance at the careworn prince, then followed her sister back to her room.

IN HER WORKSPACE at the gallery, Kat lined up two sections of framing material. She hummed while she labored, her mind lost in memories of Gamble. His hands. His body. How he made her feel—

"That could almost resemble a tune."

Kat whirled, gasping. "Armand…" She pressed one hand between her breasts. "You scared the hell out of me."

His green eyes scanned her face, implacable as always. "You look very well, Katharina. Something agrees with you." He removed his coat, then his gaze dropped to the workbench behind her. His focus shifted from her as he stepped closer to the sketch she was framing.

"It's only a—"

"Shh." All his attention centered on the sketch, until he spotted two more. He picked up first one, then the other.

Kat would have stood for this from no one else. Armand was as knowledgeable a collector as she'd ever met; still, this was personal. He was her closest friend, but she felt somehow naked.

And not simply because she was naked in the sketches.

"Gamble Smith?" he asked.

Unsigned though they were, Armand recognized them.

"Yes."

He stood motionless, focused on the drawings. Kat felt like nothing so much as a schoolgirl called into the headmaster's office.

She laughed. "Shocked? Not you, surely." Nothing could dampen her mood. In an hour or so, she'd be with Gamble. Probably naked again.

God, she hoped so. She was far from having her fill of him yet.

"Were I ever easily shocked, you'd have cured me of that by now." The faintest trace of something she couldn't quite pinpoint prowled through his voice. He turned to her, oddly intent. "Be cautious, Katharina. This one will not take it well when you decide to move on to greener fields."

"Maybe I won't—" She stopped in shock.

Armand appeared just as startled. After a long pause, he cocked one dark eyebrow. "I see." He glanced away, and Kat waited to hear more.

One muscle ticked in his jaw as he stared at an empty wall. She was surprised by a strong need, however foolish or unexpected, to have his understanding. His approval. The feeling was most unusual. And unwelcome. "Armand, it's none…"

"None of my business? I suppose that's true." Again, the odd note. "Unless you consider that I happen to be concerned about your welfare."

She went stiff. "Your investment is safe. I won't run away to Texas and abandon the gallery."

Disappointment painted the curve of his mouth, deepened furrows between his eyes. "I wasn't thinking of my money, Kat." His use of her nickname was almost as surprising as the tenderness in his voice. "It's your heart that concerns me."

She snorted, safe in the euphoria that had kept her head buzzing for days. And nights…nights unlike any she'd ever known. Just the idea that she'd be with Gamble again tonight had the power to muddle her thoughts. She'd lost a lot of hours to daydreams lately, though she'd never voice a one.

But beneath the glare of Armand's scrutiny, her euphoria slipped, melting away as fog in noonday sun.

"My heart's the same as it ever was."

"Your capacity for self-deception has always been remarkable."

"What the hell is that supposed to mean?"

Smiling like a damn Cheshire cat, he returned his attention to the sketches. "Will you hang them in the gallery?"

Her response was emphatic. "No."

That eyebrow again. "These would sell for a pretty penny, my dear."

"Don't 'my dear' me. You make yourself sound a thousand years old."

"I seem to recollect being called fatherly."

She grinned. "You can't hold me responsible for what I say when I'm mad."

"What about when you're in love? Are you to be held accountable then?"

"Love?" she scoffed, even as a shiver rippled up her spine. *Don't fall in love with me, Kat. I won't be good for you.* She resorted to reliable defenses. "Love and I are not on speaking terms." She reached for the sketches, no longer comfortable with Armand's perusal. "Go get your own dirty pictures, Delacroix. The peep show's over."

One hand touched her arm. "I'm sorry if I'm making you uncomfortable, Katharina. They're stunning. Certainly you are aware of that."

She wasn't confident of anything. Too much was jumbled up inside her now.

"You're right not to hang them here. They're much

too intimate." True to the gentleman he had always been, Armand stepped away. "Have you decided on your next show?" Smoothly, he shifted the topic.

She should have been grateful. Instead, she felt the sting of conflicting urges: to demand that he retract the ridiculous idea that she could be falling in love with Gamble Smith. And the equally strong desire to lean her head against his shoulder, just for a moment. To ask him for advice.

Ridiculous. If he didn't laugh at her, she'd definitely do so herself.

So Kat grasped at the conversational lifeline he'd thrown. "The bedsprings are still available."

Armand glanced over his shoulder, a frown already forming. Then he saw her grin, and chuckled, nodding as if the idea were worthy of consideration. "It would definitely establish your credentials."

Her eyebrows lifted. "As—?"

"Someone who refuses to knuckle under to the tyranny of good taste."

Kat laughed, and Armand laughed with her, all discomfort forgiven. It felt so good that she should have left well enough alone, but that would be a stretch she'd not yet managed. Poking sticks into anthills was one of the things Kat did best.

Their laughter slid away, and the urge to know seized her and wouldn't let go.

"Armand, have you ever been in love?"

The green eyes she'd trusted as no others shied away from hers, another swift spear of darkness lancing through them. For the first time, Kat realized she had the power to hurt this good man. It was a revelation: the urbane, ever-controlled Armand Delacroix was not made of stone. "I'm sorry. It's not my place—"

"That's true. It's not." Seconds passed, the air between them shimmering with more than she knew how to interpret.

Then she remembered the way he'd looked at Tansy, and felt ashamed of herself. No matter how beautiful or sweet Tansy was, a man of Armand's sophistication would be acquiring a lifelong burden with her care.

"Never mind." She returned to her workbench, put up her tools. There would be no more creation tonight. All at once, she yearned to be with Gamble, to indulge in the flesh and let her mind rest from the turbulence Armand had introduced.

"Yes."

"What?"

He chuckled faintly. "Try to keep your mind on the questions you're asking, Katharina. Yes, I've been in love."

"Did you do anything about it?"

"I've never married, if that's what you're asking."

"Why not?"

"My mother would tell you that I'm a romantic." A faint frown crossed his face. "One day I might have to admit to her that she's correct, I'm sorry to say. Watching my parents conduct a forty-five-year love affair has perhaps kept my standards too high. I've never been willing to settle for less. Never thought I'd find a woman who wouldn't bore me over the course of a lifetime. Then I found her, but…" His tone was wry and world-weary. "Not that it's any of your business, but the lady is not available to return my affections."

"And you're just leaving it at that?"

Armand smiled. "Sometimes you're so young."

"Don't patronize me," she snapped.

But his smile only widened. "Has it never occurred to you that you are a romantic to the bone, Katharina?"

If he'd slapped her, Kat couldn't have been more shocked. "That's absurd. You're dead wrong, Armand." Her fingers fumbled on her tools, and she dropped one.

He was there first with a lightning, muscular grace she seldom remembered he had. Usually, he moved as though he possessed all the time in the world and might miss something delectable if he hurried.

He placed the awl in her hand. Kat felt the brush of warm fingers. Armand touched her only rarely, and somehow the impact was too strong for everything else tangled inside her tonight.

He stepped back, his voice carefully neutral. "Think what you will. We seldom see ourselves clearly." His gaze flicked to his wristwatch. "I have to go. Shall I escort you home first?"

She could hear his impatience and felt an absurd re-luctance to let him depart.

Gamble. She had to see Gamble. A round of fast, hot sex would make everything tumble into place. "No," she said, "but thank you. I still have a few things to do around here."

"Before you go to him."

She tilted her chin higher. "Yes."

He nodded evenly. "I won't ask you again to be care-ful. It would be asking a bird to walk instead of fly." That darkness flashed again, so briefly she might have imag-ined it. "I will, however, ask you to remember that I am your friend. Call me if you need me."

So gently was it said that Kat felt the prick of tears. All at once, she saw him as she never had. *He's lonely.* A wealthy man who could not have what he most wanted. "Armand…"

His gaze met hers, too full of something unsettling.

"Same to you. I'm here if…" She didn't attempt to finish.

Sorrow flickered, was quickly banked. "Good night, Katharina." He shrugged on his coat.

"Good night, my friend." She found a smile for the man who was indeed her best friend.

She heard his footsteps across the wooden floor, then the soft click of the outside door of the gallery and the turn of his key in the lock. She fought the urge to run and summon him back.

The silence pressed in, the gallery, for once, filling none of the empty spaces inside her. Kat stared sightlessly at her tools, then laid them down and readied herself to leave and seek out Gamble's warmth.

CHAPTER FOURTEEN

MONA WAITED UNTIL after dinner to phone her father. "Daddy?"

"Desdemona, my heart," he said in his usual expansive manner. "How are you?"

"Just fine," she answered out of habit. "How about you?" For one treacherous moment, she flirted with the impulse to be there with him, to lay her head on his shoulder and let him be the father he'd never been, and tell her what to do. But he had already launched into a recounting of rehearsals that day, how gifted Julie was, how the director was too young to know the proper way to treat a cast, how his understudy was a fool.... Mona listened with half an ear, murmuring in appropriate places, while her own heart sank. Her father had never been a refuge.

Finally, he wound down. They spoke for a minute about the gala. Then she discovered her opening. "Daddy, I saw Tansy today, and she said something that concerned me."

"What was it?"

"Why would she be distressed about someone taking her away? She begged me not to let it happen. What could she be talking about?"

The length of the pause began to dismay her. His voice was grave when he spoke. "Carlton is more uncomfortable about her safety, since I am gone every day now. He would like to move her to his apartment—"

"That's impossible. You can't be seriously considering it."

"He's redecorating it with her in mind. He'll give her a wonderful studio space—"

"In a couple of months, you'll be around every day again. Why—"

"I'm uneasy about Titania. I'm not getting any younger. As his wife, she would be in Carlton's care."

"Wife? Daddy, we've talked about this. It's insane! He's old enough to be her father!"

"I am worried about Lucas Walker, Desdemona. We still don't know where he is. What if he decided to try again to harm her?"

And then it hit her. The painting of Tansy's prince. "Oh, my God…"

"What?"

"Have you seen the painting of her prince?"

"Once, but it wasn't finished. Why?"

"It is now. Go look at it. I'll stay on the line."

"What's this about, Desdemona?"

"Check it out, Daddy, and tell me if that's not Lucas Walker."

She heard his sharp intake of breath. "No."

"I didn't realize when I viewed it today. He's changed a lot, but I think it's him."

"What do we do?" Suddenly, her father sounded every year of his age.

"Double-check first. I could be wrong. I had other things on my mind and wasn't really paying attention."

She heard him set down the phone. In a couple of minutes, he was back.

"There is a strong resemblance."

"Has Tansy been shown a picture of him since he went to prison?"

"I don't believe so."

Mona's throat tightened. "Then she's encountered him. He must be here."

"I'll summon the police."

"And tell them what? They don't have the manpower to keep watch over her, and he's committed no crime." *That we know of, anyway.* "I doubt they'd be able to do anything." Her heart beat faster at the thought of Lucas Walker meeting Tansy in her current state. He could do anything….

"I'll call Carlton right now," her father said. "He'll handle this."

Mona rebelled. "No—we don't need Carlton. I can handle everything. First thing tomorrow, I'll have a bodyguard hired. Don't let Tansy leave the apartment until then."

"But Carlton—"

Might use this as a reason to convince her father to let him assume responsibility for Tansy. He might be very good at it, but Tansy was Mona's sister, and she would take care of her own.

She resorted to flattery. "Daddy, you have a lot on your mind with rehearsals. Your performance is too important for you to be distracted. Let me help you with this. Please. I'd be happy to do so."

"Well…if you really think…"

"I do. We're making assumptions right now with no proof. Perhaps it's no different than Paris, simply Tansy's imagination, or maybe we're grasping at straws. We'll be sure she's guarded until we know. She'll be happier where she is, though. Promise me you won't let Carlton spirit her away. He's not family."

"He's the next thing to it."

His pride would kick in if she forced a confrontation. "Please, Daddy. I promise you I'll ask for help if I need it."

"You're a good daughter to an old man, Desdemona."

Kat would sneer, but Mona's heart thrilled to the words. "Thank you. I'll be in touch in the morning as soon as I have things worked out. I'll have someone there before you must leave, and I'll explain it all to Tansy."

"I don't want Walker's name mentioned to her. I won't put her through this again."

"I'll think of something."

"All right, then. Good night, sweetheart."

"Good night, Daddy."

As Kat emerged from the train, she shifted the bags in her hands and realized, to her amusement, that she was humming again.

Good Lord. How had this happened? When had this outrageous contentment spread beneath her skin? Gamble Smith had done what no other man had: he'd turned a vixen into a well-loved woman, with the sappy smile to prove it. Not that he'd ever said the word *love*, but there was more than hot sex between them, though God knows they could melt polar ice caps from the heat that exploded every time they touched.

Love, Kat mused, rolling the taste of it around on her tongue. Could she, queen of the vampires, have taken the fatal fall?

Denial didn't leap as quickly to her lips as it once would have. That very realization made something inside her quiver like a newly baked custard.

Kat Gerard. Love. The words danced before her as Salome before a king. In them lay a beautiful and seductive danger. Inexorably, her thoughts flew toward Gamble, the raw power of him. The allure of the volcano simmering deep inside. He was a magnificent and fiery lover who was also surprisingly tender at times. The discovery of that seemed to shock him, too.

The baguette sticking out of one sack shifted as she dodged a trash can, and reminded her that she'd surprised herself, as well. She didn't cook for men; she hardly cooked for herself, though Nana had taught her all the basics. Kat could whip up a good down-home Texas meal with the best of them, if inclined—but she seldom was. So what was she doing, bringing food to Gamble Smith?

She'd gone soft in the head, obviously. Becoming a leather-bedecked June Cleaver, for God's sake. Never in her life had she envisioned herself feeding a man. Feeding was one step from slavery, one pace down the rocky road her mother had walked until there had been nothing left of the Juliette who had taken Hollywood by storm.

The hell of it was that Kat thought she understood her mother better than ever before in her life. That scared her witless.

But as she rounded the corner to Gamble's building, deep inside her some damnable Pavlovian response turned Kat as warm and soft as melted chocolate. Anticipation bubbled in her blood as she imagined all the ways she would touch Gamble and he would touch her. Images of past days—and nights—danced before her eyes, and her nipples tightened, just at the notion.

Food would come later…much later.

She let herself in with the key he'd given her. He'd

said he might still be working. If so, she would sit quietly and wait.

Or, she smiled inwardly, perhaps she would seduce the painter.

That smile had made it to her lips when she walked inside Gamble's loft—

And heard an unmistakable moan.

Just before she saw them.

The groceries in her arms grew as heavy as the stone Sisyphus rolled up the hill. Her muscles held on a bit longer as though the burden were precious, while Kat's eyes took in the sight of Gamble Smith's powerful muscles rippling as he thrust inside the body of another woman.

And Kat's painting—the one that bared her soul— was five feet away, watching over them.

The bags hit the floor with a thud.

Gamble's head jerked around, his eyes as wild and beautiful as they'd been with her—

"You bastard." Kat couldn't tear her gaze away, even to protect her ripped-open heart.

The woman shrieked, and Gamble pulled out of her, the glistening juices of their joining so beautiful and familiar and murderously painful that Kat wished for a knife to plunge into his black heart.

But the expression on his face was not surprise.

He'd known she was coming. He'd wanted her to see this.

Then he performed the coup de grâce and reached for his pants. To cover himself. From *her,* the son of a bitch.

Even as Kat excoriated herself for forgetting all that she'd learned about men, she experienced a moment of absolute clarity, of utter calm. As Gamble donned his pants and the woman scrambled to find her clothes, Kat closed the distance between them. From within the eye of the storm, she observed herself pick up the painting from the easel and turn.

"You said it was over," the other woman accused.

Gamble ignored her. "Kat…"

She was proud of herself that from somewhere down in the chaos that was her insides, she could still summon a laugh, sucked dry of merriment though it was.

"Goodbye, asshole." Humiliation stirred, white-hot and screaming. She was almost to the door when she heard him following. She raced down the stairs as though the hounds of hell pursued her.

Gamble kept coming. Kat gripped the canvas more tightly.

Gamble grabbed her arm and whirled her around.

Kat bared her teeth and held out the canvas. "I'll smash it on that pole if you don't let me go."

He dropped her arm. "Kat…"

There was nowhere she wanted to look less, but she was no coward. Tilting her chin upward, she met his gaze. "A lie, all of it?"

He stared at her for an endless moment. Then he swore beneath his breath, his stance belligerent. "I told you I didn't have room in my life for you."

Kat grasped for a complacency that was light-years away, hearing the crash at her feet, the dull thud of her folly. "Yes, you did, didn't you?" Bile rose in her throat. "More the fool me that I didn't listen."

That she couldn't summon the strength to kick him in the nuts and walk away was a sign of just how far she'd gone over the edge. Instead, she bled.

Then sour laughter burned its way out of her chest. "It ought to be funny, you know? I'm the one who decides when it's over, the one who discards. It's been that way for a long time. There are a lot who'd say this is my just desserts."

"Kat…" Guilt flickered over his face. And pity. He grasped for her. She recoiled as if from a leper. He dropped his hand. "It went too far. I can't…" He exhaled in a gust. "You made me feel things I can't afford."

"Why not?" Kat summoned the strength to ask what she should probably let be. "Just answer me that. Surely you owe me that much."

Gamble's fingers raked through his hair, leaving it sticking up all over. With the heels of his hands, he rubbed his eyes, his whole body echoing resignation.

"Because I'm married."

After the first shock hit, Kat slapped him hard. She stared at the red imprint of her hand on his cheek even as the pain in his eyes burned its way into her heart, scorching all the promise of recent days. All the fun and heat and hope vaporized like the drops of water Nana used to fling from her fingers to test a hot griddle.

In that moment, Kat was surprised to discover that she hadn't outrun her West Texas upbringing. She found herself unable to say to a man who mattered too much that his marriage didn't, and detecting such a middle-class sentiment inside her was a blow to her sense of herself. She'd had married men before and never cared—but this time was different. Before it had been sex and amusement and boredom.

With Gamble, she'd thought it was more.

It had been more to her, but she couldn't bear to think about it now. She'd made the dumbest mistake of her life. Forgotten to keep her heart out of the equation.

When she was alone, she would let the pain in, but right now, she had to survive this moment and the next. And a lot of moments after. She would heal, but it would hurt like hell first.

What was worst of all was knowing that if he opened his arms right now, she couldn't promise she wouldn't fall into them like a grateful, shipwrecked sailor crawling onto the sands of home.

Kat held Gamble's gaze for long enough to savor one last moment with him, one final connection.

Then she closed her eyes, squeezed them shut hard

to begin the process of cutting him out of her life. "I'm not giving this back," she said of the painting.

"It's yours," he said, his voice raw. "Kat…"

"No," she answered, staring down at the grimy sidewalk that had, for a time, been the yellow brick road.

She wanted badly to ask him why. Then she realized it didn't matter. She turned away, then stopped. "Where is she?"

"Back in Texas."

"You bastard." Her voice went guttural. "What the hell are you doing in New York?"

"It's complicated." He glanced away. "I couldn't paint there. I couldn't breathe."

Shades of her father, so self-absorbed. Convinced that his art counted most.

"So you just walk out, do you? Simply forget her?"

"No," he said, voice hollow. "I don't forget."

"Go home, Gamble," she said, suddenly too weary for anger. Awkwardly, she dashed tears with the back of one hand. Then she gathered herself to leave.

"Kat." Gamble's hoarse voice stopped her. "Find someone who deserves you. Quit screwing around." He pointed to the woman in the painting. "Let her live. She deserves better."

Kat cast one last glance at ravaged blue eyes, praying her knees wouldn't betray her. Then, fragile as an old lady, she shuffled into a night that suddenly frightened her.

LUCAS DREAMED OF JULIETTE. On his narrow cot, haunted by Juliette's daughter, he twisted. Turned. Sought peace.

He was in her kitchen, which always smelled of spices. When he remarked upon it, Juliette graced him with a sad, sweet smile. "I tried to reproduce the way my mother's spice cabinet smelled. There's this one just to the right of the sink, and when you open the door, it's like entering Aladdin's cave. My memories are there in her kitchen. She had a green pottery bowl with a band around the top and a basket weave carved into it. She made rolls in it and mixed cakes. She'd hold it just so, tipping to the side, blending batters and doughs and puddings." Juliette glanced up. "She made tapioca pudding for me, and I can still taste it, so cold and creamy, the smooth dark sweetness of pure vanilla."

Lucas was transfixed. He wanted to sit there all day. No, for days and days without eating or sleeping or thirsting except for more of Juliette's bounty, the love she dispensed with abandon to her children and, miracle of miracles, to Lucas himself.

He worried about the day when she would see him for what he truly was. When that moment came, it would be over, this bright respite when all the world seemed crafted of hope and dangerous grace.

Sometimes, he thought it only fair to warn her who he really was. Hadn't his father told him on numerous occasions that he was nothing? Hadn't his mother shown him it was true? And hadn't he learned well how to hate, how to hurt? He'd wished his father dead over and over. Knew that he bore enough malice to be the instrument as soon as he was big enough.

It would hurt her when she understood how black he was inside, and he could not bear to bring harm to Juliette of the Sorrows, too kind and lovely to stay long in this world where ugliness waited to taint her. So he didn't tell her, hoping for a miracle that would make him the person she believed him to be.

"Lucas." She turned to him, her blue eyes more serious than he'd ever seen them. "You have more experience of the world than my children do." She reached for his hand, and he felt the thrill of it. Every time, it was as if he'd touched a live wire. His every nerve burst into life, and he longed to be more than he was. Yearned to be the hero who would save her.

She clasped his bony fingers, already so much larger than hers, between hands so fine and delicate that he wanted to remove his so he wouldn't defile her.

But instead, she folded his fingers over one of her hands and covered them with the other. "Lucas." Her voice was a siren call he wouldn't deny, even if he could. "They'll need you one day when I can't protect them." Her eyes held a zealot's fire. "Will you guard them for me? Will you be my champion when the world tries to hurt them?"

Lucas shifted on his cot, restless with the fire of how

much he'd wanted to do anything, anything at all that Juliette would ask of him—along with the gnawing dogs of knowing, deep in his heart, that he was doomed to fail her. That violence was the music of his blood. That he was forever tainted.

Lucas...Lucas...guard them...be my champion....

He jerked to consciousness, sat up on his cot, ground his knuckles into his eyes. Lucas stared out into the weak morning light spilling down the stairs, then deliberately placed his bare feet on the cold concrete floor as penance.

The feel of Juliette's hands still surrounded his, burning his flesh with the knowledge that he had indeed failed her. He had tried, but in the end, Juliette's son was dead. Her daughter lost. And Juliette herself had died, unaware of the rape, thank God, still trying to believe that Lucas hadn't meant Paris's death to happen.

Mercy. Juliette had died, still with faith in him, mortal and flawed as he was. Lucas drove fingers into his hair and groaned from the depths of his soul. She had asked only this of him in exchange for her love.

No one in his life had given him love except this woman and her golden twins. She was gone. Paris was gone. The bright promise of those years was no more.

But Tansy remained. And for whatever misbegotten reason, she felt safe with him, cruel and wrong as that was, for no one had failed her more. His body hungered for a woman who was little more than a child, and in its hunger had betrayed them both. He could not have her, regardless of what he'd once dreamed.

Despite all that, Lucas rose from his cot and dressed with haste. Like Juliette's mercy, Tansy called him to return.

Rusty armor and all.

CHAPTER FIFTEEN

MONA WAS AWAKE at dawn, too keyed up to sleep. In her bathroom, she pondered the box with the pregnancy test. Her hand hovered over it, but she didn't touch. She wasn't ready to use it. Knowing for certain would open up Pandora's box. Once she knew, she would have to act. Either tell Fitz or deliberately hide it. Make decisions about what to do. Despite her inner sense, she could tell herself she was imagining things and do nothing. Perhaps Tansy's mist was comforting and secure. Mona craved one of her own.

She withdrew her hand and slid it into the pocket of her robe. She'd focus on Tansy for now and deal with her own problems later. She'd placed some calls last night, longing to include Fitz among them, to confide in him about Walker and Tansy. But she hadn't. So far he hadn't come by to get any more of his things, and she was afraid to disturb the balance, no matter how desperately she desired his counsel. Counsel, hell. She smirked at herself. She missed Fitz, all of him—the messes he trailed all over the apartment, the crumbs on the counter, the socks on the floor. The sound of his tuneless humming when he was concentrating on his laptop.

To sleep with him again seemed the finest luxury she could imagine, but she couldn't see him yet, not until she'd worked things out in her mind. She could never keep a secret of this magnitude from him, and until she was sure what she should do, she couldn't afford to tell him anything.

Mona didn't bother trying to fool herself that he'd ever forgive her if he was aware that she'd had an abortion. Once, maybe. Now… Regardless of his passionate belief in a woman's right to choose, in his current state of mind he'd be delirious with joy to realize that his child grew in her belly. For him to learn that she'd taken that away from him would be the death knell of their marriage, she felt it in her bones.

So she had two choices: terminate the pregnancy she believed was all but a foregone conclusion and never tell him…or bear the child Fitz wanted so badly. She couldn't honestly say she was ready to do either yet.

So she would think, instead, about Tansy. When things were settled there, she'd make herself take the test and face the consequences. But not yet.

Mona dressed quickly and left a message on Gaby's voice mail, then headed for her father's apartment to stay until the security people came. She'd used her contacts to arrange, after hours, a firm that assured her Tansy would never have to be aware she was being followed. The longer Mona considered it, the more she believed that was the right way to approach this. Tansy's range was already too restricted by her own hand; to deny her further movement would be to harm Tansy's soul. She should be able to live much as she always had until they could determine if Lucas Walker was actually in contact with her. Once they knew, they could bring in the authorities and hope to have Walker arrested, maybe as a stalker. He'd be sent away to jail again—with luck, for the rest of his natural life.

When she arrived, however, Carlton's limo was idling outside, and Mona's temper kindled. She paused on the sidewalk and dialed Kat's number on her cell phone, planning to leave her sister a message, since lately she was always at Gamble's.

But Kat answered, her voice groggy. "Hello?"

"What are you doing there? I assumed you'd be at Gamble's. Is he there?"

"No." Kat's voice sounded odd.

"What's wrong?"

"Nothing. He…he just had work to do."

"Are you all right?"

"Of course I am," Kat snapped. "Why are you calling me at this ungodly hour?"

"It's Tansy."

"What's wrong with her?"

"I think Lucas Walker has been in contact with her."

"What? That son of a… Have you called the police?"

"I'm on top of it, Kat. I don't have time to explain, but I need you to get over here. I'm outside Daddy's apartment and Carlton's here. Daddy wants to let Carlton move her to his place—"

Kat exploded in vicious swearing.

"It's worse than that. He's softening on letting Carlton marry her so she can be taken care of when he's gone."

"That bastard. I'll be there in twenty minutes if I have to fly."

"I've got security arranged for her, and they'll arrive soon. I can handle it myself, but I wouldn't mind reinforcements."

"The Mounties are on their way, honey bun."

"Thanks, Kat." Mona disconnected and entered the building.

Mrs. Hodgson answered the door, her face troubled. "Mona, he can't do this. My little Tansy should be here where things are familiar."

Mona squeezed the older woman's shoulder. "Tansy's not going anywhere, don't you worry. Where is she?"

"She's still asleep, poor darling. She's been having nightmares lately."

"I'll handle it, Mrs. Hodgson. There will be a gentleman showing up later who'll be guarding her, and Kat is on her way." She saw the housekeeper's grimace. "Kat's a fierce fighter, and Tansy may need all of us."

Mrs. Hodgson nodded grimly. "You're right about

that. Kat and I don't see eye to eye, but she loves her sisters more than anything in the world." She wiped her hands on her apron. "They're in the living room. I'll bring you coffee."

Mona's stomach lurched. "I'd better pass." To spare the housekeeper's feelings, she lied. "I've already had plenty."

Mona straightened, gathering dignity around her like a robe. Then she entered the living room and kissed her father's cheek, noticing his nervous glance. She turned and offered her hand. "Carlton, how nice to see you."

Arrogance intact, Carlton returned the shake and went straight to the point. "Mona, I'm surprised to find that you don't grasp the obvious sense in my plan. None of you has my resources to protect Tansy from that criminal. I'm shocked that you'd be so cavalier with her safety."

Kat had never liked Carlton, but Mona had always been able to deal with him well enough. Both of them had tolerated him because he was so important to their father, but he'd crossed the line now. "It was under your tender care that our sister was raped and our brother murdered."

His eyes narrowed. His nostrils flared.

Martin intervened. "Desdemona, that's uncalled for. Carlton couldn't have predicted what happened, and he tried to save both of them."

She smiled for her father's benefit, but her eyes spoke

to Carlton. "Nonetheless, he cannot promise that she will be safe there any more than she is here."

"Of course I can. I have enormous resources to place at my disposal."

"I've already arranged for security for her, and you can't give her what she has here—the comfort of familiar surroundings. Your place is filled with terrible memories."

"I'm redecorating. I can re-create her entire room there, and I will, if that's what she wants."

"There's another thing you can't provide. If Walker is in contact with Tansy, he's got to be doing it somewhere nearby because she stays so close to home. The only way we'll catch him is to keep her here."

"You would use her as bait, your own sister?" Carlton wore a look of horror.

"I don't want to. But you're not getting anywhere in finding him, are you? She's vulnerable until we find out where he is. Are you suggesting we wait until he decides to show himself openly? It could be years."

"She will be safe with me, and I'll be sure she's happy."

"She will never be happy without Paris."

Carlton dismissed that. "It's an illusion. Paris isn't in the park."

"Tansy believes he is. Are you prepared to take away the one thing that means more to her than anything in the world? She's already so far away from us…can you assure us we won't lose her for good if she's robbed of that refuge?"

Mona turned to her father. "Daddy, you can't seriously be contemplating letting him do this. Tansy doesn't want to go. She told me that. She was afraid, really afraid."

"If we explained why she should go…" Martin began.

"No!" Carlton declared. "We can't explain this. The doctors told us not to force her to remember."

Mona smiled in triumph. "Then how do you propose to explain to her why she should live with you?"

Kat's voice chimed in from the doorway. "And why in the hell would she ever agree to marry you? That's disgusting."

Mona turned to her sister and smiled.

"Katharina, what are you doing here?" Martin asked.

"I told you Mona and I would be responsible for Tansy. She's our sister. You can't abandon her to Carlton again."

"See here, young lady—"

Mona noted the outrage on her father's face and wished she hadn't weakened and called Kat. She'd just about had it all sewed up; now her father was steamed, and Carlton looked dangerously grim. She reached out to stem any argument from Kat, but another voice intervened.

"What's going on?" Tansy asked, sounding sleepy. "Is something wrong?"

Carlton was the first to speak, crossing the room to

her side. "Nothing at all, my dear. I just dropped by to see your father. He's very busy just now, and he thought you might like to stay with me for a few days. Now that Kat and Armand have shown you how much fun it could be to go to new places, we thought you might enjoy another new adventure."

Furious at his deceit, Mona observed Tansy shrinking from him slightly. Standing there in her white cotton gown and pale-lavender robe, bare toes peeking out, she seemed unbearably young and fragile.

Tansy eyed Kat. "I had fun with Kat and Armand, but I don't want to leave Daddy."

"But your father won't have much time for you until the run is over."

Tansy shrugged. "I'm fine right here. I don't get lonely. Paris and I…" She glanced around uncertainly.

"Of course you prefer to stay here." Mona stepped between her and Carlton. Kat flanked Tansy's other side.

"This is your home. And if you want a new adventure, maybe you'll decide to visit Kat's apartment or mine. Perhaps we could have a slumber party one night." Mona tried not to smirk at Carlton, but Kat showed no such restraint.

Mona continued. "I thought I'd visit for a while this morning, since Daddy has to leave. Would you like that?"

Tansy smiled. "Could Kat stay, too?"

"You bet," Kat said. "We'll engage in some hen talk."

Tansy's lips curved fondly. "Nana liked hen talk." But her eyes still held shadows.

Mona met Kat's gaze, then nodded toward the hallway leading to Tansy's bedroom.

Kat signaled her comprehension. "Why don't you brush your hair, sweetie. I'll accompany you, and Mona can join us in a minute." She escorted Tansy out of the room.

Mona spoke to her father and ignored Carlton. "She'll be fine. We'll stay here until the security people arrive."

"You won't let her go to the park, will you?" Martin asked.

"That's probably where she's been meeting him, Daddy. How do you propose we explain to her that she can't go there, when it's part of her daily routine?" She patted his arm. "We aren't even sure that any of this is warranted, remember. Maybe the painting is just a trick of Tansy's mind. But she'll be guarded by a team, and they know who they're looking for."

"You may wind up very sorry that you've treated your sister's welfare so casually," Carlton warned. "No security is ever fail-safe."

Mona stemmed a shiver. She was betting a lot on the security company; they were supposed to be the best. For a moment, doubt assailed her. If anything happened to Tansy…

But then she recalled the plea on Tansy's face. *Don't let him take me away.* Which was worse?

She hoped she wasn't making a huge mistake, one for

which Tansy might pay, when she'd already sacrificed too much. Gripping her father's hand, Mona faced Carlton. "My point exactly. Even your security wouldn't be fail-safe, and Tansy would be in a place she doesn't wish to go, with the added risk of forcing her to remember things that might make her much worse. If you want to hire extra security, be my guest, but it seems to me the only kind thing to do is to let her stay in familiar surroundings."

Enmity shone in Carlton's eyes, but she could also spot her victory.

"Very well." He addressed her father. "I'll investigate Mona's arrangements myself and if I'm at all dissatisfied with what I find out, I'll arrange for any necessary improvements."

Mona gritted her teeth and remained silent. They all sought the same thing, after all: Tansy's safety.

"I'm very appreciative, Carlton," her father replied.

"As am I," she forced herself to say. "Mrs. Hodgson can show you out."

Outrage at being dismissed flashed in his eyes, but Carlton nodded regally. "I'll talk to you later, Martin."

"Why don't you get ready for rehearsal, Daddy." Mona patted her father's arm, though she longed to punch Carlton in the nose. The thought made her smile. Kat wouldn't have hesitated, and Mona could see the appeal.

"Are you certain we're doing the right thing, Desdemona? Titania must be safe. Juliette would never forgive me if—"

"Mama would do exactly what we're doing. She made this place a home for all of us, and she'd want Tansy to stay where she feels secure."

"I hope you're right," her father said. He left the room.

Mona watched him go. *No more fervently than I do.*

RIVERSIDE PARK on this day had decided that spring would die stillborn. The wind whipping off the Hudson cut through Lucas, knife-sharp. His chances of encountering Tansy today were slim and none. If he had a brain in his skull, he'd get back on the next bus, go to Al's and make a big pot of thick, hearty soup. The few customers they'd have would thank him.

He would leave soon, but first he would sit on Mt. Tom and try to conjure up that feeling of peace he'd known with Tansy on one bright, spring-hopeful day.

He found Darla on her usual bench. "It's too cold to be out today, Darla."

The old woman smiled. "I've sat here through worse. The sun feels good."

Lucas scanned the tiny patch of sunlight and knelt beside her. "Would you like to go with me to have a cup of coffee?"

She studied him fondly. "Tansy's right—you are a prince." But she shook her head. "My squirrels would miss me."

Lucas stayed with her a few moments longer, helping her feed her squirrels. When he failed to persuade her to leave and seek shelter, he gave up and continued toward Mt. Tom.

It was there, perched on the bald knob, that he spotted his enemy, Carlton Sanford, for the first time in twenty years.

And he knew why he'd had to come.

There was some comfort in noting Sanford's slower stride. Slight satisfaction in noting the gray shot through his hair. But Sanford still bore himself as though he had some divine right to take what he wished, to destroy lives at a whim, to focus on his own pleasure, no matter the cost to others.

Conflict raged within him. He longed to race down the slick stone, grab Sanford and take out on him twenty years' worth of a boy's desecrated dreams, of a grown man's knowledge of failure. He burned to avenge Tansy and Paris, the ruin of two shining lives. If he could destroy Sanford, all Lucas had lived through would be worthwhile, no matter that he himself would not survive it.

But there was Tansy to consider, Tansy the beautiful innocent. She'd lost twenty years, too, and she was still in danger, no matter that no one was aware of it but him.

As Lucas contemplated his nemesis on this cold, sun-starved day, he clenched his hands in a futile wish to turn back time. To be not Galahad—too blinded by ideals to recognize true evil—but the Michael Tansy thought him, avenging archangel and protector of those whose hearts were too pure to guard themselves.

Like Tansy.

Sanford stopped outside the car and surveyed his surroundings as if scenting the breeze for his prey.

Lucas shivered, but it was not the cold he felt. As he watched Sanford enter his limousine, he recognized that his chances of surviving the coming confrontation were almost nil. Sanford had the power; Lucas had only longing…and old dreams doomed to die.

His own survival wasn't important, but Tansy's was everything. He was certain somehow that Sanford was here because of him, that like predators destined by nature and fate to be always at odds, each had a heightened awareness that the other was near.

Lucas's time incognito was coming to an end. Very soon, he must act.

As the limousine pulled away, a rusty warrior prayed to be equal to the task.

TANSY SAT VERY STILL, her gaze fixed on the window that overlooked the park, as Kat brushed her pale locks. "Your hair's so pretty," Kat said. "Maybe I should grow mine out." Or shave her head. Or take a trip. Something. Anything to make this damn shaky feeling go away.

"What's wrong?"

Kat shook her head. "I'm fine."

"You're not." Tansy's blue eyes studied her and perceived too much.

For a moment Kat hovered between confidence and collapse, her own eyes stinging. "I will be." She smiled at her sister. "Don't worry. Nothing gets me down for long."

Tansy clasped her hand. "Talk to me, sweetie."

"No." Kat jerked it away.

Tansy regarded her too closely. "You can tell me, Kat."

"I don't have to tell…" Kat almost shouted, then her voice faltered. "I'm sorry, Tansy. I'm just—" She broke off as Mona entered the room.

"What is it?" Mona asked.

Before Kat could demur, Tansy spoke, casting Kat a silent apology. "Kat's sad."

Mona's gaze narrowed. "Is it Gamble?"

"I don't want to talk about it," Kat snapped.

"Who's Gamble?" Tansy asked.

Kat stared at Mona, daring her to say more.

Tansy's eyes swept from one to the other. "We're sisters…can't we tell each other anything?"

Kat and Mona traded glances.

"What is it?" Tansy asked. "Don't you trust me?"

Mona's face softened. "Sweetheart, it's not that…."

Tansy frowned. "You feel sorry for me."

Kat spoke quickly. "No, we're just worried about—"

Mona's expression was sharp with warning.

"I'm not weak."

"Of course you're not," Mona said too hastily.

"You think I am, don't you?" Hurt crossed Tansy's features, chased by disappointment. She walked to the window and peeped out. Suddenly, she stiffened and pressed one hand to the window, a small sob escaping.

"What is it, Tansy?"

Tansy whirled to face them. "It's Paris. He's waiting for me."

Worry subsided to sorrow. "Tansy…" Kat began, but a frown from Mona quieted her.

Mona spoke then. "Tansy, please be careful about going to the park."

"I like the park. I'm safe there. Paris needs me to go there."

"I know, I know," Mona said, nodding. "Just…be careful. Don't trust strangers."

"What strangers?"

Kat spoke up. "They're not all princes, Tansy."

Tansy's jaw jutted. "My prince is a good man."

"Do you see him in the park?" Mona asked abruptly.

Tansy cocked her head and took a long time to answer. "In my dreams." She leaned forward. "He makes me feel safe. He's good, just as Mama said. He protects me."

Kat spoke again. "Please…be cautious."

"Why are you so worried?"

They traded glances again. "We only want you to be safe."

"I'm safe here. I don't wish to go to Carlton's." Her face drained of color.

"You won't," Mona assured her. "Don't worry about that."

Tansy shivered and wrapped her arms around herself. "All right. If you promise, then I won't worry." She walked to the door. "You can leave now."

"Maybe you could stay in today. It's cold outside."

"Yeah," Kat added. "The wind off the river is terrible."

Tansy considered both of them with something that resembled pity, and smiled. "I love you both. I'll be careful. Now, go away."

For an instant, Kat could almost spy the big sister hidden inside, and she grinned past all her worry. "Yeah, yeah, we're going." She dragged her other big sister along with her.

LUCAS MOVED RESTLESSLY inside his disguise, observing the two men who reeked of cop taking stock of the park. One swept the stoop of the building across the street; the other sat on a park bench, pretending to read the paper.

He felt like an idiot, but the charade was working. Neither noticed the old lady Lucas had become with Darla's help. Darla was on her way to Broadway to eat a meal courtesy of Lucas; she'd left some of her gear with him after he'd sworn on Tansy's life that it would all be safe and that he would feed her squirrels.

He had a dread that wouldn't go away, an icy prickle at the back of his neck that had saved him more than once in jail. The sight of Sanford had only increased his foreboding.

He had to talk to Tansy, needed to make sure she was all right, though he couldn't be certain she'd show up today. He kept an uneasy vigil, trying not to think what might happen in his absence.

Then he spotted her and breathed easy for the first time in hours. With effort, he remained where he was.

But when she headed his way, he could tell something was wrong. She was conversing with Paris again, agitation trembling in her frame. He cast a glance at the two men. Both had gone on alert. He had to play this cool.

"I want to stay with you, Paris," she said. "But Daddy would like me to go with Carlton. I understand that he's busy with rehearsals, but something feels wrong. I'm afraid."

Carlton. Lucas's misgivings burst into full flower. He had to force himself to remain seated until she drew near.

"Hello, Darla. Are you warm enough?"

Lucas lifted his head, finger across his lips as her eyes went wide. "Act as if I'm Darla, Tansy. I have to talk to you. It's important."

"Is it you, Michael?" she asked softly.

He nodded. "Please…will you sit by me?"

She moved in perfect trust, a giggle rising from her throat. "Why are you dressed like Darla?" A faint frown crossed her face. "Is she all right?"

"Yes. I'm minding her things for her."

"Is this a game?"

He almost said yes, not sure he could—or should—

convey to her the seriousness of the situation. Instead, he grasped her hand. "Tansy, there are men here who intend to take me away from you." He'd bet anything it was true.

She stiffened. Her head whipped around.

"Don't look, please. Just sit here with me and act as though you believe I'm Darla."

"Are you all right? Why do they—"

"Maybe they think I'll hurt you."

She scoffed openly. "That's ridiculous. You're my prince. I'll just go tell them—"

He pulled her down. "No. They can't be alerted that you see them. Don't draw attention to me. If they figure it out…"

She squeezed his hand. "I won't let them get you."

He smiled at her fervor. "Thank you." He studied her. "Has something happened today?"

"You've been gone for days and days."

He couldn't meet the hurt in those blue eyes. "I'm sorry. I missed you, too." He longed to put his arms around her, but he didn't dare.

She rested her head against his shoulder. "I'm afraid. I wish you could stay with me."

He did, too, but he was in no position to intervene. "What makes you afraid?"

"My father intends to send me away with Carlton, but Mona and Kat say I don't have to go. Everyone is mad, especially Carlton." Her eyes grew distant. "I don't want to go to his apartment," she whispered. "I want to stay with you. Paris needs me to be here."

"Why are you unwilling to go?" *How much do you remember?*

She clutched her hands around his arm. "The bad dream," she whispered, her eyes going dark.

He had to ask her—

The newspaper reader rose and began to walk their way.

Lucas was running out of time. "I have to go."

"Take me with you."

Lucas recoiled in astonishment. "What?"

The man stopped not far away, possibly close enough to hear. For Lucas to linger wasn't safe, but they had to have more time. "Do you recall how you used to sneak out through the laundry room?" he asked.

Her blue eyes went wide. "How do you know that?"

"Would you…" He stopped. The idea was insane. How would he ever care for her? But his sense of her danger was screaming, and he didn't trust anyone else. Perhaps her sisters would listen, but he had to be sure she was protected first. He spoke again, his voice low and hurried. "Once you said you'd go to new places with me because I made you feel safe."

Tansy smiled. "Yes."

"What if we did that soon?"

"All right." No hesitation at all.

"What about Paris?"

Her expression grew troubled. "I don't think he can leave." She stared into the distance, then turned back to him. "Paris told me to trust you. He would understand." Her eyes glistened with sudden tears. "Could we come back…to see him?"

Lucas almost took her into his arms until he remembered the watchers. He settled for covering her hand with both of his. "We'll come back. But Tansy, I believe Paris will always be with you in your heart."

Her smile was a thousand suns. "Do we go now?"

He shook his head. "Not yet. Tonight, can you get out the old way?"

For a second, he thought he saw something stir in her eyes, a fleeting shadow…a memory? She frowned faintly. "I won't be afraid if I'm with you," she said, but her icy hands betrayed her.

"You don't have to go if you don't want to." But how the hell would he ever protect her otherwise? Urgency seized him. He had to get her away from Sanford's control.

And then he had to secure help. The file he'd built had shown him just how much power Sanford had. Now there were rumors of an ambassadorship at stake. Lucas had to find someone who could make the authorities listen.

But first he needed Tansy out of harm's way.

She spoke up. "I want to go. What time?"

And so it was that they made hasty plans before he

had to send her back. He scribbled the bar's phone number on a scrap of paper and put it in her hand. "If anything happens before then to make you afraid, call this number."

"Okay." So much trust.

"Now, say goodbye to me as if I'm Darla and go back inside. Be sure to dress warmly tonight and don't bring very much." He forced himself to smile as though he wasn't scared as hell that something would happen before tonight.

Tansy smiled back, sweet as sunshine. "'Bye, Darla," she called out. "You go to the shelter tonight, all right?"

Lucas watched her walk away and tried to tell himself that in a few hours, she would be safe.

Please, was all he could think. *Please. Don't abandon us this time.*

CHAPTER SIXTEEN

CALL ME IF YOU NEED ME.

Kat stared out her bedroom window at the building behind, idly pondering whether Telescope Man in the apartment directly across and down three would like a peep show. In the same split second, she studied the piece of green Depression glass a hand's-width away and wondered if it would make a satisfying crash if she airlifted it against the wall.

Or if anything at all could peel this dead zone away from her heart, once so trustworthily bulletproof that she'd taken it for granted.

She'd gone by the gallery, intending to give Gregory the day off, but she'd gotten one glimpse at Gamble's paintings and known that if she stayed there, she'd burn them...along with her future.

So she came home, where the painting she'd stolen from him faced the wall. She'd circled it as a swordsman searching for an opening to an enemy's heart. Finally, she'd left it there, too afraid to turn it around, and now stood before the open refrigerator door as though inside were answers.

To *why?*

And *how?*

Cruel words with no explanations. Why this man? How had he done it to her? Why had fate sent him her way? How had she lost herself?

Why was he married? How could he betray his wife? *His wife, hell. How could he betray* me?

A small smile lifted the corners of her mouth. Even she could see the humor in feeling herself to be the one wronged.

Kat sat on the kitchen floor, chilled from air scented with mustard and old Brie and white wine.

And she mused over what had become of the groceries she'd left at Gamble's. Had he and that woman eaten them? Did they understand how she'd tucked dreams inside the tender leaves of baby lettuce? How she'd shaped the baguette with her fingers and pictured herself and Gamble tearing off great hunks and feeding them to each other when they were starving but unwilling to move from the bed? How she would have bread crumbs on her skin and he would brush them away with gentle fingers…and she would know, at last, the care she'd craved for years?

Call me if you need me.

She'd dialed Armand's number three times, listening to the message on his answering machine. But then she'd dropped the receiver in its cradle, unable to find fifteen seconds' worth of words.

Oh, Armand. I hurt so much. There's this hole that gets so big sometimes that I'm pretty sure my insides have vanished. That I'll collapse like a rag doll from the weight of all my wanting.

From the fear that no one will ever want me. Not me, Kat Gerard, vixen seductress.

But me. Really me, who used to have the prettiest long red braids I cut off with Nana's pruning shears when everybody went away.

Kat slid to her side on the cold kitchen floor and felt the chill leach into her bones. As twilight fell, the appliance light bathed her in metallic moonglow tainted yellow. She curled up tighter to preserve the tiny flame of a spirit she no longer felt able to turn into torchlight.

And when her phone began to ring, she closed her eyes and covered her ears. She lay very still, the refrigerator light keeping away ghosts.

Finally, when she couldn't stand the ringing anymore, she rose and unplugged both recorder and phone.

MONA WATCHED FROM HER office window as an unseen hand slowly adjusted the rheostat of city lights, bringing them up through the mist of watery late-winter sun. It was a time of day when she and Fitz had once checked in with each other, compared notes on the day's progress, made evening plans. Each of them often had work left to do, but they'd sometimes meet for dinner, then return to their respective offices. Or they'd both head home, and retire to work a few hours longer once they'd shared takeout.

And sometimes they'd meet and not eat at all, recharging their batteries in a different manner. Breathless and snorting laughter into the other's shoulder, she and Fitz would steal bliss on top of her desk. In the coat closet at the paper. Paying an exorbitant night's rate at the Plaza and using the room for only two hours.

She craved the feel of his thick sandy hair in her fingers, the heat of his mouth. The strength of his arms. She wanted to call him and talk about Tansy, hear him tell her she was worried for no reason. Or hear him, period. Just…savor his voice.

Her left hand, wedding ring glinting, stole down to rest on her still-flat belly. She'd meant to call her doctor and talk about…

Why did the word sound different to her now? *Abortion. Abort.* It was a harsh word, abrupt and graceless. That shouldn't be. All her adult life she'd seen it as a bright and shining word, the example of a woman's freedom from the tyranny of biology that robbed so many of hope and the futures they should have had.

But tonight she realized that inside her might be a little Fitz, a boy with the hazel eyes she loved more than anything in the world. With the long fingers that had touched her with such love…

Something inside her gave way. Just the smallest bit, but the tear was sharp and stunning, and her years of assurance of who she was and what she believed and what she wanted stumbled on once-steady moorings.

One call. It would only take that to bring Fitz back. He'd fly across the city to be with her if he knew. He'd laugh and whirl her and cover her mouth with his and hold her so tightly she'd feel safe and protected and loved. He'd pick up the phone and call everyone he knew—

And everyone *she* knew. Jack Bradshaw's face loomed before her, eyes gleaming in triumph as he moved into this office while she was on maternity leave. Took over her magazine. Mona pictured herself, ungainly and round, trying to get on and off the train quickly. Traveling back and forth to Westchester every night.

She clutched the edge of her desk with a white-knuckled hand, her chest tight. For a second, she could not breathe as terror gripped her. As much as she wanted Fitz beside her right now, she couldn't be sure that he wouldn't encase her in a silken prison. He'd been a passing-good feminist for years, but he was different now. She would be the carrying case for his new dream, to be cosseted and pampered…

And changed. Forever changed. She pictured his sisters, happily ensconced in their suburban lives. His mother who still baked from scratch.

He would wish for that, and Mona could not be anything like it.

Her mother had stepped into her velvet cage with a smile and eager eyes. Every year, she had faded. The bright splash of color that was Juliette had become the pale cabbage rose of ancient upholstery.

She loved you so much. Tansy's soft words murmured in her ear.

Maybe she had, but in the end, she'd still left.

Mona wrapped her arms around her waist, curving over until her forehead touched the cold glass of her office window. *What do I do, little one?*

She listened, listened hard, but she heard no words, no advice, no answers. Yet deep within, was a tiny warmth, a faint flickering of a light that felt strong and true and real. It could be snuffed as finger and thumb doused a candle. Quickly. Easily. Then it would all be over, and she could go on with her life.

Not yet. Something inside her spoke. *Not yet.*

All right, little one. A tad longer. That's all, though. A brief respite to find an answer.

Some of the tempest inside her receded. Part of the bite softened. It was only temporary, and she was all too aware of what would be smart and sane and realistic for someone like her, but…

Not yet. Just…not yet.

Mona uncurled her arms from around her waist and turned toward her desk, seeing it through the eyes of a stranger. As she scrambled for some distraction, her gaze landed on the card for the security company.

Tansy. She would check on what happened today. After punching numbers into the phone, she listened to the ring.

"Duncan."

"This is Mona Gerard. I'd like a status report."

"All quiet."

"Did she go to the park?"

"Not long after you left, but Walker wasn't there. She spent some time with an old bag lady, but she didn't stay long."

"And no sign of him since?"

"Not a one."

"So what happens tonight?"

"You've said she never leaves at night, but we'll have a man keeping tabs on the lobby, just in case. He'll patrol outside as well."

"Tomorrow there will be two again?"

"Yes."

"Has Mr. Sanford returned?"

"No. She's had no visitors. Ms. Hart returned with your father and is still there, but no one else."

Mona didn't enjoy knowing that the blond bimbo was there with her father so often, but she had no right to restrict his social life. "You'll call me if anything at all happens?"

The man's voice conveyed forced patience. "We'll do our job, Ms. Gerard. We take our work seriously."

"Of course you do," she conceded. "I'll talk to you in the morning, then."

"Fine." He disconnected.

Mona pondered the work on her desk and wished she could sweep it all into the trash and walk away. But she was nothing if not disciplined, so she picked up the top piece of paper, the final designs from the florist for her father's celebration.

It was better than thinking about the rest of her life.

LUCAS HOVERED IN THE shadows across the street from the delivery entrance, constantly scanning both the side and front of the building. He'd been observing for an hour, searching for any sign of the man he'd mentally dubbed Crewcut or his buddy. He hadn't seen either outside, but once when he'd moved locations to check the building entrance, he thought he'd spotted Crewcut strolling through the lobby. Other than that, the night belonged to him and one old bum sacked out on a bench.

Be careful, Tansy, he thought. The girl he'd once known could have made it down the stairs and into the basement without stirring the air, but there was so much he didn't understand about her now.

Once again he wondered just how insane he was to be doing this at all. Any of it. If the sense of foreboding would go away, he'd leave her be—but it hadn't. It was stronger than ever. As fierce as that night so long ago when, on a hunch, he'd convinced Paris to turn around and go back to Sanford's apartment. The dread Lucas had felt had overpowered the lure of their school-boy plans to sneak into a peep show down by Times Square instead of going to the movies as Paris had gained permission to do.

Lucas still wasn't sure why foreboding had pressed in so hard on him that night. For whatever reason, he'd been as connected to Tansy then as he seemed to be now, and the itch between his shoulder blades that had kept him alive in prison was eating at him again. He was afraid for her, but he was sure no one would listen. He couldn't figure out what else to do but spirit her away.

Her father trusted Sanford now as he had then, from what Tansy had said this afternoon. Lucas had tried to tell Paris back then that there was something wrong in the way Sanford looked at Tansy when he believed no one was paying attention. Paris had laughed it off. Would Tansy's sisters do the same?

Lucas had more in his file now, prepared from the re-search he'd been doing. He had a hunch, based on pris-on stories and a pattern of Sanford's investments, that some of Carlton's businesses might be fronts for mon-ey laundering. If so, he had friends more dangerous than Lucas had guessed. But no one would listen to an ex-con over a man rumored to be up for an ambas-sadorship; Lucas needed aid from someone with better sources and more credibility.

He had a candidate, a man he'd never met but whose

work he'd been studying in the newspaper archives. James Fitzgerald, husband of Tansy's sister Mona. The man had done some impressive investigations and didn't seem to mind taking a shot at sacred cows. This sacred cow was one of the city's premier philanthropists and Fitzgerald's father-in-law's closest ally, so talking to him was a risk. Lucas had held off, searching for evidence that would convince Fitzgerald beyond a doubt that Sanford wasn't what he seemed.

But Lucas couldn't wait any longer. The threat to move Tansy to Sanford's place had blown his careful plans to hell. Once Tansy was secure, Lucas would have to seek Fitzgerald's assistance and hope that the man felt protective of his sister-in-law.

Once again Lucas's jaw hardened at the idea that all of them had let her come to this, had allowed her to drift into madness. He'd been a fool to buy Sanford's assurance that Tansy would get help, but what of the rest of them? Why had they let her go so easily?

Lucas squeezed his eyes shut for a moment, overcome, once again, by a sense of his impotence to be all that Tansy deserved. A scared seventeen-year-old had believed he'd managed to protect her before. Had accepted a stiff price to keep Tansy safe—then had been betrayed. What he'd returned to find had shown him just what a fool he'd been. Why should he think he could manage any better now when he had so many strikes against him?

For a moment Lucas wavered, ready to walk away, to hold off on this half-baked plan and determine if he was only paranoid about Sanford.

But then an image rose, one burned into his brain for all time. Tansy, struggling on the floor of Sanford's library, blood smeared on her pale thighs, her eyes full of horror and pleading.

Now, just as then, he was powerless before his love for her, unable to turn away when she needed him. Then he'd been drugged and half out of his mind; now he was handicapped in a different way.

But it couldn't matter. He'd paid a high price for failing before, but the price extracted from Tansy far overshadowed his. This time, no matter the cost, he had to make sure he didn't fail again. He had to find a way to checkmate Sanford—

Across the street, the delivery door opened. A slender form eased through, bright hair covered with another of the old lady scarves. She stood out on the street, waiting for him, her expression lost and scared. He could see her knuckles tighten on the bundle slung over her shoulder.

Lucas put aside his doubts, buried his fears. It was the moment to act. He emerged from the shadows. "Tansy."

She spun to face him, joy and relief on her face.

He crossed the street with long, eager strides. Somehow, he would make this work. He would hurdle all the obstacles in their path. He would save her, as Juliette had asked him so long ago.

When he neared, she threw her arms around him and laughed, her smile transforming night into day. He pulled her close and swung her in a circle. In that instant, his heart was as light as the moon-shot silver of her hair. He met her gaze, his heart filling with dreams he had no right to. When her lashes swept down, he pressed a kiss to each lid, wanting his touch to tell her what he didn't dare say. *I love you, Tansy. You are my heart.*

"Walker—" a harsh voice shouted. "Let her go. Step away. Now."

Lucas whirled, automatically putting her behind him.

"Michael?" Tansy gasped. "What—"

The bum from the park bench was armed, and he moved too fast for an old man. Lucas had only seconds to decide.

He shoved Tansy in front of him, searching for something to use. "Run, Tansy," he yelled. He seized a nearby trash can and heaved it at the man's head. The weapon fired. Lucas heard the bullet slam into the building just to his right. He picked up another trash can and threw it, too, nodding in satisfaction as garbage flew high and wide and the man went down, spouting curses.

Lucas wheeled and ran after Tansy. He took the bundle off her shoulder, grabbed her hand and held on tight,

towing her with him as he raced around the corner and
into the safety of the night.

THE PHONE SHRILLED, and Mona grappled for the light.
It was 3:00 a.m. Good news didn't come at 3:00 a.m.

Oh, God. Not Fitz. Please, not Fitz. "Hello?"

"Desdemona." It was her father, sounding a thousand
years old.

"What is it, Daddy? What's wrong?"

"It—" His voice broke. "It's Titania. She's gone."

"Gone?" Mona sat up so quickly her head spun and
her stomach rebelled. "What do you mean, gone?"

"Walker. He has her. He stole her away, my poor
sweet angel. That murderer, he—" The air was filled
with harsh, broken sobs.

"Daddy, tell me what happened…" She heard voices,
winced as the phone crashed on the other end.

"Mona, this is Carlton."

"What are you doing there? Have you summoned the
police? What the devil's going on?"

"Calm down. You won't help your father this way."

He was right. She had to— She couldn't— "What
happened? When?"

"About an hour ago. Walker kidnapped her."

"How did he get in? The guard—"

"She left through the delivery entrance. He was waiting outside. I had a man stationed nearby, but he
couldn't get to her in time."

"You had a man?"

"Your guard sat in the lobby reading a magazine while Walker kidnapped your poor sister."

"Why didn't you tell me you'd gotten someone?"

"My input wasn't welcomed, as I recall."

His superior tone grated, but she couldn't afford that now. "What do the police say?"

"I didn't phone them."

"What? Are you insane? There needs to be a manhunt. Every second that passes without pursuit, he can take her farther away."

"She left on her own. The police won't consider it a kidnapping."

"Well, we have to do something. We can't just—"

"I never said there was no search. Leave it to me, Mona. I'll get her back."

"Why should we leave it to you? This is a family matter. I want to speak to my father."

"Your father is in no shape to talk to you. Must I remind you that he entrusted Tansy to me? That I'm to be the executor of his estate? He has asked me to handle this, and I will do so. I have resources you can't imagine."

"You have no right to interfere."

"No right?" He sneered. "I have a score to settle with Walker that is just as old as yours. He invaded my house, murdered my best friend's son before my eyes, destroyed the innocence of a girl who never harmed a soul, and wounded me in the bargain. Don't talk to me about rights—if not for me, Walker would have been released years ago. I have Tansy's best interests at heart and the resources to protect her. If you had listened to me, none of this would have happened."

Guilt ran roughshod over fury. Tansy, oh, sweet, too-innocent Tansy. Where was she? What was he doing to her?

He makes me feel safe. He's my prince.

Oh, God. She'd been wrong, Mona realized. She should have let Carlton move Tansy and keep her safe. That Mona didn't like him wasn't the issue. Tansy's safety was. She was fair game, easy prey for such a man as Lucas Walker. She had fallen for the fantasy Juliette had woven. *Knights in shining armor don't exist, Tansy. They can't keep you safe.*

Then Mona remembered the fear in her sister's eyes. *Please don't let him take me away.*

Fury fought with fear. "I'm coming over there. Daddy will need me."

"Your father has taken a sedative. Julie is with him. He's better off sleeping, Mona. Wait until morning."

"Wait until morning? Where will Tansy be then? He could transport her anywhere—oh, God, she must be so afraid…"

He makes me feel safe.

"What could he have told her that would make her leave?" she asked.

"I don't know," Carlton said, his tone clipped. "Mona, I have things to do."

"I still think we should go to the police."

"I'll handle this," he barked. "After how you've botched it, don't interfere now." His voice slid into condescension. "Get some rest. If you want to do something, call Kat and inform her. The two of you can see your father later. Right now, I have calls to make."

The click rang like a gunshot.

That bastard. Like hell she would sit, hands folded, and wait.

She needed allies. She didn't have the resources to fight him by herself. Who did? Who would care?

Fitz would, but she wasn't sure she could ask.

Kat, then. She would be crazed over this. She'd storm their father's apartment and hang Carlton up by his thumbs.

But Kat was only good for passion. They required more.

Armand. He adored Tansy, and he was as rich and well connected as Carlton. Mona would call Kat and have her contact Armand. They would get together and make plans.

She punched in Kat's number, not surprised when her sister didn't answer. On the fourth ring, though, the recorder didn't pick up. Six rings. Eight. Ten. Mona frowned. Disconnecting, she punched in the numbers again, just in case.

No answering machine. Ten more rings. Kat would sooner give up sex than her social life, with which her recorder tried valiantly to keep up.

Kat's sad. Suddenly, Mona remembered Tansy's concern. Saw again the pain and sorrow in Kat's eyes when she had asked her about Gamble. Remembered the drawings and Kat's unusual buoyancy the past several days.

She hadn't been exuberant today. A lovers' quarrel? Maybe so. Perhaps Kat had gone to Gamble's to patch things up, but if she had, Mona had no idea how to find her. She tried Directory Assistance, but no Gamble Smith was listed in any of the boroughs.

She couldn't wait until she found Kat to act.

Mona sat on the bed, holding the portable like a lifeline, her free hand wrapped around her middle. Her gaze fell on the picture of Fitz that stood on her nightstand, and in that moment, she wanted nothing more than his arms around her.

Armand had connections, but so did Fitz. He was tight with the NYPD, and he loved Tansy, too. What was wrong between them couldn't matter. He would want to know. She searched for the phone number of his hotel.

But then she thought of the small life flickering inside her and stopped in mid-dial. How could she ask Fitz for aid and lie to him while she did? Could she, who couldn't keep a Christmas present secret, see Fitz and not tell him that his child slept inside her?

Oh, God. She wasn't sure what to do.

Then she considered her sister in the hands of a killer and knew that she wouldn't turn down any assistance she could muster.

Armand first. He could assist her in locating Kat. He lived closer and could get over there faster than Mona.

"Hello?"

"Armand, I'm sorry to wake you, but it's an emergency. Tansy's been kidnapped by Lucas Walker, and I can't contact Kat. I need your help."

His reply was all business. "I'll bring her to you as soon as I can. What else do you need?"

Just like that, no questions, no doubts. "Thank you, Armand." Mona bit her lip as her eyes burned. "I—I think that's all."

"Is Fitz there with you?"

She swallowed hard and lied. "Yes. I'll be fine."

"Good. I'm sure you're frightened, but we'll get her back, don't you worry. Anything I have is at your disposal."

"Thank you." She hung up. Took a deep breath. Dialed the phone.

"Fitzgerald."

"Fitz, Tansy's been kidnapped." Then she burst into tears.

"Hang on, sweetheart," said the voice she'd loved for years. "I'm on my way. Just hold on."

"Thank you," she managed to answer. And even after he disconnected, she held on to the phone, hearing in her head the sound of that voice, clasping his words to her heart like the last fire in a cold, dark world.

Her free hand slid over her belly, and in that moment, the life inside her seemed real as it had not before. A baby. Fitz's baby.

Her baby.

THE POUNDING ON Kat's door awoke her. She stirred from the sofa, trying to remember exactly how she'd gotten there. Her head ached with every blow, and there was a taste in her mouth of cigarettes and old shoes.

"Kat? Katharina, open up."

Armand? She glanced at the clock on her VCR. Three forty-five? What the hell was this? "Go away," she shouted.

Just then, it opened. Kat stood there stupidly, blinking. "Where did you get a key?"

"I own the building."

"You...what?" She shook her head. "Why didn't you tell me?"

His eyes flashed. "Forget that. What the hell are you doing?" He grabbed her by the arms. "Mona's been calling. I've been calling. Why don't you answer your phone?"

"I didn't want to talk to anyone." The reasons crowded in, and tears threatened.

She dodged, but she wasn't quick enough. Armand grabbed her chin, turned her toward him, studying her with eyes that saw too much. "What's wrong?" he asked in a voice unbearably gentle.

She wouldn't cry. She didn't need pity. She was just fine—

Tears fell, rolling down her cheeks, wetting the hand that cupped her chin.

"Oh, Kat," he said softly, pulling her into his arms. He was only a few inches taller, but his shoulders were broad and he felt so warm, so strong. So safe. "I'm sorry."

She couldn't speak around the ache in her heart. She laid her head on his shoulder and let him embrace her. They lingered there, Armand rocking her slightly. Kat felt everything inside her crumble. "I'm such a fool," she cried.

"No, you're not. You're a beautiful, passionate woman who leads with her heart."

"I kidded myself that he loved me," she hiccupped. "I thought I loved him." The tears were a flood now; even her nose was running. "Oh, God, leave me alone. I'm so embarrassed." She tried to turn away, but Armand wouldn't let her.

She should draw back, assert her independence, but the comfort he offered was seductive. She straightened and every thought in her head vanished as she spied the unguarded tenderness that blazed from his eyes. But something else lingered in shadows. "Katharina," he said, his voice unutterably sad. "Something's happened."

Dread slicked down her spine. "What?"

"It's Tansy," he stated, his grip relenting, hands stroking up and down her arms. "I have to take you to Mona's."

Kat shivered, afraid to ask. "Why? What's happened?"

Armand's face hardened. "Lucas Walker has her."

MONA HEARD THE KEY in the lock and sought to gather her wits. She'd worn a hole in the rug, pacing. Panic wouldn't help; it was up to her to handle this, all of it. Her father was useless, and Carlton too arrogant. Tansy deserved someone without an agenda.

"Des?"

For a second, they stood there, the air between them filled with history and hope and accusations. She should play it cool. Be strong and sure.

Instead, she flew across the room into his embrace.

When they closed around her, the arms that had been all she'd ever experienced of home, Mona felt something inside her ease, something that had been coiled and tight and strained since the night he'd left. "Oh, Fitz," she sobbed.

"I'm here, babe," he soothed, his voice the slightest bit unsteady. "I'm here." He tightened those strong arms around her, clasp her hard against him. As she sobbed, he swayed in a comforting rhythm, one hand cradling her head against his broad shoulder. "Shh, sweetheart. We'll get her back, I promise. Shh…"

She started to tell him thank you, but her words were swallowed up in his kiss. The kiss went on, and it was like dying and being reborn, like losing everything and finding it again, like the breathless ascent from hell to heaven. She attempted again to speak. "Oh, Fitz, I'm so sorry. I miss you so much—"

He took her words into him as though she were the essence of life itself. His free hand roamed her body, giving and seeking comfort. Heat and hunger and love and memory clashed and coalesced, swirled around them.

The hard shell of her resistance cracked. Nothing in her life matched this man in importance. He was her soul mate, her other half. Surely there had to be a way for them to find the path back to each other.

Fitz cupped her face in his hands and rested his forehead against hers. "We have to talk about Tansy, but I can't wait to say this." He retreated a little, his gaze boring into hers. "I love you, Des. I've missed you like hell. I'm half-alive without you."

She could barely speak, but she had to try. "I love you, too. Fitz, there's so much I have to tell you."

His thumbs stroked over her cheeks, soaking up her tears. "I know, sweetheart. I pushed you too much—" He stopped, all the love in the world in his eyes as he shook his head. "We have to talk, but tell me about Tansy now."

He led her to the sofa, one eyebrow cocked as he saw the bed she'd made there because their own bed was too full of memories for her to sleep.

"I couldn't…"

Fitz smiled. "I haven't slept worth a shit since I left." He brushed the bedding to one corner and sat down with her, keeping her close. "Lay out for me the facts you have."

The doorbell rang, and Fitz rose to answer. When Kat and Armand entered and sat down, Mona began to explain.

CHAPTER SEVENTEEN

LUCAS FELT TANSY SHIVER against him as they stood in shadows across the street from Al's. He tightened his arm around her shoulders and pressed a kiss to the top of her head, but he never stopped scanning the area, even though he wasn't sure what to watch for. He was almost certain they'd lost their pursuer after ducking into a market around the corner from Tansy's. Lucas wished to God he knew more about this cloak-and-dagger stuff.

Tansy leaned against him in a posture of absolute trust that scared the hell out of him. They had jumped from the frying pan into the fire, no question. It was too late to stop. He would never see her again if he let her go now.

The time for doubts was past. He would have to make his sketchy plan work. Somehow.

First things first. Settle Tansy in his basement room. Get some sleep to clear his head. Then start seeking someone to believe him.

"Where are we?" Tansy asked, looking up with those blue eyes that reached all the way into his gut.

"Over there." He gestured. "It's not much, Tansy. Just a room in the basement beneath a topless bar."

"What's a topless bar?"

He paused, not sure how to explain.

"Oh." Her eyes widened. "Where women…"

"Only one," he said. "It's not a very successful place."

"Is she nice?"

"Who?"

"The lady who…"

His stomach churned at the thought of Gloria, of how he'd let her—

Hell.

The damn thing was, that was exactly what Gloria had been: nice. Trying to do something for a friend. He'd laugh, except there was nothing funny about it. "Yeah." He glanced away. "She's a nice lady."

"Okay." That simple. That readily accepted.

"Tansy, you're a miracle," he blurted.

Her smile was sunlight on roses, dawn after dark night. "Why?"

He'd never given her this, never told her what she meant to him. They'd been young. He'd been stupid, a self-conscious teenage boy, uneasy with words. Fists were simpler. Fights and struggle he understood. Pretty words were foreign soil.

"Your heart is good. You assume the best of everyone." He sought more. "You make me feel as though I could be a prince."

"Galahad. I told you. And now you've rescued me."

His stomach clenched. He could also be her biggest danger. As soon as possible, he had to turn her over to someone who could protect her as she deserved. For right now, she was stuck with him.

"Have you slept at all?" he asked.

She shook her head, and suddenly, he could see the smudges beneath her eyes, the slump of her shoulders. She was exhausted.

"My place is just one room with a bed. I'll find someone better to help you soon."

She clutched his arm. "I don't want to leave you, Michael."

He reminded himself that she wasn't talking to him per se. Michael was only a name that, for whatever reason, made her feel safe. If only she knew.

She *would* know at some point. She'd remember. And what would happen then?

He had to face the fact that simply being around him might prove the trigger for memories she could not survive. If the knowledge destroyed her, he'd never forgive himself.

A hell of a mess, son, he thought. *You've landed in the middle of something you considered long over.* That was okay—except that he'd taken Tansy with him.

He had to discover a path out that would end the nightmare for once and for all, but wouldn't destroy Tansy in the process. Christ, if he could just think, but he was so everlasting tired….

Logic grabbed hold. Nothing to do with what was left of the night but get some sleep. No one would show up until at least noon. For the next several hours, they would hole up and rest.

"Okay, let's go." Lucas wished she weren't wearing the bright green coat, but at least he could pull the hood over her hair and hide her face from any passersby. She wouldn't be going out for a few days, and before then he would locate her some nondescript clothing. Tucking her into his side, he hurried her across the street and opened the door as quickly as possible, then locked it behind them.

He released her and inhaled his first deep breath of the night. For the time being, they were safe. No one would locate them just yet. "This way," he said, ready to lead her to the basement stairs.

But Tansy had slipped back her hood and was gazing around the room. Lucas wondered how it looked to her. She pointed to the tiny stage. "Is that where…?"

"Yeah. That's where Gloria dances."

"Gloria." She said the name with wonder and began moving past the tables. She came to a stop beside one of the stools arranged around the small runway. One slender hand gingerly touched the wood surface, then jerked back as if it were a hot stove.

Shame washed over Lucas that he'd brought her to a place that stank of cigarettes and beer and cheap sex. "Tansy, let's go," he said too harshly.

But when she turned, it was not revulsion he saw, but curiosity. "Would it be okay if…" She peered sideways at the stage.

It took him a minute to realize she was asking to get up on the runway. Something in him rebelled. He wanted her to have no connection at all to this dark world. "No. Come on."

She cast one wistful glance back, then walked toward him, shoulders sinking. "All right."

Christ Jesus. He had no clue what to do. He felt as though he'd stolen candy from a child. She didn't know, couldn't understand, that he didn't want her tainted by his life, that he couldn't allow her to be profaned by the depths that were his natural element, not hers.

All she wished was to play pretend. She'd always been the most curious person he'd known, and her wings had been clipped for years. "It's okay," he forced himself to say. "You'd like to stand up there?"

Eyes sparkling, she nodded.

"Here, let me help you." Hands around her waist, he lifted her easily.

She stood at the end of the runway, grasping the metal pole around which Gloria had posed in a thousand sleazy ways, fueling the tawdry dreams of lonely men.

Lucas itched to yank Tansy down, wash her hands, wrap her in cotton and hold this world at bay.

But she paused there, smiling. She loosened the scarf around her hair and shook it out, the pale, shimmering mane. And she began to dance around the pole with the dainty, dreamy steps of an innocent ballerina.

At her feet, Lucas watched, mesmerized, as Tansy cleansed the room of its muck and grime with her shining presence, with the power of the goodness inside her. She was a dream herself, a pure and golden light in the darkness.

He knew in that moment that he would die for her if need be, suffer for her again if that was required. She was the best part of him, his last hope of salvation. He would guard her, not for Juliette but for herself, because no matter that she had been frozen in time, that she wasn't what the world called normal, she was what the universe needed more of, what it cried out to have. So soft and tender and kind that she could heal the wounds of every soul she touched.

It made him afraid for her. It also made him fierce.

She stopped humming and dancing and held out her arms, sliding into a graceful curtsy, her smile wide and warm and heartbreakingly lovely.

Lucas found a smile and clapped.

She rose and stepped to the edge of the stage, held out her arms and let herself fall toward him in perfect trust.

And Lucas caught her. Arms tight around the woman nestled against him, he closed his eyes and wished the moment would last forever. When Tansy lifted her gaze to his and cradled his face in her slender hands, he did what he'd wanted to do since the first day he'd met her, a lifetime ago.

With reverence and awe and whatever love could find root inside his battered heart, Lucas Walker chastely kissed the woman who was more of heaven than he would ever deserve.

MONA'S EYES WERE SO HEAVY she could barely keep them open. It was 5:00 a.m., and none of them had slept. Armand was on the kitchen phone and Fitz paced the living room, talking on his cell phone to some detective he said they could trust.

At her living room window, Kat stared out at the night beyond. *Kat's sad,* she remembered Tansy saying, and Mona could see it again as she had the day before, carving lines of defeat in Kat's usual careless abandon. She walked over to her sister and placed a hand on her shoulder. "What's wrong?"

Kat shrugged off the hand and stirred, her answer automatic. "Nothing." But Mona could spot the lie. "It's just…I'm worried about Tansy. That son of a bitch…" Her voice went low and harsh. "I'll kill him if he hurts her, I swear it." Her hands curled into fists.

But it was more than worry for Tansy that Mona saw in Kat's eyes. "What's happened with Gamble?"

Kat's expression went blank. Frost crackled in the air. "It was just…a fling. No big deal."

"Pretend with other people, Kat, but not with me. What did he do?"

She saw the slump into defeat, the suspicious moisture in Kat's eyes, quickly masked as her sister turned away.

"Kat, sweetie, it's me. You're not telling the world at large. We have to be able to talk to each other."

"Yeah?" Kat swung around. "When did we get to be so chummy, Miss Prim and Proper? When did you forget that you think I'm just a slut?"

Mona was too shaky to defend herself, for once. Their normal thrust and parry hurt too much when she was inches from being a wreck herself. "Don't," she pleaded. "Not tonight." She caught herself just before she blurted out her secret. Fitz's voice across the room slid into her awareness. She couldn't tell anyone before him.

She reached for her sister's hand, the sibling with whom she'd been stranded at Nana's so very far away from New York. "Kat," she murmured urgently, squeezing hard. "This is me, remember? We have to stick together."

All at once, Kat's eyes filled. "Please…I just—" She blinked fiercely against the tears. "Damn it, I hate crying." She averted her face, but she held tight to Mona's hand.

Mona cast a glance toward Fitz and Armand. Fitz was intent on his call, but Armand was watching, and on his face was naked pain. In that instant, she realized that he loved her sister far past friendship. Their eyes met for one blinding second in which Mona understood that Armand had patiently loved Kat for a very long time. He would be the best thing that could happen…assuming her sister ever woke up enough to see.

Dazzled by the sudden insight, Mona tried to refocus on Kat. "What did Gamble do?"

"Oh, God, don't make me talk about it here."

"They're both busy. Tell me."

"I went to see him like some romantic fool. I knew better. I always have. Love—" Brittle laughter crackled in her throat. "Jesus Christ. There's nothing so pathetic as a fool who believes she's in love."

"Love exists, Kat. There's nothing as wonderful in the world."

Kat rounded on her. "Yeah, as though you and Fitz are so happy now."

Mona recoiled, her hand going instinctively to her belly. She jerked it away. "We'll work it out." She persisted. "So what happened?"

"He was in bed with someone else."

"Bastard."

"It gets worse." She paused a beat for effect. "He's married."

"What?" Mona goggled, just for a minute. "That snake."

Kat's triumph was only a thin film over heartbreak. "Go ahead, tell me I had it coming."

"No." She spoke again, emphatically this time. "No,

Kat. You deserve better." Her mind went back to the expression on Armand's face, and she almost said something about him.

But Fitz ended his call just then. "That's all I can do tonight." He crossed the floor. "I've got a meeting at ten. Until then, I think we could all use a little sack time."

Mona started to protest that she couldn't sleep a wink, but her body chose that moment to exert its pull. Suddenly, she was so tired she could barely keep her eyes open.

"He's right," Kat conceded. "I'm headed home. You and I can go through Tansy's room in the morning...." She laughed without real mirth, running fingers through her spiky hair. "Okay, so it's already morning. Christ..." She rubbed her hands over her face.

"Come, Katharina," Armand said. "I'll take you home."

Kat stiffened. "I'm a big girl. I don't require an escort."

"Of course not," he said, handling her as smoothly as ever. "But my driver's outside."

Her shoulders slumped. "Oh, all right." She turned to Mona. "I'll meet you at the apartment at eleven?"

Mona nodded. She and Fitz walked them to the door, exchanging handshakes and kisses. The door closed behind them, and all of a sudden, there was too much silence.

Mona was so exhausted she was seeing double. They needed to talk, she knew, but she didn't have the strength. Still, she had to be fair. He'd rushed to help her without question. She owed him—

"Stop, Des," Fitz said, a faint chuckle in his voice. "Your brain's clicking so fast it's making me dizzy."

"But we—"

He embraced her, and the feel of him sank into her bones and melted them to honey. "Shh…it's time for sleep. You're out on your feet."

Her eyelids were so heavy it would take a jack to lift them. Fitz was so warm. So strong. Just for a second, she let go. She would think in a minute; she would—

And then he swung her up and carried her to their bedroom. "Fitz…" She struggled to find the words.

"Not tonight, babe. I'm going to stay with you, and we can talk tomorrow. For now, just rest."

They were the last words she heard.

ARMAND'S DRIVER WAITED for them at the curb. Armand placed one hand on the small of Kat's back and guided her toward the door.

She thought of how she'd fallen into his arms at her apartment. "I think I'll walk."

"Don't be a fool."

She recoiled. "Don't patronize me." Then she thought of his key to her apartment and took refuge in anger, poking him in the chest. "Just where the hell do you get off, not revealing to me you own my building?" Her gaze narrowed. "You better not tell me I got some kind of special deal."

His driver watched them both, his expression as

blank as Armand's. But she saw the avid look in his eyes. Knowing she could be making fodder for the gossip columns only steamed her more.

Armand, as always, kept his cool. "You're my friend."

"Friend? You don't lie to friends about something like that." She stuck out her hand. "You give me that key right now."

"Kat," he said patiently, "I own the master." He spoke as if to a child. "There are plenty more where that one came from."

Anger and embarrassment at being so vulnerable earlier spurred rebellion. "Fine. I'm moving," she announced. "I'll start searching tomorrow."

"You can't afford anyplace else." His green eyes were maddeningly calm.

She'd had all the blows her pride could take. "I'll move to Brooklyn if I have to. No!" She shoved at the arms drawing her close. "No, damn you, let me go. Don't you dare—"

"Shut up, Kat," he said, dangerously quiet. "Just shut up."

And he kissed her. No more Beacon Hill reserve. No iron control. It was a hell of a kiss, the one she'd waited for all her life. Hot and sweet and…something more.

It scared the shit out of her how much she craved to melt into his arms, how much she wanted to forget—

She pushed away, regarding him in shock. "What about Tansy?"

"We'll get her back."

"No—you can't—we can't—" she stammered. "I mean—you and Tansy. You love her."

"Of course I love her. We all do." He stopped, brow knitting, and stared. His eyes widened suddenly, and he laughed. "You're an idiot, Katharina."

His amusement sent her temper spinning, and she slapped at the hands that would draw her back to him. Then she got a good gander at his eyes. Something deep and hungry and tender blazed there.

For *her?*

"You mean…" She swallowed, looked again. And got really scared. "Armand, no. We're friends, just friends. I can't—I need you to—"

For a second, she thought she spotted pain, sharp and stunning. Then, just as quickly as it flared, the blaze was snuffed, doors slammed shut. Armand addressed his driver, his voice very calm and neutral. Too neutral. "We'll drop Ms. Gerard off on our way, Slater."

"Very good, sir."

Armand held the door open. "Climb in."

"Armand, I don't…" Stumbling around in a world gone topsy-turvy, she had no choice what to say. "I'm sorry. I didn't—"

"Just get in the car, Katharina. Now."

She wanted to battle; she was more than ready for a

fight. Anything to clear the air that had somehow become threatening. She tried to gauge his mood, but his face was as smooth and blank as glass.

Too much was changing. At once, she was as drained as she'd ever been. She said nothing, only slid into the seat.

On the drive, Armand was silent, reserve wrapping him in an impenetrable wall. She brushed her lips with one hand, remembering. *The lady is not available to return my affections.* She started to speak several times but finally gave up.

When they reached her place, she grabbed for the door handle on her side.

Armand spoke in clipped tones, barely glancing her way. "Good night, Katharina." But in his voice, she heard goodbye.

"I don't know what you want from me."

He spared her one merciless glance. For the briefest second, she thought she saw pain hover, but in the faint light, she couldn't be sure. "I'm through wanting anything from you." He continued past her stammer of protest. "I'll do everything in my power to help Tansy. Otherwise, perhaps you'll do me the favor of leaving me alone for a while."

"But…" She realized all too quickly that the stab of fear in her chest was coming from the finality in his tone, the death knell of the friendship that she'd taken so much for granted. "Armand, why are you doing this?

Can't we just go on the way we were? I don't want things to change."

"A pity. But you see, you're not the only one who wants things." Lines appeared around his mouth. He focused on her, his face set and grim. "I'm only a man, damn it. A man who…" He looked away. "Never mind. Good night."

"Armand, please don't leave. I need you. Maybe I do love you—"

He grabbed her wrist and squeezed. Fury rose, swift and hot. "Don't you dare say it," he commanded, fierce and low. "Don't you throw those words around simply because you're hurting and scared."

She was shocked by the violence in his gaze.

Armand stared at his hand on her wrist and thrust it from him. He scrubbed one palm over his face. "Get out, before we destroy what's left."

"Armand…" She touched his arm, but he recoiled. Her hand hovered in the air. "You're my best friend, don't you get that? That's worth everything."

"We could have so much more—did that ever occur to you?" His eyes blazed again, then the flame guttered. His jaw tightened. "Forget it."

Her world was crumbling, and she'd never been this frightened. Armand had been there for so long. She'd thought he always would be. Before her opened a chasm. She pictured life without Armand in it, and she sensed how deeply he was woven into what was best about it.

She wanted to argue, to talk this through, to find her place in a universe that had just shifted under her feet.

She couldn't lose him.

But she could tell that words were futile now. Kat scooted toward the door Slater held open, but she stopped at the edge of the seat. "Armand…"

He leaned his head against the seat and sighed. "Go away, Kat. Just forget this."

"I won't." One betraying quiver bled through. "There are many things in life that I don't give a damn about." She ducked to leave, but turned and leaned toward him first. "You're not one of them."

He didn't move, didn't spare her so much as a glance. Sobered by his resolve, she understood now exactly how Scarlett must have felt when she let the best part of her life walk away. "Armand, I want…"

Her voice trailed off as she heard herself, as she viewed the situation, for the first time, from his perspective. It had always been about her wishes, and he'd been strong enough, had cared enough, to give her that. "I'm sorry," she said in a small voice.

"You're always sorry." He sounded so weary. "Just go, Kat. We must focus on Tansy now." He signaled his driver to start on their way.

Slater tipped his hat to her as he closed the door, his eyes sympathetic. "Good night, Ms. Gerard."

"Good night, Slater." Kat headed toward her door, her knees unsteady, but no way would she let him see her cry. She'd shed too many tears already. It was time to sleep…and then to plan. She would fix this. She could give Katie Scarlett O'Hara a run for her money when it came to determination.

And she would. Somehow.

LUCAS STIRRED HOURS LATER on his pallet on the floor, his glance going immediately to the narrow bed he'd turned over to Tansy in the instant before it registered on him that he wasn't alone.

Bright hair spilled over his shirtfront and a slender arm encased in pale-blue wool crossed his chest. He had no idea when Tansy had left the bed and joined him on the cold concrete floor. He must have been dead asleep not to sense her, but he did now, and his body shot to instant awareness. Hunger, fiery and insistent, flashed through him at the feel of her in his arms.

He had to get away from her. Now. He needed her too much, the cravings a man's, raw and savage. Too powerful for the child-woman in his arms. He tried to ease away, but she only snuggled closer, sighing softly in her sleep.

Lucas closed his eyes and beat back the thunder in his veins. This was Tansy, innocent, damaged Tansy. She wasn't ready. Might not ever be. And he wanted to protect her, even from himself.

But, God, she was sweet and warm and soft. He could still taste her on his lips, even that one chaste kiss.

Last night's tender, magical spell shattered under the force of his body's longing to make her his, to bind her to him forever. The flesh was weak, so damn weak when combined with a lifetime of dreaming.

With care and gritted teeth, he removed himself from beneath her, then picked her up and put her back in the bed, smoothing her skirt down the legs of a full-grown woman, curvier and longer than her height would suggest. Swallowing hard, he covered her with a blanket and turned to go.

"Michael?" she said, sleep heavy in her voice. "Don't leave me."

His hands clenched into fists and he studied the ceiling. Inhaling sharply, he forced his voice to neutral. "I'm going to fix us something to eat. I'll be right up the stairs. Stay here and sleep." *Please.* He had to have a few minutes to wrestle the demon back under control. God.

She murmured and drifted off again.

Lucas headed for the steps, gratefully putting distance between them and cursing his body's inability to care that her mind was not as grown-up as her figure.

Nearly noon, he noticed as he pulled out pans and began breakfast while assembling the beginnings of a thick, hearty soup. He shivered a little in the chill air and knew that spring had decided to delay another day.

"Mornin'," Al boomed.

Lucas almost jumped out of his skin, so wrapped up in worrying over Tansy that he'd completely missed the sound of the door. "Hey, Al," he said over his shoulder. "Ready for something to eat?"

"I'd always rather have one of your breakfasts than my poor-ass excuse for cookin'."

"Have a seat. Coffee should be perked."

He expected Al to approach on his right to get a cup, but Lucas was too busy tending bacon to see what was holding him up.

And then he knew.

"Good morning," Tansy said shyly.

Lucas turned and spotted Al staring at Tansy as though she were some sort of apparition.

"Mornin', pretty lady. Name's Al."

Tansy smiled and held out her hand. "I'm Tansy."

"Al…" Lucas began, attempting to figure out how to explain with Tansy present. "I have to talk to you—"

"Not now, son. Don't want to talk to you when there's a beautiful lady here. I can jaw with you anytime." With the moves of a practiced courtier, big, beefy Al settled the fairy sprite Tansy at the table like visiting royalty, on his face wonder as though he'd just found a diamond on the sidewalk.

And Tansy was regarding Al with the same gentle cheer she gave to everyone. "My prince brought me here. Do you live here, too?"

Al shot him an expression loaded with mischief. "Your prince, eh?" He shook his head. "He's a good fella, but I ain't sure about no prince."

"He is," Tansy said soberly. "He rescued me."

"Why—"

Lucas broke in. "Here's your eggs, Al." He sought to warn him with a look.

Al nodded, then indicated Tansy. "Can't eat before the lady."

"Hers are next. Scrambled, fried or omelet, Tansy?"

"You can cook, Michael?"

Al frowned at the name, shot him a questioning glance from behind her.

Lucas shook his head quickly before answering her. "That's how I earn my living now."

Al shrugged. "He's a good cook."

"Would you teach me? Nana showed me a little, but Mrs. Hodgson doesn't like anyone in her kitchen."

You won't be here long enough, he wanted to say. But he couldn't get into that now. "Sure. Come over here and I'll demonstrate. What kind of eggs?"

"Is an omelet too hard?"

"Not a bit." He busied himself dicing onions and grating cheese. Tansy asked to grate some, so he let her while he whisked the eggs. When she gouged her knuckles, he grasped her hand and drew her to the sink to run cold water over them, struggling to ignore the feel of her hands. With practiced moves, he opened a box and bandaged the small scrape on one knuckle, resisting the urge to kiss it, aware all the time of Al's perusal.

Finally, their food was done. Al had almost finished

his plate but poured a second cup of coffee as they sat and talked. Tansy was full of questions once she realized Al was the owner, and Lucas winced more than once at the contrast of her naiveté and their surroundings.

Al cast odd looks at him again and again, but there was nothing Lucas could explain right now. Soon, the talk moved to Tansy's friends in the park, and she proved such a dead-on mimic that she had them all laughing. He'd forgotten that, her gift for mimicry, for distilling the essence of another's movements or expressions or accent.

And for a golden span of time, Tansy transformed the dreary kitchen of a third-rate topless joint into a table of friendship and foolishness, a magic circle of belonging and community that spanned race and age and background and made them an odd sort of family. Al's face glowed, his loneliness dispersed to the winds. The emptiness inside Lucas gave way to a feeling that was almost like hope.

Then the beer man showed up, and illusion shattered under the harsh light of the real world. Al left to check in the delivery, and Lucas gathered up dishes to wash them.

"May I?" Tansy asked.

"No," he said automatically, revolted at the thought of her working in this dingy place. Ready to send her back down to the basement, he noted disappointment in her eyes. "You serious?"

She nodded. "You made my breakfast. Please let me help."

"But it's..." *Dirty. Beneath you. You don't belong here.* He noted the stubborn tilt of her chin, a reminder of a headstrong young girl. "Okay. Thanks."

He got the stew going while she washed dishes and asked him a million questions about what he was doing. He let her cut up potatoes and carrots, observing graceful fingers that could make birds out of eggshells and lost feathers carve perfectly precise cubes.

With every spice he added, she wanted to sniff and taste, and he thought he'd lose his mind watching her lick her fingers, close her eyes and run her tongue over her lips. But as much as he burned for her, he yearned for her spirit more. She was a balm on his heart, a cool palm against a fevered brow, a refuge from what years of ugliness and violence had done to his soul.

So Lucas shoved away the man and became a boy again with Tansy. They played and laughed and fought with soap bubbles. Al finished with the deliveryman and rejoined them until Tansy excused herself to go change her clothes, breathless and laughing and half-soaked.

Then dark eyes sobered. "What you doin', son?" Al asked.

It was icy water dashed in his face. "I'll find someplace else to take her."

Al waved that off. "That's not what I'm askin' you. She can stay here forever, far as I'm concerned. This place ain't never held her kind of happiness." His gaze narrowed. "And you, boy. You need what she got to give you."

Lucas shook his head. "I can't…" He glanced away, tamping down all the feelings that had run riot, then looked back up. "She's in danger, Al. I had to get her away, but I don't know what the hell to do. I have to protect her."

"Cops can't help, huh?"

"No. The man who's after her can pull strings like you never saw." Lucas ground his teeth as he thought of Sanford. "I've got some stuff on him, but not enough. I need help, but I don't have anyone to trust. I was hoping to do it without involving her, but it's too late for that now." He studied the man who'd been the only one to offer him a chance. "They're after us, Al. I think I got her away without being followed, but they'll be crawling over this city with a fine-tooth comb, searching for her."

"Ain't been nothin' in the news."

Lucas breathed a little easier. "I can't count on that lasting. Her father's famous. Martin Gerard, the Shakespearean actor—heard of him?"

Al seemed only slightly offended. "Might not be no theater hound, but I read the papers. So how you get involved with her?"

Here goes nothing. "The man I went to jail for killing?"

Al frowned, nodding for him to continue.

"He was her twin brother."

Al's eyes rounded. A slow whistle escaped. "What the fuck you doin', boy?"

"I didn't do it, Al. But it's a long story." Lucas waited

for a response. When he got none, his heart sank. "You don't have to believe me, but I'd appreciate it if you'd let me stay on until I can find a secure place for her."

"What I think don't matter. Does she believe you?"

"She doesn't remember it. She thinks he's still alive. She's…she's sort of frozen in time back then."

"That why she callin' you by another name?"

"It's my middle name. She's the only one who used it. But she doesn't realize it's me—she says the name makes her feel safe."

"Jesus on a rocketship, Lucas, you don't like things simple, do you?" Al paced, muttering.

Lucas's hopes plunged. "If I could have my check, even though it's not Friday, I'll clear out my things today. I'd wait, but I'll have to have the money to get her a room somewhere."

"You ain't takin' that sweet child anywhere until we sure what's what. She got to stay out of sight while folks is here, and you got to get your young ass busy finding some help for her. But don't be talkin' about takin' her out on the streets till Al says so, hear me?"

"But you have no idea what he's capable of."

"I don't, you right. But I understand that girl is somethin' special, the likes of which you and me never met. You got to protect them that's God's special ones. None of us certain where angels hide, and me, I ain't a smart man, but even I can tell that that little girl is one of the good Lord's gifts to the rest of us sorry sumbitches." He poked a finger at Lucas. "So you get to work on findin' her some help, and I'll share watch over her until it's safe. Can you convince her to stay down there, real quiet like, while we're open?"

Relief surged. "Yes."

"All right." He turned away.

"Al…"

The older man glanced back. "What?"

Lucas cleared his suddenly crowded throat. "Thanks. I owe you."

Dark eyes bored into his. "That angel girl figures you for her prince. Don't you disappoint her."

Lucas shoved aside his doubts. "I won't. I failed her once, but I swear I won't, not ever again."

Al nodded and went back to work.

MONA TRIED TO MOVE LIMBS heavy with sleep, but they remained pinned beneath the weight of slumber. She didn't want to wake up, anyway. She was having the best dream…Fitz's big body curled around hers, one arm tucking her into his belly. She sighed softly and let herself drift.

"Des?" She thought she heard Fitz, his voice husky with morning. She opened one eye, then blinked. It was him, perched on the edge of the bed, his hip against hers, his hair wet, his face still marked with a crease from the sheets.

"Babe, we overslept, and I've got to leave now to

meet Detective Tucker." He proffered the crooked grin she'd missed so much, but his eyes looked worried.

Tansy. "Oh, no—" Mona bolted up straight, shoving her fingers through her hair. "What time is it? I've got to—"

"Easy." Fitz chuckled. "Almost ten now. Here—I made coffee."

"I can't—" *Drink caffeine,* she started to say, but he was already rising to his feet. "Thanks."

He donned his bomber jacket, his eyes somber. "I'd like to come back tonight." He paused, and she saw real regret. "I wish I could make you understand what that experience taught me, but I also know I pushed you too hard, Des. Nothing means a thing without you. If you don't want kids—" His cell phone rang, and he cursed ripely. "I'm sorry. I'd better take this, in case it's about Tansy. Fitzgerald," he snapped.

He listened for several seconds. "Hold on to it. Don't let it out of your sight. I'll be right there."

"What is it?"

He didn't respond for a moment, and her heart seized. "Is it Tansy? Has she been found? Oh, God—"

Fitz shook his head, slid his hand over her hair. "No. It's a package for me, delivered to the paper just moments ago."

"Who's it from?"

"Lucas Walker."

Mona blinked. Then her mind started racing. She

jumped from the bed, headed for the shower. "I'm coming with you."

"You're supposed to meet Kat in an hour."

"Fitz, I have to—"

"Des, think about it. The clock is ticking. We don't have much time to find her. Every second counts." He raked fingers through his shaggy hair. "It's not as if we have an excess of help. It's more effective to split up and hit on two fronts. We need to discover if there are any clues in Tansy's room, too." He sighed. "But you can come if you want."

"No, you're right. I just…"

"I understand. I promise I'll call you the second I've read it." He crossed to her, pulled her close. "I love her, too, Des."

Mona sank against him. "I know."

"You're not alone, honey."

She turned her head up to his. "Thank you." She gazed into his eyes, finding the man she'd loved for so long waiting there, and she wished she could share her news now. "Come back soon, Fitz," she urged. "We need to talk."

"I will, babe. I love you."

"I love you, too."

Fitz lowered his mouth to hers in a kiss of unbearable sweetness, then he left.

Mona watched the door close and leaned her forehead against it, her hand resting over Fitz's child.

CHAPTER EIGHTEEN

WHEN FITZ CALLED LATER, Mona and Kat had already been through much of Tansy's room. "Found anything?" he asked.

"Nothing. What about you?" Mona replied.

Kat moved closer, chewing on a fingernail.

"How much background do you have on Sanford, Des?" he asked.

"Not that much, just that Daddy trusts him completely. Why?"

"Walker has assembled some pretty interesting stuff here. I'll check with other sources, but he's found a pattern that doesn't fit too well with Sanford's reputation as a patron of the arts and doer of good deeds."

"What does that have to do with Tansy?"

"Walker says he never raped Tansy, that it was Sanford who did it."

"What? That's absurd—"

"He says he and Paris were going to a movie that

night and Tansy was supposed to be with your dad, but at the last minute plans got changed. Lucas says he had a bad feeling about her being there alone with Sanford and convinced Paris to go back. Sanford offered them the same drugged wine he'd given Tansy. The two boys passed out, and the next thing Lucas knows, Tansy's screaming and Sanford is on top of her."

"That's ridiculous. Carlton may be a pompous jerk, but he would never—"

"Why would Walker lie about it now?"

"He was never charged with her rape. Maybe he's afraid of going to jail for it now."

"Can't happen. Statute of limitations has passed."

"I don't care. If he'd murder Paris, why should we believe he wouldn't rape Tansy?"

"He says the shooting was an accident. Paris jumped at Sanford just when Walker fired the gun."

"Why didn't he tell anyone if it was true? Why would he plead guilty if it was an accident?"

"I have no idea." They were both silent for a moment.

"What's he saying?" Kat demanded. She stopped her restless pacing and stared at her sister.

When Mona filled her in. Kat just snorted. "The bastard's lying."

Fitz overheard. "What's the motivation?"

Mona couldn't answer that. "But why would he let them put him in jail if what he says is true? Wouldn't they have charged him with less than murder?"

"Yeah, probably. He sure wouldn't have served so much time."

"This makes no sense, Fitz. Why would he go to jail for twenty years for something he didn't do?"

"I can't tell you. He says in his note that he took Tansy last night to keep Sanford away from her. Says he'll bring her home if we convince him that Sanford will never get his hands on her."

"I just can't imagine…" But as Mona relayed the rest to Kat, her mind was racing, recollecting how Tansy had never liked being around Carlton. "She always acted afraid of him, but we all assumed it was because she was afraid to remember that night."

Kat shook her head violently. "You're not buying this, Mona, surely."

"Think about it, Kat. Carlton doesn't want us to call the police—why?"

"He said—"

"Forget what he said—but why, after all these years, did he get so insistent about moving Tansy in with him? It was only recently, when Walker was nearing the end of his sentence, that Carlton started talking to Daddy about it again. What if—"

"It's ridiculous, Mona. I mean, I can't stand the guy, but look at who we're talking about. Mr. Philanthropy."

Mona was holding the receiver so Fitz could hear, too. He spoke up. "Which is exactly the reason I need to dig into this. If Walker's right, Sanford has a whole lot to lose. That ambassadorship would go right down the drain. It's the word of an ex-con against a pillar of society at the moment, but if Walker can somehow trigger Tansy's memory of that night, and she agrees with him, Sanford would be ruined."

"You said there was other information. What kind?"

"Walker's done a lot of research on Sanford. Some of the companies he owns would be great for laundering money. Anybody ever figure out what Sanford does to get the funds he throws around so freely?"

"Maybe Daddy has. I never paid any attention."

"There's something else. Walker included a copy of an old newspaper photo of Sanford and your mother. I'll check the dates, but I think this was taken before your parents ever met."

"That could be. He introduced them. Why is that important?"

"The look he's giving her in the photo isn't that of a man who'd want to share her with your father."

"What are you saying, Fitz?" But Mona couldn't quit thinking about Carlton's expression when she'd caught him with her mother's photograph. And he'd said he'd intended to marry her, but…

"I'm not sure what to make of it. The pieces don't all fit."

"Why would Lucas send it to you? What's he after? No ransom note, just clippings?"

"He says he can't trust your father to guard Tansy,

that he didn't protect her from Sanford before and he won't now. All Walker seems to want is to convince us that Sanford isn't who we think, and that she's in danger from him. Walker demands assurance that she'll be protected from Sanford, permanently."

"That's easy enough," Mona said, consulting her sister, who was listening in and nodded vigorously. "I told Tansy we wouldn't let Daddy send her away. Why didn't she believe us?" But in her mind, she kept hearing Tansy say, *he makes me feel safe*. "What if…" She shook her head. "No way."

"What, Des?"

"If he really did defend her once, maybe that's why she says she feels safe with him now."

"But if she recalls that, why doesn't she remember that he killed Paris?" Kat demanded.

"I can't begin to guess. We have to talk to Tansy. Fitz, tell him to bring her back."

"I can't. I don't have any means to contact him. He says he'll call me."

"When?"

"I have no idea."

"And meanwhile, Tansy's his prisoner."

"Maybe not, Des. Maybe he really is only interested in protecting her."

"We need to confront Carlton with this."

"Not a good idea, babe. If any of this is true, Sanford is not someone you should mess with unless you have ammunition. If he's laundering money, God knows who he's in bed with. You think he's going to simply confess?"

"So what do we do?"

"I talk to Detective Tucker, fill him in. And let's hope to God Walker calls soon. Meanwhile, we figure out how to find him."

THE PHONE WAS ANSWERED on the second ring. "Fitzgerald."

For an instant, Lucas froze. This was the whole ball game—this call and his ability to convince this man.

"Hello? Anyone there?"

"It's Lucas Walker."

"Hold on—just a second. Let me—"

"Forget attempting to trace this." Lucas fought his temper. "Don't you care that I'm trying to help Tansy?"

"Are you?"

His spirits sank. "You don't believe what I sent."

A long sigh. "I don't have a clue what to believe. It doesn't make sense. Why would you go to jail for twenty years when you didn't have to? Why didn't you tell anyone, if that's what really happened?"

Lucas watched the seconds tick away. "I—it would require too long to explain." He exhaled in a gust, exhaustion overtaking him. "All I want is for her to be safe."

"She was safe at Martin's."

"Her father left her in Sanford's hands before. He can't be trusted."

"Then bring her to me."

"I can't do that, not until I'm sure Sanford's not a threat. Will you help me put him away?"

"I—it's complicated, Walker. It's not up to me."

Despair weighed him down. "Forget it, then. I was hoping her sisters or you would be concerned enough to listen. I've got to figure out something else—"

"Don't hang up! Walker, we do care—don't—"

"She's in danger. I can't risk it." Lucas raked his fingers through his hair. "Goddamn it, don't any of you pay attention to her? She was supposed to get help—the bastard promised. Why didn't anyone help her? I thought it was over…" He exhaled in a gust. "Goodbye."

"Walker—wait. Here's my cell phone number. Call me back, please. I'll meet you. You name the place. Please…tell Tansy we love her."

"I love her, too," Lucas whispered, weary to the bone. "I'll tell her," he said louder.

Then he hung up. His head sagged in defeat, coming to rest against the hand still gripping the receiver.

LATE THAT NIGHT, Lucas trudged toward the stairs after he'd closed down the kitchen, his steps heavy with the weight of his failure to convince Fitzgerald. The police would be searching for them. He couldn't imagine why Tansy's disappearance hadn't hit the news yet.

No matter; he couldn't hide her for long. Locked up in the basement, she'd wither and die. Already, he could tell the toll on her. She'd sent a message through Al when Lucas had returned from his call, asking to be left alone. He hadn't seen her since early afternoon, isolated in that dingy basement room. Surely a creature of air and light such as she would be withering by now, robbed of everything familiar.

But he couldn't abandon her, didn't trust taking her back. He could see no solution but to run with her, but would she leave the island? What would it do to her to leave Paris behind? How would she hold up to the pressures of being poor and away from everything familiar?

If only someone would listen. Her father wouldn't— he'd as soon see Lucas dead. Her sisters were mysteries—he'd known them only briefly before they'd been sent to Texas. Kat had been too young to notice, Mona too prim. He hadn't been concerned with them back then.

He was now. Extremely. Even if he'd never promised Juliette, he would still feel responsible for Tansy.

Maybe he'd try Fitzgerald one more time…. But the most convincing argument was one he would never use.

Just then, the basement came into view and his breath caught. He'd have seen the glow from the top of the stairs if he hadn't been so distracted.

Lucas stopped on the bottom step. And gazed in wonder. He'd thought she was despondent and needed time alone.

Instead, she'd created magic.

She'd made her hours alone count. On a crude and

ugly basement, Tansy had cast a spell. Butcher paper wrapped the walls, covering the bare concrete. On it, she'd painted a mural, a prince rescuing a fair maiden. The maiden resembled her.

The prince looked like him.

Trees and vines and flowers spilled forth in brilliant watercolors. Bees buzzed. Birds flew. Butterflies danced.

Lucas turned in a circle, trying to take it all in, shaking his head and smiling.

Smiling. After a day of abject failure.

"Tansy," he said, seeking her out. "You're amazing."

Her face was the most beautiful thing of all. "Al got me the paper and paints and candles." Stuck in everything from cans to buckets, candles cast a golden glow from every corner. "You really like it?" Her expression was shy.

His heart too full to speak, Lucas only nodded. He crossed to where she stood, perhaps lost in mists but still the most powerful force in his lonely world. She'd always been bigger than her size in impact. Always been unlike anyone he'd ever known.

Maybe her mischief had become something more gentle. So she shied from memory and sought oblivion—it didn't matter. The power that lived within her shone bright.

And with it, she brought beauty into the lives of every soul she met.

"It's stunning."

Tansy whirled and clapped, her face alight, then held out her hands. "Dance with me."

"I don't… I can't—" He'd never even attended a school dance. And prisoners didn't waltz.

"Come on, anyone can do it." She put his right hand on her hip, clasped the left one in her right. Placing her other arm on his shoulder, she slid into a step. "Follow me. One, two, three…one, two, three…" In a lilting voice, she began to hum.

"Tansy, I…"

But her lips parted in a smile and her eyes were filled with hope, so Lucas did his best to follow, grateful that they had no audience.

Her steps were light and graceful. Beside her, he felt a lumbering oaf. But Tansy was happy, and he'd do much more than this for her. Sooner than he would have believed, he was circling the room in something resembling a dance.

"It's like Cinderella," she said, eyes twinkling with mischief.

"Except I'm the one who'll be in rags at midnight."

Tansy laughed, and his heart lightened. For a span of time, there was no world outside. No danger, no threats, only Tansy's song…and blue eyes locked on his. He'd sell his soul to freeze time forever.

Then she stopped, slid her arms around his neck—

And kissed him.

So soft. So sweet. Lucas's heart stuttered. He held her close and slanted his mouth to deepen the kiss.

Tansy sighed against his lips, slipping her hands into his hair. Everything in him cried out to hold tight and never let go.

With enormous effort, he forced his hands loose and retreated.

Tansy protested, her grip surprisingly strong. Her head lolled back, eyes closed, exposing her long white throat. He could see the pulse beating beneath her jaw. Reverently, he placed a kiss at the tender, vulnerable spot where her life force flowed. Tansy moaned in pleasure and wriggled closer.

Ah, God, he wanted. Craved to the point of madness. "Tansy," he groaned.

She burrowed against him, every curve of her body pressed against his length. He attempted to resist, to let her go. She didn't know, couldn't know…

Kiss after kiss she tenderly brushed against his jaw, exquisite gentleness healing the wounded places inside him. Between kisses, she murmured his name as though it were a benediction and not a shame.

Lucas stood there, arms by his sides, quivering. Trembling with the force of his need for her love, struggling to hold back from grabbing what he wanted most in life. What he'd dreamed of since he was fifteen years old. What he'd long ago sacrificed.

When she kissed the scar on his face, and he tasted her tears…

He broke. Just broke. Years of loneliness, eons of sorrow burst like a dam under pressure. Lucas embraced Tansy as though she were salvation, every touch of her hands, of her lips, a blessing, a mended tear in the ragged edges he'd held together by force of will alone.

He sank to the floor with her in his arms, head bowed as he clung to all the goodness that was left in his life. She was the shining beacon, the morning star, the welcoming fire at the end of the road.

I'm sorry, I'm sorry, I'm sorry, his heart cried as his memory burned with images of terrified eyes, of pale limbs shuddering against brutal thrusts. He hadn't saved her. He hadn't been strong enough, old enough, smart enough. Grief for her lost innocence ravaged his heart. Twenty years was not penance enough.

Long-held tears leaked down his cheeks, burning like acid. He averted his face in shame.

Tansy clasped his head and kissed them away. Lucas rocked mournfully, holding her close. Closer. Everything he valued in the world was here in his arms. In the flickering candlelight, he made a vow from the depths of his soul.

"I'll keep you safe, Tansy." *If it costs me my life.*

"I know you will." Blue eyes shone with perfect trust. *You don't know that. You can't. But I will. I promise.*

Tansy stared at him solemnly, then rose to her knees and melted against him, her lips opening over his, her tongue tracing the crease of his lips, artless and tentative and more devastating than the most practiced kiss.

He couldn't stop his fingers from tightening in reflex as desire roared through him.

"Please," she murmured. "I want…"

Oh, God. He couldn't do this. She didn't understand—

He had to think. Swiftly, he disentangled them, then backed away.

Hurt blue eyes studied his. "You didn't like it? I didn't do it right?"

He knelt before her, clasping her hands, smoothing her hair. "Shh…no. You did it right, sweetheart. Perfect…" He fought to calm his racing heart. He cupped her jaw. "So perfect."

"Then why…?"

Why indeed? When his body raged with the need of her, when the dream of years long-standing was here in his grasp, why didn't he take it?

Because it was some misguided idea of a prince she was kissing, not him. Not Lucas Walker.

And because he was bone-deep afraid. What memories might be released when bodies met? What horrors unshackled? What if touching her destroyed her defense against recollections of that night? She might not survive it.

He settled for a version of the truth. "It's been a long day. I'm very tired."

Instant sympathy shoved past confusion and hurt. "I'm sorry. I didn't consider—"

He kissed the delicate fingers, looking around the

room once more. "You created magic here, Tansy." His gaze met hers. "You have a gift."

Long lashes swept down, her mouth curving in a shy, proud smile.

Swinging her into his arms, he stood and crossed to the small bed, laid her down carefully, then turned to walk away. "It's time to sleep."

She grasped his hand. "Don't go."

Lucas studied her for a long time, then finally nodded. To lie with her when his body craved so much more would be agony, but he would do it, just until she slept. He owed her that and more. Endless more. Circling the room, he blew out the candles. Tansy watched him every step of the way, blue eyes refusing to let go. Finally, he returned to her side and stopped. Holding out her arms, she scooted against the wall.

Lucas took off his shoes and lay down beside her, trying not to touch. Crawling half over him in innocent trust, she slid her fingers through his hair. The feel of her slim hands on his scalp was both blessing and curse. The scent of her…the feel of her slender curves… Lucas stifled a groan.

Tansy grasped a lock of his hair and wrapped it around the fingers of her left hand. Snuggling closer than air, she sighed softly…

And slid into slumber.

For a time, Lucas suffered the sweet ache of desire unspent, but oh, how good she felt against him…. He picked her up and resettled her over the length of his body. In slumber she wiggled until hardness found shelter against softness, and Lucas thought he'd die.

Then she sighed again, her breath warm on his throat, and sprawled across him, boneless in trust.

Lucas lay there, stone hard, sweat breaking out on his forehead.

And fought the urge to smile, anyway. He'd found another piece of the girl he'd once known.

Lost in the mists though she might be, at her mischievous best, Tansy couldn't have devised a better torture.

CHAPTER NINETEEN

"LUKE—PSST, LUKE—" Al called quietly from the stairs.

Lucas stirred against the weight on his chest, fought his way through the fog. Turning toward the stairs, he frowned at Al but nodded acknowledgment.

Then he realized the picture they made. Tansy still had his hair in her hand as though afraid he'd vanish. She wiggled against him in sleep, and he winced. He'd been rock hard for hours and now his bladder was about to burst. Carefully, he slipped her onto the sheets, then gently disentangled his hair from her grasp.

She muttered in her sleep and frowned. He bestowed one kiss to her nose, then rolled to get up.

"Don't go," she murmured.

"Sleep," he whispered. "I'll be back."

She smiled then and curled up. Tenderly, he covered her and tiptoed across the floor, glancing around the room at the mural and smiling.

When he saw the concern on Al's face, the smile vanished. "What is it?"

Al shook his head, nodding toward Tansy. "Upstairs."

Lucas grabbed his shoes and followed, unease prickling. At the top of the steps, he stopped. "Talk to me."

"Trouble, boy. Trouble's here."

"What do you mean?"

"People asking around about you and the girl. The wrong kind of people."

Lucas frowned. "I don't understand."

"Your man, the one you're hidin' that girl from? He dangerous in ways you don't know. If he connected to these boys, it ain't the police you got to worry about, nossir."

"Tell me what you've heard."

"Talk is that there's a price on your head. Stiff one. Don't matter if you found dead or alive, though. The girl's to be taken unharmed if possible."

"If possible?"

Al clucked his tongue. "You done pissed off the wrong shark, son. Tell me how you got crossways with this fella."

He shook his head. "No time now. I've got to move, and fast." He studied Al. "You don't have a reason in the world to trust me, but I need to borrow enough money to leave the city today. I swear on Tansy's head that I'll pay you back."

Al waved him off. "I know you will."

Gratitude warred with worry. "I don't want to involve you anymore. There's no telling what he'd do if he found out you were helping us." One thought occurred to him. "Can I leave her here with you for a little while? I have to make one call and gather a few supplies. I'll be back in two hours, max, then we'll get out of here."

Al gripped his shoulder. "I got me a pistol in the office. Nobody's taking that girl while you gone."

Lucas looked Al straight in the eye. "I don't know how to repay you."

"Just keep that angel safe, boy. And keep yourself alive."

Lucas nodded, his mind racing ahead to all he must accomplish before they left. If his call was successful, maybe Tansy could come back to New York soon.

But he never would. Last night's dreams were just that, vanished under the glare of daylight. There was no future for him with Tansy, never had been. He would get her away safely, but as soon as Sanford was no longer a threat, he'd bring her back to the loving arms of her family, to the life she deserved, not the pitiful excuse for one he could give her.

He followed Al to the office and left his dreams sleeping in the basement.

EXHAUSTED AFTER TRYING to reason with her father, Mona slumped on the sofa. He'd never sounded so weak or confused, but he insisted that the bimbo was taking good care of him. It was useless to argue with his faith in Carlton. Between her father and the nausea that had

come to signal mornings for her, what she craved was
a return to bed, to bury her worries beneath the covers
and welcome a few hours of oblivion.

But she couldn't rest now, not when Tansy was still
missing. She heard Fitz's cell phone ringing. Normally, she wouldn't answer, but he was in the shower. What
if it was Walker?

Her hand hesitated over it. Voice mail would pick it
up, but would Walker leave a message? She made the
grab. "Hello?"

"Where's Fitzgerald?" The voice was rough and angry.

"He can't come to the phone right now."

She heard a low curse. "Tell him to call them off,
damn it."

"Call who off?"

"The goon squad. Make Sanford call them off."

Her heart thudded. "You're Lucas Walker."

"Who are you?"

"Mona Gerard. Tansy's—"

"Sister. She's not hurt. She's doing fine."

Damn him for sounding reasonable. "Listen to me,"
she pleaded. "Just bring her back. If it's Carlton you're
concerned about, I won't let him have her, I promise.
She's my family, not his."

"You Gerards think he walks on water."

"Not this Gerard."

"Do you believe me, then?" There was an oddly wistful note in that rugged voice.

"I don't know."

He exhaled in a gust. "Forget it. I'm taking her away where he can't find her, before it's too late. I don't have any choice now."

"What do you mean?"

"Your net won't catch us. I won't let it."

"What net?"

"I wondered why it hadn't been in the news. Should have realized Sanford would go for a hit squad."

"What?" Horror froze her throat. "What are you saying?"

"You expect me to believe you don't know?" His tone was pure contempt. "It shouldn't surprise me. It was your family who let him have her in the first place."

"Tell me what you mean."

"Word's out on the street, a reward if they find us. Me, dead or alive—no sweat, I can take that. But when he starts threatening Tansy…"

"Carlton wouldn't do that." Would he? "He intends to marry her."

"So he can control her—so he can have her at his mercy. You'd let her go through that again? To be an ambassador, he has to keep his reputation lily-white. I'm a threat to that, and if she ever remembers that night, she's a threat, too. That's why I have to go."

"So why didn't you ever tell anyone? And if he raped her, why did you kill Paris?"

His voice went cold and hard. "Paris's death was an accident."

"So why did you plead guilty?"

"Because…" His breath escaped in a huff. "It doesn't matter anymore. All that's important is Tansy and getting her away where she's safe."

"No, please, you can't. She's not—she can't make it out there."

"I didn't want to do this, but he forced me." Anguish laced his tone. "We had a bargain, but he broke his end. Now I'm breaking mine. I can't risk letting him near her, ever again." Lucas Walker's tone went hard. "Why didn't you get her help? Who let her slip away? I was a fool to believe him when he promised to take care of her, but what's your excuse?"

"Daddy and Carlton had her seen by specialists…." Mona stopped, wondering why she was defending her father from accusations she'd leveled herself.

"Your mother would never forgive this."

"Don't you talk about my mother," she snapped. "You were her biggest mistake."

"You think I don't know that?" The bitter defeat in his laugh surprised her. "Tansy tries to make me into some kind of prince, no matter what I tell her. I couldn't save her before, and I'm not sure I can now."

"So bring her to me. Please, Walker."

Sorrow bled through his tone. "I'll do that—just as soon as your husband exposes Sanford so he isn't a threat."

"I can handle Carlton," she said.

The chuckle was soft and sad. "I thought that once, too. Goodbye, Ms. Gerard."

"Walker, wait, I'll make sure—"

But she was too late. He was already gone.

ARMAND OPENED MONA'S DOOR, and Kat dropped her gaze, unsure what to say to him now. She'd lost her footing in their old relationship and hadn't yet figured out her new plan.

"Good morning, Katharina." He lifted her chin with one finger. "You didn't sleep." Concerned green eyes studied her. He was almost the old Armand—except for the dark wariness shadowing his gaze.

Shame made her awkward. Gingerly, she sought a safe path. "I just keep thinking about how scared Tansy must be."

"We'll find her." He squeezed her shoulder, and Kat felt a powerful temptation to burrow into his chest.

But he'd already turned away. Still out of breath from running up the stairs instead of waiting for the elevator, she faced her sister. "I came as soon as I could. Has he called back?"

Mona shook her head, dark circles under her eyes stark against the too-pale skin. She twisted her fingers together and paced, glancing over at Fitz watching some other man conferring on a cell phone.

"Who is he?"

"That's Detective Tucker. He's talking to his boss."

"Katharina." Armand held two mugs in his hand. He extended one to Mona. "Coffee?" he asked Kat.

"Thank you." The look in his eyes undid her. Not all her tossing last night was over Tansy. If she lost his presence in her life, she would grieve more than she'd ever dreamed. To fight the knot in her stomach, she sought out Mona. "So what the hell are we doing? Why are we all just sitting here? We should be—"

"Kat…" Armand's voice became velvet-edged steel. "Your sister is upset enough without you yelling at her."

"I'm not yelling, I'm—"

"It's all right, Armand. I understand. I'm scared, too." Mona set her cup down abruptly and dropped her head in her hands. "I don't know what I should have done. I tried to make Walker understand that we'd take care of her, that we didn't want to let anything happen to her, either." Her voice broke on a sob.

Armand started to her side, but Fitz got there first. He stroked her back, leaning over to talk to her. "Don't, Des. You did as well as any of us could. He has it in his mind that Tansy's in danger, and nothing we say is getting through."

Walker's accusations had taken up a drumbeat in Kat's head. During the long, sleepless night, she'd thought about the clipping he'd given Fitz, of Mama and Carlton. An old, hazy memory had reared its head. "Maybe he's right."

Mona frowned. "What do you mean?"

"Did you ever stop to wonder why Carlton was always around?"

"He was Daddy's friend and patron."

"I suspect he was obsessed with Mama."

An odd expression crossed Mona's face. "Why do you say that?"

Kat drew a deep breath, aware of the eyes on her. "I've never liked him, but I couldn't have said why. Last night I was thinking about the picture Fitz mentioned, and remembered something that happened years ago."

"What was it?"

"I was under Mama and Daddy's bed, hiding from the rest of you to get you in trouble because you said I was too little to play with. Carlton came into their bedroom and closed the door. She asked him to open it. He said he would in a minute, after they'd talked. She walked around the bed. Her voice was scared." Kat gripped the fingers of one hand in the other.

"He followed her. I could see his feet on either side of hers, really close. I didn't understand what they were doing then. I realize now that he was kissing her."

"What did she do?" Mona asked.

"She shoved him away and slapped him. It was loud. He pulled her close, and I saw her feet slip. She had on really high heels, red ones. His ugly black shoes looked like they would crush hers." Kat shook her head. "She sounded frightened. I was going to crawl out from under the bed, when I heard her tell him she would scream if he touched her again. That she would tell Daddy."

"What did he do?" Mona asked.

"He used some names for her I'd consider mild now. I'd never heard them before. They fought and he said things that didn't make sense to me then. Something about forgiving her if she'd leave Daddy." Kat smiled. "I was shocked when she cursed. She said he could go to hell. That she'd spill it all to Daddy if Carlton ever came near her again."

Every eye in the room was on her. Even Detective Tucker had concluded his call.

"He laughed and said that he owned Daddy. I remember that word because the idea was funny, owning someone. He said Daddy loved his fame more than any of us." Kat caught Mona's eye. "He wasn't wrong about that."

Mona grasped her hand. "How did Mama respond?"

"She said maybe so, but that she would go to the papers, expose him."

"How did he react?"

"His voice was mean. He said…" Kat frowned, trying to retrieve the words. It hadn't made sense at the time. She covered her eyes with her fingers, struggling to go back to that long-ago time. "I didn't understand. It didn't fit. Something about us, about the kids."

Armand's hand settled on the small of her back. "Just relax. Draw in a deep breath and don't try too hard."

But she couldn't help thinking it was important. "I

have to. Damn, if only I could remember." It tickled at the back of her mind, frustration building.

Mona seemed troubled. "The other day I went to his place for a meeting. I didn't wait to be announced. He was holding a photo of Mama I'd never seen, and he had the strangest look on his face." She frowned. "When he noticed me, he tried to shove it in a drawer, but I asked for it."

She squeezed Kat's hand. "He said he'd planned to ask her to marry him once he got better established, but then she went to Hollywood, and soon, she met Daddy." Her expression grew thoughtful. "His face, though…"

Kat shook her head. "What do we really know about him? We've taken him for granted for years because he was always around and so important to Daddy. But he's been pulling strings all our lives. He's the one who talked Daddy into leaving us in Texas and bringing Paris and Tansy back to stay with him while you and I—oh, God." Memory hit. She covered her mouth with shaking fingers. "Oh, God." Suddenly, she heard him again, his voice cold, so cold. Heard her mother's breath catch.

Kat lowered her fingers. "It was Tansy. He was talking about Tansy. How could I have forgotten? It made no sense, but I—"

Mona rose. "Damn it, Kat, stop babbling. What did he say?"

A chill shuddered through her. "He said that Mama

could be a fool if she wanted, because he wouldn't need her anymore…because Tansy was growing up to look just like her."

AL BURST OUT on the sidewalk as soon as Lucas neared the bar. "I thought you'd never get here. She's gone, Luke. She slipped out while I was fixing breakfast."

"Tansy?" His breathing stalled. "She's…gone?" Like an automaton, Lucas followed him inside.

"I didn't know where to look. I been up and down these blocks over and over, talkin' to everyone. She headed toward Broadway. Someone said he saw her goin' down to the subway, but another fella spotted a woman in a green coat like hers gettin' pushed into a car. I'm sorry, Luke. She must have overheard us. She was askin' me questions about if you were in danger. I was sure I put her at ease. I swear I never considered she'd run away."

Terror roared through Lucas. He wanted to curse God, to strike out so this awful, tearing grief would drown in bloody, numbing pain. He opened his mouth to lash out at Al for letting her walk into danger—

One glimpse at Al's devastation silenced him.

"I'm so sorry. That angel's in danger and it's all my fault."

"No," Lucas said. The bags in his hands dropped to the floor. He leaned his head against the wall. "The responsibility is mine. I forced his hand. If I'd never come back, maybe she'd be safe." And he would have to live with that, whatever happened. He'd endangered the one soul in the world he loved, the only person who cared if he lived or died.

Some Galahad he was.

But now was not the time to think about his mistakes. He shoved away from the wall, kicking the bags aside. It was time to get even. "You said you have a gun?"

"What you got in mind?"

"I'm finishing what I should have done long ago."

"You ain't no murderer, son. Don't get yourself sent back upstate."

Lucas lifted one eyebrow. "No one else ever believed me, you know. Except Juliette. At least she believed it was an accident."

"Who's Juliette?" Al had retrieved the gun from behind the bar and handed it over.

Lucas accepted it and nodded thanks. "Another angel, who trusted me to take care of her daughter. I'll do it now, whatever is required."

On his way to the door, he stopped. His fate didn't matter, but he should obtain backup for Tansy. "I want you to call this number." He rattled it off. "Talk to Fitzgerald. Tell him Sanford has nabbed her, and I'm going over to his apartment. Someone should be with her, after."

"I don't like the sound of this. You have no idea what the hell you're walkin' into. Maybe we should call the police."

"I've waited too long already. Twenty years too long." He tried to reassure Al. "Let Fitzgerald summon the cops, if he thinks he can convince them. They're not going to listen to me." Lucas caught Al's gaze. "Just make sure there's someone there for Tansy, whatever happens."

"Be careful, son," Al called out. "That angel needs you alive, not a martyr."

Lucas paused. "You've been a good friend, Al. Not many would have given me a chance."

"You come back, Luke Walker," Al said gruffly. "I can't cook worth a damn, and I'll lose all my new business."

Lucas tried for a smile. Then he stepped into the street and hailed a cab.

CHAPTER TWENTY

IF KAT DIDN'T QUIT prowling the apartment Mona thought she would scream. Of course Kat didn't want to be here. Neither did she. But someone had to keep an eye on Daddy with that Julie creature hovering so close.

"Martin, honey, why don't you lie down. A little nap would do you good," Julie suggested. Her normal effervescence was missing, her voice revealing the strain they all felt.

Mona saw Kat whirl, ready to pounce on the interloper. She stood up quickly to intercede. Tearing at one another would do Tansy no good. "Perhaps it is a wise idea, Daddy. We'll have to be at our best when Tansy's found."

Their father's gaze rose from the volume of Shakespeare on his lap. "'My child is yet a stranger in the world,'" he quoted from *Romeo and Juliet*. He looked so tired and old. "What will happen to my poor Titania?"

Mona moved toward him, but Kat reached him first. Shooting a glare at Julie, Kat spoke up. "Let's go back where it's quiet. I'll read to you for a few minutes."

Mona couldn't credit what she was seeing. Apparently, Kat's loathing for the woman over whom their father had become a fool superceded Kat's years-old fury at Martin. Mona was still staring when her cell phone rang.

"Des," Fitz said. "I just heard from some friend of Walker's." He paused slightly. "I don't know how to tell you this."

Mona gripped the phone. "Just say it, Fitz." She sensed Kat moving up beside her.

"He says Tansy's been snatched, and Walker is sure it's Carlton's men. Walker's gone after her."

"What? She's at Carlton's?" Mona heard Julie gasp. She glanced over, surprising an odd expression on the blonde's face, but she couldn't think about it yet. She focused on Fitz.

"I'm going there now," he said. "I'll call you as soon as I have more information."

"I'm coming, too."

"No. Stay there. I've phoned Tucker and he's going to meet me. I won't have you caught in the middle of whatever this is."

"Fitz, she's my sister—"

"Des, I don't have time to argue. Please—I'm worried about you. You haven't been feeling well."

"Fitz, it's not—" She stopped herself. She wasn't going to explain to him now, not this way. It was a private matter between them, one they should be face-to-face to discuss. "I'm fine, and I want to be there."

"Des, please. Let the cops handle it. I'll contact you the second I know anything."

She started to protest again but couldn't risk the distraction concern for her would cause. But he wouldn't prevent her from going. "Fitz, be careful. I love you."

"I love you, too, babe. I never stopped." Then he was gone.

Clamor erupted immediately.

"Desdemona, what's the meaning of—" Her father rose unsteadily to his feet.

"Tansy's at Carlton's?" Kat asked.

Julie said nothing, but she'd gone very pale.

Mona stared at her, but Kat interrupted. "I'm going with you."

"A friend of Lucas Walker's told Fitz that Tansy has been kidnapped. Walker believes Carlton did it."

"At Carlton's…thank God. She's safe now," Martin said.

Kat and Mona traded loaded glances.

"I hope you're right, but I'm not so sure, Daddy."

"What do you mean?"

"Kat remembered something last night, something about Carlton that…" It was too complex to explain. She shook her head. "I have to go now. I'll call you later."

"Desdemona, finish what you were saying." It was his old voice, the tone of command.

"Daddy, it's not…" She glanced away, then back,

speculating. "Why didn't you bring all of us home from Texas?"

"What?" Martin blustered. "What does it matter now?"

"Just answer her," Kat demanded. "Why did you only bring Tansy and Paris back?"

"I don't…" Brow wrinkled, he continued. "Carlton had the idea that it would help your mother to have them here—the twins were special to her. He was gracious enough to offer to house them himself because he knew that I needed to concentrate on your mother and getting her well. Four children, however, were too many to expect him to handle. You were better off with Juliette's mother."

Mona ignored the stab of resentment. "Didn't Carlton date Mama before you met her?"

"I suppose he might have. He did know her first. He's the one who introduced us, but—" He broke off. "Why does this matter?"

"He was obsessed with Mama. I think he still is. Your career was his way to stay involved in her life. And when she rebuffed him, he turned his attention toward Tansy."

"That's preposterous," her father declared. "Juliette would never have encouraged him. She loved me, not him."

"Oh, my God."

Mona heard Julie's gasp. She glanced over to see the younger woman pale. "What is it?"

"You're right. About your mother, I mean. He was in

love with her, almost possessed. And he was determined to bring Tansy to his place. He—he promised me the role if I'd keep Martin too involved to interfere."

"Interfere with what?" Kat demanded.

Julie's expression was grave. She turned to Martin. "I'm sorry, Martin. I didn't understand when it started. He just found me and offered me the understudy role. Told me I should keep you happy because you needed this run to be good to cap off your career. I've always admired your work so much, and there was the possibility that the other actress would get sick…."

"What are you saying?" Martin's hand trembled in Mona's.

"A few days ago, he told me I wasn't working hard enough, that if I handled you properly, I could be moving in with you, and you wouldn't care if Tansy went to live with him."

"But why?"

Kat spoke up. "He and Mama had a fight, years ago. He wanted her to leave you. He was rough with her when she resisted."

Martin sat down heavily. "Leave me? Juliette would never have—"

"She told him she wouldn't go. That she would tell you if he ever came near her again."

"What does this have to do with Titania?"

Kat's voice went hard. "He told Mama that she could be a fool if she wanted because soon he wouldn't need her."

"Why not?"

"Because," Kat said, "Tansy was growing up to be her spitting image."

"What's your point?"

"What if Walker's telling the truth?" Mona asked. "What if he wasn't the one who raped Tansy? What if Carlton's drive to get her under his roof is about controlling her in case her memory comes back? Walker's been insisting she's in danger from Carlton."

"Carlton? No. No, it can't be…" He sank into a chair, suddenly old.

"I can't argue about this now. We have to go." Mona faced Julie. "I think you should leave now."

The actress straightened. "Perhaps so, but the least I can do is stay here with Martin." She placed one hand on his shoulder. "He won't want to be alone."

Just then, Martin stood up, an aging lion once more. "I won't be alone," he said. "I'm going with you."

"Daddy, I don't think—"

But Kat surprised her. "We don't have time to argue. I'm calling Armand to let us use his car."

LUCAS SLIPPED INSIDE the service entrance of Sanford's building right behind two men lugging a sofa and cursing its bulk. "Here, let me help you with this," he said.

One man grunted assent. The other started to protest, but then nodded instead. "It's one heavy bastard. Thanks."

He rode up in the service elevator, but remained behind when they left. Once outside Sanford's apartment, he knocked.

"Who is it?" a voice asked.

"Groceries," he said, gambling.

The door swung open. "I wasn't expecting—" the young man said.

Lucas shoved past him and raced through the kitchen.

"Hey!" the man shouted. "I'm calling the cops—"

Lucas never paused, charging down the hallway, scanning side to side.

A figure stepped out of the library, scene of the long-ago nightmare. Carlton Sanford.

"Where is she?" Lucas demanded.

"Well, well…" Sanford said. Peering behind Lucas, he smiled over the houseman's protests. "Not to worry, Hanson. This…person doesn't really want to hurt me, do you, Walker?" His smile was a shark's, gleaming and false. "Oh, but perhaps you'd first check him over to be sure he's not carrying anything as unseemly as a gun?"

Lucas tensed to resist. *Tansy,* he thought, forcing himself to be still. *Don't do anything rash until you know where she is.*

Hanson patted him down and removed the gun from the back of his waistband. Lucas stood rigid, blood roaring in his ears.

"Tut-tut," Sanford clucked. "What can one expect from a mongrel, after all?"

"Where is she, Sanford?"

"Sir, don't you want me to call the police?"

Sanford shook his head, eyeing the gun with distaste. "No. Merely remove that thing from the premises. I'm sure Mr. Walker doesn't want to worry my other guest." He turned to his houseman. "I have the situation well in hand. As a matter of fact, why don't you take the rest of the day off."

"Sir?"

His face was a study in neutrality. "My guests and I require privacy."

"If you're sure," Hanson said. "I'll finish up and be gone."

Sanford looked at Lucas smugly. One hand swept toward the library. "Please. Join us. Tansy and I were just having a little reunion."

"If you've hurt her..." Lucas's hands gathered into fists.

"Ah, yes...ever the protector. I've been hearing about Tansy's prince." His smile was chillingly calm. "But she doesn't realize who you are, does she?" He gestured inside. "Please. I'm sure you want to see her."

"You first." Lucas had learned better than to turn his back on this man.

Sanford shrugged elegantly. "Very well." He strolled through the door as though he had not a care in the world. "Tansy, you have a visitor."

Lucas spotted her, huddled in a corner of the sofa.

When she noticed him, she exploded from the couch and threw herself into his arms. "Michael, some men grabbed me. I was going to see Paris so he could tell me how to help you, but I didn't know I needed money for the subway, and this man was going to help, but then he shoved me into a car…."

She was shivering feverishly. Lucas cradled her tightly and glared at Sanford. "You son of a bitch…"

Sanford stopped beside his desk. "My, such language. But you always were a crude one, weren't you? A cur. I told Juliette she was making a mistake trusting you, but she never listened, I'm sorry to say."

"Juliette?" Tansy repeated, turning toward Sanford, then back to Lucas. "What does Mama have to do with you?"

"You don't recognize him, Tansy?"

"Don't do this, Sanford," Lucas growled. "Don't make her remember…."

"Remember what?" Tansy stepped away, her eyes hurt and confused.

Just then, angry voices sounded in the hallway.

"Mr. Sanford has guests—"

"Tansy, where are you?"

"Sanford, is Walker here?"

"Walker?" Tansy said. "Who is…"

Lucas couldn't take his gaze off her, even as his heart sank.

Sanford spoke. "Please allow me to introduce an old

friend to you. Lucas Michael Walker, your brother's murderer."

"Lucas? No, he's…" She shook her head. Her eyes darkened in confusion.

"Tansy…" He stalled, unsure what to say. Then he glanced at Sanford, and his heart stuttered.

Sanford was holding a gun. It appeared to be the same one. "Don't move, Walker."

He heard the gun cock, and all he could think was, *It's happening again.*

Desperate to protect her, Lucas shoved Tansy out of harm's way, then dived forward. As he threw his shoulder into Sanford's chest, he chopped at the hand holding the gun. It clattered to the wooden floor.

He went down with Sanford, landing blows to his face. Violence sang a siren song. This was the man who'd stolen twenty years of his life, the man who'd ruined Tansy….

Voices crowded in.

"Walker, stop it—"

"Let him go!"

"Police, Walker—freeze!"

But Lucas was lost in the past. He saw Sanford looming over him with the gun. Heard Tansy's screams….

Suddenly, he heard her again. His head jerked up.

Whimpering like an animal in pain, Tansy knelt before the gun, her eyes unblinking.

Lucas let go of Sanford and froze. "Tansy…"

Her sister Mona rushed toward her.

"No!" Lucas snapped. "Don't. You don't under-stand…."

Like a zombie, Tansy picked up the gun.

"Tansy, give it to me," he said, stepping closer.

"Tansy, don't!" Sanford gasped.

"Walker, I said freeze!" A voice rang out.

All he could see was Tansy, the devastation in her gaze. He moved a step closer, aware that every eye in the room was on them—

Sanford lunged at his back, knocking him to the ground.

WITH A SNAP LIKE GLASS shattering, memory crashed in and Tansy saw it all anew.

The gun in her hand.

Carlton's fists.

Michael's grunts of pain. Blood, so much blood. Carlton was killing him.

Burning…where Carlton had hurt her. Blood ran like acid down the inside of her shaky legs. She staggered to the desk, where she knew Carlton kept a gun—

Gun.

In her hand.

Carlton rising over Lucas, his face black with hate—

Squeezing the trigger and…

Tansy couldn't breathe. Her vision wavered, and she swayed.

Paris leaping across the open space and—
Paris. *Oh, Paris, no. Oh, no—oh, no—oh, no—*

LUCAS PINNED SANFORD beneath him. The stronger one now, he knew he could kill him. He wanted to. Craved retribution for every minute of hell Tansy and he had endured.

Sanford's breath came in gasps. Lucas only squeezed his fingers tighter around the man's neck, rage and heartache howling in his ears—

Until Tansy screamed.

"No…! I killed him. I killed Paris. Oh, no. Oh, no—"

Lucas looked up just as she collapsed. He barely heard the cries of shock around him. Barely noticed Martin Gerard sink into a chair. All he could see, all he cared about was Tansy.

He covered the space between them. Her agonized sobs tore at his heart. On the floor, she rocked, the pistol drooping in her hand. "I did it, I did it, I did it…." Her moan was unearthly, her expression pure agony. "I killed Paris. Oh, God, he's dead and it was me—"

Lucas grasped her shoulders. "Tansy, listen to me. It was an accident. You saved my life. Sanford was trying to kill me."

She curled into a ball. He simply picked her up and placed her in his lap, wrapping her tightly in his arms. "You didn't know Paris would leap just then. He got in the way, that was all. You couldn't have predicted it."

She didn't seem to hear him. Vaguely, Lucas sensed

movement in the room, heard someone reading Sanford his rights. A hand touched his shoulder, and he stared into the ravaged face of Martin Gerard.

"She always believed in you, my Juliette." The man looked ancient, his eyes shell-shocked. He glanced to the side, where Sanford was being handcuffed. "How…why—" Horror filled his gaze. "What have I done? Carlton. It was Carlton all along." He turned toward where Sanford had been, but the police had already led him away.

Mona knelt beside her sister, tears in her eyes. One hand hovered over Tansy's hair, then stroked. She spoke to Lucas. "We couldn't figure out why you'd go to jail for twenty years if you didn't do it. You were trying to protect her, weren't you? So she wouldn't have to face it."

Lucas had no idea what to say. Tansy had gone mute, her eyes empty.

Kat knelt on Tansy's other side. "Tell us what happened."

"It doesn't matter now," he said.

Tansy stirred in his arms. Tried to sit up. Lucas loosened his grip but kept her close.

She was silent for endless moments, but finally, she spoke.

"It does matter." Voice shaky, she swallowed hard. "Carlton raped me. You protected me. You didn't do anything wrong."

She turned shattered blue eyes on him. "You've been

in prison for twenty years for Paris's murder?" Tears spilled down her cheeks, and she lifted one hand to his face. "Why didn't you tell anyone the truth?"

Her touch was too intimate. He couldn't stand all these prying eyes.

A man whose voice he recognized as Fitzgerald's spoke up. "Tansy was his leverage, wasn't she? You said to me that she was supposed to get help, that he'd promised." He studied Lucas. "Sanford cut some kind of deal with you, didn't he?"

Lucas shook his head. "Not now. Not while—" He glanced at Tansy.

Her eyes were wet and filled with pain, but they were clear now in a way he hadn't seen in years. "You don't have to shield me anymore."

His own eyes stung with shame. "I've done a lousy job of it every time I've tried." He wanted away from everyone but her. Out of range of all their questions, all the stares that forced him to remember. To confront the waste his life had been.

Only Tansy's soft, precious weight kept him in place.

Then Martin Gerard spoke, his forehead in his hands. "You did a better job than I. I gave her into the keeping of a monster."

Lucas saw Kat and Mona trade glances.

Mona started to soothe. "Daddy, you didn't mean—"

"No." Kat held up her hand. "Don't you dare excuse him for what he's done. If he'd ever cared about any of us as much as he did his damn career, none of this would have happened."

The room hummed with a charged, heavy silence.

Martin sat back in his chair, his age-spotted hands slack on the arms. "She's right. I never should have married, never had children. I was no good with them. My career would have been enough for me, but it meant so much to Juliette to have them. It was selfish of me to want to capture her, but oh, if you could have seen her then. She was life at its most radiant. No man could have resisted her...." His face was transformed by memory.

Then the present rushed in, and he sagged visibly. He glanced from one daughter to the next. "What I did can't be forgiven, nor can it be fixed."

Last, his gaze landed on Lucas. "I need to understand what happened. Will you tell us?"

Lucas frowned.

"Please, Lucas," Tansy asked. "Tell them. I—I can't."

And so he began.

LUCAS STIRRED, wondering at the cries, the desperate, inhuman sobbing. He tried to move, but his limbs were weighted as if he were pinned under a boulder. Darkness moved in at the edge of his vision, and he slid beneath the heavy blanket of unconsciousness once more.

The sobs broke into a jagged, anguished wail, then

a tortured whisper. "Please…stop. Please—" Her voice cracked. "Michael…Paris…please…help me."

Tansy. It's Tansy, but she sounds all wrong. What…what's happening? He opened his eyes, but the room kept whirling. In the corner of his vision he saw motion, saw limbs entwined, saw—

Oh, God—Tansy. Naked. Fighting. A beast loomed above her, a big man, still clothed—

Lucas rolled to his side, rose to hands and knees, struggled to stand….

Blackness swept over him. He swayed, barely able to feel his hands or feet. What the—

He battled the darkness, fought the sickness back, made it to his feet and staggered across the floor, to throw himself at the man—

The man shouted his rage, struck backward, sent Lucas flying to the floor. His head slammed against the wood, and he lay there, everything whirling in front of him in a grotesque merry-go-round. Then he saw who it was.

Carlton Sanford spared him barely a glance, already reaching out toward her again. Tansy skittered backward like a crab, a smear of blood on her thighs, her face crazed and desperate. Sanford grabbed her, pulled her back, thrust into her again. "Juliette…" he groaned.

Tansy slapped at him, tried to get away. He hit her once, viciously, and she fell backward, whimpering helplessly, keening with an awful, blood-chilling grief.

Lucas heard Paris stir, saw him struggle to rise, then fall backward. Suddenly, Lucas remembered the wine they'd felt so adult sharing.

Sanford had drugged them. All along, the beast Lucas had sensed beneath the polish had been there. He hadn't imagined it.

With effort, Lucas brought himself to his feet again, lurched forward. Grabbed Sanford around the neck and jerked back hard. With a bellow, Sanford wheeled on him, shot out a fist, launched himself at Lucas.

"Paris—wake up! Call 911," Lucas yelled, everything a blur of flailing fists, of ringing ears. Tansy's whimpers. Sanford's shouts. Endless, bone-racking pain.

Still Lucas fought to buy time. From the corner of his eye, he saw Tansy crawl across the floor toward the desk, gasping, trying to cover herself. A blow from Sanford's fist snapped his head the other way. He saw Paris attempt to come to his knees, confusion giving way to horror. "Now, Paris. Goddamn it, now!" Lucas threw himself into the fight with renewed determination, though Sanford outweighed him by a good fifty pounds.

Ever after, Lucas could not remember which came first when he shoved Sanford upward, before the blow that knocked him out:

The shadow of Paris, launching himself into the fray.

Or the sound of the shot.

But Lucas knew that he would never in his life forget the look on Tansy's face as her twin slammed to the ground.

Dead from the bullet meant for Carlton Sanford.

HE WOKE ONCE, saw Sanford dressing a wooden, unblinking Tansy as tenderly as though she were a child. The coppery tang of blood stung the air. Sanford rose, walked to the desk, used the phone to report a break-in. His voice filled with convincing horror, he requested an ambulance. Lucas tried to rise, must have made a noise. Sanford turned his head and smiled.

Then he lifted the gun and fired.

WHEN LUCAS REGAINED consciousness, he was in the hospital with a gunshot wound, charged with the murder of Paris Gerard. His fingerprints were on the weapon that Sanford had given to the police. The nurses and cop on duty outside his door had no interest in his protests of innocence, and his first visitor was Carlton Sanford, chairman of the hospital board.

Sanford stopped Lucas's furious protests too easily. He'd played two cards against which Lucas had no defenses: Tansy and Juliette.

Tansy had gone mute, the horror of killing the other half of herself too much for her to bear. What would happen to her if she were forced to face it, if the news media caught wind of it? Sanford asked. She'd be an object of curiosity and pity for the rest of her life. Even her family would shun her, unable to forget that she'd killed her twin, however unintended.

And what of Juliette? As sick as she was, how would she survive Tansy's pain as well as her own? he queried. It was horrible enough to lose one twin, to see the other so destroyed…but what of the agony a sensitive woman would feel, understanding the inner horror Tansy was suffering now?

"You raped her," Lucas retorted furiously. "She acted in self-defense. Paris was an accident. This is your fault. You can't escape that."

"Who will believe you, a young nothing, over a solid citizen like me?"

"I didn't fire the gun."

"Oh, but you did. The residue is on your hand. I retrieved the cartridge from the firewood myself. The evidence is overwhelming. You'll go to jail for the rest of your life. You've murdered the son of the most beloved actor of our time, a boy who was his parents' shining hope, his very ill and beautiful mother's reason to live. That mother took you in, gave you her affection, treated you as a son, but you were always a bad seed. Who's going to listen to you instead of me?"

"Tansy knows what happened. She'll speak up for me."

"Tansy isn't talking. She remembers nothing." He let that sink in. "I'm going to make you an offer. I've spoken to my lawyer, who has conferred with the D.A., a big fan of Martin's. He's been half in love with Juliette for years. If you will plead guilty to Paris's murder, the rape will not be a part of the charges, and Tansy will not have to face that. The family will throw its weight behind mercy and ask for a lesser charge. You will be given a light sentence of seven years, with parole possible in two."

"I didn't do it! I can't go to jail."

"You can plead innocent. Of course, Tansy will have to testify. She'll be forced to relive that night in public, and the media will have a field day. Meanwhile, Juliette will have to sit by helplessly, having already lost one child. Tansy is fragile enough now that it might drive her over the edge. Of course we'd watch her, but she's bereft of the most important person in her life, and the strain might take her mother, too. Juliette is very sick, you understand, and I'm glad I can provide the funds for the doctors to save her, but…"

In his eyes, Lucas could see the threat. Juliette's death, maybe even Tansy's, would be on his head.

"Why didn't you just kill me?"

Sanford's smile was chilling. "You have the devil's own luck, young man. A few minutes more and…" He shook his head and sighed deeply. "Well, no matter. What's done is done."

He leaned over Lucas, his eyes glittering. "You can, of course, fight this. You'll lose, but you'll cost me precious moments with Juliette, and I can't have that. She's very ill, and I won't waste what time I have with her. If you truly care about her and Tansy, you'll play along. If you don't…"

Lucas thought of the last sight he'd had of Tansy, as though all the light in her had gone out. She'd looked so fragile, the laughing, mischievous girl vanished. Paris and she had been connected by a bond so strong, Lucas truly feared for her. He'd loved Tansy since the day he'd met her. Juliette had given him a mother's care.

Two years. He could survive two years to protect them.

"You have to agree to stay away from Tansy, to never touch her again," he demanded of Sanford. "If I do this, you will leave her alone or I'll tell Martin what you did. He'll never forgive you."

Sanford smirked. "Martin does what I tell him. He thinks you raped one child and murdered the other. Martin needs me to save his beloved, to keep his career afloat."

Only Tansy could tell them differently. Lucas could not put her through that. Still, he stuck to his guns. "You have to make sure she gets help, and never touch her again or—"

"Or what? What can you possibly do?"

From somewhere inside Lucas came the steely voice of a full-grown man with intimate knowledge of a brutal world Sanford's manicured hands would never touch. With barely suppressed violence, he spoke. "If I ever find out that you've laid one finger on her again, I'll see that you pay. No matter how long it takes."

Maybe Sanford recognized the part of Lucas's father that crouched inside the youth, waiting to emerge. He was silent for a long time. Finally, he nodded, stuck out his hand and shook.

Lucas entered his guilty plea as promised, his heart a boy's then, clinging shakily to his resolve in the face of the hell that waited. *For you, Tansy. For you and Juliette...*

And in the jumble of his thoughts, he needed a moment to realize that he'd been suckered, that the D.A. wasn't going to ask for less.

He listened with horror as the judge decreed that Lucas Walker would be imprisoned for a minimum of twenty years.

WHEN HE FINISHED, the room fell silent. Tansy had drawn away, huddled on the floor with her knees against her chest. Despair swept over him. It had all been for nothing, everything he'd done to protect her from the agony of remembering.

The look of her destroyed him. If she'd been fragile before, she was barely a wisp of fog now. And her eyes...dear God, her eyes.

Agony gave him a voice. "Tansy," he said fiercely, leaning over her. "It was an accident. You saved my life. You didn't know Paris would leap in the way."

She didn't speak, but tears trailed down her cheeks, a silvery river of hopelessness.

He couldn't stand it. Somehow, he had to get through

to her. No matter that he'd have to leave her soon, he had to touch her, comfort her. "Tansy," he murmured, kneeling beside her. "Paris isn't gone, not really. He's still there inside you. He loved you more than his own life. That's why he tried so hard to save you."

"I didn't mean—" she sobbed brokenly.

"Of course not. You would have given your life for him, wouldn't you?"

"Yes," she whispered.

"You saved me. It's my fault, not yours. I felt something wrong about it. I never should have let Paris talk me into leaving once I found out you weren't going with your father that night. Sanford always made my skin crawl."

"Why did he—" Her breath hitched. "I didn't want— I was so scared and he wouldn't stop—" Her hand seized his shirt. "He kept calling me by Mama's name."

"He was obsessed with your mother. He's a sick, evil man, but you never have to be afraid of him again." Heart cracking in two, Lucas tried to fasten on her future. "You'll go back now to your family, but you'll be all right. You won't ever have to worry again."

She lifted her face to his. "Where will you be?"

He swallowed hard. "I don't know."

She gripped his arms. "You can't leave me. You're my prince, and I need you." Her eyes were wild and sad.

"Tansy, I'm not a prince. You see that now. I'm that super's kid with no future, turned ex-con working in a bar. I'm the last thing you need."

"I can't make it without you. Paris is gone and I don't have anyone."

"You have your family. And you're strong, Tansy. You were the strongest one. Paris understood that." Lucas sought down deep for the confidence she'd require. "You'll be fine. You'll get some help and you'll rest up and one day soon you'll forget all about me and see that this is best."

"But I love you. Don't you love me?"

The expression in her eyes almost broke him then. He had to stay strong. He had nothing to offer her. "Tansy, I—"

"No— You can't leave me now." She drew his head down and kissed him, a woman's kiss, untutored perhaps but full of the fire of the passionate, reckless girl he'd once known.

Oh, God. His arms fastened around her, and he wanted her so badly, craved nothing more ever in his life than this, just this. Tansy, the fiery one, the girl who'd dare anything.

He ended the kiss and buried his face in her neck, his longing more than he could bear. If only there was a way, but—

Quickly, before he could change his mind, Lucas thrust Tansy into Kat's arms and walked away.

CHAPTER TWENTY-ONE

Mona sat up in bed when she heard Tansy's sobs.

"Des? What is it?" Fitz asked, reaching for her.

"It's Tansy. Nightmares, I'd guess." She leaned down, snuggled against him for a second. "It's okay—go back to sleep." She consulted the clock. They'd only been in bed for an hour.

"You sure?" he said, exhaustion heavy in his voice.

She brushed back his thick hair and kissed his cheek. "Yeah. I can handle it."

She shuffled through the loft, steps quickening as she heard Tansy whimper again. Tansy had grown too agitated about going back to their father's apartment after the endless hours of police questioning, so they'd brought her home with them.

In the faint streetlight, Mona could see her huddled into a ball. "Michael," Tansy wept. "Don't go."

Walker. Why had he left when Tansy needed him most?

Mona gathered Tansy into her arms. "Shh, it's all right. I'm here. It's just a dream."

All serenity had fled her sister's face. Agony and despair had banished it.

"Mona?"

"Yes, sweet," she soothed. "You're in our loft. You're safe."

Tansy clasped the sleeve of Mona's robe but turned her face away. Tears slid slowly down her cheek. "Paris. He's…gone." All the light that had been Tansy was gone, too, and it tore at Mona's heart.

But they couldn't ignore the truth anymore. "Yes," she said, smoothing Tansy's hair away from her face. "He's gone. But we remember him, don't we? He'll be with us as long as he's in our hearts."

Tansy gripped harder. Curled more tightly. "I don't know how to be alone," she cried. "How do you stand it? He was always there, always part of me, and it's as if someone ripped out my insides." She whipped her head around to stare at Mona, who thought she'd never witnessed so much hopelessness in a person's eyes. "I…shot him, Mona. The other half of me, and I…killed him." Horror bloomed as her voice dropped to a whisper. "How do I live with that? How do I survive without him?"

Mona pulled Tansy's trembling body close as her own eyes stung. "You let us love you until it gets better." She squeezed her sister, willing her own strength into her wire-tight frame.

"I want Michael so much," Tansy said. "But he's gone, too."

"I know, sweetheart," Mona said as she stroked her back. "I know." She stared into the darkness and once again cursed Lucas Walker. She soothed her sister until the exhausted Tansy relaxed in her arms.

Mona eased Tansy's head onto the pillow and stood.

"Mona?" Her voice was heavy with sleep.

"Yes?"

"I have to go back tomorrow."

"Back?"

"To visit Daddy. He'll be lonely."

Oh, Tansy. Ever the gentle soul, she couldn't even punish the man whose selfishness had led to the destruction of her life. "Are you sure?"

There was a long silence. Mona thought Tansy was asleep until she spoke faintly. "He didn't mean for any of it to happen. And…he lost Paris, too. All of you did." Grief thickened her voice.

"Oh, honey…" Mona sat down beside Tansy. "Remember what Lucas said—it was an accident. No one blames you. Please don't blame yourself." She touched Tansy's cheek and felt tears on her hand. "We'll get through this, I promise."

She petted Tansy's hair until she was sure Tansy had fallen asleep. Then, worn-out herself, she headed for her bedroom, fighting a wave of dizziness. Quietly, she crept through the darkness to their bathroom. Holding on to the counter, she filled a glass with water, willing her head to steady and her stomach to stop rolling. *Not now,* she begged. *Not—*

"DES?" She woke up on the floor, Fitz's eyes wild on hers. "Stay right there—I'm calling an ambulance—" He started to rise.

"No—"

"Goddamn it, something's really wrong. Just stay right there while I—"

She grabbed his arm. "I'm not sick, Fitz."

"Bullshit," he shouted. "You're losing weight and you're pale and—"

"Pregnant."

"I don't care what—" He stopped dead. Whirled, eyes wide. "What did you say?"

"I'm pregnant."

He sank to his knees beside her. "But…how—"

"The usual way, I think," she said, smiling.

Fitz tugged her into his arms, joy flaring in his eyes. Then he went still. "Are you going to…" He cleared his throat. Looked away, then back. "I meant it, Des, when I said that you're what's most important. If you're not happy about this—"

She pressed one hand to his cheek. "I'm happy." She laughed, certain at last that she really was. "Scared bone-deep, yes. I don't know if I can be a good mother, Fitz. I can't give up everything the way my mom did, and I don't want to do this wrong." She took his hand

and kissed the palm, then placed it over her belly. "But I do want your baby." She saw his eyes fill, felt her own burn. "I'm sorry I…"

Then she could say nothing more as he embraced her and kissed her within an inch of her life. Mona responded fervently, clutching at his broad back.

Then he drew away. "You're sure?"

She studied the hazel eyes she loved so much, listening, too, inside herself. Then she nodded. "Yes. Yes, I'm sure."

Fitz whooped and scooped her up, grinning. "I am so good with babies, you won't believe it."

She put a cautionary hand on his chest. "No commuting, though," she warned. "Don't press your luck."

He laughed, the old Fitz laugh, the one that was free and easy and all hers. "No commuting. Scout's honor."

His arms tightened, and his face grew solemn. "Sweetheart, I…" His voice crackled with emotion. "We'll make it work, I promise. You won't regret this."

Mona's own eyes grew damp. "Let's go tell Tansy."

KAT EMERGED FROM THE CAB in front of Armand's Gramercy Park brownstone, fighting the urge to go back, think some more, come up with some foolproof strategy. She'd been absorbed, as they all had, with Tansy after her world had collapsed once more. The shrink Mona had called hadn't pulled punches. Tansy was in for a fight. There would be bad days, and she would have to grieve properly for Paris. She would have to learn to live without her other half, but Dr. Samuels was optimistic that, with love and support, Tansy would make it. The only problem was that she was pining as much for Lucas Walker as for her twin.

Kat was thinking very hard about bearding the lion in his den. Walker was still in New York, Fitz said, but not for long.

But Kat had her own lion to beard first, right here in this brownstone. As she walked up the steps, she almost backpedaled around. She wasn't ready. She hadn't figured out the perfect words, but Armand was leaving tomorrow for Europe, and her gut told her this couldn't wait. *You never used to be a coward, Kat.* Before she could chicken out, she pushed the doorbell.

Travers, the ancient butler from the Delacroix Beacon Hill mansion, opened it. "Miss Gerard," he noted without warmth. He'd come to New York with Armand almost twenty years ago, certain that the young master needed him to provide a touch of civilization in the melee that was New York. He'd never left. Though he was far past retirement age and did little of substance anymore, he was devoted to Armand, and Armand would never ask him to leave. Travers's expression made it clear that his down-the-nose assessment he'd made of Kat the first time they'd met hadn't changed.

It had never bothered her before, but tonight she could use an ally. "Is he here, Travers?"

"Mr. Delacroix is engaged in preparations for his trip, miss."

Her stomach clenched. "Does he plan to be gone long?"

He looked askance. Need-to-know basis only was what he conveyed.

It only fueled Kat's fears. She gripped Travers's forearm. "I have to stop him."

Thick white eyebrows snapped together. He looked down at her hand, then back at her face.

She couldn't afford to care. "Lighten up, Travers. I screwed up, okay? I love him. I'm sure you think I'm the worst possible person for him, but he loved me until two days ago—but I didn't realize it. I have no idea if I can make him love me again, but I can't let him leave. If he does, I'm scared that—" To her horror, her voice cracked. She took her hand off his arm and stepped back, humiliated and blinking away tears. She faced the door.

Her hand was on the doorknob when she heard his voice, that frosty, patrician tone. "Miss Gerard." He cleared his throat. "I believe you'll find Mr. Delacroix in the garden just now."

Kat gripped the knob, fighting the urge to run. Or bawl like a baby. She looked back. To her surprise, his usually stern gray eyes held a flicker of warmth. "Thank you, Travers."

"Very good, miss." Dignity resumed its proper position on that ancient face, and he stepped out of her path. "As you know your way, perhaps I'll resume packing."

Kat ignored the jitter in her stomach and remembered Scarlett. "Take your time, Travers." She straightened and tossed her head. "If I do this right, you'll only have to remove it all."

She thought she saw the faintest twitch of his lips as he motioned her forward.

Kat descended the steps to the kitchen of the four-story brownstone. Just one room wide, each level's rooms opened onto each other, Armand had explained. The kitchen floor, once frequented only by servants, was Kat's favorite by far over the more formal parlor, living area and dining room above. She'd never seen the bedroom levels or the rooftop terrace.

The kitchen was warm and welcoming, as was the breakfast nook and sunroom. Through the expanse of glass, she saw Armand in his garden. She'd teased him often about being a gentleman farmer, but in truth, he'd wrought miracles, all through the labors of his own hands. He refused to hire a gardener, saying that digging in dirt was therapeutic, that it kept him in touch with the rhythms of the seasons. It was incredibly peaceful, yet brimming with life even in these early days of spring.

But Armand didn't look at peace now. His handsome face was pensive as he brushed one hand over a patch of vibrant red tulips.

When she cracked the door, he glanced up. Immediately, he came to his feet with that easy, muscular grace of his. Concern tripped over his features. "Is Tansy all right?"

Kat didn't answer for a moment, studying this man who'd been the most important part of her life since the day they'd met. Newly awakened, she wondered how she'd missed it for so long, how she'd been so blind. Armand was the furthest thing possible from her father. He'd paid attention to her for years, gently but steadily urging her away from the worst of her excesses, always there to pick her up when she wouldn't be dissuaded from them.

"Katharina?"

She stared into the green eyes she trusted more than any in the world. "It's not Tansy," she said. "It's me."

His dark brows drew together. "What's wrong? Has something happened?"

"Yeah," she admitted with rue. "You might say that I finally got my head out of my ass."

He went very still but said nothing.

He wasn't going to make this easy. She drew a deep breath to steady herself. "Is it too late, Armand? For us?" She stepped closer. "Because I can't allow it. You can't leave now, not just because I was stupid. You've seen me be an idiot a thousand times and you didn't walk away then."

Armand turned slightly, looking out over his garden.

She grabbed his elbow and pulled, but he was too strong. Too solid. He'd always been solid. Always been there.

"Damn it." If he wouldn't face her, she'd go to him. "I won't let you do this. You can't just run off to Europe."

Arms crossed over his chest, Armand lifted one patrician eyebrow. "I have business interests in Europe. I believe you're the one who's perfected the art of running."

Temper did a tap dance on her control, but these were high stakes now. "You can't insult me." She sniffed. "I'm not going to get mad."

"A first." He headed toward a patch of crocuses. "You must be proud."

Kat shut her eyes, counted to ten. Okay, five.

Then she raced across the stepping stones and slipped in front of him. "I get it. Paybacks, that it? I've been a jerk, so you're going to outjerk me."

His beautiful mouth tilted at the corners, and all at once, she wanted another kiss, to see if she'd imagined the punch of the first one.

"I think one child in a relationship is more than enough."

Desperate to erase the distance, Kat crowded him. She slid her fingers into his hair and dragged his head down, sealing her mouth to his. At first he stood there, wooden, so she pressed her body to his and poured every ounce of skill she'd ever developed into kissing the socks off him.

For long seconds he didn't respond. Her bravado evaporated, and a creeping sense of despair filled her.

She drew her mouth away. "Armand, what do I have to do? I can't bear it if you go. Please don't leave me."

"Damn you, Kat," he muttered, yanking her back. Then he was kissing her with a hunger that made his first one seem child's play.

Relief swept over her in a cooling wind. Kat forgot about keeping the upper hand, or protecting herself, or any of the games she'd played with any other man. This was Armand, and she'd almost lost him—

She stopped abruptly, placing one hand on his chest. "I didn't blow it all the way, right? You're not giving up on me yet, are you?"

"Christ, Kat, you do try a man's patience." He shook his head, then traced her mouth with one long finger. "Katharina. You were aptly named for Shakespeare's shrew."

"I won't be a shrew anymore, not with you. Cross my heart, hope to die, stick a needle—" She drew an *X* over her heart, but before she could finish, Armand took her fingers in his hand and brought them to his lips, chuckling.

"Of course you will. Don't make promises you can't keep." His eyes grew solemn as he touched their entwined fingers against first her heart, then his. "But for whatever misbegotten reason, I seem to have a taste for shrewish redheads with evil tempers and no impulse control."

"Oh, Armand…" As the cold fear leached from her

bones, Kat felt suddenly drained. She leaned her head against his chest. "I'm so sorry. It's just—I saw what happened to Mama and to all of us, and I was terrified of surrendering myself to any man."

He stroked her hair. "And now?"

"Now there's—" one hand fluttered "—this."

"This?" His eyebrow arched.

"You know." She shrugged. "Us."

"Is there an us, Katharina?"

She shivered at the chance she was taking. "If those kisses are any example…" She cocked her head. Grinned. "Maybe I need another sample to be sure I'm not judging too quickly."

Armand's smile was wide and warm and everything she could have wished. "Allow me to demonstrate again."

TANSY HAD KISSED MONA goodbye in the cab, refusing to let her sister run interference for her any longer. Mona was radiant with her joy about the baby. It was time for Fitz and her to celebrate, not be dragged down by Tansy's sorrow.

"Afternoon, Tansy," the elevator operator said. "You ready for your father's big night?"

"Getting close," she agreed, doing her best to smile.

The apartment was dark when she entered. "Daddy? Mrs. Hodgson?" Silence bore down, and she pressed one hand against the entry wall. "Daddy?"

No answer.

She walked slowly toward the living room, plunged into shadows except for one small opening in the heavy drapes.

Her father sat there motionless, staring out over the park.

"Daddy?" She stepped closer, heart beginning to pound. "Why aren't you at rehearsal?" She came up beside him and saw his eyes, fixed and open, and for a moment, fear clawed its way up her throat….

Then she saw it. One tear, trembling on his lashes. He blinked, and it spilled over, winding a lonely trail down his weathered cheek. He looked a thousand years old.

"I can't." His voice was barely a whisper. "My fault…all of it. Paris…Juliette. Gone, both gone. My poor Titania…so hurt."

With one trembling hand, she reached out, letting it hover over his head. For a moment, she contemplated the park, no longer her place of magic. No longer Paris's home. Her vision blurred, and she glanced away.

She straightened her shoulders. Let her hand settle on the curve of his skull.

And rest there. "You must go back. You have to finish."

"Why?" His voice was gritty with pain. "Why are you here, Titania? After what I've done, why would you come to me? There is no pardon for what you've suffered at my hands."

For a long time, she studied him without speaking,

this man who'd loomed so large in her life. Finally, she knew what to say.

She spoke softly at first, searching for the words. "'The quality of mercy is not strain'd, it droppeth as the gentle rain from heaven upon the place beneath.'" Her voice gathered strength, and she stroked her father's head with one hand. "'It is twice blessed; it blesseth him that gives and him that takes....'"

An agonized moan convulsed her father's frame. His head fell forward, his shoulders shaking.

Tansy knelt and wrapped her arms around him.

WHAT HE OWNED MADE a pitiful stack, Lucas thought, as he folded the few clothes he'd gathered during these brief weeks. Just as well. He'd need to travel light. No room in his life for belongings.

Who was he kidding? There was nothing but room in his life. Endless emptiness. Days stretching out into weeks and years with no purpose. For over half his life, Tansy had been the backbone of his days, the spine of his dreams and goals, no matter how hard he'd tried to make it different. Even surviving each day of hell in Attica had been for one reason—to serve out the sentence he'd been assessed to protect her. He'd told himself a thousand times that he couldn't wait to get away, to leave the past behind and get started on his future.

It was all bullshit. Without Tansy, there was no future, no reason for joy. He would miss her forever.

Lifting out the last T-shirt, he saw the envelope, faded and ancient. It had formed his purpose for so long, and now that purpose was over. He lifted it with fingers that weren't quite steady, then sank to the cot, holding it in both hands. Pondering the graceful feminine handwriting, as familiar as his own.

Finally, he opened it.

Dear Lucas,

Carlton says that you murdered Paris, but I don't believe it. I can't. The young man I know loved my twins. You promised me you would protect them, and I've placed my trust in you. You would not betray me. The agony of Paris being gone would eat at you, too. In my heart of hearts, I am certain of that.

You've had a difficult life, Lucas. There's goodness in you; I can't believe you intended it to happen. I've asked Martin to help you, to forgive you as I do. If something went wrong, it must have been an accident. I'll believe that to my dying day. You came to me as a boy, half-wild and so hungry for love. Paris and Tansy loved you, Tansy most of all. She's trapped in silence, Lucas. Half her heart is lost. After this is over and you've been cleared, I'm invoking the promise you made me. Protect her, Lucas. Help her heal. When I am gone, she will need you even more.

Juliette

He closed his eyes and lay back on the cot, clutching the letter to him.

THE CRACKLE OF PAPER startled him awake. He bolted up, feeling his hand empty.

Then he saw her. "Tansy…" He blinked, positive he was dreaming.

She lifted her head, and it was not the same Tansy. He'd never met this woman before. Her face had fined down to hollows; her blue eyes were layered in shadows.

She held out the letter. "Mama was sure you were innocent." Pain darkened her gaze. She rose, wrapping her arms around her waist. "If she'd realized that it was me…"

Lucas rose, too. "It was still an accident."

Tansy studied a patch of the floor. "It doesn't seem real. How can he be gone and I'm still alive?" She raised weary eyes to Lucas's. "We were always together. I can't remember a time when I didn't feel his heart beating, didn't hear his voice inside my head. I have no idea how to be alone," she whispered. "But I have to learn."

Agony burned raw and deep. "You're not alone, Tansy. You have a family who loves you. You'll go places, meet new friends now. You'll have a full, rich life, and you'll always keep his memory alive inside you."

"But I won't have you, will I, Michael or Lucas or whatever I'm supposed to call you?" she snapped. "Never mind that I love you and you love me, you're still going to leave, aren't you?"

He stared, dumbfounded. "Tansy, I'm trying to do the right thing—"

"Are you? What's right about walking away from the people who care about you? Do I have to live the rest of my life wondering where you are and if you're lonely or hurt?"

"You don't understand…"

She stopped suddenly, her shoulders bowing. "I don't comprehend a lot of things. All I know is that I need you and you're leaving because you think that you're doing what's best for me." She raised a haunted gaze to his. "Maybe it would be easier for you to go. God knows you've earned your peace. You've suffered too much. I have no right to ask you to stay. I'm working to get better, but it's all such a mess inside me. I can't blame you for not wanting to take it on."

"That's not it."

Her head popped up. "What is it, then?"

How did he explain? For so many years, his only thought had been survival. Then there was Tansy, bright and shining, the princess he'd longed for since he was fifteen years old. Had he fought through everything else, only to let her go without a fight? "I'm not afraid of your problems."

"Then what do you want, Lucas Michael Walker? What means more to you than light or air or water? Because that's what you should grab, no matter what. You deserve so much more than you'll ask for. You've lost too much of your life to settle for less."

So fierce she was, this Tansy. So much she offered, standing there, furious and beautiful and oddly strong.

Like a petitioner with more understanding of punishment than joy, he slowly stretched forth his hands, palms up. Holding out an ancient, weary heart, bereft of the words he needed to tell her.

"Say it." She leaned forward, only a breath away. A wish away. A dream.

Blue eyes crackled with impatience, and they were the most beautiful sight he'd ever seen.

"You," he finally said in a low, hoarse voice. "All I really want is you."

Her mouth opened once, then closed without a sound. Her eyes shimmered with a rush of tears. Slowly, she laid her slender, delicate hands in his big rough ones and gripped them.

She looked up at him. "I knew this boy once who would dare anything...." She paused, swallowed hard. Tried again, and he saw a faint twinkle of the old mischief. "I double-dog dare you, Lucas Michael," she said, her voice unsteady but valiant, her blue eyes flashing. "Take me. Grab me and hold on. Help me find my way home."

His throat too full to speak, Lucas could only nod.

And hold on.

Everything you love about romance...
and more!

Please turn the page for Signature Select™
Bonus Features.

Bonus Features:

Signature Select™

BONUS FEATURES

MERCY

4

THE NIGHT BEFORE
by Jean Brashear

KAT PACED across Mona's living room until she reached its limits.

Then she paced back.

"Stupid," she muttered. "Barbaric custom."

Tansy laughed. "You don't have to wear it if you don't want to." She proffered the veil in her hand, not a veil for Kat's wedding to Armand tomorrow, but one Tansy had made for their bachelorette party tonight.

It might be her finest act of creativity: a froth of tulle, attached to a wreath Tansy and Mona had spent hours concocting.

Snickering every second.

"I mean—" Tansy shrugged one shoulder, and it was all Mona could do to keep a straight face "—unless you're, well, chicken."

"What?" Kat's head whipped around. "Oh. That. Give it here." She snagged it from Tansy's hand and plopped it on her head.

Backward.

"No, no. Let me fix it." Tansy winked at Mona over her shoulder, then adjusted the headpiece so that the nosegay made of condoms and baby charms was front and center.

"Okay, now we're ready to hit the bars." Mona rose, barely suppressing her amusement.

"You can't drink while you're nursing. Baby Fitz will have a hangover at my—" Kat screeched as she caught a glimpse of herself in the mirror. "What in blazes is this, Tansy?"

"Your veil for the bachelorette party," Tansy replied, all innocence. "You agreed, sweetie." She winked outrageously at Mona.

"And here's your bouquet." Mona thrust the tangle of bows at her sister, mementos from the only shower Kat had allowed them to give her. Lingerie, the more wicked the better, Kat insisted. No way was she becoming an old married lady.

The attendees had done their best. Fitz had been so impressed with Mona's choice, he'd whispered lavish and delicious promises to her about what would happen if she'd buy a duplicate for herself. Mona wasn't quite ready for that display until she lost a few more pounds, but she had to agree that her nursing-mother breasts might, for once, rival Kat's killer figure.

"You have to be joking." Kat regarded the haphazard bouquet as if it were something dead.

"You left the arrangements up to us," Tansy pointed out.

Mona watched as Kat assumed that careful manner they all still donned too easily with Tansy. Ten months had passed since the illusions that protected Tansy for twenty years had shattered. She'd made big strides in coming to grips with the reality that her twin, Paris, was truly dead and, more importantly, that his loss at her hands was an accident. She would probably always feel that a part of her was missing, but more and more, Lucas filled the emptiness.

"Tansy, I really appreciate all the work that went into…" Frown lines formed between Kat's eyebrows as she searched for diplomacy, never one of her strong suits.

Mona and Tansy's gazes met. Mona's mouth twitched.

Tansy lost it. Laughter burst from her lips. "Gotcha!" She grabbed her sides and fell back on the sofa.

Mona was torn between her own amusement and a catch in her heart at the welcome sight of Tansy's long-lost impishness.

Kat's eyes narrowed. "You brat." She grinned, yanked the veil off her head and tossed it to the floor.

Then her eyes filled. "It's not funny. I'm about to make the worst mistake of my life."

Instantly, Tansy sobered. "Oh, sweetie, you know that's not true." She slid one arm around her much-taller sister's waist. "Armand is the best thing that ever happened to you."

"Don't you think I know that?" Viciously, Kat swiped away the moisture. "But I can't be what he wants."

Tansy cast a worried glance at Mona while patting Kat's back. "Maybe we should call Armand to come over."

"No!" Kat's head jerked up. "It's bad luck."

Mona rolled her eyes. "Not until tomorrow. Or we could call him. Talking on the phone doesn't count."

"I can't. I don't want him to know I'm—"

"A nervous wreck?" Mona sighed. "I think he figured that out the third time you broke the engagement."

"I can't help it. I'm going to screw this up. I will, you just watch."

"Get a grip, Kat." But Mona planted herself on her sister's free side. "I understand, really I do."

"How? You can't possibly relate—you couldn't wait to marry Fitz."

"True. But I was terrified of having Jamie." Even the mention of her three-month-old son's name made her go all soft inside. "Fitz and I nearly divorced over the prospect of children because I was so sure I had no idea how to be a mother."

"You're wonderful with him," Tansy said.

Kat nodded. "You're a bowl of mush where he's concerned."

"I know." Mona blinked back tears. "I never dreamed it could be like this. I'd die for him." She sniffed hard. Blew her nose. "Worse, I'm even considering the suburbs."

"Dear God." Kat shuddered. "See? My point exactly. If I show up tomorrow, I'll be living on Beacon Hill and wearing St. John knits before you know it." She sank to the sofa. "Stepford Wives, both of us." She buried her face in her hands.

Mona's watery chuckles died off when she glimpsed Tansy's expression.

Sad. Wistful.

"Tansy, what's wrong?"

"You two don't—" She threw up her hands, walked away.

Kat leaped from the sofa. "Talk to us."

Now it was Tansy who paced. "You have no idea how lucky you are." She whirled, and Mona was shocked to see anger on her face.

A new breakthrough. Tansy used to have quite a temper, but she hadn't been angry in twenty years.

"What do you mean?" she asked carefully.

"You—" Tansy stabbed a finger at Kat "—have an incredible man who has waited years for you to grow up enough to appreciate him. Armand will lay the world at your feet if you'll let him, and he would never, ever ask you to be anyone but who you are."

Kat's mouth opened and closed again, but before she could utter a word, Tansy had turned on Mona. "And you have not only a man who loves you, heart and soul, but the most precious child on earth. How dare you, either of you, take your blessings so lightly?"

Mona rose, instantly ashamed but also worried. "Has Lucas done something to you?"

Kat's voice was a growl. "If that man has laid one finger on you, I'll—"

"Of course he hasn't hurt me. He'd tear his heart out and lay it on the ground for me to grind into the pavement first. He just won't—" Her mouth slammed shut. She stared at the floor. "Never mind. I'm going to get my coat."

She stalked from the room. Mona started to follow her, but Kat grabbed her arm.

"No, don't. Give her a minute."

When Mona would have resisted, Kat stepped in front of her. "Think about what she said. I know we hated Lucas once, but we were wrong. He went to prison for twenty years to protect her. He's not going to harm her now." Kat sighed. "I think that's the problem. He's afraid of hurting her."

"Oh, my." Mona subsided. "He's as aware as the rest of us that Tansy's only sexual experience was her rape." She shook her head. "We all keep doing it, don't we? Treating her as if she'll shatter at the slightest provocation?"

"Yes," Tansy said from the doorway. "You do."

"So what's going on with you two? Lucas won't do the deed?"

10   "Kat!" Mona shoved past her. "Honey, it's understandable that he'd be concerned…."

"I think I've become an obligation, someone too pathetic to stand on her own." Her eyes glittered. "I guess I am pathetic—a thirty-seven-year-old virgin who's not—"

A virgin. No thanks to Carlton Sanford, the man whose obsession had cost Tansy—and Lucas—so much. Mona glanced at Kat, who returned the bewildered look. How to handle this delicately?

Kat didn't try. "Tansy, has he ever kissed you?"

"All the time. Until I think I might die. He's…" She shivered. "Incredible. He drives me out of my mind, and I'm positive he, well, he wants me, too. He just—" Her cheeks were a hectic red. "You know. Won't press the issue."

"Ah." Kat smiled. "That's very good." She rubbed her hands together. "Okay, you're in my territory now. What I don't know about pressing the issue hasn't been discovered. Is he still living in that dreary basement?"

"What are you thinking, Kat?" Mona asked. Her sister might have cut a wide swath through New York's men, but that would never be Tansy's style. Before that tragic night, Tansy had been a daredevil teen, but never with Kat's edge.

Kat waved Mona off. "Is he?"

"Yes," Tansy responded. "Because he has a record, even if it's totally unjustified, he can't hold a liquor license, but for all intents and purposes, he's running the place for Al now."

"Fitz says his exposé on Carlton has had its effect. The governor's office is paying attention," Mona said. "He thinks Lucas will definitely receive a pardon."

"Lucas should get every last cent Carlton ever made, too," Tansy muttered. "But he doesn't want to sue. Instead, he's saving every penny he can earn to start over. I think the only reason he's still in New York is for me."

Mona didn't want to think about Lucas leaving and taking Tansy with him, so she didn't. "What about all the book and film offers?"

"They keep coming, but he turns them all down. He's afraid of the cost to me of dealing with the publicity. I've told him I'll be fine, but…"

"The man's too noble for his own good," Kat observed. "Ergo, your current state of frustration."

"Kat—" Mona warned.

But Tansy grinned. "I haven't the faintest idea how

to seduce a man. If I did, Lucas and I would be much more relaxed by now." Her tone was light, but in her eyes, Mona saw nerves.

Kat dismissed that concern with an airy wave. "That's what you have me for." She turned to Mona. "Suite at the Plaza, you think?"

"It would be dreamy," Mona agreed. She turned to Tansy. "But I don't think he'd be comfortable there, do you?"

Tansy shook her head. "He still sees himself as the super's kid. Even if I can get him to accept the offers, I don't think that will ever change."

"Okay." Kat tapped one fingernail on her chin. "We don't have time to wait to convince Lucas to go out to some cozy inn. I won't be able to leave on a monthlong honeymoon unless this is put to bed." She grinned. "Literally."

They shared a laugh. "But, Kat, your wedding is tomorrow—" Tansy's protest faded as Kat's face lit with inspiration, and she raced from the room.

"Let her," Mona advised. "This is taking her mind off her jitters."

"What about mine?" Tansy pressed one hand to her abdomen.

Mona sobered. "Honey, are you sure you're ready?"

"If I get any more ready, I won't be fit to live with." Tansy's eyes softened. "I'm okay, Mona. I'm not afraid of Lucas." Her whole face glowed. "I love him. He... When I'm with him, it's almost like the way it was with Paris all our lives, like we're halves of one whole." Then she smiled and winked. "Only better."

"I'm glad. He loves you so much. When you're together, he can't take his eyes off you, as though you'll vanish if he looks away for a second."

"Well, now, ladies, he's going to be focused on her for a different reason. Ta-da!" Kat brandished a concoction of lace and ribbons not nearly scarlet-woman enough for her but definitely beyond the demure nightgowns of Tansy's past.

"Wow." Tansy's eyes widened. "But I can't possibly wear anything that would fit you." Kat was a nearly six-foot-tall sex goddess; Tansy was a slender sprite.

"I bought it with you in mind."

"Me? But how could you know?"

"I didn't, not your current situation, but any fool could see that Lucas isn't leaving your side for the foreseeable future. I fully expect the two of you to be following us down the aisle. I just didn't know I'd need to apply the boot to your rears."

Tansy reached out tentatively and stroked it. "It's white but not virginal."

Kat nodded. "No, it definitely has an edge. Go try it on."

Tansy clasped it to her and hurried from the room.

"Don't rush her, Kat."

"She's ready, Mona. Stop coddling." Kat snickered. "Lucas is the one we should be worrying about."

"That thing is evil."

"Yeah. Man won't know what hit him." She turned. "There's more. I called Travers while I was in the other room. Armand owns this boutique hotel on the East Side. Very low-key, luxurious but no ostentation to put

Lucas off. We go over there, fix up the room Travers is reserving. You call Fitz and tell him to hold up on the liquor, if he and Armand and Lucas were planning a bender tonight. Ask for Lucas and tell him you're worried about Tansy, give him the address. He shows up, Tansy opens the door—voilà! His goose is cooked."

"I like it," Tansy said from the doorway. She opened Kat's robe that she'd donned. "And I really like this."

Kat and Mona exchanged glances. "Lucas is so dead," Kat said. "Wow, Tansy—I did good!"

"Really?"

For all that she was the eldest, Tansy had spent most of her years trapped in girlhood. Once she'd operated on sheer bravado, frequently the ringleader when she and Paris got into mischief. Tonight, Mona could see traces of that bolder Tansy mingled with her nerves.

"Honey, you're going to blow off the top of his head."

"Yeah?" Delight danced over her features.

"Oh, yeah." Kat applauded. "Lucas Walker is toast."

Tansy bit her lower lip. "I'm scared to death." Then her grin flashed and she executed a quick dance step. "But...no guts, no glory."

"All right, ladies," Kat said. "Operation Sex Kitten is officially underway. Mona, call Fitz. Tansy, take that off and help me gather up candles. We'll head for the hotel, get the stage set, then...the rest is up to you."

She was halfway to the kitchen when Tansy waylaid her with a hug. "Thanks, Kat." She turned. "Thank you, Mona. I don't know how—"

"Think nothing of it." Kat winked. "What are sisters for?"

14

* * *

"MONA SWORE Tansy is safe," Fitz reminded Lucas as the cab hurtled down the street.

She might not be in danger, Lucas thought, but Mona said she needed him. Tansy was making real progress in dealing with all had happened to her, but she still had agonizing days her family didn't know about. His sense of urgency ratcheted. "You didn't have to come with me," Lucas replied. "You and Armand could go on with the evening."

"We weren't doing a very good job of carousing, anyway. I wonder if he'll sleep much tonight, since Kat refused to stay with him."

"He'd be wise to put a tail on her. Make sure she shows up."

Fitz grinned. "That's the truth. I love Kat, but, man…he's got his work cut out for him with that one."

"He's up to the task." *Come on, come on,* he urged the cab silently. "Why did they pick this place for a bachelorette party? I thought they were hitting the bars."

"Who knows? Maybe Kat has finally gotten her fill of the wild side. Anyway, Mona sounded ready to call it a night and go see Jamie, even if he's fine with my mom."

Lucas could hear eagerness in Fitz's voice, too. "No need to pretend you're not dying to see the little guy yourself."

Fitz shook his head. "Hell of a deal, huh? First night out after three months of baby boot camp, and I can't wait to get my hands on the kid. I wanted him a lot,

Lucas, but I never imagined how he'd wrap my heart up in those tiny hands."

"I envy you, man. You've got it all."

Fitz's gaze sharpened. "You could, too. Tansy loves you, and you can't tell me you aren't crazy about her."

Lucas shrugged it off. He'd stay until Tansy was completely well. That's all he could plan for now. "She's still fragile. And she could do better than me."

Fitz snorted. "Bullshit. You saved her life. Twice."

"She's been through too much she shouldn't have. If only I—"

"Can it, Lucas. She's had it rough, yes, but Carlton created all of it, not you. And Tansy's doing much better. She's stronger than you think."

"She's still lost without Paris."

16

"But she has you." Fitz peered at him. "Or are you again considering running away because you think that's best for her?"

Lucas bristled. "It's not running away to give her a chance at the life she deserves."

"You are some piece of work. Tansy doesn't want money or fame or anything else but you—and you could provide very well for her if you'd stop being so noble and take even one of the offers that have been thrown at you."

"I'm not exploiting Tansy for money."

Fitz rolled his eyes. "It doesn't have to be exploitation. You can control the content. Or follow the other avenue open to you and sue Carlton for every penny he has."

"Uh-uh. I'm not exposing Tansy to that or giving my

life up to years in court. I just want—" He subsided. *To be free. To go somewhere no one knows me and start over.*

With Tansy, though, not without her. But a prison record and very limited funds meant life would be hard for a while, and Tansy should be pampered.

"You still want to leave New York, don't you?" Fitz asked, as if he could read Lucas's mind. "You're going to get the pardon, if it's the last thing I ever do."

"I owe you for that."

"No, you don't. You were wronged. It's what I do, expose corruption. And anyway—" he lifted one shoulder "—you're family."

Lucas hadn't had a family since he was eight years old, except for those too-brief, shining years when Tansy's mother made him part of their magic circle.

He craved that sense of belonging far more than he wished for money, but he'd take Tansy on any terms. He was trying very hard to be patient and wait for her full recovery, but some days the heat and longing between them was nearly more than he could bear.

Yet no way was he risking reminding her of that night when all their lives were changed forever.

He could wait. He'd endured twenty years in a cage; he could do this.

Even if wanting her was a constant fire in his gut.

"She could be a good partner, you know, if you'd ever stop treating her with kid gloves. And she's got a trust fund she'd gladly share."

"I take care of my own," Lucas snapped.

"Your call. Hey, there's the place." Fitz pointed and

clapped him on the shoulder. "A word of advice—don't let your pride rob you of the best thing that ever happened to you. That woman loves you. Give her a chance to show you what she's made of."

They emerged from the cab. Fitz instructed the driver to wait for him until he retrieved his wife. Lucas tried to hand Fitz cab fare, but Fitz refused. "You paid for the first one tonight."

Lucas barely noticed the interior of the hotel, so focused on Tansy was he. All the way up in the elevator, he remained silent, jittering inside as he wondered what Tansy was feeling, what had her upset.

Fitz accompanied him to the door, but instead of waiting for Lucas to knock, he rapped hard, twice. "I think you can take it from here, my friend." He retraced his steps to the elevator.

"But what about Mona?" Fitz waved behind his back.

The door opened. "Mona's not here."

Lucas heard Tansy's voice a split second before he turned to ask—

His jaw dropped. His eyes nearly popped from his head. "Tansy?" His voice cracked like a teenager's.

"Are you going to stand out there all night?"

"But they said—Mona called Fitz and—" He slammed his jaw shut. "What's going on?"

She captured his hand and drew him inside. The room glowed golden from the light of more candles than he could count. The beige carpet was thick beneath his feet, the walls were covered in creamy fabric, the mahogany bed was a lake of bronze satin.

It was the kind of place Tansy deserved.

And he'd never be able to give her.

Don't let your pride rob you of the best thing that ever happened to you.

Fitz's advice didn't matter. Pride was all Lucas had, and that was in short supply. He was about to tell Tansy he had to go, when he got a good look at her eyes.

Despite the jut to her chin, she was scared half to death.

"Tansy, are you seducing me?"

"Is it working?"

"You've always had more guts than sense." But he could sense that she was starting to lose her nerve.

Don't be an idiot. You want her, and she wants you.

"You take my breath away. Let me look at you." He snagged her hand and twirled her around, perusing the skimpy concoction of white lace and satin ribbons clinging to her slender curves, granting occasional, enticing peeks of smooth, ivory flesh.

Sweet mercy.

She tried for casual, but her expression told another story. "Like it?"

"Like? If I can ever manage to pick my tongue up off the floor, I'll see if I can come up with a better word."

Her smile was quick, and he noted a trace of her old mischief in her gaze.

"That thing you're barely wearing is surely illegal in several states."

"Kat found it."

"Remind me to fall to my knees the next time I see

her." He struggled to maintain a light banter and glanced around the room again. "This is amazing, Tansy. It reminds me of the night—" *No. Don't go there.*

But she completed his sentence. "When I decorated your basement."

Their gazes locked. Remembered. "Yeah. You took something miserable and turned it into magic." He'd carefully preserved her butcher paper mural of the princess and her champion that bore their features.

"No place is miserable if I'm with you, Lucas." At the advice of her therapist, she'd put effort into making the switch from the Michael she'd called him so long ago.

Sometimes he mourned the loss of it.

He couldn't dodge the issue any longer. "Tansy, are you really certain you're ready for this? I'm not sure you are."

She was silent so long that he began mentally to prepare himself to leave yet again, before he did anything to frighten her. To bring back that night of horror.

Lost in his own thoughts, the smack of her palm on his chest caught him up short. "What are you doing?"

Her look was pure go-to-hell. "I'm sick of it, do you hear me? I'm not an invalid, and I'm not pathetic. Stop treating me like I can't know what I want." She clenched her fist, and he grabbed her, more to protect her hand than because she could hurt him.

"I'm only trying to make sure—"

"I *am* sure, Lucas Michael Walker. Don't you get that? You're driving me insane, I want your hands on me so badly. If you don't make love to me right here and now, I'm—I'm—" She burst into tears and buried her face in her hands.

Oh, God. Tears. He couldn't bear to make her cry. "Tansy, take it easy. Let's just sit down and talk about—"

She shrieked.

His Tansy. Like a harridan. He goggled.

"You're driving me nuts, you and your stupid, stubborn sense of honor." She lifted her head, her eyes glittering, her stance defiant. "I know you only want to protect me, but, Lucas, of any person in the world, you're the last one I need protection from. You'd cut your own heart out before you'd hurt me. I know that, so why don't you?"

She unclenched her fingers, and her voice softened. "I'm not afraid for you to make love to me, and it won't remind me of what happened. How could it? You're my prince, the man I've loved since you were a boy."

"I'm no prince, Tansy." His voice was rougher than he intended.

She clasped his hands as if pledging fealty. "You are to me," she whispered. "Please stop letting the past come between us. You told me once that all you really wanted was me." She spread her arms wide, still gripping his hands. "Well, here I am, waiting for you to take me."

With shocking suddenness, she pressed his palms to her breasts. Looked at him with her heart in her eyes. "Please, Lucas…give us both what we're dying to have. Make me yours. Bind us together with this last step."

She was so slender, so fragile. So goddamned brave.

She was his dream, the flame that had kept him alive for so many dark, hopeless nights.

And she felt like pure heaven.

"I'm not selling your story for money, Tansy. That means I'll never be rich. I'm a hard worker, but what you see here is all I have to offer. Be certain."

"Lucas, I never needed money or fame. All I absolutely require is you. Let me have you, Lucas. Let me give you myself, tainted though I might be—"

He hushed her with a hard kiss. "Yours is the purest beauty I've ever seen," he vowed against her lips. "You're the dream I held close every single day of those lost years. I tried to forget you because I knew it was best for you, but—"

"Hush." She stopped his words with her own kiss, sweet and rich.

She was everything of paradise he'd ever hoped for, every wish of his life come true. All he had to do was risk as much as a small, courageous woman had already done.

So, with a groan of mingled thanksgiving and hunger, Lucas at last surrendered.

Swept her up in his arms, carried her to that soft and welcoming bed. Gave his heart and his life into Tansy's keeping. "I'll work hard, Tansy, to provide for you. I'll guard you with my last ounce of strength. You'll never spend one second wondering if you're cherished." He rose above her and began, with trembling fingers, to untie all those amazing ribbons.

She watched him with blue eyes as wide as the horizon. "I'll make you a home, Lucas Michael Walker.

You'll never be alone again, and—" here she took a deep breath "—I'll follow you to those wide open spaces you crave."

"Tansy, I can't ask you to leave your family."

"We'll keep in touch, but you'll be my family, you and—" She caught her lip in her teeth.

"And who?" he asked.

"Our babies. Do you want to make babies with me, Lucas?"

Emotion swamped him. His eyes burned. "You bet I do."

Her smile was incandescent. "Then—" she slid her arms around his neck and drew him down "—we'd better get started."

She laughed, if a little watery, and Lucas laughed with her.

Soon there was nothing between them but skin touching skin, heart touching heart. Lucas made love to Tansy, and she made enthusiastic love to him. With more of the tiger than the timid, Titania Gerard seduced Lucas Walker into forgetting that she was fragile, until they both hovered so close to the edge they could barely breathe.

"This is it," he warned as he poised above her. "I'll never let you go after this."

"Thank God," she murmured.

Then gasped at the feel of him. And sighed, eyes wide with wonder.

She held on tight, and he gathered her closer.

And together, Lucas and Tansy found their way home.

* * *

ARMAND PROWLED through the rooms of his brownstone.

Damn that woman. For all he knew, she was halfway to Miami or Paris or Timbuktu.

He'd been patient with her, hadn't he? Taken more guff from her than any sane man should, but—

He loved her to distraction, and distraction she indeed was. Good thing his various enterprises had management teams in place; he'd certainly been worthless lately, so close to having the life he'd never have dreamed he wanted, yet certain every minute that Kat would back out on him again.

His world had been simple before he'd met Katharina Gerard. She was the single most annoying, impossible creature on the planet, given to grand gestures and flagrant behavior, to shooting the world the finger and daring fate to settle the score, but—

He loved her. There it was again, and why, despite all her foibles?

Because, behind her bravado, Kat was terrified no one could really love her. Because she would do anything for those she loved, and for many she didn't. Her gallery could have made money long before, except that she kept doling out rent money to starving artists when she could barely feed herself, or buying paintings she'd never show, simply to help someone through hard times.

Her heart was as big and bold as her reputation. She'd led him on a merry chase, yes, but he hadn't spent life as a monk, either. The past was the past and done now.

If she didn't show tomorrow—today, actually—he'd strangle her with his bare hands.

He stopped short at the French doors and realized somehow he'd made it to ground level.

Well, hell. If he couldn't sleep, he might as well do something productive. Weeding the garden by moonlight was only slightly less insane than marrying Kat.

He stalked outside.

And froze. "How did you get here?"

She opened one palm. "Key, remember? I live here." Her body was stiff. Awkward.

"Do you, Katharina?" *Or are you going to break my heart?*

"You know this is crazy, right? Your family hates me, your friends think you've lost your mind, I'm going to make your life miserable—"

He smiled. *I'm going to* was all he heard. "Come here."

"Uh-uh. I can't think when I'm near you."

"That's just too bad." He went to her instead.

She stepped back, held out one hand. "It's bad luck for you to see me. We're doomed now, you know that. We'll probably be divorced in six months."

He snagged that hand and yanked her close. "Not on your life." He lowered his mouth to hers, tortured them both.

She tried to dodge, but her breathing was uneven. "You should be running for the hills. It's your last chance, Armand."

"Easy come, easy go."

"No wonder your family couldn't keep you on Beacon Hill with a cavalier attitude like that."

He pressed their bodies together. "Nothing about me feels too cavalier right now."

A smile teased at her lips. "You're not going to let me save you, are you?"

"No, but I'll have a medal made to celebrate your heroism in the attempt." He touched the upper curve of one breast. "We'll pin it." His fingers traced the shape of her. "Right about…here." Then he seized her in a kiss that was nakedly carnal and straight from his heart.

Kat answered in kind, and the madness that swamped them every time poured over them again.

He gripped her, spun. Started for the door.

"Wait—if seeing me is bad luck, what will making love to me do?"

He started to laugh but saw the honest worry in her eyes. He faced her again. "What it will do, my love, is calm both of us down."

She snorted. "You've never made me feel calm in bed, Armand."

He grinned. "Point taken. But afterward—" He broke off. Went for honesty. "I need you, Kat. I want to sleep with you tonight before the circus begins in the morning, and—" he crooked one eyebrow "—I want you where I can watch you."

"We should have eloped."

"Protest all you want, but you're going to be a beautiful bride, and you'll thank me someday." He edged her toward the house.

"You ever get tired of being a know-it-all, Armand?"

But she laid her head on his shoulder. His arm circled her waist.

"Not really." His grin was as quick and light as his heart had earlier been tormented.

Kat threw back her head and laughed. "We are surely the most mismatched couple ever—" She sobered and stroked his cheek. "But you're stuck with me, pal. You waited too long."

"I did indeed." He kissed her. "But that's over now. You're not going anywhere."

"But your bed."

"Our bed," he corrected.

"Know-it-all."

"Harpy."

Smiling, they took the stairs two at a time.

FITZ COPPED A FEEL on the way back down the aisle.

"Fitz! Everyone's watching."

His grin was unrepentant. "Are you kidding me? They're still trying to decide if that was really Kat." He drew her into a shadowed corner of Armand's garden, which had been transformed into a wedding bower.

"She's a beautiful bride."

His eyes were fond. "Yeah. Who knew she could dress demure?"

"'Demure' is overstating it," Mona responded. "But the simple lines of that slip dress are stunning."

"Stop talking about clothes and kiss me to tide me over."

Mona readily complied.

"Can't we ditch the reception and go make out until Jamie's next feeding?"

Mona felt the telltale tingle. "Too late."

Fitz groaned. "I'm dying here. Tell the kid to take a number."

She jabbed him lightly in the gut. "He's a baby. And you got yours last night." She winked and turned to go.

"But it's today now," he called after her.

She was laughing as she left.

"You two-timing me, Fitzgerald?"

He yanked himself from contemplating his wife's lovely behind. "Hey, it's the blushing bride. Do I get the first kiss?" He swept her up in a hug, pausing only long enough to plant a hearty one right on her mouth.

"I think Armand beat you to it. How come you wait until I'm married, hotshot?"

Fitz laughed. "I can't believe you pulled it off." He shook Armand's hand. "Welcome to the family." He looked at Kat. "Jitters all gone?"

"Up yours, smart aleck."

"Ah, that's our Kat." He exchanged grins with Armand.

"Look at them," Kat said. Fitz followed her gesture.

Tansy and Lucas stood together, surrounded by wedding guests, yet they were obviously in their own world.

"I've never seen Lucas that relaxed," Fitz remarked. "Good for you, my friend."

"Amen," Armand said. "If anyone on this earth deserves happiness, it's the two of them."

"She could light up a planet with that glow," Kat noted. "She's so beautiful she's going to steal my thunder." She wiped away a tear. "I couldn't be more thrilled."

Armand turned to her. "Katharina, we should see to our guests."

Her sigh was dramatic. "I told you I'm no Miss Manners, pal." But her smile was wide as she slipped against his side.

Fitz spotted Mona approaching with the other light of his life in her arms and moved to meet them both. As she and Kat passed one another, Kat nodded toward Tansy, and Mona grinned at the sight.

Tansy's attention was caught then, and she smiled at them both shyly, nestling closer to the man who looked as if someone had just handed him the winning lottery ticket.

Armand and Kat moved on, but a few steps later, she paused. Then, in typical Kat disdain for proper procedure, she winked at Tansy—

And launched the bridal bouquet straight at her.

THE END

A conversation with
JEAN BRASHEAR

Tell us a bit about how you began your writing career.

Unlike most of the writers I've met, I didn't always know I wanted to be one. People told me I wrote great letters, but as a matter of fact, if you'd asked me what my "someday when I get time" dream was, during the whirlwind child-rearing years, I would have said it was to have time to paint!

But I've always been an avid reader and had the sort of "wouldn't it be amazing?" thought many people have about the idea of seeing one's name on the cover of a book. Thus, when my youngest was in high school, and my husband and I were having a "what do we do now that the nest is nearly empty?" kind of chat and I voiced that thought, he urged me to give it a try. And he did much more than that, actually—we were running our business with no support staff, yet he offered to do so alone a couple of hours a day so I could write, and was my constant cheerleader (and still is).

Beyond high school English I had absolutely no training for writing fiction, so I was anything but methodical in my attempt. Somehow, six weeks later, I had about 300 pages that seemed to form a coherent tale, a story I now understand was romantic suspense but had no idea what to call at the time. I made about every greenhorn mistake possible as I fumbled my way toward understanding the business of writing as well as the craft, but from the beginning I got feedback that I had talent, if very raw and unpolished. I persisted, though I wanted to give up a million times, and, glory be, if a little over two years later, I didn't sell my first book!

I'm a living example that it's never too late to follow a wild hare—dust off those "someday" dreams and go after them!

Do you have a writing routine?

I'm an early riser (sigh...I would so love to be a night owl), so I sometimes write very early in the morning, but my more usual routine is to get up, have a cup of tea and read for a few minutes, then, after breakfast, go for my walk, then settle down to write. I write all morning and into the afternoon if needed for a deadline, and I turn off the phone while I'm doing it so as not to be interrupted in sinking deep into the story. Afternoons (and however many more hours are required) are reserved for the business details of writing—promotion, answering fan mail, etc. Evenings my brain goes off the clock, sadly. That's when I kick back and read for pleasure, but I fancy, in my next life, being one to write in the deep, dark hours when the rest of the world is sleeping. Midnight oil and all that...seems so glamorous.

When you're not writing, what do you love to do?
Spend time with my husband, numero uno, and read, read, read. I hyperventilate if I don't have a book at hand at all times. I also enjoy doing needlework, swimming and my daily walks with a dear friend, and lately, I've pulled out my guitar to see if I can remember how to play it. You'd be deeply impressed to hear my stirring rendition of "Wild Thing."

What or who inspires you?
In my writing, I can seldom recall the seed of inspiration that leads to the final story, but it can come from anywhere: a guy I see on a street corner, and I start building a "wonder how he got there?" story....a snippet of conversation I'm compelled to finish after the speakers are long gone...an image I see that triggers heaven knows what in my brain. I'm inspired by good writing from others, by the ability of poets to convey so

much in a hundred words when I have trouble staying under four hundred pages, by art, by music...and most of all, by human nature and its astonishing variety.

In life, my mother and grandmothers, who have shown a remarkable ability to endure hardship with grace, inspire me deeply. I greatly admire, as well, the ordinary folks of this world much more than superstars. The people who may never receive recognition (though they should) for doing the things we too often take for granted: go about their lives, simply working every day, raising their families, caring for their communities...serving as the backbone of society, the bedrock that makes it possible for all the whiz-bang glamorous stuff to happen. They're the heroes: the grocery clerk, the plumber, the garbageman, the carpenter, the teacher, the pastor, the cop...those who give our society, too often blinded by celebrity, its real meaning. These are the people we should be celebrating and revering.

If you had to choose between the two, would you pick mercy or justice?
Tough one. My immediate reaction is to choose mercy, though I would hope it would not have to be at the expense of justice. (Justice being defined as fairness, not revenge, I hasten to add.)

What are your top five favorite books?

I have read so many books in my life that it's very hard to limit the choice to five (and I'm positive I'm forgetting some I'll kick myself for later). As a child, I loved the L. Frank Baum Oz series, and adored *Little Women* (doesn't every female writer secretly imagine herself as Jo? Hmmm...maybe I should have realized back then that this was my true calling!)

As an adult, anything by Deborah Smith, whom I consider a goddess (*On Bear Mountain* is a particular favorite). The Outlander series by Diana Gabaldon (especially *Voyager*—how can you not love that reunion scene?). Oh, Jeez...only five? This is killing me! *Beach Music* by Pat Conroy. *Earthly Paradise* by Colette. *Honest Illusions* by Nora Roberts.

Other writers whose work I enjoy enormously: Patricia Gaffney, Luanne Rice, Barbara Delinsky, Elizabeth Berg, Rosamund Pilcher, Laurell K. Hamilton, Jacqueline Carey, Linda Howard...I could quite easily go on for pages. In case you can't tell, I read A LOT.

What matters most in life?

Love. Family. Loyalty. Friends. Integrity.

I guess my philosophy boils down to this: it isn't the lot of most of us to change the world in any massive way or by one impressive act, but each of us can focus on lighting our little corner of the world by the way we live each day, by the kindness we demonstrate in the tiniest of ways—saying thank you readily and often, giving the store clerk a compliment on her smile (or smiling at her even if she isn't), taking the time to tell someone he did his job well, waving a fellow driver in line instead of making a rude gesture and charging on. By the love we share and the compassion we spread in a thousand everyday instances, both to those we know and love and those we do not. I believe that one person *can* make a difference in the world. Ripples spread from these actions, and there is great power in them.

If you weren't a writer what would you be doing?
Oh, wow. Do I have to? Having spent too many years not writing and now mourning not having started sooner (though I wouldn't trade for the years nurturing my family), I would love to keep writing until I keel over in front of the computer...or ride off into the writer's sunset, still trying to figure out the best way to describe just what it looks like—in new and compelling prose, of course.

Marsha Zinberg, Executive Editor, Signature Select™, spoke with Jean last July.

The Writing Life

SMALL TOWN GIRL MEETS MANHATTAN

I GREW UP in a town of five thousand, and I live in a bigger small town now. In between, I've lived in cities, but none of them begin to compare to New York (well, nothing can, really). I've read a zillion novels set in Manhattan and yearned to see it for myself, but, being from West Texas, where cows outnumber people and the sky is endless, even my current tree-covered small town makes me feel a little claustrophobic at times. So I admit to feeling intimidated at the prospect of being plopped down in the midst of all those...people. Big buildings. No sky. No air?

And then, of course, there are the stories of how unfriendly New Yorkers are, how crime-ridden it is, yadda yadda. So when I ventured to make my first trip there—alone, I might add—it was not without trepidation. Would I panic, being surrounded by such crowds? Would I get mugged? Would I be the ultimate rube?

The answers are no, no, and...probably yes.

But I can tell you this: it was love at first sight.

I still haven't done the touristy things, even though I've made other visits since. No Statue of Liberty, no Empire State Building, no Broadway shows. On that trip and the succeeding ones, I've spent most of my time wandering the neighborhoods, seeking the flavor of the real Manhattan, not the tour guide version. I felt so instantly at home that my editor at the time was teasing me about my Bataan Death March assault of the city—by the time I saw her thirty-six hours into my trip, I'd covered a whole lot of ground and already learned to walk like a New Yorker. (In other words, lights and cars and crosswalks be damned.)

Mercy is set in Manhattan, and this was my researach trip. The Gerard apartment mimics one in which a friend of mine lived on the Upper West Side, near the part of Riverside Park where I found Mt. Tom, and not far from the small hotel (and boy, do they grow hotel rooms small on that very crowded island) where I stayed. The bathroom was so tiny there wasn't even room to hang a toilet paper roll. (And we won't discuss the kind of cushy room I could have gotten for the same money elsewhere!)

But I also learned one of the basic survival skills of a trip to Manhattan—immediately upon your arrival, locate the nearest diner and deli, and you're set. I began a major love affair with bagels and ate as inexpensively as I could anywhere else in the country. I learned about carrying my purse strap across my chest. I got pretty good at stepping right out in the street to hail a cab (but why, oh why, did I never learn a proper ear-splitting whistle?).

And I squealed when I bought my first Metrocard (I still have it, too.) Yep…one of my first official rube acts, to the vast amusement of everyone around me. But there it was, my very own ticket to ride the subways I'd read about for years, and I ask you, what's a girl to do but celebrate such a watershed moment? I rode the trains all over kingdom come by myself and never felt unsafe. Coming from Texas, where we're all married to our cars, I am now a huge fan of mass transit.

Of course, that was also the scene of my second act of egregious rube-ism. I'd met my agent in Chelsea for lunch at a to-die-for French restaurant, then wandered around the area some more. When I was ready to head back uptown, I went down in the tunnel, only to find the #9 train running the wrong way. (Is this where I should admit that my sense of direction leaves a bit to be desired?)

So I stood there for a few minutes, puzzling over the signs, then spotted a subway cop. I walked over and asked him if the 1 and 9 sometimes went both ways because I needed to go that way (use your imagination here) but the one that just came through was going the other way. He looked at me and said, "Lady, where are you from?"

"Texas."

"It figures." Sigh. "Go back up the stairs to the street and go down the other side."

Ooops. When hearing this story later, my husband remarked that it takes a certain amount of arrogance to assume that the trains are running the wrong way. Okay, okay. I mentioned that sense of direction problem, right?

While meandering through the area earlier, though, I had a couple of other experiences that made their way into the book. I left early enough to find the place where I was to meet my agent, then spent some time wandering around. I wound up outside a warehouse in what might have been the Meatpacking District and got a little lost (yeah, yeah...but this time I hadn't deluded myself that I knew where I was) and found myself being stalked by a front-end loader as I skirted the barrels of freshly stripped bones. For a vegetarian, not the most delightful experience, but thrilling all the same. (Interspersed with thoughts of how my very protective husband would be having a heart attack right about then.) So I tripped the light fantastic across the cobblestones and headed back toward the restaurant.

Somewhere along the way, I wound up in the reception area of the offices of Barnes & Noble's Web site, *bn.com*, but beats me how. I also encountered the fascinating Chelsea Market.

Lunch, while fabulous and yummy and interesting, was almost too tame after all that.

Oh, yes—and I stumbled across the infamous Hogs and Heifers bar, though it was morning and not open and the windows were so covered with stickers I couldn't see a thing. So the interior views of Kat and Gamble's meeting in a bar much like it cannot be taken for anything but a writer's imagination, sad to say.

That thing about New Yorkers being unfriendly? Forget it. Bunch of hooey. Okay, so I might have gotten a fair number of odd looks because I kept making eye contact (a particular no-no on the subway) and smiling at people as I walked down the street. And so I insisted on striking up conversation with perfect strangers at the drop of a hat...but people would talk back. We'd visit. Yes, they were in a hurry (everyone's in a hurry) but I found New Yorkers to be very friendly folks and kind to a stranger. God knows what they said when I left.

My lovely New York friend was generous enough to meet with me several times while I was there, and we strolled through Central Park from the Met one day (oh, sweet mercy, surely one of the sublime places on this planet!) heading to the Oak Bar at the Plaza, which she thought I needed to see. I was captivated by crocuses (oh, how I wish I could grow them where I live! Such friendly little flowers poking up from the snow), and the very thought that I was here, right here in Mecca—Central Park in New York City, for goodness' sake—just about had me expiring from rapture. It was an astonishing place, too; you walk fifty feet into the park, and it's like all those millions of people don't exist. I'm convinced that Central Park is the key to sanity for anyone living there, but that might be my West Texas need for space and quiet speaking.

So my friend and I are walking along, having a great time laughing about how neither of our husbands would be able to enjoy the stroll because they'd be too busy looking for dangers to us, while we were having a ball (and I promise, guys, we weren't negligent...okay, not very negligent). We arrive at the south end of the park, and I see this big golden statue of a man on a horse. I walk around to see who the hero is and—Rube

Moment Extraordinaire—blurt out, without thinking, "Ohmigod, they've built a statue to the Antichrist!"

The horse-drawn carriage drivers laugh. Everyone within hearing laughs. My friend chalks it up as another snapshot she'll be able to relate to her husband, who's in California but calling in every day to see What Jean Has Done Next.

But seriously, folks, it was a world-turned-upside-down experience. These people think William Tecumseh Sherman is a hero, for cripes' sake! Anyone raised south of the Mason-Dixon Line knows he's the devil incarnate.

A definite *I don't think we're in Kansas anymore, Toto* moment.

The small-town girl has been to Manhattan a few times since and looks forward to many more visits. I mean, one of these days, I have to actually hit the tourist trail, right? Catch a show, hit Ellis Island, all that jazz?

You could visit New York for a lifetime—heck, you could visit the *Met* for a lifetime—and never see it all. I once remarked that New Yorkers were the only people with egos as big as Texans about the place where they live, and it's indeed so—but we both have good reasons for feeling that strongly. It is, in some ways, the biggest small town in the world, while being an ever-changing panoply of sights, sounds, tastes, smells...a crazy quilt of human experience and a city unlike any other in the world.

This small-town girl fell head over heels for New York...and I don't expect to recover anytime soon.

Signature Select™
SPOTLIGHT

National bestselling author

JOANNA WAYNE

The Gentlemen's Club

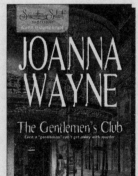

A homicide in the French Quarter of New Orleans has attorney Rachel Powers obsessed with finding the killer. As she investigates, she is shocked to discover that some of the Big Easy's most respected gentlemen will go to any lengths to satisfy their darkest sexual desires. Even murder.

*A gripping new novel...
coming in June.*

HARLEQUIN®
Live the emotion™

**Bonus Features,
including:**

Author Interview,
Romance—
New Orleans Style,
and Bonus Read!

COLLECTION

Nothing is what it seems…

SMOKESCREEN

**An exciting NEW anthology featuring
talented Silhouette Bombshell® authors…**

Doranna Durgin
Meredith Fletcher
Vicki Hinze

Three women with remarkable abilities…

Three explosive situations that
only they can defuse…

Three riveting new stories that you will love!

Silhouette®
Where love comes alive™

THE FORTUNES OF TEXAS™: *Reunion*

The price of privilege. The power of family.

Your favorite family returns in a twelve-book collection with a new story every month starting this June.

$1.00 OFF

the purchase of *Cowboy at Midnight* by *USA TODAY* bestselling author Ann Major.

RETAILER: Harlequin Enterprises Ltd. will pay the face value of this coupon plus 8 cents if submitted by the customer for this specified product only. Any other use constitutes fraud. Coupon is nonassignable. Void if taxed, prohibited or restricted by law. Void if copied. Consumer must pay any government taxes. Mail to Harlequin Enterprises Ltd., P.O. Box 880478, El Paso, TX 88588-0478, U.S.A. Cash value 1/100 cents. Limit one coupon per customer. Valid in the U.S. only. Coupon expires July 30, 2005. Redeemable at participating retail outlets in the U.S. only.

FTRCUS

5 65373 00076 2 (8100) 0 11159

Visit Silhouette Books at www.eHarlequin.com

©2005 Harlequin Enterprises Ltd

Silhouette®
Where love comes alive™

THE FORTUNES OF TEXAS: Reunion

The price of privilege. The power of family.

**Your favorite family returns
in a twelve-book collection with a
new story every month starting this June.**

$1.⁰⁰ OFF

the purchase of *Cowboy at Midnight*
by *USA TODAY*
bestselling author Ann Major.

**Visit Silhouette Books
at www.eHarlequin.com**

Silhouette®
Where love comes alive™

©2005 Harlequin Enterprises Ltd